D0090245

THE INSIDER

ALSO BY STEPHEN FREY

The Takeover

The Vulture Fund

The Inner Sanctum

The Legacy

THE INSIDER

STEPHEN FREY

BALLANTINE BOOKS
NEW YORK

A Ballantine Book
Published by The Ballantine Publishing Group

http://www.randomhouse.com/BB/

LIBRARY OF CONGRESS CATALOGING-IN-PUBLICATION DATA
Frey, Stephen W.
The insider / Stephen Frey. — 1st ed.
p. cm.
ISBN 0-345-42827-7 (alk. paper)
I. Title.
PS3556.R4477I55 1999
813'.54—dc21 99-14358
CIP

Text design by Mary A. Wirth

Manufactured in the United States of America
First Edition: September 1999

10 9 8 7 6 5 4 3 2 1

Once again, to my wife, Lillian,
and our daughters, Christina and Ashley,
who make every day special for me

ACKNOWLEDGMENTS

I thank the following people for their significant contributions to, and support of, *The Insider*:

Peter Borland, Cynthia Manson, Gordon Eadon,
Bill Oberdorf, Mike Pocalyko, Bill Carroll,
Mike Crow, Bill Kelly, Bob Wieczorek,
Steve Watson, Kevin Erdman, Barbara Fertig,
Scott Andrews, Marvin Bush, Jim O'Connor,
Tim and Diane Urbanek, Walter Frey,
Pat and Terry Lynch, Mike Attara,
Alex Bushman, Vivian Herklotz, Jim Galowski,
Gerry Barton, and Emily Grayson.

PROLOGUE

AUGUST 1994

Like distant headlights, pale yellow eyes burned the water's surface, reflecting in the beam of the high-powered spotlight that cut through the Louisiana night. Moths swarmed about the bulb while the man held the spotlight aloft with one hand and guided his Boston Whaler over the murky depths with the other. He smiled, satisfied at the number of eyes dotting the surface. He knew alligators as long as fourteen feet lurked beneath—apex-of-the-food-chain predators capable of ripping apart a human in the blink of an eye. He wiped away beads of perspiration dripping down his forehead with a red bandanna. It was August, and even at two o'clock in the morning the heat and humidity of Bayou Lafourche were stifling.

A large moth landed on his upper lip. He grabbed the insect, crushed it, and tossed its fluttering carcass to the water. Almost instantly something rose from the depths and inhaled the moth in a swirl of black water. The man was momentarily distracted, and the Whaler's fiberglass bow struck a thick tree stump almost submerged by the high tide. The impact, though not violent, still caused him to pitch forward. The outboard engine, which had propelled the sleek craft across the bay to Bayou Lafourche from Henry's Landing on the docks of the tiny shrimping town of Lafitte, stalled. He caught himself on the chrome steering wheel, cursed, refired the Mercury engine, once more aimed the spotlight on the water ahead, and proceeded slowly, guiding the boat around the stump.

The brackish channel, which a quarter mile back had narrowed to only twenty feet, widened again, making his progress easier. He flashed the spotlight on the muddy bank, then up into the cypress limbs looming over him. They were draped by thick Spanish moss, silky spiderwebs ten feet across, and an occasional water moccasin lying in wait to ambush a bird or a rodent. Behind the trees were marshy fields and desolate swamps, all crisscrossed by an intricate labyrinth of waterways. Other than a few energy-industry employees and fishermen, humans rarely ventured this deep into Bayou Lafourche. The only significant inhabitants were alligators and coyotes, which hunted white-tailed deer and nutria—a strange, orange-toothed cross between a rat and a beaver. This was the middle of nowhere, and it was perfect.

The boat's engine stalled again as water lilies thickened on the surface and wrapped around the Whaler's propeller, ensnaring it like a boa constricting about its prey. The man turned off the spotlight and for several seconds stood behind the steering console, listening. Without the constant throb of the engine, Bayou Lafourche was deathly still save for the groggy symphony of frog and insect calls and the gentle lap of water against the boat's smooth hull. He glanced toward a hazy, moonless sky, then back over his shoulder toward New Orleans. The city was only fifty miles away, but it might as well have been five hundred, so desolate was this place.

"Hello."

The man's head snapped to the right and he flicked the spotlight back on, aiming it in the direction from which the voice had come. Paddling toward him was a thin, elderly man sitting in the aft seat of a battered metal canoe, a grizzled hound standing like an oversized hood ornament in the bow. The dog was wagging its tail excitedly and panting in the oppressive heat, its pink tongue dangling obscenely from glossy black jaws.

"I thought I was the only person within ten miles of here," the elderly man called out in the odd drawl of his singsong Cajun accent. As he pulled alongside the Boston Whaler, he shielded his eyes against the spotlight's fierce glare. "Name's Neville," he announced, exhibiting two rows of crooked, coffee-stained teeth beneath the brim of a soiled Mack Truck cap. "This here's Bailey." Neville pointed at the sad-eyed hound, which had placed its front paws on the gunwale of the man's boat. The dog was sniffing intently, fixated on a large canvas sack lying in the Whaler's bow. "What the hell are you doing out here this time of night?" he asked.

"I'm an inspector with Atlantic Energy." The man scrutinized Neville's weather-beaten face for signs that this was anything but a random encounter. "Just checking gauges on the wellheads."

Neville removed his cap and scratched his bald head. "I don't remember Atlantic having no rigs out in this part of Lafourche." He replaced the cap on his bare scalp, then dug into a crusty leather pouch attached to his belt, removed a dark, leafy wad of chewing tobacco, and stuffed it between his cheek and gum. "And I ain't never met no energy-company inspector out here at this time of night. Even the state fish-and-game boys are in bed by now."

"There's always a first for everything," the man replied tersely. He had noticed Neville subtly eyeing the canvas sack as well as the .30-06 Remington rifle and the cinder blocks lying next to it.

"Mmm." Neville glanced at Bailey. "Easy, pup," he said gently. The dog was agitated, whining and wagging its tail furiously. "Quite a rifle you got there, mister."

"I never come out here without firepower. You can't be too careful this deep in Lafourche."

"I guess so," Neville agreed. "Christ, that thing would bring down a charging bull elephant with one shot. You wouldn't have any problem at all stopping an alligator with it. Not even them big territorial males."

"That's why I've got it." The man was impatient to be on the move, but first he needed information. "What are *you* doing out here this late?"

"Checking my nutria traps," Neville replied defensively.

On top of a large red cooler positioned between Neville's knees lay a revolver, what looked like a Ruger .44 Magnum. The odds were excellent that Neville was really hunting alligators, which was illegal until September and probably why he was paddling through Bayou Lafourche in the dead of night. "You live out here?" the stranger asked.

"Yeah," Neville said warily, checking the hunting rifle in the bow of the Whaler once more. He spat tobacco juice over the side. Instantly it spread out like a drop of oil hitting the water. "Why?"

"I assume when September gets here you'll be hunting alligators." The man knew that Neville could earn a significant amount of money selling the valuable skins and meat to black-market buyers on the docks of Lafitte—buyers who didn't care that the strictly controlled and hard-to-obtain state game-and-wildlife tags weren't impaled in the alligator tails. "I'm out here on a regular basis and I've seen quite a few giants. Gators that would bring a nice price in Lafitte. Several were over twelve feet, and I've seen them in the same places over and over."

"Oh?" Neville tried not to sound interested. But one twelve-foot alligator could bring him almost three hundred dollars cash at the docks in town, close to what he earned in a week as a deck-hand on the shrimping boats. "Where were they?"

The man shook his head. "I'd have to draw you a map. You'd never find the spots without it." He picked at his cuticles for a few seconds, then looked up slowly. "I could come by your camp sometime if you tell me where it is."

Neville was uncomfortable giving away the location of his home, but he wanted that information about the large alligators. "Twelve feet, huh?"

"Yeah. And I'd be grateful if you got them. I don't like those big ones swimming around out here while I'm trying to check gauges."

After a few moments Neville nodded cautiously. "Back down the way you come, then left at the first canal. Up there about two miles in a grove of willows. I got one of the only cabins this side of Lafourche. Now that I think about it, it might be nice to have a little company once in a while."

The man nodded. He had what he needed. "Okay." He leaned down and gunned the Whaler's engine in reverse, ridding the propeller of the choking water lilies. Bailey quickly retreated to the canoe. "Adios!" the man yelled above the roar as he powered forward once more and steered away.

Twenty minutes later, when the man was certain he had left

Neville and his too-curious hound far behind, he cut the engine and dropped anchor. For several moments he aimed the spotlight about the water's surface and counted ten sets of yellow eyes reflecting in the glare. He moved to the front of the boat, removed a body from the canvas sack, and, with thick chains, affixed the cinder blocks to the body's neck, wrists, and ankles. He caught his breath for a moment, then, with a herculean effort, rolled everything over the side of the boat. The body and the cinder blocks splashed loudly in rapid succession. By the time the man retrieved the spotlight and aimed it down on the black water, only a few bubbles remained. The alligators would feast that evening.

The man turned and headed back to the steering wheel. He was going to take Neville up on his offer to stop by—probably a little sooner than the Cajun had anticipated. Neville wouldn't see sunrise.

■ ■ ■

The Gulfstream IV climbed off the St. Croix runway into the night, roared over the lights of a sprawling oil refinery, and headed north for a hundred miles out over the Atlantic Ocean. Then it turned west, toward Miami.

The mood on board was somber. That afternoon the five senior executives now sitting quietly in the jet's passenger compartment had made an exhaustive presentation to a wealthy individual living on the island. Several days earlier he had expressed a preliminary interest in their company. The executives needed money desperately and had flown to St. Croix immediately to persuade him to become their partner. For all intents and purposes their company was insolvent, though only a few individuals outside the senior management team knew how dire the situation was.

At the conclusion of the presentation the investor had decided against making what was marketed to him as the opportunity of a lifetime. He had sensed desperation seeping through the executives' conservative suits and too-confident, too-cavalier demeanors. Their answers to his questions were unspecific and evasive, and they had traveled too quickly to see him. An experienced investor, he had learned that people who were overly accommodating usually had pressing needs, and more often than not pressing needs were a precursor to financial distress—something he wanted no part of.

Time had run out for the executives. The company didn't have enough money in its checking account to meet the payroll at the end of the week, no more availability under its bank line of credit, and only a dwindling stream of customer payments trickling in. The next day the chief executive officer would call the lawyers in New York and request that they file the appropriate bankruptcy documents. There were no options left.

The CEO gazed out his window into the darkness. The bankruptcy filing would buy time, but little else. Without a significant slug of fresh capital, the company was doomed. Ultimately it would be liquidated for salvage value by creditors who would be lucky to receive fifty cents on the dollar for the assets—a scenario that would net the original equity investor nothing. The CEO shut his eyes tightly, trying not to think about how difficult the telephone call to that man would be.

The bomb had been armed moments after takeoff by a wire running from where it had been planted in the baggage compartment to the nose-gear uplock switch. When the wheels had fully retracted into the fuselage, the countdown began automatically, set to expire thirty-two minutes later, when the jet would be over an area of the Atlantic where the seabed was deep and the currents strong. Where all remnants of the plane and its occupants would be lost forever only a few minutes after the crash. Where the emergency locator transmitter would die twenty-four hours later without guiding rescuers or investigators to the sight—if its electronic pulse even survived the explosion.

The man scanned the starry sky from the deck of the sailboat, listening intently. He knew the plane should be close, and as the seconds ticked by he worked hard to control his anticipation—and his anxiety. Finally he heard the whine of engines and moments later observed a tiny flash of light when the bomb detonated. Then he saw a larger flash as the jet's fuel tanks caught fire and exploded, sending the decimated craft plummeting toward the water's surface in a shower of twisted metal.

He let out a long, slow breath. He had executed two extremely sensitive missions in rapid succession. His superiors would be pleased. The cause would live on.

CHAPTER 1

JUNE 1999

"How much do you make?"

"Salary or total compensation?" Jay West asked deliberately. He never disclosed sensitive information until he absolutely had to, even in a situation like this one, where he was expected to answer every question quickly and completely.

"What was the income figure on your W-2 last year? A W-2 is that little form your employer sends you each January to let you know how much you have to report to the IRS."

"I know what a W-2 is," Jay answered calmly, displaying no outward irritation at the interviewer's sarcastic tone. The young man on the opposite side of the conference room table wore a dark business suit, as did Jay. However, the other man's suit was custom-made. It was crisper, was crafted of finer material, and followed the contours of his muscular physique perfectly. Jay had purchased his suit off the rack, and it bunched up in certain spots despite a tailor's best efforts. "The commercial bank I work for provides me certain fringe benefits that don't appear on my W-2, so my income is actually more than—"

"What kind of fringe benefits?" the interviewer demanded rudely.

For a moment Jay studied the unfriendly square-jawed face beneath the strawberry-blond crew cut, trying to determine if the confrontational demeanor was forced or natural. He had heard that Wall Street firms often made prospective employees endure at least one stressful interview during the hiring process just to see how they reacted. But if this guy was acting, he was giving an Academy Award performance. "A below-market mortgage rate, a company match on my 401K plan, and a liberal health insurance package."

The man rolled his eyes. "How much can those things be worth, for Christ's sake?"

"The amount is significant."

The man waved a hand in front of his face impatiently. "Okay, I'll be generous and add twenty thousand to the figure you quote me. Now, how much did you make last year?"

Jay shifted uncomfortably in his seat, aware that the figure wouldn't impress the investment banker.

"Hello, Jay." Oliver Mason stood in the conference room doorway, smiling pleasantly, a leather-bound portfolio under his arm. "I'm glad you could make time for us tonight."

Jay glanced at Mason and smiled back, relieved that he wasn't going to have to answer the income question. "Hi, Oliver," he said confidently, standing up and shaking hands. Oliver always had a sleek look about him, like an expensive sports car that had just been detailed. "Thanks for having me."

"My pleasure." Oliver sat in the chair next to Jay's and put his portfolio down. He gestured across the table at Carter Bullock. "Has my lieutenant been grilling you?"

"Not at all," Jay answered, trying to seem unaffected by Bullock's third degree. "We were just having a friendly chat."

"You're lying. Nobody ever just chats with Bullock during an interview." Oliver removed two copies of Jay's resume from the portfolio. "Bullock's about as friendly as a honey badger, which is what he's affectionately known as around here," Oliver explained. "Badger, for short." He slid one copy of the resume across the polished tabletop. "Here you go, Badger. Sorry I didn't get this to you sooner. But I'm the captain and you're just a deckhand on this ship, so deal with it."

"Screw you, Oliver." Bullock grabbed the resume with his thick fingers, scanned it quickly, then groaned, crumpled the paper into a ball, and threw it toward a trash can in a far corner of the conference room.

"Do you know about honey badgers, Jay?" Oliver asked in his naturally aloof, nasal voice. He was smiling broadly, unconcerned by Bullock's less-than-positive reaction to Jay's resume.

Jay shook his head, trying to ignore the sight of his life being tossed toward the circular file. "No."

"Most predators aim for the throat when they attack their prey." Oliver chuckled. "Honey badgers aim for the groin. They lock their jaws and don't let go, no matter what the prey does. They don't release their grip until the prey goes into shock, which, as you might imagine, doesn't take long, especially if the prey is the male of the species. Then they tear the animal apart while it's still alive." Oliver shivered, picturing the scene. "What a way to go."

"Screw you *and* your mother, Oliver." But Bullock was grinning for the first time, obviously pleased with his nickname and his tough-as-tungsten reputation.

Oliver put both hands behind his head and interlaced his fingers. "Don't let me interrupt, Badger."

Bullock leaned over the table, a triumphant expression on his wide, freckled face. "So, Jay, how much *did* you make last year?"

Oliver Mason's appearance wasn't going to get him off the hot seat after all. "A hundred thousand dollars," Jay answered defiantly, staring at Bullock's flat nose. The figure—salary plus bonus—was actually closer to ninety.

Bullock rolled his eyes at the number. "Do you live in Manhattan?"

"Yes." Jay had been prepared for the negative reaction. He knew that Oliver Mason and Carter Bullock earned many multiples of his salary as senior executives at the boutique investment banking firm of McCarthy & Lloyd.

"How the hell do you survive on that in Manhattan?" Bullock wanted to know.

"A hundred thousand dollars is nothing to scoff at," Jay retorted. He was proud of how far he'd come in life.

"Are you married?" Bullock asked.

Jay shook his head.

"Where do you live?"

"Upper West Side."

"Do you rent or own?"

"Rent."

"One or two bedrooms?"

"One."

"Got a car?"

Jay nodded.

"What kind?"

"A BMW," he answered, aware that Oliver and Bullock wouldn't be impressed if they knew his real mode of transportation was a beat-up, barely operational Ford Taurus. "A three-twenty-eight."

"Do you park it in the city?" Bullock asked.

Jay nodded again, then flashed a quick glance at Oliver, who was staring into space, probably thinking about a deal that would net him millions.

Bullock reclined in his chair and contemplated the ceiling. "So let's think about this," he said, stroking his chin with his thumb and forefinger. "You make a hundred thousand dollars a year, which, without any deductions or exemptions other than yourself, is about seventy thousand after taxes. I'll be generous and assume that you clear six thousand dollars a month." He tapped the arm of his chair, clearly enjoying the analysis. For Bullock, Jay thought, life came down to numbers and little else. "You're probably paying about four thousand a month for your rent, utilities, car loan, parking, and insurance. I'm sure you have a significant amount of school loans, too." Bullock glanced at Jay for confirmation.

But Jay gave no indication that Bullock was right on target. No indication that each month he was writing a hefty check to slowly repay the forty thousand dollars—plus interest—he had borrowed to finance his four years of college.

"That leaves two thousand a month for groceries, clothes, a social life," Bullock continued, "and to save for the house in the suburbs you'll have to buy when you meet that perfect girl and she wants to start nesting. The problem is that you'll only have enough to buy her a two-bedroom box in Jersey City and not the sprawling mansion in Greenwich she'll require." He snickered. "And at a commercial bank your upside is limited. You'll receive inflation raises for the next forty years, then retire with a gold watch and medical benefits. Maybe." Bullock shook his head. "You're poor, pal. You're a hamster on a treadmill, and there's no way off."

Jay didn't flinch despite the accuracy of Bullock's back-of-the-envelope analysis. A hundred thousand dollars a year sounded like a lot of money, but within fifty miles of New York City it didn't go very far. He had almost nothing to show for six years of working at the National City Bank of New York as an account officer making loans to medium-sized companies. And though the upside opportunity at the bank was better than Bullock had described, it wasn't great.

"Oh, wait a minute." Bullock spoke up, touching his forehead. "I almost forgot about all those wonderful fringe benefits you mentioned. Like that below-market mortgage rate you can't take advantage of because you can't afford to buy a place."

Jay felt Oliver tap his shin with the point of a shiny black tasseled loafer.

"Told you." Oliver was refocused on the interview. "My buddy Bullock is a ball-buster, isn't he? We don't let him out in public much, but he's hell on the trading floor." Oliver chuckled. "Badger operates on the golden rule: He who has the gold rules. Remember that. Live every day of your McCarthy and Lloyd career by that simple tenet and you'll be successful."

Jay eyed Oliver. He was thirty-eight, ten years older than Jay. His handsome face was deeply tanned from weekends spent sailing his fifty-foot sloop on Long Island Sound. His dark brown eyes were in constant motion, darting about, taking in everything around him so that his brain could process as much information as possible. A got-the-world-by-the-short-hairs grin was etched onto his thin lips, and his long, jet-black hair was combed straight back and kept fastidiously in place with a generous amount of gel, revealing a wide, sloping forehead. Navy blue suspenders divided his starched white shirt into three distinct sectors, and a brightly colored Hermès tie fell smartly from his neck, a perfect divot in the middle of the knot.

Jay gave Oliver a quick grin. "His nickname does fit."

Bullock folded his arms across his chest, satisfied that he had accurately dissected Jay West's personal financial statement and, by doing so, established rank.

"We all know that commercial banks don't pay anywhere near what we do. They can't afford to because they don't take real risks." Oliver broke into his take-charge-of-the-meeting voice, more nasal than normal. "But that isn't what we're here to discuss. We're here to discuss Jay's joining McCarthy and Lloyd to work for me on the equity arbitrage desk."

"But why him?" Bullock pointed at Jay, then at the crumpled resume lying beside the trash can. "No offense, kid, but you've got an average resume at best." Bullock was thirty-three, only five years older than Jay, but he was perfectly at ease addressing Jay as "kid" because he made so much more money. "You went to Lehigh." Bullock tilted his head back. "It's a good school but certainly not A-list, not Ivy League. And you haven't even been to graduate business school yet."

"Hey, I—"

Bullock kept going. "There's a ton of young people out there with sterling-silver resumes." He waved nonchalantly at the window. "People who attended Princeton, Harvard, or Yale. People with the experience and background we're looking for. We can attract the cream of the crop. Why should we bother with you?"

"That's enough—"

"Why would you hire him, Oliver?" Bullock ignored Jay's second attempt to turn the tide. "Forget about where he went to school, or didn't—he's never had any arbitrage experience. He has no idea how to identify or value potential takeover stocks. He's a damn lending officer at a run-of-the-mill commercial bank making dog shit for a living."

"Exactly!" Jay slammed his fist on the table.

Oliver and Bullock both flinched, caught off guard by the sudden, loud noise.

"I'm hungry." Jay suppressed a smile at Bullock's startled expression. "I'll work twenty-four seven. I'll dedicate myself to this firm. I'll do whatever it takes."

"Yeah, yeah," Bullock said, smirking. "Everybody wants to be an investment banker these days, but—"

"And I do know how to find and value potential takeover stocks." It was Jay's turn to interrupt Bullock. "I'm not just a lending officer. I've acted as a financial advisor on several takeovers at National City in which I initiated the transactions for our clients. They were small, private deals, I'll be the first to admit. Not the sexy deals, splashed all over the *Wall Street Journal*, that you guys are involved with, but my bank still made a great deal of money." Jay drew in a quick breath without giving Bullock a chance to cut in. "Numbers are numbers. Your deals just have a few more zeros than mine. But I've made a good reputation for myself at National City."

"That's true," Oliver agreed. "The senior people at National City love him, Badger. I called a few people and checked him out." Oliver put a hand on Jay's shoulder. "He's talented."

Bullock shook his head. "I'm not convinced. Let's hire a Harvard Business School grad and cover our asses. If the HBS person doesn't work out, we'll have a lot less explaining to do. If this guy doesn't work out"—Bullock pointed at Jay again—"we'll be in hot water with the man. He'll want to know what in the hell we were thinking about." Bullock paused. "I really liked that woman we saw last night. What was her name?" He snapped his fingers several times.

Jay's eyes narrowed. "Why are you so concerned with where I went to college, Badger?"

"Huh?"

"Your boss here," Jay said, gesturing at Oliver, "went to City College. City College is about as far from the Ivy League as anyone can get, and he's done pretty well without the privilege of attending one of those highbrow schools."

Oliver bit his lip to keep from smiling. Bullock might possess the relentless determination of a honey badger, but in a different way Jay West was equally formidable. Jay was street-smart. He knew how to obtain sensitive information and was willing to use it. That was the word on him. And he came from a lower-middle-class background, so he was financially motivated. It was the perfect combination for what Oliver needed.

"I know you went to Harvard, Badger," Jay continued. "I know you're a Crimson man."

"Yeah, so?" Bullock asked hesitantly.

"But it isn't as if your family and the Ivy League are synonymous. There is no Bullock Hall at Harvard, Badger. Quite the opposite. Your mother went to a community college, and your father never even graduated from high school. He's a mechanic, just like my father is. Though I'm sure my father's better." Jay winked at Oliver. "In fact, Badger, we have more in common than you'd probably like to admit. We're both from way-past-their-prime steel towns in eastern Pennsylvania."

Bullock bristled. "How the hell did you find out all that?"

"I have—"

"It doesn't matter how he found out," Oliver interrupted. "What's important is that he did. It's obvious to me that Jay can access information when he needs to, which is the most important quality someone can have in the arbitrage business." Oliver thought for a moment. "And he's hungry. An HBS grad is likely to have a trust fund we don't know about, Badger. When the going gets tough and the days get long, that person might bail out on us. Jay won't. He'll do whatever it takes to make money for McCarthy and Lloyd." Oliver glanced at Jay. "Won't you?"

"Yes," Jay answered forcefully. "Whatever it takes." He sensed that this was the deciding moment. "Whatever it takes," he repeated.

"I worked with Jay on a transaction and I liked what I saw. I've been talking to him about this position for three months while I've been doing my background checks. I have confidence he would do very well here at McCarthy and Lloyd."

Bullock shrugged, unimpressed by his superior's argument. "You asked me to meet this guy and give you my honest opinion, Oliver." Bullock eyed Jay skeptically. "I don't think you should hire him." He hesitated. "But you're the boss."

"Good, then it's settled." Oliver shook Jay's hand. "You've got the job."

Jay's body relaxed, as if he'd finally been able to let go of a great weight. "Really?"

"Yup."

"That fast?"

"I'm the boss." Oliver waved a hand in Bullock's direction. "I wanted to give Badger a chance to rage. Things have been pretty calm around here the past few days, and he gets out of sorts if he doesn't have an opportunity to get angry once in a while."

"What can I say except thanks?" Jay shook Oliver's hand again. "I accept." He gave Bullock a subtle victory smile.

Bullock stood up, shook his head, snorted, and exited the room without saying goodbye.

"Not a very friendly guy," Jay observed, watching the strawberry-blond crew cut disappear into the hallway.

"Does that bother you?"

Jay exhaled heavily. "No. I want to work at McCarthy and Lloyd to make money, not friends."

Oliver nodded approvingly. "That's what I wanted to hear you say." His expression turned serious. "I had to put you through all that because I needed to see how you reacted under pressure. I asked Badger to make things rough on you before I came in. It can get crazy around this place when deals unfold. You did great, like I knew you would." Oliver rubbed his hands together. "Now let's talk about McCarthy and Lloyd."

Jay closed his eyes and allowed himself a moment of immense elation. He had made the jump to the major leagues of the financial world. "Okay," he said calmly.

"As we've discussed, I run the equity arbitrage desk. My mandate is simple: to make money by speculating on publicly traded stocks." Oliver flipped Jay's resume over and scribbled something on the back. "Sometimes we buy stocks of companies that are 'in play,' " he continued. "Those are situations in which a company has already received a takeover offer, and we bet that it will receive another, higher offer from a second bidder or from the original bidder. Perhaps several more offers surface from several more bidders. Ultimately, I sell our shares to the highest bidder. The risk for me in those situations is that no other bidders surface or that the target's management can't goose up the original bidder. Then I probably lose a couple of bucks a share when the stock price settles back down, because it usually pops above the initial offer price when the deal is first announced."

"That makes sense." Jay watched Oliver scribble again on the paper. He was constantly making notes to himself, carrying on the conversation with Jay and thinking about several other things simultaneously.

Oliver finished writing, then carefully replaced his Mont Blanc pen in his shirt pocket. "We'll also buy shares of companies that my people and I think would make particularly attractive takeover candidates—situations in which a takeover *hasn't* yet been announced, but we think it will be in the near future. If a takeover is announced, we benefit when the price of the stock we hold runs up toward the offer price, which, as you probably know, is always above the current trading price because acquirers must pay a premium for control."

"Sure."

Oliver smiled as if he were consuming a delicious dessert. "It's beautiful when we buy a stock before the first offer is announced, because that's where the real juice in the takeover game is. That's when the stock price can double or triple overnight. After the first offer, subsequent bids are usually only a few dollars higher." He laughed. "We sit back and watch the stock price soar. Ultimately we make millions, sometimes tens of millions in those deals."

"It's got to be tough to hit on many deals where you buy the stock even before the first offer is announced," Jay pointed out. "You'd have to have privileged information to do it consistently."

Oliver's eyes narrowed slightly. "Do you mean *inside* information?"

Jay hesitated, aware that he had stepped into no-man's-land.

"Trading on inside information would be illegal," Oliver said quietly after an uncomfortable silence. "Listen to me and listen to me good. We are absolutely ethical around here. If a deal smells at all, we don't get involved. It's like that piece of week-old meat in the refrigerator that doesn't look or smell too good. Some idiots are willing to risk food poisoning because they can't bear to see the meat wasted. So they eat it and end up in the hospital. Here at McCarthy and Lloyd, we don't care. We make enough money that we don't have to take those kinds of foolish risks. We toss the rotten meat out and make a fresh kill. Our chairman wouldn't have it any other way. All you have in this business is your reputation, Jay. We want to keep ours pristine."

"Of course," Jay agreed. "How many people work in the arbitrage group?" he asked, quickly steering the conversation in a different direction.

"Right now three professionals, a secretary, and an administrative assistant. You'll be the fourth professional." Oliver hesitated. "We may hire one more at some point. Anyway, I run the desk, and my title is managing director," he continued, gesturing at the door. "Bullock is a director, one title below me, and my right-hand man. We also have an associate. Her name is Abigail Cooper. You'll be a vice president, the title between director and associate, and report to Bullock, as Abby does."

Jay nodded. It wasn't going to be much fun reporting to Bullock, but then, life couldn't be perfect. And Jay knew Bullock's attitude would improve if Jay made money.

"Now let's focus on compensation," Oliver said.

Here was the crux of the issue. The reason Jay was willing to have no life outside of McCarthy & Lloyd.

"Your annual salary will be fifty thousand dollars."

"Excuse me?" Jay's exhilaration faded.

Oliver saw the disappointment evident in Jay's expression. "Yup, fifty grand. That's what every professional at your level makes here at McCarthy and Lloyd."

"But I earn more than fifty thousand a year now."

"And we don't make any fringe benefits available to the professional staff," Oliver continued, ignoring Jay's objection. "No health or life insurance, no 401K plan, not even a pension."

"Are you serious?"

"Absolutely."

Jay looked down.

"But I will make you one promise, Jay West."

"What's that?"

"I'll guarantee you a minimum bonus of a million dollars,

and I'll guarantee it to you in writing. You show up on the arbitrage desk every day until the end of the year, and on January fifteenth McCarthy and Lloyd will stroke you a check for *at least* a million."

Jay managed to control his show of emotion despite the anticipation tearing through his body. "Really?"

"Absolutely." Oliver watched Jay's reaction carefully, vaguely disappointed that the younger man hadn't been more outwardly affected by news of the huge bonus. "And I want you to consider two things. First, it's already the middle of June, so that million dollars represents compensation for only half a year's work. I'll let you do the math." Oliver paused as if to allow Jay a moment to double a million. "Second, if you do more than simply come into the desk every day, your bonus next January could be well in excess of your guarantee. If you come up with a couple of stocks that end up being taken over and the firm makes some real money directly as a result of your contribution, your actual bonus in January could be multiples of what I've guaranteed you."

Jay curled his fingers around the arms of the chair. A million dollars in one lump sum. His life would change dramatically with that deposit. His annual salary at National City had been seventy thousand dollars and his last bonus twenty-three. He had been at the top of his peer group in terms of the bonus amount and considered himself a success. Now he realized how wrong he'd been.

"You're lucky," Oliver remarked. "Around here we like to say that we eat only what we kill. But in your case, you'll have a guarantee. At least for the first year. Of course, if you don't produce, you'll be out on your ass."

"I understand," Jay answered. "But I'll earn the million."

Oliver leaned back and yawned, as if a million was nothing to be particularly impressed with. "Bullock earned three million last January," he said casually.

Jay's heart rate jumped several notches, but he made certain Oliver detected no sign of his excitement. Being too excited about anything, even the possibility of a huge bonus, could be taken as a sign of weakness.

"He does an outstanding job, and I recognize him for it because I don't want him jumping ship for another firm. He made McCarthy and Lloyd almost thirty million dollars last year using very little of the firm's capital."

"I won't let Bullock know that you told me what he makes," Jay said.

"I don't care if you tell him. He's proud of it. Wouldn't you be?" Oliver hesitated. "There aren't any secrets about what people earn around here. We want the figures to be out in the open. It makes you work harder." His eyes flashed. "See, that's the way Wall Street operates. We bring life down to its most basic element, survival, and its most powerful motivator, incentive. We make every day an all-out competition. If you win, you win big. If you lose, you find out pretty quickly and you get out. Or you get fired." Oliver's smile broadened. "But you strike me as a winner."

"I am," Jay said confidently. He had left his office at National City that night not knowing what to expect, and the last half hour had been an emotional roller-coaster ride. But the interview had ultimately turned out far better than he could have imagined. Taking the cut in salary would be a small, short-term price to pay for that million-dollar guarantee.

Oliver picked up Jay's resume. "Let's go meet Bill McCarthy. He's the chairman of McCarthy and Lloyd."

"I know who he is."

Everyone in the financial industry recognized the name Bill McCarthy. Ten years before, he and Graham Lloyd had left promising careers at one of Wall Street's most prestigious investment banks to strike out on their own. Now McCarthy was chairman of one of the Street's most profitable private firms, a firm that executed stock and bond trades and provided financial advice to America's wealthiest individuals as well as the world's bluest-chip companies and most stable governments. McCarthy regularly counseled senior White House officials and prominent CEOs. *Forbes* had estimated his net worth to be half a billion dollars, and he counted the governor of New York and the mayor of New York City as friends.

"Hurry up." Oliver beckoned to Jay from the conference room doorway. "Oh, one thing," Oliver cautioned, holding up his hand.

"What?"

"Everything that goes on at McCarthy and Lloyd stays within the walls of the firm. You know what Bullock's bonus was last year, but that figure doesn't get to anyone who isn't employed by McCarthy and Lloyd. Just the same way you wouldn't discuss proprietary information about one of our clients with anyone outside the firm. If someone is caught discussing any of our business with anyone on the outside, it's grounds for immediate dismissal. We are privy to very sensitive information around here on an almost hourly basis. We need to protect our clients' privacy, and as the saying goes, loose lips sink ships."

Only in times of war, Jay thought.

"Bill McCarthy is a stickler on that issue, and people have been terminated for violating the policy," Oliver continued. "For getting drunk in a bar and saying things they shouldn't have. Got that?"

Jay heard an ominous tone in Oliver's voice. "Yes."

"Good." The warning was over and the friendly tone returned. "Let's go." Oliver moved out into the hallway, and Jay hustled to keep pace. "It's the press that's the real problem," Oliver called over his shoulder. "They're so damn hungry to find out about this place."

"I'm sure." Jay was well aware that details of what went on inside McCarthy & Lloyd were not generally available to the outside world. The *Wall Street Journal* had nicknamed the firm Area 51 after the top-secret Air Force base in the Nevada desert where the government developed next-generation weapons and was rumored by conspiracy zealots to have interred the Roswell aliens. And reporters had dubbed Bill McCarthy "Howard Hughes" for his total abhorrence of publicity.

"Of course, our desire to maintain a low profile only feeds the press's appetite." Oliver smiled. "Bill is a smooth operator. We get more publicity by saying nothing than we would by advertising."

The hallway suddenly opened up onto McCarthy & Lloyd's huge trading floor—over an acre in size. In front of the two men lay row after row of lunch-counter-like workstations, each twenty feet long and facing a bulkhead, on the other side of which was another workstation of equal length. Four to five people sat elbow to elbow on either side of the bulkhead like patrons at a diner. Each chair was known as a "position" on the floor. In front of each position, and supported by the bulkhead, were several computer screens providing up-to-the-second data concerning stock, bond, currency, and derivative markets around the world. Also in front of each position were telephone banks with multiple lines so that the trader could buy and sell securities instantaneously. Televisions tuned to CNN were positioned throughout the room to give them information on world events, because a coup in Russia could trash U.S. markets as quickly as chaos at home—and vice versa. There was little decoration around the room, just a small country flag or two on top of the bulkheads of the foreign-exchange areas signifying the currencies traded there. Overall it was a bland and uninviting environment. But decoration was superfluous, and the people there didn't have time for nonessentials. They were there to make money and that was all.

Oliver stopped and pointed toward a far corner. "Over there," he said, having to speak loudly over the dull roar of many voices, "is the equity desk—"

"Desk?" Jay asked.

"Yeah," Oliver replied. "We don't use the word *groups* or *divisions* on the trading floor. We call them *desks*."

"Okay."

"Those three workstations in the corner comprise the equity desk—salespeople as well as traders using house money. Along that wall is the fixed-income desk, and beside them is—"

"Oliver!" A short, dark-haired young woman rushed toward them down the open corridor paralleling the length of the trading floor. She was clutching a single piece of paper.

"Hi, Abby," Oliver called.

"I've got the offer sheet ready for that block trade." Abby smiled politely at Jay, then looked back at Oliver. "I'm going to fax it over."

"Good." Out of the corner of his eye Jay noticed Oliver's and Abby's fingers intertwine momentarily. Then she rushed away and the scent of her perfume drifted over him.

"Abby's a sweet girl," Oliver said. "A tremendously hard worker. She'll be here until at least ten o'clock tonight." He glanced at Jay. "Abby is the associate on the arbitrage desk I mentioned earlier. You'll like her."

"I'm sure." Jay checked Oliver's left hand and saw a wedding band.

"Hey, pal, I saw you checking Abby out, and I've got to say I agree with your taste." Oliver gave Jay a friendly punch on the upper arm. "But don't get any ideas. She's spoken for." He turned and began moving forward again. "As I was saying, the capital market desk is over there, next to the fixed-income people, and our home, the equity arbitrage desk, is positioned in the far corner. We have only one workstation, but we make more money than anyone else on the entire floor." He waved toward the desk casually. "The difference between us and the equity guys in the far corner is that we trade *only* takeover stocks. They trade all other stocks."

Jay followed Oliver's gesture and caught a glimpse of Bullock sitting in front of a computer, studying one of his screens.

"Hey, it's God!"

Jay's head snapped right. A young trader twenty feet away had directed the remark at Oliver.

"You the man, Oliver!" another yelled.

"What's that all about?" Jay asked.

Oliver gave the two traders a friendly nod. "The arbitrage desk has performed tremendously well since I arrived here five years ago," he explained immodestly. "As I said, we're small in terms of people, but we make more money than any other desk. The fixed-income desk those two guys work on didn't do too well last year. In fact, they lost money for the firm, but they still received decent bonuses because my desk, the desk you are about to become a part of," Oliver emphasized, "tore the cover off the ball. Again," he bragged.

"There goes the king!" someone yelled.

Jay shook his head. It was like accompanying royalty.

"Upstairs are the merger-and-acquisition, corporate-finance, and project-finance groups," Oliver continued, ignoring the last accolade. "Bill doesn't like those groups being located on the trading floor because of the potential conflict of interest. Like it isn't a conflict of interest to have the arbitrage desk on the same floor with the equity traders," he said smugly. "They hear about takeover bids before almost anyone except the M and A people, and it would be very easy for one of them to run over to us and give us the inside scoop so we could trade on it. But hey, it's Bill's firm. He can do what he wants."

Jay scanned the floor. Most of the several hundred individuals talking into phones, checking computer screens, or conversing with each other were men, and the few women on the floor were young and attractive. He noticed the way most of them nodded deferentially to Oliver, and how Oliver acknowledged very few of them.

"You will sign a contract with us tomorrow," Oliver remarked. "You probably never did that at National City, did you?"

"No."

"Don't worry, it's standard stuff. It'll spell out in detail the financial and legal terms of your employment." Oliver clapped his hands and laughed. "It'll stipulate that you can't sue us for anything. That any dispute you ever have with McCarthy and Lloyd will be settled by an industry arbitrator. Probably by someone who owes Bill a big favor. A lot of the big investment banks have gotten away from that policy and have allowed employees to sue them, but not us. We don't have to." Oliver slammed the wall with his open palm. "What a crock of shit that is, huh? But what difference does it make? Everybody understands that you're here to make money and if you don't, you'll be fired. If you want a comfortable living, Jay West, sell sofas and easy chairs. And for Christ's sake, don't tell the human-resources person that you need to have an attorney review the contract. That's a big red flag."

"I won't."

Oliver turned down a hallway leading away from the trading floor, and the dull roar subsided. "What's today?"

"Tuesday," Jay answered, glad to be of even trivial assistance to a man who had just guaranteed him at least a million-dollar payday in a little over seven months.

"All right, then you'll start on Thursday."

"I can't."

"What?" Oliver stopped abruptly and whipped around, hands on hips, his face twisted into an expression of intense irritation.

Jay blinked slowly. "I want to give the people at National City the standard two weeks before I leave. I want them to have plenty of time to put someone on my accounts and make the transition smooth."

"Bullshit, Jay!" Oliver bellowed, furious. "Son, I've just guaranteed you a million-dollar bonus in January from my personal operating budget. I want you in this building ASAP. Not next week, not the week after, but Thursday. I think I'm being pretty damn generous to give you two days to get your personal house in order. For a million dollars you ought to be planting your ass on the desk and getting to work for me as soon as you finish speaking to Bill McCarthy. Every day you're working for National City, you're not working for me."

"It's just that the people at National City have been good to me," Jay said quietly. "They're my friends. I want to leave there on good terms. I think that's important."

"Not half as important as pleasing me, pal," Oliver replied coldly.

Jay gazed at Oliver for several moments. The senior executives at National City weren't going to be happy, but Oliver Mason had offered him the opportunity of a lifetime. He had no choice. "Okay, I'll be here first thing Thursday morning."

"That's the right answer. You had me worried for a second, son. Remember, no matter what anyone tells you, life is a one-way street. That one way is straight ahead. Keep your eye on the target, move directly at it any way you can, and don't waste time worrying about people who can't do anything for you anymore. As of this moment, those idiots at National City are in the past. Fuck 'em." Oliver saw that Jay was struggling with his decision to leave National City so abruptly. "You don't have any children, do you?" he asked.

"No."

"Get some," Oliver advised.

"Why?"

"They're the only people who will ever truly appreciate you."

"What do you mean?"

"They don't know any better. Unfortunately, even they catch on at some point." Oliver shook his head. "Yup, get yourself some children, Jay, but don't misunderstand me. I'm not suggesting that you get a wife." He continued down the hallway. "Here we are," he announced suddenly, pushing open a door without knocking. "Hello, Karen."

"Hi, Oliver."

Jay watched Oliver stride to the desk, take the hand of a woman sitting behind it, then lean down and gallantly kiss the backs of her fingers.

"Oh, Oliver." The woman turned her head to the side, delighted with Oliver's attention.

"Jay, meet Karen Walker." Oliver gestured at Karen. "She is Bill McCarthy's very capable executive assistant."

Jay judged Karen to be in her fifties. She was the first woman even close to that age he had encountered at McCarthy & Lloyd. "Hello."

"Hi," she said politely, then quickly turned her attention back to Oliver. "How is that lovely wife of yours?"

"Just fine, thanks."

"Hello, Oliver." Bill McCarthy's voice boomed out as he appeared in the doorway of the inner office, shirtsleeves rolled up above his elbows and what little remained of a lit cigar clenched between his teeth. He was a bear of a man with a large nose, meaty cheeks, and an unruly head of shaggy blond hair.

"Hello, Bill." Oliver held up a black leather cigar case. "I've got something for you."

"What?" McCarthy asked in his deep southern drawl.

"Davidoff Double R's." He pulled two out of the case and handed them to McCarthy. "Twenty bucks a pop. Best cigar this side of Cuba."

McCarthy snatched the cigars from Oliver without a word, then walked directly to Jay and shook his hand. "Bill McCarthy."

"Jay West."

"Follow me, Mr. West," McCarthy ordered gruffly, heading back into his office.

Jay stepped toward the office doorway through which McCarthy had disappeared.

"Have fun," Oliver said quietly. "But don't say anything stupid, like you can't leave National City for another two weeks because the people there have been so good to you."

"Aren't you coming in?" Jay asked, ignoring Oliver's remark.

"Nope. You won't be in there very long. Find me when you're done."

"Right."

"Come in," McCarthy growled when Jay hesitated at the doorway of the spacious office. It was a corner office with a panoramic view of lower Manhattan and New York Harbor beyond. Lights from ships anchored north of the Verrazano-Narrows Bridge shimmered in the distance with dusk falling on the city. "Shut the door," McCarthy instructed, sitting down behind his massive desk, cluttered with newspapers and Styrofoam cups half full of black coffee.

Jay pushed the door shut, and it clicked behind him.

"Let's get a couple of things straight right off the bat," McCarthy began. "Don't call me Mr. McCarthy or sir. Call me Bill. This is a collegial firm."

McCarthy's southern accent was heavy, and Jay had to listen carefully to make certain he understood. "Okay . . . Bill."

"Don't kiss my ass with any false respect crap, either. And, yes, I'm worth north of five hundred million dollars. Actually, well north. North Pole north, in fact." He chuckled. "And I do talk to one of the president's senior advisors every few days. The governor's and mayor's offices as well. They are constantly looking to me for guidance. The *Forbes* article you probably read to prepare for your interview was accurate; in fact, it didn't really paint the whole picture. I'm even better-connected than it reported, and that is for two very good reasons: I'm almost always right when I give advice, and I'm generous with my contributions. Give politicians money and they'll do anything for you. They are the most predictable people in the world that way." McCarthy took a puff from his cigar and tossed the Davidoffs Oliver had given him onto the cluttered desk. "Now sit down," he directed again, pointing at a chair in front of the desk as he began to search through the mess before him.

Jay moved to the chair and sat.

McCarthy glanced at the younger man as he rummaged through papers. Jay was tall and lanky with straight, layered dirty-blond hair, parted on one side. It fell over his forehead almost to his dark eyebrows in the front and to the bottom of his collar in the back. His face was thin but strong, dominated by large dark blue eyes, full lips, and a nose that was slightly crooked—probably broken at one point, McCarthy assumed. And under one eye was a faded half-inch-long scar, the only imperfection on a smooth complexion that still needed shaving only twice a week to keep a sparse cover of whiskers at bay. But the characteristic that struck McCarthy most wasn't physical. What impressed McCarthy so strongly, and gave him the slightest seed of concern, was the steely self-assurance evident in Jay's measured manner.

McCarthy drew himself up in the desk chair. "You need a haircut," he blurted suddenly.

"Excuse me?" Jay had been taking in the view of the harbor.

"Your hair's too long. I don't like that."

"All right." Jay stole an inquisitive glance at McCarthy's own longish hair.

McCarthy continued hunting through the papers on his desk. "I know Oliver sent me your resume in the office mail, but I can't find it in this pile of crap." He abandoned the search and reclined in his large leather chair. "So give me the audio version, and make it the abridged one."

"Okay. I'm from Bethlehem, Pennsylvania. I graduated from Lehigh six years ago last week with a degree in English. And since then I've been working for the National City Bank of New York as a corporate finance specialist."

McCarthy removed the stub of thc cigar from his mouth and pointed it at Jay. "You mean you've been working as a lending officer."

"Pardon?"

"All you people at commercial banks claim you're corporate-finance specialists," McCarthy said testily. "But to me, a corporate-finance specialist is someone who underwrites public debt and equity deals, which I'd be willing to bet a lot of money you've never done. You've made loans, right?"

In six years at National City Jay had never experienced a

personal confrontation or had someone call into question his abilities. At McCarthy & Lloyd it had happened three times in the last twenty minutes, and he wasn't even officially an employee yet. "I've done my share of deals," he responded evenly.

McCarthy thought about digging deeper, then decided against it. "I'll be blunt. Oliver's taking a big chance on you. I told him he ought to hire somebody from Princeton or Harvard, but he wants to hire you." McCarthy shrugged. "Oliver's instincts are excellent. He runs the arbitrage desk and has made lots of money doing that for me over the past five years. If he wants to take a chance on you, it's his business. But let me tell you something." McCarthy leaned over the desk. "People will be watching you closely, and Oliver's reputation will suffer if you don't work out. He's made me a great deal of money, but I don't much care about the past. I care about today. Remember that," McCarthy said forcefully. "Oliver is under an immense amount of pressure, as everyone around here is. But in return for dealing with that pressure Oliver owns a vacation home in the Caribbean, sails his fifty-foot boat out of the Westchester Yacht Club in the summertime, drives expensive cars, sends his kid to the finest private school in the area, and takes vacations most people only hear about from Robin Leach." McCarthy smashed the glowing end of his cigar into a crystal ashtray sitting atop a stack of folders. "Oliver wants to guarantee you a million dollars in January. Personally, I can't see why. However, it's his budget and he has the authority to do it." McCarthy held up his hand. "It's his budget, but ultimately it's my money. If you don't produce, you'll be gone and Oliver will have a big problem, because I detest wasting money. For me it's like hearing fingernails screech slowly down a blackboard. It makes my skin crawl." McCarthy paused. "Oliver has stuck his neck out on a chopping block for you. He's given you an opportunity a great many people would kill for. You better appreciate that."

"I do," Jay said calmly. Now he understood why Oliver had exploded at the idea of Jay's taking two weeks to leave National City. At McCarthy & Lloyd you were expected to produce immediately. The pace there would be frenetic from the opening bell and would only intensify after that. Losing would not be tolerated. "I won't forget what he's done for me."

"Good." McCarthy checked his watch. "I've got to get to a dinner at the Waldorf. Do you have any questions?"

"Just one." Jay held up his forefinger. "What's it like to have half a billion dollars?"

McCarthy glared at Jay for several moments, then stood up and walked around the desk until he was standing directly in front of the younger man. "Maybe you'll find out someday," he growled, then grinned in spite of himself. He took Jay's hand. "Welcome to the club, Mr. West."

CHAPTER 2

Jay placed his briefcase on the arbitrage desk, then removed his suit coat and hung it neatly on the back of his chair. Jay, Bullock, Abby, and a secretary had seats on this side of the bulkhead, while Oliver's spot was on the other side of the computer monitors and telephone banks beside an administrative assistant. On either side of Oliver's chair were two unused positions. He had mentioned the possibility of bringing people on board to fill the vacant spots several times; however, Jay had now been at McCarthy & Lloyd for just over a month and nothing had occurred to make him believe Oliver really intended to hire anyone. Hiring more people meant sharing the wealth, something Oliver was loath to do.

"Hello, Abby," Jay said cheerfully. It was early, a few minutes after seven-thirty, and she was the only one on the desk. He peered over the computer screens but couldn't determine if Oliver had arrived. A rumpled suit coat was slung over the back of his chair, but Jay noticed that it was the same one Oliver had worn the day before. "How are you this beautiful July morning?"

Abby stopped tapping on her keyboard and looked up from the jagged historical graph of the Dow Jones Industrial Average climbing from left to right across one of her monitors. "Hot."

"I know what you mean." New York City was suffering through an oppressive heat wave, and the subway ride from Jay's Upper West Side apartment down half the length of Manhattan to Wall Street on the number 2 train had been muggy and unpleasant. "This heat is incredible."

"Especially when your air conditioner goes on the blink."

Jay glanced down at Abby. She was short—a few inches over five feet—and had olive skin, dark brown hair with red highlights, an engaging smile, and a voluptuous figure. Her face was plain, but her constant smile made her ordinary features seem unusually attractive. "That's no good." Abby lived across the East River in a one-bedroom apartment on the fifth floor of a Queens walk-up. She had invited Jay to a small get-together a week after he had joined the firm to introduce him to several of her friends. With the window unit on the blink, her place would be a steam bath in this heat. "I'd be happy to come over and take a look at it," he offered. "I'm no engineer, but my father taught me a thing or two about moving parts."

"I bet he did," she teased, raising one eyebrow and giving Jay a sly, suggestive once-over before bursting into laughter.

He eased into his chair, grinning. He and Abby had become good friends over the past month. She hadn't been resentful at all about his joining the arbitrage desk from the outside as a more senior person than she. In fact, she had gone out of her way to make him feel comfortable. Unlike Bullock, who was still doing his best to make Jay's first few weeks hellish.

"Don't worry about the air conditioner," she said. "My

father's coming over tonight to try to fix it. If he can't, he said, he'll get me a new one. But it's nice of you to be concerned."

"No problem."

"Oh!" Abby snapped her fingers and picked up a pink message slip. "I think you better talk to this guy. He's called three times in the last ten minutes."

Jay took the slip from Abby. "Brian Kelly." He read the name aloud. "Kelly works at Goldman Sachs. He brokers common stock to institutions. Oliver went on a rampage last night trying to reach Kelly." Abby had taken the previous day off and hadn't been around for the fireworks.

"Why was Oliver trying so hard to get Kelly?"

"It had to do with the Bates Corporation," Jay explained.

"Bates is the company that's been trying to fight off a hostile takeover bid from that British conglomerate. Right?"

"Yes," Jay confirmed. "The Brits offered sixty-five a share for Bates two weeks ago."

"Didn't Oliver buy a large block of Bates shares the day after the takeover bid was announced?"

"That's right. Oliver was sure another company was going to come in and make a higher bid for Bates than the British conglomerate. He thought we could make a few dollars a share very quickly. But so far nothing's happened. Nobody else has made a bid for Bates."

"What does Brian Kelly have to do with it?" Abby asked.

Jay glanced around furtively. "Oliver got a phone call last night here on the desk from somebody telling him that General Electric was going to be making a rival bid for Bates." Jay touched the scar beneath his eye. "A bid way in excess of the Brits' bid."

"Who called him about the GE bid?" Abby asked suspiciously.

"I don't know," Jay admitted.

"He never does say, does he?"

"No." Jay had wanted to ask Oliver about the source of the GE information, but hadn't because it seemed clear that Oliver didn't want to talk about it. "When Oliver heard about the GE deal last night, he tried to reach Kelly right away. Kelly had told Oliver earlier in the day that Goldman had some Bates shares to sell. But Oliver didn't like the price Kelly was quoting, and at that point Oliver didn't know about the GE deal. When Oliver called Kelly last night, no one at Goldman could find him. I guess he'd already gone home for the evening. Oliver was yelling into the phone at the top of his lungs."

"Really?"

"Yeah. You should have heard him. He was going crazy. The veins were bulging out of his neck. When he couldn't get Kelly, he tried all of his other good contacts on the Street, but no one had any Bates shares for sale." Jay exhaled heavily. "If there are shares at Goldman available and we don't get them, Oliver will go ballistic." Jay stood up and checked the floor. "Has Oliver or Bullock come in yet?"

"No," Abby answered. "I've been here since five-thirty, and I haven't seen either of—"

"Five-thirty?" Jay asked incredulously.

"I couldn't sleep. My apartment was about a hundred degrees."

"Oh, right, the fritzed air conditioner." Jay checked the trading floor again. Oliver would be furious if they missed the double-down opportunity on Bates and General Electric announced a huge takeover. Leaving money on the table was a more serious crime than murder to Oliver. It ranked right up there with sharing the wealth. But he'd be equally as angry if Jay purchased the shares at too rich a price and the GE offer never came. "Do me a favor, Abby," he said calmly.

"Sure."

"Get Kelly on the phone. Find out where he's offering the Bates shares and how many he has." Jay stood up. "I need to go check something."

"Okay," she said hesitantly. "But remember, Jay, I don't have trading authority."

"I know." He touched her arm reassuringly. "I'm not going to put you in a bad spot. Just get the information. If Kelly starts yelling and telling you that he has to know what our decision is immediately, hang up." Jay turned and moved off.

Five minutes later he was back. "Did you get Kelly?"

Abby nodded. She seemed shaken.

"And?"

"He has a million Bates shares to sell," she said, her voice trembling slightly. "It was like you said, Jay. He was yelling at me from the get-go that I had to make a decision right away. He said he's got other buyers interested. He wants to do the deal with Oliver, but time's running out."

"What price did Kelly quote for the shares?" Jay asked, grabbing his phone and checking his computer for an off-hours price.

"Seventy-three," she answered nervously.

"Bastard," he whispered.

"What's wrong?"

"Kelly's gouging us," Jay answered. "The price on the screen is only seventy dollars a share, which is the same price our equity guys quoted me a minute ago." He considered his options. "But a million shares is a big block, and Oliver mentioned that the GE bid is expected to be in excess of eighty dollars a share."

Abby's eyes opened wide. "Eighty dollars?"

"Yes." Jay gazed at her. "If we buy the Bates shares from Kelly at seventy-three and GE offers eighty, we make seven dollars a share. That's seven million dollars if we buy all million shares. And we could make that seven million dollars overnight. Literally."

"But the British company's bid is only sixty-five," Abby pointed out. "If you buy a million shares at seventy-three and the GE bid never comes, McCarthy and Lloyd will *lose* eight dollars a share. That's eight million bucks." Abby shook her head. "You'd have based your purchase of Bates shares on nothing but a rumor. And we all know that rumors in the takeover world are worth about as much as presidential promises of fidelity."

Jay smiled wryly as he dialed Kelly's number. "This could get interesting." He motioned for Abby to pick up on her extension so she could listen.

"Hello!" The line hadn't finished its first ring.

"I need to speak to Brian Kelly."

"This is Kelly."

Jay heard commotion on the other end of the line. "Brian, this is Jay West at McCarthy and Lloyd."

"Yeah? Where's Oliver? I want to talk to him."

"Oliver isn't in yet."

"Great," Kelly groaned.

"I can make the decision regarding Bates," Jay said calmly.

"Yeah? Well, you've got three minutes to do it. Oliver's been a good client in the past, but I'm not waiting around for him."

"Give me the offer," Jay demanded.

"I told whoever it was who called a minute ago. The price is seventy-three."

"Bid seventy-one," Jay said quickly.

"I guess we don't have a deal." Kelly snickered.

Jay felt Abby's long fingernails digging into his right arm. He whipped around, gazed at her for a second, then grabbed the paper she was holding out.

"I'm waiting," Kelly said smugly.

Jay scanned the paper.

"The silence is really loud," Kelly added, pushing. "I'm hanging up and selling to—"

"Seventy-one for five hundred thousand shares," Jay cut in.

"I've got a million shares!" Kelly shouted. "I told the woman who called from your shop before that it's a block sale. A matched set. No breaking it up. A million shares or nothing."

"That's my bid," Jay said evenly. "And it's final."

"I'm gonna count to three, Jay West, and if I don't hear seventy-three for a million shares, I'm gone!"

"You can count to a *hundred* and three if you'd like, Kelly. But the bid won't change. I'm sure Oliver will be happy to learn how accommodating you were. I've been here only a month, but I know how much volume he puts through you and how much money you make off us." Jay paused. "I wouldn't count on that gravy train continuing."

The silence now came from Kelly's end of the line.

"Kelly?"

Still no answer.

"Well, have a nice day," Jay said politely.

"All right!" Kelly yelled. "Done. Five hundred thousand at seventy-one. Damn it!"

Jay winked at Abby. "Good. The operations guys can settle up later. Nice doing business with you, Kelly." But all he heard was the sound of the phone being slammed down in his ear.

"Nice going, Jay." Abby smiled as she put down her phone. "You were great."

"You saved me, Abby." He leaned back in his chair and took a deep breath. "I would have purchased all one million shares if you hadn't reminded me that a million shares would have given us more than five percent of Bates."

When a single entity owned 5 percent of a company's shares, the purchaser was legally bound to report its share position to the Securities and Exchange Commission—a disclosure that would have been available to anyone checking SEC filings. Oliver had strictly forbidden anyone on the arbitrage desk to make a purchase that would give McCarthy & Lloyd more than 5 percent of any company. He didn't want anyone knowing what he was doing.

"Thanks."

"Don't mention it," Abby said.

Jay gazed at her. She had quickly become quite a good friend. He had no doubt that Bullock would have let him purchase the million shares, then left him to endure Oliver's temper, which Jay had witnessed several times in the past few weeks. Volcanic explosions that sent the innocent scurrying for cover and the target cowering. But Abby would never set him up that way. He smiled at her. Strangely, there was no sexual tension between them. She subtly made it clear to everyone that she wasn't available. But she had never mentioned a boyfriend and didn't seem to receive calls from suitors on the desk.

"Good morning."

Jay and Abby swiveled at the sound of Oliver's nasal voice. He stood before them, his face emitting a healthy bronze glow.

"You look nice."

"Thanks, Abby." Oliver ran his eyes over her legs. "I spent the weekend on the sailboat. It was great. A nice breeze and not a cloud in the sky the entire time. I must have picked up some color."

"You definitely did." Abby looked at Jay. "That's what we have to look forward to when we become senior managing directors: Sundays sailing on Long Island Sound picking up tans." She let out a frustrated breath. "But for the time being we toil in obscurity earning minimum wage and spending summer weekends in Central Park because that's all we can afford."

"Uh-huh."

Jay glanced at Oliver. Despite all of his bluster about how everyone at McCarthy & Lloyd knew what everyone else earned, Oliver had ordered Jay not to tell others about the January million-dollar-bonus guarantee. "So you took your wife sailing this past weekend," Jay said pleasantly.

Oliver shook his head. "No. Barbara was away at a horse show," he explained curtly.

"I see." It was strange. During Jay's first day at work, Oliver had played the part of a proud father, escorting Jay around the firm to meet the important players. They had eaten lunch in the firm's formal dining room with Bill McCarthy and enjoyed a delicious rack of lamb served on sterling-silver trays by an attentive staff. But since that day a month before, Oliver had turned cool. Not unfriendly, but not cordial, either.

"What was going on here?" Oliver asked suspiciously, pointing at the phones. "As I was walking over, it looked like a lot of action."

"Jay just pulled off a great trade," Abby volunteered. "He bought a bunch of Bates shares from that guy Brian Kelly at Goldman."

"How many?" Oliver asked quickly. "Don't tell me you went over the five per—"

"Relax," Jay interrupted. "Kelly was trying to sell us a million, but I only bought half. We're still under five percent. No disclosures to be filed."

"Good boy. I'm glad you remembered that in the heat of battle. Shows you're learning."

Jay pointed at Abby. "Abby reminded me. I can't take the credit."

"What did you pay for the shares?" Oliver asked, ignoring Jay's honesty.

"Seventy-one."

"That sounds expensive," Oliver snapped.

"Not if GE comes through," Jay countered.

Oliver rubbed his chin, thinking. Finally he gestured to Abby. "Why don't you and I find a conference room so we can go over that proposal I'm going to make to Bill this afternoon?"

"What?" A confused expression flickered across Abby's face.

"The proposal," Oliver repeated tersely. "The one we talked about Friday afternoon."

"Oh, right." Abby rose quickly from her chair, grabbed a manila folder, and followed Oliver through the maze of the trading room floor.

Jay watched them go. It was only seven-thirty, but already the floor was crowded, and they had to dodge their way through traders shouting buy and sell orders over telephones. Finally they ducked into a hallway at the far end of the room. It was odd. The folder Abby had picked up appeared to be empty.

When they had disappeared, he turned back around to face his computer screens. Fortunes could be made using the information on these screens, especially at a firm such as McCarthy & Lloyd, which provided its people generous dollar amounts to trade with. The trick to making that fortune was simple: find the right stock to bet on. But so far he hadn't pulled the trigger on a single trade—except for the Bates shares, which he wouldn't get credit for, anyway, because Oliver had made the initial purchase two weeks earlier. He sensed that Oliver's standoffish demeanor was in part a reaction to this slow start. Jay clenched his jaw. He wanted to make money for Oliver and the firm, but he didn't want to lose any, either. He was acutely aware of the importance of early wins versus early losses. Reputations were made or lost based upon the success or failure of the first few trades.

"Good morning." Bullock tossed his suit coat over the bulkhead behind his computer screens, loosened his tie, rolled up the sleeves of his dark blue shirt, and sat down in a chair beside Jay.

"Morning," Jay answered warily. Bullock rarely opened the day with a friendly greeting.

Bullock placed a plain brown bag on the desk, extracted a bran muffin, slapped a generous amount of butter on top, and took a huge bite, pushing nearly half of it in his mouth at once. "Any hot stock tips for me?" he asked through the mouthful, crumbs falling to the floor.

Jay heard a sarcastic tone through the muffin. Oliver hadn't yet vocalized his displeasure at Jay's slow start. Bullock, on the other hand, rode him constantly. "Yeah, the company that makes that muffin you're inhaling. You must eat five of them a day."

"Three," Bullock corrected.

"And the company that makes Slim-Fast," Jay added. "You're going to add a couple of points to its stock price on your own when all that fat starts bloating your waistline."

"That's where you're wrong. I work out twice a day, every day—before I come here in the morning and at night when I get home. It's all I can do to keep the weight on, kid."

"Why do you work out so much, anyway?" Jay asked, irritated that Bullock was still referring to him as "kid." Bullock liked to advertise his muscular build, wearing his shirts a size too small so they stretched tightly across his chest. "Are you trying to make up for other deficiencies we can't see?"

"Why do you ask so many stupid questions?"

Jay smiled. "There's the Mr. Congeniality I'm accustomed to.

I was a little worried when you said good morning. You actually sounded friendly."

Bullock finished chewing and wiped his mouth with a napkin. "You aren't gonna be giving me that cocky little smile when Bill McCarthy wants to know why you haven't made any money for his arbitrage desk."

"Don't worry about me, Badger," Jay shot back.

"I'm not worried about you at all," Bullock assured Jay. "In fact, I'm going to thoroughly enjoy myself the day Bill stomps out here and starts screaming about your lack of performance in front of the entire fucking floor. And that day will come soon. He hasn't screamed at anyone in a while, and you're the perfect candidate. If you think Oliver is impatient, he's nothing compared to Bill." Bullock paused. "And guarantees aren't always guarantees, even when they're written."

"What do you mean by that?" Jay asked.

"You figure it out."

Jay leaned back in his chair, wondering if McCarthy & Lloyd could renege on his bonus. "Oliver wouldn't screw me that way."

"Don't be so sure," Bullock muttered.

"And anyway," Jay said, "I'm working on a couple of things that will make us a significant amount of money."

"Like what?" Bullock pasted more butter on the muffin and took another large bite.

Jay shrugged. "I'll tell you when I'm about to pull the trigger." He didn't trust Bullock. The guy could easily follow up on the company, buy the shares, preempt Jay, and take credit himself when the stock price rose.

"I'm your direct superior, and I want to know what you're working on—right now," Bullock insisted.

"It's still preliminary. You know as well as I do that the more people who know about an opportunity, the better the odds are that word will leak out. And if word gets out on the Street that we're looking at a stock, the price might run up before we can buy shares, and there goes the opportunity."

"You're blowing smoke," Bullock sneered. "But it's a false alarm. There's no fire. You don't really have a line on anything."

"You'll—"

"Mr. Bullock."

Bullock and Jay glanced up at the sound of the voice. Before them stood Karen Walker, Bill McCarthy's executive assistant. Beside Karen was a tall woman with long blond hair swept off the creamy skin of her face and arranged in a neat bun at the back of her head. Instinctively Jay and Bullock rose from their seats. There was an unmistakable presence about this woman.

"This is Sally Lane," Karen explained. "I believe Oliver was expecting her this morning."

"Yes, he was." Bullock stepped forward and took Sally's hand. "Good morning." A smile spread across his wide face. "It's nice to have you aboard."

Jay's eyes flashed to Bullock's.

Bullock gave Jay a subtle glance, then turned his attention back to Sally. "You're a welcome addition to the arbitrage desk."

"Thank you. I've been looking forward to this morning." She let go of Bullock's hand and turned to Jay. "Sally Lane."

"Jay West." He met her aqua eyes head-on, masking his surprise that there would be a new member of the team. "Welcome to McCarthy and Lloyd."

"Thank you."

Sally was about five-eight, Jay judged, six inches shorter than he, and slender. Her face was slim, her nose slightly narrow, and her lips thin. She wore almost no makeup, yet it was obvious that she took great care with her appearance. Her dark blue dress, which fell slightly below her knees and fit her slim body perfectly, was plain but tasteful. Her light hair shimmered, and her face exuded a fresh, natural look.

"Sally will be joining us as a vice president," Bullock announced, a triumphant smirk on his face. "Just like you, Jay."

"Great," Jay said cheerfully. He wasn't going to give Bullock the satisfaction of seeing his irritation at not being kept in the loop. "Welcome aboard, Sally."

"I'm thrilled to be here."

Karen spoke up. "I need to take you up to human resources, Sally."

As the two women walked away, Jay turned and moved off through the trading floor, threading his way around the long workstations, making his way to the supply room. So they'd hired another professional for the arbitrage desk. Another vice president. Perhaps Oliver was more irritated about Jay's slow start than he seemed and was going to replace him with Sally Lane. He shook his head as he walked away from the trading floor and down a hallway toward the supply room. That didn't make any sense. He had been there only a month. Oliver would have had to spend at least a month interviewing Sally and doing background checks. That meant he would have had to begin interviewing her at the same time Jay arrived.

Jay ducked into a doorway and walked down a dimly lit, twisting hallway, past cardboard boxes filled with old files. Of course, Bullock had made that crack about guarantees not always being guarantees. Yes, he had signed an employment contract on his first day that guaranteed him a million dollars in January, but the firm might hold up the payment if Oliver and Bill McCarthy weren't satisfied with his performance. He had blindly taken Oliver's advice and skimmed the thirty-page contract himself without having an attorney review it, then signed it immediately.

Perhaps there were loopholes in the document that would allow the firm to renege on its obligation. He took an irritated breath as he turned into the supply room and reached for the light switch. He was usually so careful.

Jay froze. Coming from a room at the end of the hallway he heard muffled voices, one obviously a woman's, rising in fear. He backed out of the supply room and moved slowly over the carpet to the doorway at the end of the hall. The door was slightly ajar, and he could just see into the room. The lights were off, but a small window provided a feeble gray light, enough for him to see Oliver pinning Abby against the far wall with one hand and reaching beneath her short dress with the other.

"Oliver, please," Abby begged, pushing his hand away. "Please don't do this."

"What's the problem? Don't you like my attention?"

Jay swallowed hard, stunned by the sight of Oliver accosting the young woman. He glanced over his shoulder down the dim hallway, then back into the storage room.

"Not here at work, Oliver!" Abby struggled to fight him off.

"So you wouldn't have any problem meeting me at the Plaza Hotel later." Oliver pulled her pantyhose down to her knees, then worked his tasseled loafer between her legs and rolled the hose down to her high heels.

Abby leaned down and attempted to pull them up, but Oliver caught her and pushed her back against the wall roughly. "I want you to be at the Plaza at six o'clock sharp," he ordered. "Understand?"

"Oliver, I love you, but I don't think I can do this anymore."

Jay hesitated. He'd been about to push open the door, but Abby had said the word *love.*

"Why not?" Oliver pulled the dress up to Abby's neck and pressed himself against her. "Why can't you do this anymore?"

"You're married," she said softly, no longer struggling.

"That little complication hasn't gotten in the way for the last few months. It didn't stop you from spending this weekend on the sailboat with me."

Jay pursed his lips. The scene on the trading floor a few moments earlier had been a charade.

"Please, Oliver," she sobbed.

Oliver stepped back, and Abby's dress fell to her thighs. "I could fire you so easily," he whispered. "You'd be on the street by lunchtime, and you wouldn't get another job in the industry." He straightened his tie. "I know how poor you are, Abby. You need this job." He paused. "And don't think I wouldn't fire you. I'd do it in a heartbeat."

Abby gazed up at him, suddenly incensed. "That wouldn't be a very wise thing to do," she snapped through her tears. "Remember, I know about you and your friends. If you fire me, I wouldn't have any problem letting the proper people in on the secret. I'm sure they'd take care of me in return for that kind of information."

"You don't have any information."

"You know I do."

Oliver pressed a fingertip into her face. "That would be a very stupid thing for you to do, Abby."

"Is that a threat?" She pushed his finger away.

"Take it any way you want to," he hissed.

For several seconds Abby gazed up at Oliver, then her chin dropped dejectedly. "I can't believe you're saying these things to me." Her voice was barely audible. "I thought you loved me."

He reached out and brushed a tear from her cheek. "Likewise."

"I do," she sobbed. "With all my heart. I've told you so many times."

Oliver moved closer and took her face in his hands. "Then do what I want and everything will be fine."

For a time Abby remained motionless. Finally she slid her hands around Oliver's neck and kissed him deeply. "I can't resist you," she murmured, pulling back and allowing her head to come to rest against the wall.

Jay stepped back from the doorway. For several moments he stood in the darkness feeling his heart beat rapidly, uncertain of what to do. He didn't condone their action, but it wasn't any of his business, either. Finally he turned and quietly retraced his steps, carefully avoiding the file-filled boxes. As he emerged from the hallway, he nearly ran into Bullock.

"What the hell were you doing back there?" Bullock asked suspiciously.

"Looking for legal pads," Jay answered quickly.

Bullock glanced at Jay's empty hands, then past him and down the hallway. "Where are they?"

"What?" Jay asked unsteadily. Did he mean Oliver and Abby?

"The pads."

"Oh, I couldn't find any," he said, trying to sound convincing. "I'll have to tell whoever is in charge to reorder."

"You do that." Bullock looked over Jay's shoulder once more. "I suggest you get back to the desk. You've got a few messages."

Jay brushed past Bullock and hurried down the corridor toward the trading floor. Bullock seemed to have checked the hallway as if he knew what was going on in the room at the end of it. As if he knew that Oliver was in the storage room with Abby. Oliver and Bullock were good friends, and Oliver had paid Bullock a three-million-dollar bonus the past January. Bullock had every incentive to protect Oliver, Jay reasoned.

He stopped when he reached the trading floor. What the

hell had Abby meant by her threat to tell the proper people about Oliver and his friends?

■ ■ ■

After several moves, the wire transfer into Victor Savoy's account at Bank Suisse had come from a dummy corporation in Antigua, so the odds were damn good that the money was already clean because Antigua was the new financial black hole of the Caribbean. Now the money had reached Switzerland, and the chance that it had been successfully laundered had risen to almost a hundred percent. However, Savoy was a careful man. He knew that only through painstaking attention to detail and extraordinary patience would he remain beyond the reach of the FBI, the INS, Scotland Yard, and law enforcement units in Eastern Europe, which were under intense pressure from Washington to find him.

"Sign here," the young woman behind the desk instructed, holding out a pen.

"Certainement," Savoy answered in perfect French, taking the pen and scribbling the alias of the day on the withdrawal order.

"All right, now this is yours." The young woman held out a small box.

"Merci." Inside the box were fifteen million Swiss francs—about ten million dollars—in large bills. He took the box and placed it in his jacket pocket, then stood up, leaned over the desk, shook the woman's hand, and walked calmly through the bank's ornate lobby.

When he had made it through the revolving doors and out to the street, Savoy checked his watch. It was ten of three. There was still plenty of time to redeposit the money. He turned right, hurried a hundred yards down the Paradeplatz to the entrance of the Bank of Zurich, and hustled inside. He was carrying a massive amount of money, and though he prided himself on maintaining total control over his body in any situation, he could feel that his pulse rate was slightly above normal. For a few minutes—while he was on the sidewalk between banks—the money had been vulnerable to anyone on the street, including a common thief with a gun. But now that he was once again inside, it and he were safe. Better still, the money was almost certainly beyond the reach of the authorities. Even if they had somehow been able to follow the maze of wire transfers to Bank Suisse—U.S. regulators could now pierce Switzerland's once-impenetrable veil of secrecy—the trail ended at that account like footprints in the middle of a snowy field.

At the Bank of Zurich, Savoy deposited the fifteen million francs into two separate accounts in unlike amounts—so that authorities wouldn't see the same amount coming out of Bank Suisse and being deposited minutes later at the Bank of Zurich—on top of fifty million already amassed in accounts that bore names different from the one at Bank Suisse. Now there was but one more transaction to execute. He would withdraw the money from the Bank of Zurich in the form of certified drafts, in odd amounts, and take them to a bank in Liechtenstein, where other accounts were waiting. At that point he would feel completely certain that no governmental authority could possibly have traced the movement of money that had originated in New York City.

Finished with the deposit, Savoy walked out of the bank and back into the sun-scorched afternoon. He watched a trolley roll past, relieved that he no longer had the massive amount of cash on his person. He would execute the last transaction the next day in Liechtenstein, before flying to Afghanistan.

Now he had to contact the team training on the farm in Virginia to make certain all was proceeding on schedule. For the last week they'd been practicing under the direction of his second in command, an able man who knew his craft well. However, Savoy always worried when he wasn't in direct control of everything. As he hurried past the many shops lining the street leading to his hotel, the Baur au Lac, he remembered something his mother had said many times during his childhood: If you want something done right, do it yourself. She would be so proud of him for following her advice.

■ ■ ■

Jay stood leaning against the arbitrage desk talking on the phone. It had been fifteen minutes since he had returned from the storage room. He spotted Abby returning to the arbitrage desk. It seemed to him that her dress was wrinkled and that she was upset, but perhaps it was simply his imagination, fueled by what he knew had happened within the walls of the storage room.

He ended the call abruptly as Abby neared him. "Hey there."

"Hi," she answered curtly, collapsing into her chair.

Jay picked up his soda and took a sip. "Are you okay?"

"Fine." She leaned down, opened a drawer, and pulled out her pocketbook.

"So what kind of presentation is Oliver making to McCarthy this afternoon?" he asked, noticing that she didn't have the manila folder.

"It concerns a company he's thinking about buying into."

"Since when did Oliver have to ask for McCarthy's permission to take a position?"

"It's a big purchase. Maybe up to two hundred million dollars."

Jay whistled. "That is big. Still, I—"

"Listen, I've got to go to the ladies' room," Abby interrupted, pushing her chair back and heading past him.

Jay caught her gently by the arm. "Anything you want to talk about?" he asked. Her dark red lipstick was smudged and he noticed blotches on her neck.

She hesitated, glaring at him, her chin pushed out defiantly. Then her expression softened and her eyes glazed over. Finally she opened her mouth, about to say something, when her gaze flickered past Jay. Instantly she shook free from his grasp and darted away.

Jay turned and saw Oliver walking toward the arbitrage desk. As Oliver made his way through the traders, Jay heard Bullock call out loudly from the open corridor paralleling the floor. Bullock's voice was like a foghorn, and it easily cut through the noise of the large room. Oliver stopped and waited while Bullock trotted across the floor. They were only twenty feet away, but now Bullock was speaking quietly, his words masked by the roar, one hand over his mouth so his lips were hidden.

Jay picked up his phone and dialed distractedly while he peered at Oliver and Bullock. He paid no attention to the recorded message telling him that he had reached a nonworking number. Oliver glanced up, directly into Jay's eyes, and Jay looked quickly away. When he looked back, Oliver was once again heading toward the arbitrage desk—staring directly at him—and Bullock was walking in the opposite direction.

Jay sat down and pretended to be in conversation with someone at the other end of the phone as Oliver made it to his position on the opposite side of the bulkhead.

Oliver grabbed his phone and dialed. "Jamie, it's Mason," he shouted. "I want to buy a hundred thousand shares of Pendex. Right now, you got it? A bid for Pendex just came across the wire."

Jay glanced up at Oliver, who had his thumb beneath one

paisley suspender. Unlike Abby, Oliver seemed his typical, unflappable self.

"I know that's more than thirty million dollars' worth, you little puke!" Oliver bellowed. "You think I can't fucking add?" He pulled on the suspender and then let it snap back against his starched white shirt. "Just execute the trade." Oliver punched several keys on his computer. "And while you're at it, buy me ten thousand August calls. The forties . . . What? Of course I've got my approvals. Just do your job, you got that? . . . Good! And I don't want to pay more than thirty-one for the shares. Call Badger with a confirm. I'm gonna be off the desk for a while." Oliver slammed the phone down. "Jay!"

"Yes?"

"You and I need to talk. Let's go." Without awaiting a response, Oliver wheeled around and took off.

Jay raised his eyes to the tiled ceiling and recited a quick prayer. Bullock must have said something about the storage room. Perhaps his short stint at McCarthy & Lloyd was about to come to an end.

When Jay reached the conference room, Oliver was already seated with his feet up on the table and a cigar hanging from his mouth. He motioned for Jay to close the door while he held a lighter to the end of the cigar. "Have a seat."

As he gazed at the loafer he'd watched Oliver jam between Abby's legs, Jay heard a friendly tone in Oliver's voice that hadn't been there since Jay's first day at McCarthy & Lloyd.

"Come on, sit down." With his foot Oliver pushed out the chair next to his and rolled it toward Jay. "Want a cigar?" He pulled his black leather cigar case from his pants pocket, removed the top half, and held it out. Two cigars protruded.

"No, thanks." Jay sat down slowly, not taking his eyes from Oliver, half expecting an ambush. Oliver's sudden display of camaraderie could be simply a diversion from the attack that was coming.

"They're really good, pal. Davidoffs."

"No, really."

"Suit yourself." Oliver replaced the top and jammed the case back in his pocket. "So, how are you?" He took a long puff from the cigar.

"Fine."

"Sure you are." Oliver turned his head to the side and coughed. "Look, I know I've been kind of preoccupied since you got here. It's just that we've been working on a couple of very big deals like the one I'm going to pitch to Bill this afternoon. We could double our money in a couple of weeks on that one." Oliver beamed. "It would be a hell of a deal."

"I agree." This didn't sound like the start of a being-fired speech. "You've also been working on hiring an addition to the desk, I found out this morning," Jay said.

"You mean Sally?"

"Yes."

Oliver waved his cigar. An ash fell to the carpet, but he paid no attention. "Yeah, I should have told you about her, pal, but like I said, I've been busy." He took another long puff. "What are you working on these days?"

Jay shrugged. "A couple of things. I've been looking at a company based in Nashua, New Hampshire, called TurboTec. I told you about it two weeks ago. My friend from college works there in the marketing group. His name is Jack Trainer." Jay didn't mind telling Oliver about the deal. Oliver had no incentive to steal the idea the way Bullock might. Oliver was compensated on the overall profitability of the desk, no matter who had the idea. "I really think we ought to—"

"I told you, I don't like that firm," Oliver interrupted.

"But I found out that a Japanese company has been accumulating shares in the past two weeks. TurboTec's price is up fifteen percent since we last spoke about it, but there's still plenty of room for a big pop if the Japanese announce an offer to acquire the whole thing. Which I believe they will."

"No. You can never count on the Japanese. Just when you think they're going to do one thing, they do the opposite. They're smart that way." Oliver smiled. "Don't be disappointed, Jay West. I like your thinking, but I've got a better idea."

Jay glanced up. "What?"

"A company called Simons. It's headquartered in the Midwest somewhere. Green Bay, or maybe Milwaukee—I'm not really sure. Anyway, do some quick research on it. Make certain there aren't any major problems. No deadly viruses or ticking time bombs. When it checks out, buy fifty thousand shares. Understand?"

"I'll get right on it."

"Good." Oliver dropped his feet to the floor and leaned toward Jay. "That ought to help you out with what you have to admit has been a slow start here."

Jay recoiled slightly. He hadn't been prepared for that.

"I know you bought the Bates shares this morning, but that wasn't originally your idea."

"I know."

"Of course, I'll kick your ass if you've stuck me with five hundred thousand additional shares and that GE offer never materializes."

Jay said nothing.

"Two more things, pal," Oliver said quickly. "First, I want you to take tomorrow off and come up to Connecticut for a day of sailing. The weather is supposed to be absolutely beautiful. Hot, but beautiful. I'll have a car pick you up around eight o'clock in the morning at your apartment."

"I don't think Bullock will be too happy about that."

Oliver flashed a smile. "Fuck Badger. Remember, he takes orders from me."

"I don't know. . . ."

"They'll be no further discussion. It's a done deal," Oliver said confidently. "It'll be a good opportunity for us to get to know each other better. And you can meet my wife."

"Okay." He wasn't looking forward to facing Oliver's wife. She probably had no idea what Oliver did with Abby in his spare time.

"Bring your swimming trunks and some nice clothes, too. A blazer, khakis, and a tie." Oliver stood up and headed to the door.

"You said there were two things, Oliver."

"Oh, right." He stopped in the doorway. "Tomorrow when you come up to the house, I'm going to lend you a hundred thousand dollars to tide you over until bonus day."

"What?" Jay wasn't certain he had heard correctly.

"Yeah." Oliver nodded. "I know you had to take a cut in salary to come here, and I'm going to help you out personally. I'll loan you the money. You can repay me on bonus day."

"You don't have to—"

Oliver held up a hand. "I don't want you driving around in that broken-down Taurus anymore." He flashed another broad smile. "You don't look good in that thing. You'll look much better in that Beamer you told Bullock and me you had when we interviewed you." And then he was gone.

For several moments Jay stared at the vacant doorway. Finally he leaned back, took a deep breath, and rubbed his eyes. Oliver Mason was a man of many surprises.

CHAPTER 3

Tony Vogel stood in the foyer of the Plaza Hotel suite, an anxious expression on his face. "Oliver, I'm worried." Vogel was a short, stout man with thinning hair and puffy purple bags beneath his sad eyes.

Oliver studied the neatly arranged hair plugs in Vogel's scalp. They resembled rows of newly sprouted corn. "What about, Tony? The new hair's not taking?" He glanced down at the envelope in Vogel's hand.

"I think the people downtown know something," Vogel replied gruffly, ignoring Oliver's wisecrack.

"No way. I would have heard."

"Just the same," Vogel argued, "we need to be careful. Maybe it's time to curtail this thing for a while. Maybe permanently."

Oliver laughed loudly. "We've been at this for almost five years and nothing's gone wrong in all that time. Why are you suddenly getting cold feet?"

"The others feel the same way," Vogel responded, avoiding Oliver's question.

"All of them?"

"All of them," Vogel confirmed. "Particularly Torcelli."

"But there's no way we can get caught," Oliver protested. "There's no money trail. It's perfect." He sniffed loudly several times in quick succession. "Besides, we can't stop. You know that."

"We can do anything we want." Vogel hesitated. "It might be time to cash in."

"What?"

"Yeah."

"Are you saying—"

"You know exactly what I'm saying."

Oliver's jaw clenched involuntarily. "You've gone off the deep end this time, Tony. Way off."

"We think this would be a neat way to wrap up the whole affair and get our money out at the same time. This way we cut all ties and cover our tracks."

"Give me the envelope, Tony." Oliver patted Vogel on the shoulder, then snatched the envelope. "Why don't you go down to the Oak Bar and have a drink on me? A nice stiff one."

"Oliver, I—"

"You what?" Oliver's temper suddenly careened out of control. "You fucking what?" he exploded.

Vogel realized he'd pushed too far. "I—I mean we—"

"You little bastard."

"Look, I'm sorry." Vogel's tone turned deferential, then apologetic. "We're looking out for our best interests. And yours."

Oliver snorted. "You and the others go behind my back, make a bunch of unilateral decisions, and expect me to fold like a pup tent and go along. I'm the one taking the monster risks. I'm the one dealing with the pressure." He was talking quickly, like a man possessed. "I set the whole thing up. You four are simply along for the ride. You don't make the decisions. I do."

"We provide the information," Vogel protested.

"Big deal. I could replicate the system with four other people in less than a week." Oliver smiled. "And where would that leave you, Tony?" His smile faded. "Nowhere. That's where." He tilted his head back. "Or maybe you'd take me out, too."

Vogel held his hands up, palms out. "Never, Oliver."

"Shit, you wouldn't even know how to go about it." Oliver laughed. "Why should I worry? All four of you are from lily-white backgrounds. Where are you going to get the guts to commit murder?"

"I don't know." Vogel's head dropped down.

"Exactly." Oliver shook his head. "Get out of here right now and I might be willing to forget we had this conversation."

Vogel swallowed. He was well aware that Oliver wasn't going to take this well. But he had been instructed to make the sentiments clear. "The others aren't going to be happy, especially Torcelli."

"You tell the others to call me," Oliver said evenly. "Especially Torcelli."

Vogel glanced at the white powder spread out across the glass-topped coffee table in four six-inch lines. "Okay."

"Good." Oliver opened the suite door and gestured toward the hallway. "Don't let the door smack you in the ass on the way out. And keep your head down. Don't look anyone straight in the eye."

"I was just the messenger, Oliver," Vogel mumbled as he darted through the doorway. "Please remember that."

Oliver slammed the door, then moved to the couch in front of the coffee table, put the envelope down, picked up a short red straw, leaned over, and inhaled the powder. After finishing the first line, he paused for a breath. When he had finished the second one, he dropped the straw on the coffee table and leaned back slowly until his head came to rest against the couch. He sat there for a few moments until he began to feel the familiar nasal drip at the back of his throat and the medicinal taste in his mouth. Then he shut his eyes, groaned softly, and smiled as euphoric sensations of supreme power, absolute control, and total confidence overtook him. He was a man who controlled vast amounts of money and had many people at his whim, and he loved it. He was bulletproof. He was untouchable.

Oliver picked up the envelope he had taken from Vogel, extracted the single piece of paper, and gazed at the name on the page. *Beautiful,* he thought.

■ ■ ■

Abby lay on her side, naked beneath the covers as Oliver had instructed, her back to the bedroom door. She knew he was out in the living room doing the last of the cocaine. She pulled the covers up over her shoulders and shivered. It was like an ice cube in there because he had turned the air-conditioning up so high.

She had been in there for fifteen minutes waiting and she was barely able to keep still. She was also barely aware that her toe was madly tapping the mattress and that she was grinding her teeth. She thought only about how happy she was.

As they were snorting the cocaine together on the living room couch, Oliver had promised that he would ask his wife for a divorce and leave his Connecticut mansion. He had promised that he and Abby would move into an Upper East Side apartment together and live happily ever after. Abby giggled, then pushed her face into the pillow so Oliver wouldn't hear. She'd always been such a good girl. Through college and her first few years on Wall Street, she'd never touched drugs or been with a married man. Never even considered things like that. However, Oliver had come on to her like a hurricane, and now she was engaging in sinful acts her Brooklyn parents would be mortified by. But she'd never experienced anything in her life like Oliver. Suddenly she was living on the edge, and every moment was exhilarating. Oliver seemed to know all about the finer things. He was a man who lived each day as if it were his last. He was a god—or more likely the devil—but she didn't care. She just wanted to be with him. And she had confidence that, given enough time, she could change him. She had already made so much progress.

The door creaked, and Abby's body tingled as she heard Oliver remove his clothes. She felt the covers pull back and his warm body against hers. She turned to him and for several minutes they kissed wildly, the cocaine pulsing through their systems. Then he moved on top of her, spreading her roughly with his knees. She reached between his legs and her small fingers closed around his huge organ. She arched her back and screamed as he entered her and his lips closed around her dark nipple. He was so large it hurt for the first few seconds, but then the intense excitement of being with this man she idolized brought down her wetness, and she wrapped her arms around him and moved against his body.

"You should be wearing something," she moaned. "It's getting close to that time."

"I don't wear condoms," he gasped. "You know that. I hate them."

"Still."

Oliver rose up and stared down at her, breathing hard, his chest glistening with perspiration.

"Don't stop," Abby begged. "It was feeling so good."

Oliver smiled. "I'm going to make it feel even better."

"What do you mean?"

Without answering he reached beneath the pillows and produced two neckties. "Give me your wrists," he demanded.

"Wh-What?" she stammered.

"Your wrists. Give them to me."

Abby turned her head to the side. "Oliver, no."

He curled his fingers around her thin neck. "Don't say no to me," he hissed.

"I'm sorry, I'm sorry," she said, holding her hands out obediently.

Quickly he bound her wrists together and lashed them to the headboard. Then he wrapped the second tie around her neck, knotted it, and pulled it tight.

"Oliver, please," Abby gasped, her voice barely audible. She tried to struggle, but with her hands secured to the bed she was helpless.

Oliver's upper lip quivered as he saw the veins in her neck bulge. He pushed himself inside her again and began moving, slowly and methodically at first, then hard and fast. As his excitement increased, he pulled the tie around her neck tighter and tighter.

Abby pulled desperately against the tie, panic setting in, but her struggles were useless. Then suddenly, as she gazed up into his dark eyes believing that she would soon lose consciousness, she felt herself beginning to climax. The orgasm began as a spasm as he ground himself against her, then seemed to grow like a tidal wave, swelling higher and higher until it could go no further. The wave curled; perched atop its crest, she contracted uncontrollably around him, biting into his palm, which he had clamped over her mouth. She rose higher and higher as Oliver pulled the tie around her neck tighter and tighter, cutting off her oxygen, until finally the wave came crashing down and overwhelmed her in a sea of pleasure, and she blacked out.

Abby came to a few moments later. Oliver was standing beside the bed, buttoning his shirt. Her throat was on fire, but she felt as if she were floating on a cloud. Her entire body was relaxed. "What happened?" she whispered groggily.

"You passed out." Oliver sat down in a chair beside the bed to put on his socks.

"I've never experienced anything like that." She could feel his semen inside her. He had finished as she lay unconscious beneath him. "Where did you come up with that?" She tried to move, but her hands remained secured to the headboard.

"I get around," he answered smugly.

"I'm sure." She tugged at the tie again, coming to full consciousness. "Undo this, will you?"

"Nope." He slipped into his loafers. "I want to see how resourceful you are." He stood up and moved to the bedroom door. "If you don't make it into work tomorrow, I guess I'll have my answer."

"Oliver!"

He put his head back and laughed, then moved to the bed, knelt on the mattress, undid the tie, and dropped it to the floor. "Just kidding."

She rubbed her wrists for a second, then wrapped her hands around his neck, pulled him close, and kissed him, relieved to be free.

When their lips parted, Oliver gazed into Abby's eyes. He wasn't a sentimental man, yet she was making him feel things he had never thought he could. She was having an effect on him, much as he hated to admit it. He stroked her cheek for a moment, then kissed her.

"That was nice," she murmured. "I wish you would do that more often."

"What do you mean?" He lay down next to her.

"Kiss me the way you did just now. Gentle like that. It seems like the only time you kiss me is when we're actually in the act."

"I'm sorry."

"It's okay," she said softly. "You just haven't been with a woman who knows how to treat you."

He stroked her cheek gently, thinking how right she was. "I'm sorry about . . ." His voice trailed off.

She put a finger to his lips. "It's okay."

"I'd never hurt you."

"I know." She was changing him, slowly but surely. She had almost given up on him earlier in the day as he groped her in the storage room, but now she knew more than ever that she loved him.

He kissed her again. "I've got to go."

"Where?"

"Home."

"No. I won't let you. I don't want you going home to her."

"I have to." Oliver kissed her once more, then stood up, headed to the door, and was gone.

She stared at the doorway for several moments, then pulled a pillow close. When she heard the hallway door open and close, she rolled onto her side. It was only eight o'clock, and McCarthy & Lloyd rented the suite year round. There was no need to hurry out of it. This king-sized bed was so much more comfortable than hers. And her father had a key to the apartment, so he could get in to take a look at the air conditioner without her being there. She closed her eyes and felt herself drifting off.

At first Abby thought she was dreaming, but the feeling around her neck was too intense. She opened her eyes wide and reached for her throat, clawing and tearing at the material now cutting into her neck, scratching herself with her long red fingernails and drawing blood. "Oliver!" she choked. "Not again, please."

But now she felt a great weight on her back—a knee pressing down on her spine, keeping her belly pinned to the bed. She tried to push her attacker away by reaching behind herself, then tried to roll, but to no avail.

She twisted her head from side to side and tried to wedge a finger between her neck and the tie, but she couldn't. She felt her windpipe closing and she clenched the sheet, ripping it away from the mattress. Then she felt her upper body being lifted off the bed and bent back against the knee still jammed into the small of her back. She struggled, but her strength was fading with the prolonged lack of oxygen. Finally her arms relaxed and her eyes rolled back in her head.

For several minutes the attacker maintained the grip, twisting the tie tighter and tighter even as Abby's body went limp and she no longer attempted to defend herself. Then her head fell to the pillow and she was gone.

CHAPTER 4

An hour earlier Manhattan had disappeared in the rearview mirror, and now Jay was entering a world where simply being comfortable was tantamount to being poor. Where if you knew exactly how much you were worth, you weren't worth much, and where social status was measured by the private school your child attended, the country club you belonged to, and whether you drove to work or were driven.

Through tinted windows Jay surveyed the Connecticut estate from the backseat of the navy blue Lincoln Town Car that had picked him up in front of his apartment building. Maple trees towered over either side of the estate's long driveway, blocking out bright sunshine. Whitewashed four-slat fences parsed fields of timothy and clover into neat rectangles dotted by pairs of Thoroughbred horses, standing shoulder to haunch, flicking long tails to ward off insects from each other's eyes.

Jay moved forward on the leather seat as the main house came into view. Tucked into the side of a hill and surrounded by beautifully manicured gardens and lawns was a three-story mansion made of dark stone, standing at the end of a circular driveway. To one side of the mansion was a four-car garage, and parked in front of the garage were a hunter green Mercedes sedan, a red Suburban, and a white Austin Healey 3000.

The driver eased to a gentle stop before the main entrance, then hopped out and hurried around the back of the car to Jay's door.

But Jay had already emerged. He stood, hands on his waist, admiring the huge structure. On either side of the many white-trimmed windows were dark green wooden shutters, and in front of the windows were black flower boxes bursting with colorful blooms. He glanced up and counted four chimneys rising from the slate roof, then his eyes dropped to the entrance and the long, wide covered porch before it. The house was absolutely beautiful.

"I was going to get your door," the driver said apologetically.

"Not necessary." Jay took in the grandeur before him, trying to understand how it must feel to live in such a place. A grim expression came to his face as he glanced at the garage. The house he had grown up in easily would have fit inside. "Thanks for picking me up."

"You're welcome." The driver moved to the trunk, retrieved Jay's bag, and slung it over his shoulder. "Shall we go inside, sir?"

"I'll take that." Jay pulled the bag from the other man's shoulder. "There's no reason for you to have to carry it."

"Hello, Jay West."

Jay looked up. Standing in a doorway to the side of the mansion's main entrance was a woman he assumed to be Oliver's wife.

"I'm Barbara Mason," the woman called, coming down the steps. She wore a plain white top and a pair of khaki shorts. "Please come in."

Jay bid the driver goodbye and moved toward her.

"How are you?" Barbara met Jay on the lawn. "I've heard so much about you." She patted him on the shoulder. "All good, I assure you."

"I'm glad." Instantly Jay noticed a detached confidence about Barbara. The "dollar demeanor," he called it—an aura of independence born from never having to worry about money. "I wouldn't want Oliver spreading the truth about me."

She squeezed his arm and smiled coyly. "Of course not."

At one point Barbara had been an attractive woman. She was blond and of medium height, and her face was pretty and her smile charming. But as Jay studied her closely, he was vaguely surprised to see age lines at the corners of her mouth and a barely discernible sadness in the crow's feet around her green eyes. Her legs were tanned and toned, but he saw the onset of varicose veins and noticed that her hands seemed prematurely wrinkled. She was probably the same age as Oliver, late thirties, he thought, but she seemed older. And as he pictured Oliver standing beside her, they didn't seem right for each other. He had expected a flashier, more exotic woman, perhaps because he had witnessed Oliver's powerful sex drive the morning before in the storage room. His gaze dropped to the ground as the image of Oliver pressing himself against Abby flashed through his mind.

"We're going to have a perfectly wonderful day on the sailboat," Barbara said, pulling him across the lawn toward the side door and a young boy standing there. "Meet my son, Junior."

"Hello." Junior held out his hand, fingers spread wide.

"Hi." Jay took the boy's small hand and shook it. "You've got quite a grip," he said as he followed Barbara into the mansion's kitchen.

"Thanks. Can I go now, Mom?"

"Yes, honey. But go check in with the baby-sitter."

"Where's Oliver?" Jay asked, watching Junior dart away.

"Upstairs getting ready." Barbara moved to a counter on top of which was a large picnic basket overloaded with food and supplies. "Oliver didn't tell me you were so handsome," she said matter-of-factly.

Jay grinned. "And Oliver didn't tell me you were so forward."

"I say what I think when I think it," she replied unapologetically, pulling several items from the basket and placing them on the counter. "Sometimes it gets me into trouble with the girls at the club, but I've always followed that philosophy and I can't stop now. I guess I inherited it from my father. He can be pretty direct sometimes."

Jay glanced around the large country-style kitchen, stocked with top-of-the-line appliances and every cooking gadget imaginable. "Is your father on Wall Street?"

Barbara exhaled heavily, as if her father's occupation wasn't something she wanted to discuss. "My father once owned a company named Kellogg Aviation. That's my maiden name, Kellogg. The company is a—"

"A feeder airline for one of the big carriers," Jay interrupted. "It was purchased a few years back for quite a bit of money."

"How did you know that?"

"I was involved with an investment group that was trying to buy it when I was at National City. I was going to provide the bank financing, but when the large airline came into the picture, the group I was working with backed off." Jay hesitated. "So your father is Harold Kellogg." According to *Forbes*, Kellogg was extremely wealthy.

"That's right," Barbara confirmed.

"Well, it makes more sense now," Jay muttered under his breath.

"What does?"

"Oh, nothing."

"Come on."

"It's really none of my business."

"Out with it," she demanded, winking at him. "Or I'll tell Oliver that you told me he was fooling around with someone at the office."

Jay's eyes flashed to Barbara's, wondering if that comment was a test. "All right, all right," he agreed, smiling too broadly. "It's just that I know what real estate goes for up here. This farm must be a hundred acres if it's—"

"A hundred and fifty, and my father owns another two hundred on the other side of the hill."

"And the house is probably ten thousand square feet."

"Something like that."

"Right." Jay raised his eyebrows, impressed. There were commercial office buildings in his hometown that weren't as big. "I'm sure Bill McCarthy pays Oliver very well, but this is—well, it's beyond the means of even most investment bankers."

"That's true," Barbara agreed. "The farm was a gift from my father. Oliver couldn't have afforded it on his own."

For the first time Jay thought he heard a trace of sarcasm in her voice, or perhaps it was bitterness.

"And I know it bothers him every time he comes up the driveway," she continued. "Every time he sees what my father accomplished." Her lips formed a tight smile. "Unfortunately, I didn't figure all that out until after we moved in," she admitted ruefully. "They don't get along very well. My father can be, well, pretty abrasive. Oliver's always been resentful of him. I guess it's because of Oliver's background." She was silent for a few moments. "I've probably told you more than you wanted to hear," she said quietly. "Maybe more than I should have. But I warned you." Her voice rose to its natural tone. "I say the first thing that pops into my mind."

"I'm glad you did." Without realizing it, Jay ran his finger along the scar beneath his eye. It was a habit he couldn't break. "How did you and Oliver meet?"

Barbara shot him a sly look. "You mean you're interested in understanding what a society girl like me is doing with a boy from the wrong side of the tracks."

He shrugged, slightly embarrassed. She'd hit the nail on the head.

"I told you, Jay. I don't pull any punches."

"No kidding." He checked the hallway for Oliver. "So tell me."

"Oliver's quite a charmer when he wants to be." She gazed down at her French manicure. "I met him at an East Side cocktail party twelve years ago when he was a rising star at J. P. Morgan. I was fascinated to find out how a young man who had grown up in the Bronx projects could be so successful at a blue-blooded, white-shoe firm like Morgan—fascinated to find out how he even got himself into the cocktail party, because only establishment types had been invited. By the end of the evening I was fascinated with just him. He's a dynamic man. He begged his way into Morgan after graduating from City College, and the rest, as they say, is history. Once you give Oliver even the slightest opportunity, the tiniest opening, he takes full advantage. I've never met a person who can master so many things so quickly, or at least make you believe he has. He's the real deal, but at the same time he's the biggest con artist you've ever met. He's an enigma and a constant contradiction, and even though I'm married to him, I've never truly figured him out," she continued. "Which I guess is one reason I still love him." She sighed. "Why I put up with him."

Jay stared at Barbara for several moments, struck by her honesty.

"Damn it!"

"What's wrong?" Barbara's outburst had startled him.

"Oh, I forgot to get gin for the outing. Oliver loves his Beefeater and tonic on the sailboat." She rolled her eyes. "He'll go nuts when he finds out I forgot to get a bottle."

"We can stop on our way to the boat," Jay pointed out.

"No." Barbara shook her head. "Once Oliver gets going, he doesn't like to stop. It drives him up a wall to do errands on the way to the club. And I don't want to hear about how incompetent I am because I didn't remember to tell the housekeeper to buy the gin. He's always telling me I should make lists, but I hate lists." She moved to a row of hooks attached to the side of the refrigerator and removed a set of keys. "Be a dear and go get me some. There's a liquor store in a little shopping mall a couple of miles back down the lane that goes past the end of our driveway," she explained, tossing the keys to Jay. "Make a left at the end of the driveway."

"I remember seeing the store on the way out here. Are these the keys to the Suburban I saw out front?" He could tell they weren't by their shape, but wanted to politely give her a chance to switch keys if she'd made a mistake.

"No. Those are to the Austin Healey parked next to the Suburban. Driving the Healey ought to make the errand more fun."

Jay smiled. "Great."

"The car's all warmed up," Barbara said. "Oliver had it out a little while ago."

"Okay. I'll be right back."

Jay headed out the door and moved quickly to the flashy British sports car. He pulled its canvas top back, slipped behind the steering wheel, and fired up the six-cylinder engine. Then he was off, flying down the mile-long driveway, wind whipping his hair back, the white speedometer needle nudging seventy before he finally leaned on the brakes, locked up the polished chrome wheels, and skidded to a halt as driveway met country lane. When the car had screeched to a stop, Jay put his head back and laughed, then slapped the dashboard and smelled the rich leather scent emanating from the car. Oliver was living the dream.

Jay checked in both directions, then slammed the stick into first gear, punched the accelerator, and sped down the twisting road. The car hugged the tight turns as he ran through the gears, centrifugal forces pressing his body into the seat as the speed increased. Finally the road straightened out and he pushed the car to its limit. Too soon the liquor store appeared. For a moment he considered racing past and taking the car for a drive, but he slowed down, not wanting to keep Oliver and Barbara waiting. He ran back through the gears, then coasted across the small shopping mall's gravel parking lot to a stop.

As Jay unsnapped the seat belt, he was startled by the ring of a phone coming from inside the glove compartment. He leaned across the passenger seat and opened the compartment door. It was probably Oliver, he thought, calling to warn him against driving his baby too fast. He grabbed the slim cell phone from atop a black folder and pressed the answer button. "Hello."

"Oliver, it's Tony! Thank God I got you. Listen, don't use that information I gave you yesterday. There's a problem. We want to review the situation face-to-face first. Understand?"

Jay said nothing, listening to the sounds of traffic coming from the other end of the line.

"Oliver?"

Still Jay was silent.

"Shit!"

The line clicked in Jay's ear. Slowly he brought the phone down and stared at it. Finally he leaned across the passenger seat and replaced the phone in the glove compartment atop the folder that he assumed contained the car's service records, registration, and insurance information. As he did, he noticed a computer disk beside the folder and an unsealed envelope beneath it. Acting on impulse, he yanked out the envelope and removed the single piece of paper from inside, staring at the name on the page for a long time. Bell Chemical. Bell was one of the largest specialty chemical manufacturers in the country.

Out of the corner of his eye Jay noticed a red Suburban in the side mirror. It was tearing down the long straightaway toward the shopping mall. He shoved the paper inside the envelope and replaced it in the glove compartment just as Oliver guided the Suburban into the parking spot beside the Healey.

"Hey, pal," Oliver called through the Suburban's open window. He turned off the engine, hopped out of the SUV, and met Jay behind the Healey. "Glad you could make it out here."

"Thanks for having me."

"Sure." Oliver was dressed in a polo shirt, khakis, Docksiders, and a pair of Vuarnet sunglasses. "We couldn't have asked for a nicer day."

"Absolutely," Jay agreed. "What are you doing here?" He noticed that even though Oliver was wearing casual clothes, he still emitted an in-charge, businesslike manner.

An irritated expression twisted Oliver's face. "Fucking Barbara. She's so inept sometimes. She forgets to buy my gin, then forgets to tell you to pick up sunscreen. I must have reminded her ten times this morning about it. Still she forgets. Can you believe it? Like I told you, Jay, get children but not a wife."

"Why didn't you just call me on your cell phone?"

"Huh?"

Jay noticed Oliver tapping his thigh madly. He did the same thing when it got hectic on the arbitrage desk. "Your cell phone is in the glove compartment." Jay pointed toward the Healey. "You could have just called to tell me to pick up the sunscreen. Why did you drive all the way out here?"

"How did you know my cell phone was in the glove compartment?" Oliver asked angrily. "Just because Barbara gives you the keys to my car doesn't give you the right to go through it."

"The phone rang," Jay answered calmly. "I thought it was you, so I picked up."

"Oh. Who was it?" Oliver asked tentatively.

Jay shrugged. "I don't know. The guy said something about not using information he gave you yesterday. I think he said his name was Tony. He hung up when he figured out it wasn't you at the other end of the line. It was strange."

"Oh, yeah." Oliver waved a hand as though batting a bug. "I met Tony in the Oak Room after work yesterday. He's a real-estate agent. I'm thinking about buying an apartment in Manhattan, and he's representing me. It's a beautiful place right on the East River, but I'm having a tough time getting into the building. The president of the co-op board doesn't like investment bankers, especially ones from the Bronx. Anyway, Tony dug up some dirt on the guy, and we were going to use it against him. You know, a little friendly influence so he can see things my way. I realize all that doesn't sound very good, but sometimes people in those buildings can be pretty snobbish. Sometimes they need a push." A pained expression cut across his face. "I guess Tony got cold feet."

"I guess."

Jay and Oliver stared at each other for a few moments. Finally Oliver pulled out his wallet and stuffed a hundred-dollar bill into Jay's palm. "Get me the gin and the sunscreen, will you, pal?"

"Sure."

"And give me the keys to my baby."

"Huh?"

"The keys to the Healey." Oliver gestured at the car, then held out the keys to the Suburban. "Here."

Jay pulled out the keys to the Healey and they made the exchange.

"Thanks." Oliver hurried to the driver's side of the Healey and lowered himself in behind the steering wheel. "I love driving this thing," he shouted. "See you at home."

Jay watched Oliver back the Healey out of the parking spot, then peel from the lot. He glanced down at the hundred-dollar bill in his palm, then back at the sports car racing away.

Twenty minutes later Jay eased the Suburban to a stop alongside the Healey, grabbed the bag with the gin and sunscreen off the passenger seat, and hopped out. He hesitated, tempted to check the Healey's glove compartment. He eyed the side door of the house, then glanced back at the car. The top was still down and it would be easy to check. He reached for the compartment's knob.

"It's a beautiful car, isn't it?"

Jay whipped around, almost dropping the bag.

"I'm sorry if I startled you."

"N-No, not at all," Jay stammered. Sally Lane stood before him wearing a plain black golf shirt and a pair of Nantucket-red shorts that fell almost to her tanned knees. Her long blond hair and aqua eyes shone in the morning sun. "I didn't know you were coming today."

"Oliver asked me yesterday at lunch," Sally explained. "He thought it would be a good chance for us to get to know each other. You know, outside the office." She clasped her hands at the small of her back. "He wants us to work closely together. He said I could learn a lot from you."

"Uh-huh." Jay hadn't seen much of Sally the day before. She'd spent most of her first day with Oliver, meeting other people at the firm, as Jay had during his first day at McCarthy & Lloyd. "I'm glad you could come."

"I really love this car." Sally's arm brushed against Jay as she moved past him. "My father had a Healey when I was young. Only his was red." She stopped at the rear of the car and turned to face Jay. "We had to get rid of ours because the salt air caused it to rust so badly."

"Where did you grow up?"

"Gloucester, Massachusetts." She pushed her long hair behind her ears. "It's north of Boston, on the ocean."

"I know." As she had the day before, she was wearing very little makeup. Jay found her natural look extremely appealing. "Gorton's of Gloucester and all that."

"That's what everyone says. It's so embarrassing."

"Why?"

"It's like I ought to walk around all the time in a rain slicker and a floppy yellow hat carrying a box of frozen fish sticks." Sally pretended to model a box by cupping her hands, turning to the side and giving Jay a come-hither look. "What do you think?"

"Perfect. If the arbitrage desk doesn't work out, you'll always have a job selling seafood." He instinctively liked Sally even though Bullock had spent the better part of the afternoon the previous day convincing him that she was direct competition—that Sally also had a million-dollar guarantee, and that Oliver was going to pit Sally and Jay against each other, then fire the one who didn't measure up by December so he only had to pay one bonus. It all sounded too much like Oliver for Jay to ignore. And Sally had a pedigree—Yale undergraduate and Harvard Business School plus two years at an elite financial consulting firm in Los Angeles. The kind of pedigree Bill McCarthy had referred to the evening Jay had been hired. A pedigree Jay didn't have.

"I guess I shouldn't poke too much fun at the fishing industry," Sally said. "That's how my family got its start in this country."

"Really?"

"Yes. We came here back in the 1870s from Europe and settled out there in Gloucester. My great-great-grandfather was on the ocean almost every day, according to the stories I was told. It all started with one small boat, and pretty soon he had a fleet."

"Does your family still live there?"

Sally shook her head. "No my mother and father moved away." She lowered her head. "They were living in Florida, but they died in a plane crash about a year ago."

"I'm sorry." Jay heard a door open and glanced over his shoulder. Oliver was lugging the huge picnic basket toward the cars with Barbara tagging along behind.

"You two ready to go?" Oliver called.

Sally brushed past Jay, their arms touching again, and jogged across the lawn, taking one of the basket's handles and helping Oliver carry it to the Suburban.

Jay watched them carefully, searching for any sign that Oliver had more than a professional interest in Sally.

"Open the door, pal," Oliver called as he and Sally neared the Suburban.

Jay opened the back of the truck, placed the bag with the gin and sunscreen inside, then helped Oliver and Sally lift the basket in.

When the truck was packed, Oliver turned to Jay and

handed him the keys to the Healey. "Here, you and Sally take the fun car. Barb and I will take the boring one."

"I thought you didn't like other people driving your baby," Jay teased.

"I never said that."

"You didn't have to."

"You're right. But this is a special occasion. Go ahead and take it."

Jay and Sally needed no urging. They hopped into the sports car and followed Oliver and Barbara down the driveway.

"Do me a favor," Jay yelled above the wind as they turned onto the country lane. He had intentionally lagged behind the Suburban. "Make sure Oliver put the registration and insurance certificate in the glove compartment. I'd hate to get pulled over and not have them."

Sally opened the small door and withdrew the black folder. After a few moments she located the registration and insurance information inside it and held up the documents for Jay to see.

He nodded. When she had opened the glove compartment, he'd noticed that the computer disk and the envelope were gone.

CHAPTER 5

"On the count of three, say money!" Oliver aimed a Polaroid camera at Jay and Sally, who were leaning together in the sailboat's cockpit, and snapped the picture. "Nice smile, Jay," Oliver remarked sarcastically, handing the developing photograph to Barbara.

"Now you get in there, Oliver," Barbara suggested, shielding her eyes against the late-afternoon sunshine reflecting brightly off the blue water. "I'll take one of all three of you."

"All right," Oliver agreed, picking up his half-full gin and tonic and forcing himself between Jay and Sally.

Barbara snapped the picture, then put the camera down beside her.

"Jesus, Barbara!" Oliver shouted. "It's wet there." He scooped up the camera and pictures and searched for a dry place to put them. An afternoon breeze had kicked up on Long Island Sound, and the cockpit had been soaked by salty spray.

"Here." Jay handed Oliver a backpack he had brought on board.

"Thanks." Oliver quickly stowed the camera and two photographs inside, then moved to the helm of the fifty-foot craft christened *Authority*. It was a magnificent sailboat. Its white hull and cabin were trimmed with royal blue, and its huge mainsail towered over them as they ran along a port tack. "All right, both of you overboard," he ordered to Jay and Sally, holding his glass aloft like a torch. "Into the water, I said."

"Here?" Sally asked dubiously. The boat was rolling several degrees to the left as it sliced through the choppy waters.

"Right here!" Oliver bellowed, slurring his words slightly. "I'm the captain, and on the *Authority* what I say goes."

"Don't make them go in if they don't want to," Barbara protested, clinging to Oliver as the boat rolled further to port. The waves had become larger in the last few minutes.

Jay slipped his T-shirt over his head, dropped it on the deck, and nudged Sally. "Come on." She looked perfect in her one-piece black bathing suit. "It isn't as if Oliver's going to leave us out here," he whispered. "Even he wouldn't do that."

"What makes you so sure?"

"It'll be all right."

She glanced anxiously to the north. Connecticut was still visible, but it was a long way off, almost obscured by the haze of the hot July afternoon. "I don't know about this," she said tentatively.

"Come on, Jay West!" Oliver yelled. "Are you afraid of a little water? I can understand Sally's being scared. After all, she's a girl."

"Stop it, Oliver." Barbara slapped Oliver's wrist playfully. "Don't be so demanding. And chauvinistic." She grabbed him, spilling most of his drink, and kissed him on the cheek. "I love you," she whispered.

"Thanks, hon," he answered automatically, not taking his eyes off Sally. "Last chance, West," Oliver shouted. "If you don't go in, I'll know you're a pussy."

Jay grinned at Sally. "Kind of a juvenile ultimatum, but I guess I don't have any choice. After all, he's the boss."

"I guess," she agreed halfheartedly.

Jay moved to the safety ropes encircling the cockpit, stepped over them, and dove in. The water—a bathwaterlike seventy-five degrees—still felt refreshing. It was almost four o'clock—they'd been out on the Sound since eleven—and he was ready for a swim. He burst through the surface, wiped water from his eyes, and quickly spotted the boat moving away over the rolling waves. He searched the deck for Sally, but she was nowhere in sight.

"Hey!"

Jay whipped around. She was behind him treading water. "So you did it," he said, nodding approvingly. "I didn't think you would."

"I couldn't let the other vice president on the arbitrage desk show me up. Oliver would never have let me live that down." She turned her head to the side and smiled. "You never know what Oliver will consider important at the end of the year. I want my bonus as badly as you do."

"I'm sure." Jay chuckled softly. Oliver was a master manipulator.

"It sure gets lonely out here in a hurry when you're in the water," Sally observed. The coastline was no longer visible.

Jay gazed at her delicate face bobbing above the waves. "Do I detect a little anxiety?"

"A little," she admitted.

"Oliver'll be back," Jay assured her. He wasn't as certain as he sounded, but the coast was only a few miles away. It would be an arduous swim, but he had no doubt they could make it if they had to.

"Are there sharks out here?" Sally asked apprehensively.

"Sure. Tiger sharks, great whites—"

"All I wanted was a simple yes or no, Mr. Marine Biologist." She moved closer to Jay, searching the water for the boat. "Why do you think he made us do this?"

"Power," Jay answered automatically. "The same reason his sailboat is named *Authority*." He rolled onto his back and floated, arms and legs outstretched. "Oliver is one of those people who constantly needs to reassure himself that he's in command."

"I guess you're right. Oh!" she shrieked.

"What is it?"

"I felt something slimy go by my leg." Her eyes were wide as she plowed through the water toward him. "Jesus, there it is again." She threw her arms around Jay's neck instinctively and pressed herself against him.

"It's all right. You're just imagining things." Jay glanced at her gold bracelet glittering in the sun. He hoped she was just imagining things. If she felt whatever it was again, that bracelet was going to the bottom of the Sound, no matter how much it cost. He knew that sharks and other predatory fish were attracted to shiny objects.

"Sorry," she said sheepishly, backing away slightly but still close enough that their fingers touched occasionally as they were treading water.

"Don't worry." Her arms had felt wonderful. He kept reminding himself that she was the competition, that he ought to keep his distance from her, but that was becoming more difficult by the minute. Jay had already noticed her watching him that day on the boat, as she had caught him watching her.

"Here they come," Sally said, pointing across the water at the *Authority*. "Thank God."

Jay spotted the impressive, white-hulled craft cruising toward them and was vaguely disappointed. He'd wanted this to go on a little longer.

As the *Authority* passed, Oliver tossed them a safety line. Then he slackened the sail and, after Jay and Sally had pulled themselves to the boat, dropped a rope ladder over the side so they could climb aboard.

"That felt great, didn't it?" Oliver was beaming. "Just what you both needed."

Sally grabbed a large towel and wrapped it around her slim frame. "Yeah, great, except for the shark that brushed against my leg."

"Oh, no." Barbara brought both hands to her mouth.

Oliver moved back to the helm and tightened the main sail. "Probably nothing but a damn bluefish."

Jay gazed at Oliver and Barbara, now that they were side by side again. They just didn't look right together.

"What are you staring at?" Oliver asked belligerently. He'd finished off another gin and tonic since ordering them into the water.

"Nothing," Jay answered.

Oliver glanced skyward, then back at Jay. "Want a better view?"

"What do you mean?"

Oliver pointed at the top of the mast, seventy feet off the water. "I'll be more than happy to crank you up there in the bosun's chair if you want to take a man's look around."

Jay sucked the insides of his cheeks. It was a long way to the top, and the boat was pitching and rolling in the choppy sea.

"Unless you're scared of heights," Oliver added loudly so that Sally and Barbara could hear.

"I'm not crazy about heights," Jay admitted. "But what the hell." He stared back at Oliver defiantly. "I'll go for it."

Oliver nodded slowly. He hadn't expected Jay to accept the challenge so readily. "Good."

Moments later Oliver had attached the bosun's chair—a plank of wood a foot and a half long and ten inches wide—to the starboard jib halyard with a canvas strap that looped beneath the seat and came together at the end of the halyard. Jay slipped onto the seat and grabbed the canvas straps knotted at his chest.

"Why don't you give him the harness seat?" Barbara called from the cockpit.

"What's the harness seat?" Jay asked, glancing up at Oliver, who was making certain the canvas straps were fastened securely to the end of the halyard.

"It's a more modern version of what you're sitting in. There's no chance of falling out of it." Oliver patted Jay on the shoulder. "Unfortunately, it's back at the yacht club."

"It doesn't do much good there," Jay yelled, grabbing the straps as Oliver began to crank the winch. Within moments he was halfway up the mast, almost forty feet in the air.

"That's high enough, honey," Barbara called.

"Be quiet," Oliver muttered, continuing to crank. Finally he stopped. Jay was only a few feet from the top of the mast. "How you doing, pal?" Oliver shouted. "Nice enough view for you up there?"

"Beautiful!" Jay yelled back. "I can see all the way to New York City." He grinned down at Sally, who was squinting against the sun. "You ought to try this, Sally. It's not so bad."

"No way," she called, turning to Barbara. "He's crazy."

"Definitely," Barbara agreed. "Certifiably insane if you ask me. Or just fearless."

"We'll see how fearless," Oliver cracked, cranking the mainsail tighter and changing course so that the *Authority* caught as much wind as possible.

As a large swell broadsided them, the craft heeled over precariously. Jay clung to the straps, feeling his heart rising in his throat.

"What a ride!" Oliver yelled, clutching the wheel tightly. The afternoon breeze gusted and the *Authority* picked up speed. "This is great. He'll do anything I tell him to do. I love it."

"Bring him down," Barbara screamed.

"He hasn't asked to come down yet," Oliver protested. The boat heeled again, further this time, to almost thirty degrees. "He's fine."

"Oliver!" Barbara yelled.

"You had enough, Jay West?" Oliver laughed, pleased with himself. "Ready for me to save you?"

"Don't bother!" Jay yelled back. As the *Authority* leaned far to starboard once more, he let go of the straps, put his hands above his head, moved forward on the wooden seat, and slipped from the bosun's chair.

"Look out!" Sally screamed, pointing up.

"Jesus Christ!" Oliver let go of the wheel and scrambled forward, certain Jay was going to smash into the deck.

But he didn't. He plunged just past it and splashed into the water, bobbing quickly to the surface and waving to signal that he was fine as the sailboat slid past.

Minutes later Jay climbed the rope ladder to the deck and smiled at the other three, water dripping from his body. "That was great." He brushed his soaking hair straight back and gestured at Oliver. "Now it's my turn to crank your ass up the mast on that little wooden seat."

For several moments Oliver glared at Jay. He could hear Barbara giggling over his shoulder. She knew what his answer would be. Finally Oliver broke into a grin. "Not on your life, Jay."

CHAPTER 6

"Hello, Savoy."

"Hello, Karim." Savoy checked up and down the darkened street several times, then glanced back at the dark-skinned, acne-scarred face in front of him. Karim was a chameleon, able to operate in dangerous worlds without being recognized as a traitor. He had begun his life of violence in the Khad—the Afghan arm of the KGB—then smoothly shifted his allegiance to the mujahideen freedom fighters just before the Soviets invaded Afghanistan in December 1979. Now he was in bed with the Taliban. Karim had a knack for picking the winning side. And for surviving. "Will I be satisfied?" Savoy asked.

"Absolutely." Karim nodded. "Come this way." He gestured with a quick jerk of his thumb. "I like your ponytail," he called over his shoulder softly to Savoy. "It almost looks real."

Savoy's eyes narrowed, but he said nothing as he followed Karim through the streets of Konduz—a small city of seventy thousand located 250 kilometers north of Kabul across the Hindu Kush.

Karim stopped before a small building, produced a set of keys, opened the locks of the front door, beckoned Savoy inside, then relocked the door. He led Savoy down a narrow hallway and through another padlocked door. The second door opened into a small warehouse reeking of oil and mildew.

Savoy smiled, and the gold tooth he had affixed over his real one sparkled in the flashlight's gleam. "Your office, I presume."

Karim grunted his affirmation, then walked across the hard dirt floor in his swaying gait to a tarp. He threw it back with a violent motion, revealing wooden boxes stacked against the wall. With a crowbar he pried the top off one. "Here." He aimed the flashlight on the contents.

Savoy moved to the box, bent down, and removed one of the assault rifles, inspecting it carefully.

"Avtomat Kalashnikov, model forty-seven," Karim muttered. "Mikhail Kalashnikov's little contribution to world peace. I also have several boxes of the AK-seventy-four. It fires a smaller bullet, five point forty-five millimeters versus the forty-seven's seven point sixty-two. However, the smaller bullet begins to tumble faster, causing more damage to the target. The seventy-four also has less recoil and doesn't climb when fired on automatic."

"The safety mechanism is still difficult to operate." Savoy recognized that Karim was subtly beginning to negotiate. But they had already agreed on price. "And loud." He caressed the banana-shaped, thirty-round magazine. The Kalashnikov wasn't a particularly pretty gun, but it was durable. It could be buried in mud or sand for a long time and remain operational, which was why it was still so popular after all these years. "What else do you have for me?"

"Armalite AR-eighteens." Karim had a feeling that the mention of this weapon would strike a resonant chord.

Savoy glanced up, unable to hide his satisfaction. "Really?"

"Yes. That should make your client happy."

"How do you know what should make my client happy?" Savoy placed the AK-47 back in its box and stood up.

"I have my ways." It had been an educated guess, but now he knew for certain.

"I see," Savoy said, trying to sound indifferent, realizing that he might have just given something away. "Do you have more?"

"RPG-sevens and SAM-seven Strelas. The exact kind of rocket-powered grenades and surface-to-air missiles you requested." Karim paused. Savoy's subtle signs of eagerness when Karim mentioned the AR-18s told the arms broker much, as he knew which group favored that weapon. He couldn't help taunting Savoy with that knowledge, and he said, "Just don't put them on a ship named *Claudia* and sail it out of Libya." He grinned, unable to hold back. Now he knew the ultimate destination of the weapons.

Savoy's jaw tightened at the mention of that unsuccessful arms-smuggling endeavor from his past. "The trucks will be here tomorrow evening at nightfall," he said. "Be ready."

"Headed to Karachi, I assume."

"Yes." There was no reason to deny the observation. Karachi was the only logical place the trucks could have been going. "The other half of the money will be in your account at the Bank of Suez in the morning. And don't think you're going to get a penny more than what we've already agreed to." He turned to go, then paused. "We'll be wanting more, Karim. A steady stream of weapons. My clients aren't small-time, as you might believe. They are very well funded and willing to go to great lengths to disrupt the peace accord. Even you would be surprised at what is being planned." For a moment he thought about his team training on the remote Virginia farm. "This situation could prove to be very profitable, or it could lead to your undoing. Don't believe for a moment that my clients wouldn't kill a traitor. They would. And they'd go to any lengths to find you."

CHAPTER 7

Refreshed after a shower, Jay emerged from the men's locker room of the Westchester Yacht Club wearing a sharp navy blue blazer, a freshly pressed light blue oxford shirt, pleated khakis, and a healthy glow—a result of the hot day on the water beneath a cloudless sky. He nodded at several club members as he strode confidently through the great room and out onto the porch. It overlooked the club's harbor as well as Satan's Finger, a narrow spit of land extending into the Sound on which were constructed several multimillion-dollar homes. Faint traces of expensive perfume, suntan lotion, and sea air mingled to constitute an intoxicating aroma, and Jay stood in the doorway absorbing the atmosphere. After a few moments he moved down the porch and sat in a large green wicker chair. He ordered a gin and tonic from a waiter wearing a white dinner jacket, and gazed out over the water, considering how far in life he'd come.

Bethlehem, Pennsylvania, Jay's home, wasn't far from there—

no more than a hundred miles to the west—but the wealth oozing from these grounds would have been inconceivable to his blue-collar parents, who still lived in the small steel town. They had provided Jay and his siblings with a decent upbringing. They had always had a roof over their heads and at least two meals a day, though all too often the roof had been leaky and franks and beans had dominated the weekly lunch and dinner menus.

He and one brother had made it past public high school to college, but Kenny had lasted just two years at East Stroudsburg before dropping out to work as an apprentice crane man in the Bethlehem Steel plant. Only Jay had made the jump to the white-collar world. In their own subtle ways, he suspected his siblings resented him for his success. But that was life, Jay figured, and he felt no animosity toward them.

"Your gin and tonic, sir." The waiter placed the glass on the table to the side of Jay's chair.

"Thanks." Jay fished a lime wedge out of the ice cubes and ran it around the rim. "Put this on Oliver Mason's account," he instructed. "His membership number is three-seventeen." Oliver had his monthly bill sent to McCarthy & Lloyd, and Jay had spotted the account number on an invoice lying open in front of Oliver's position one day the previous week. He grinned. Oliver wouldn't be angry at all about his using the membership number without asking. In fact, he'd be impressed. Oliver was always impressed with people who obtained sensitive information. "And give yourself a ten-dollar tip."

"Thank you." The waiter hurried off.

Jay relaxed into the comfortable green-and-white striped cushions. He took a long sip of the cool drink and watched dusk settle over the Sound. This was the good life. This was why he was willing to work grueling hours in a hostile environment and endure Carter Bullock's constant crap.

He admired a particularly large house on Satan's Finger. *Money, the root of all evil,* he thought. *The road to ruin.* That was just senseless drivel from weak-minded people who couldn't handle money and would have made a wreck of their lives even without wealth. From snobs who'd never had to go a day wanting anything. Bad advice from well-meaning but pitifully naive people, like blubbering Oscar winners clutching their statuettes and imploring all the destitute, struggling actors in the world to hold on to their dreams when what they really should have been advising was to wake up and get a real job because the odds of ever really making it were so astronomically stacked against them.

The mansion on Satan's Finger blurred before Jay's eyes. He'd seen firsthand what money and power could do. It had turned Oliver Mason into a man who would force himself on a young female subordinate in a storage room and threaten her with loss of her job unless she submitted to his sexual demands. There was no question in Jay's mind that money, or the psychopathic pursuit of it, was at the core of Oliver's personality disorder. Jay's gaze dropped to the lime. And here he was accepting a drink from that man, working for that man, wishing in some ways that he could be like that man. "I wouldn't let that happen to me," he whispered.

"Enjoying the conversation?"

Jay's eyes flashed up. Sally stood before him wearing a sundress that ended halfway up her thighs. Her long blond hair tumbled down one shoulder, and her skin had a radiant glow, matching his. He glanced around casually. She was turning heads. "I was just going over some figures in my mind," he explained sheepishly, standing up and pulling out the wicker chair next to his. "About a deal I'm working on."

"Sure." She waved at a waiter, pointed at Jay's glass to indicate that she'd have the same, then sat down. "Crazy people talk to themselves, and I know you're crazy."

"What are you talking about?" Jay couldn't help stealing another glance at her long legs. Now that she was sitting, the dress was riding even higher on her thighs. "I'm not crazy."

Sally rolled her eyes. "No sane person jumps out of a bosun's chair from seventy feet."

"It wasn't a big deal."

"And you didn't even seem nervous."

"Wanna bet?"

"What do you mean?"

"When I came out of the water I was dripping wet, right?"

"Yes."

"That was pure perspiration."

Sally laughed as she took her gin and tonic from the waiter.

"Same account, sir?" the waiter asked.

"Yes," Jay confirmed. "And another ten-dollar tip."

"Thank you." The waiter noticed that Jay's glass was almost empty. "I'll bring you another, too."

"Much appreciated."

Sally held her drink out, and they touched glasses. "You seem quite at ease," she observed, taking a sip. "Did you grow up around here?"

"No." He learned long ago that there was no point in attempting to be someone he wasn't. "I'm the son of a mechanic who's only ever been to a private club to fix golf carts and isn't familiar with Austin Healeys, just Plymouths and Chevys."

"I see."

He tried to gauge her reaction to the news that he was the product of a blue-collar home. She didn't seemed put off. "Tell me about you," he said.

"There's nothing very interesting in my background. Just standard stuff."

"Come on," Jay urged. She seemed hesitant to talk about herself, which he liked. He didn't appreciate people who spouted off about themselves every few minutes like Old Faithful. "Bullock tells me you're a Yale undergraduate and Harvard Business."

"Yes."

"And after HBS you worked at a financial consulting firm in Los Angeles for a couple of years."

Sally shook her head. "No, I was in the San Diego office. The firm is headquartered in Los Angeles."

"What's the name of it?"

"It's a small West Coast outfit," she replied quickly. "You probably wouldn't recognize it."

"Try me."

She kicked his leg gently with her sandal. "Jesus, where's the bare lightbulb and the polygraph machine?"

Perhaps he was pressing too hard. "Sorry." He looked away, then back at her. She was staring straight at him over the top of her glass. Suddenly she seemed even prettier than she had the day before.

"Hey, pal!" Oliver shouted from the porch doorway, bringing several conversations at surrounding tables to an abrupt halt as people looked around to see who had shattered the evening's calm.

Jay waved back.

Oliver grabbed a waiter by the elbow, ordered a drink, then hurried down the porch, pausing to commandeer an empty chair from two elderly ladies at the table next to Jay and Sally.

Jay watched the women reluctantly agree to cede the chair, and noticed them checking out Oliver's slicked-back hair and fire-engine-red shirt beneath his blue blazer. Oliver walked in stark contrast to most of the members, who were more conservatively groomed and attired. Yet Jay saw that the women were quickly won over by Oliver's effusive manner and charm. When he left them, they were laughing and clasping him on the arm.

"What did you say to them?" Jay asked as Oliver pulled the chair close to Sally's and sat down.

"I told them I wanted them," he answered, leaning forward so the ladies wouldn't hear. "Both of them." He grinned, and a dimple appeared in his left cheek. "At the same time."

Sally put a hand to her mouth, almost spilling her drink.

"I told them to meet me later in one of the upstairs guest rooms," Oliver continued, putting a hand on Sally's bare knee. "They agreed. Apparently they've heard . . ." He hesitated, squeezing Sally's knee and winking at her. "That my nickname in college was Big Dog."

Sally put her head back and laughed again.

Oliver glanced at Sally and pointed at his prominent Adam's apple. "They say you can tell by looking at a man's hands, but this is the only real way to tell without actually seeing it." He turned to Jay. "Oh, by the way, pal, General Electric announced an eighty-two-dollar offer for Bates," he said casually.

"That's gre—"

"But don't try to take credit for those shares you bought yesterday," Oliver warned. "In fact, you shouldn't have paid as much as you did. That guy Kelly at Goldman took advantage of you because he knew I wasn't around. I could have gotten them for at least a dollar a share less. Maybe two. Kelly would never want to lose my business." Oliver grabbed some nuts from a bowl in the middle of the table. "At the end of the call he probably had you thinking you'd won. Probably yelled and screamed and hung up on you, didn't he?"

Jay said nothing.

"Kelly's a hell of an actor. He roped you in like a treble-hooked tuna." Oliver tapped the table several times, glancing quickly at Sally, then back at Jay. "I'm surprised I had to tell you about GE's bid, pal. Didn't you see that Bloomberg terminal outside the men's locker room?"

Bloomberg terminals provided up-to-the-minute financial news on markets and companies around the world. There were several positioned around the Westchester Yacht Club so its wealthy members could check their investment portfolios at any time.

Jay nodded hesitantly. "I saw it."

"Well, you should have used it instead of admiring it," Oliver snapped. "Jay, you've got to be constantly thinking about the transactions we're working on." He turned to Sally. "Here's a good lesson for you. Even on a day like today, when it's very easy to forget about Wall Street and the arbitrage desk, you've got to keep our deals in the back of your mind." He glanced back at Jay. "Understand, pal?"

"Yes," Jay answered, noticing Bullock standing in the porch doorway, dressed in a dark suit, obviously having come straight from McCarthy & Lloyd. "Is Bullock a member here, Oliver?" he asked, disappointed to see the strawberry-colored crew cut and the broad, square-jawed face.

"What?" Oliver looked up, then back over his shoulder as he followed Jay's eyes. "Hello, Badger," he called, standing up. He glanced back at Jay and Sally. "I asked him to come out for dinner. I knew you two wouldn't mind."

Bullock waved and moved quickly down the porch to where they were. "Hello, Sally." He took her hand and smiled warmly, then shook Oliver's and finally gave Jay a curt nod. "How are you tonight, Oliver?"

"Great," Oliver replied. "We had a wonderful day out on the Sound. Too bad you couldn't join us, but I'm glad you could at least come for dinner. This will be fun."

"It should be."

"Everything all right on the desk?" Oliver wanted to know. "I assume there weren't any major emergencies, because I didn't hear from you on the cell phone."

"Everything was fine."

Oliver nodded. "I owe you one, Badger. I hope you made good use of Abby." He laughed. "I told you she was your personal slave for the day."

Bullock blinked slowly, as if he was carefully considering what he was about to say. "Abby didn't come in today."

"Huh?"

Jay noticed a flicker of concern cut across Oliver's face.

"She didn't come in," Bullock repeated.

"Why not?" Oliver asked angrily. "Was she sick?"

"I don't know."

"What do you mean, you don't know?"

"She never called," Bullock explained.

Bullock's face appeared flushed, close to the color of his hair.

For several moments Oliver and Bullock stared at each other, as if they were silently communicating. Then Bill McCarthy appeared at the porch door with Barbara on his arm, and moments later the entire party headed to the Quarterdeck Restaurant for dinner.

The Quarterdeck overlooked the veranda and the water, and as the sun dipped below the horizon, the yellow, green, and red running lights of the sailboats and yachts moored in the harbor lit up, creating a beautiful display. The dining room wasn't particularly crowded, and when the meal ended and coffee was served, Oliver and McCarthy broke out cigars. Cigars were not typically allowed in the dining room, but the club's commodore—a senior partner of a Wall Street law firm—had informed Oliver that smoking would be acceptable that evening. The commodore had hopes of making McCarthy & Lloyd a good client.

When he had finished lighting his cigar, McCarthy—at one end of the white-linen-covered table—turned to Jay, seated to his right. "What are you working on these days, Mr. West?" Even though McCarthy demanded that everyone at the firm call him Bill, he almost always addressed others by their last name—everyone except Oliver. It was his way of subtly reminding everyone that he was the top dog.

Jay hesitated.

"It's all right, Mr. West. You can speak freely. We're all friends here."

Jay glanced at McCarthy's shaggy blond hair. Despite his rigid requirement that everyone else at the firm wear their hair conservatively, he often went months without a haircut himself. And he often wore suit pants that were frayed at the pockets. Jay had come to learn that despite McCarthy's millions, he was ridiculously cheap. "I was concerned about that table over there," Jay said, gesturing at a party of four sitting nearby.

"Don't worry," McCarthy assured him. "They're far enough away. They won't hear you."

"Okay." Bullock was seated to Jay's right, and out of the corner of his eye Jay saw him lean closer. Jay also noticed Oliver disengage from his conversation with Sally and Barbara. "I'm following several situations, but two in particular," he began in a low voice. "The first is a company called Simons." This was the company Oliver had suggested he buy shares of the previous morning in the conference room. "It's headquartered in Green Bay, Wisconsin, and manufactures cleaning products. I'm performing due diligence now, calling people in the industry and crunching numbers. It appears to be a decent takeover candidate. The stock is cheap and there aren't any major share concentrations." He hesitated, sensing Oliver's vexed expression without even looking at him. "But the earnings prospects aren't great."

"That doesn't sound very exciting," McCarthy observed between puffs. "A sleepy company in a boring industry. Have we purchased any shares?"

Jay shook his head, feeling Oliver's wrath like heat from an open oven. "Not yet."

"What's the other situation?"

"A company called TurboTec in Nashua, New Hampshire." Oliver had nixed the idea, but here was a chance to resurrect what Jay still believed was an excellent opportunity. "Their engineers design intraoffice computer networks for medium-sized businesses. Few Wall Street analysts follow TurboTec, so its stock price has lagged behind the performance of the NASDAQ index. But it's a great company."

"I like the idea." McCarthy's voice was animated. "How'd you find out about it?"

"A friend of mine from college works in the marketing department. His name is Jack Trainer."

"Any external factors that make the company attractive from our standpoint?"

Jay understood what that meant. McCarthy wanted his arbitrage desk in and out of a company's shares quickly. TurboTec might be a nice firm, but if the share price wasn't going to pop quickly, he didn't want to bother with it. "A Japanese company is accumulating shares."

"How do you know that?" McCarthy asked suspiciously. "Look, I realize that you're new to the firm," he continued without giving Jay a chance to respond, "but you should appreciate by now that I run an absolutely clean operation. We are ethical to a fault at McCarthy and Lloyd. I don't want to hear about even a whisper of impropriety on the arbitrage desk. Or any other area of my firm, for that matter." He pointed his smoking cigar at Jay. "If the Securities and Exchange Commission or the United States attorney's office came knocking on my door, I would cooperate fully with any investigation. And if they found irregularities, I'd personally assist them in throwing the guilty party in jail." His voice had risen to such a pitch that Sally and Barbara had stopped talking. "I can't have that kind of black mark on my firm. I'd lose my access to Washington."

"I understand," Jay answered quietly. He caught a glimpse of Bullock's smug smile. The bastard was enjoying this.

"Good," McCarthy said adamantly.

"I'd never put you, Oliver, or the firm in that kind of compromising position."

"Double good."

"The fact that the Japanese company has accumulated a position in TurboTec is public information," Jay said calmly. "But the information wasn't in any U.S. publications, which is probably why the stock hasn't reacted more quickly. The accumulation announcement was a tiny blurb in an Osaka newspaper. I know that because I have an acquaintance who works in National City's Tokyo office. National City is the bank I was with before I came to McCarthy and Lloyd."

"I remember." The harsh edge in McCarthy's voice had dissipated.

"My acquaintance in Tokyo thought I'd be interested in the information because she knew I had a friend at TurboTec. She cut out the article, attached an English translation, and sent it to me. The information is certainly important, but it isn't in any way proprietary. It's in the public domain." Jay leaned back, gave

Bullock a triumphant narrowing of the eyes, then smiled subtly at Sally before looking back at McCarthy. "I've been following the stock for three weeks and in that time the price has risen fifteen percent, but there's plenty of juice left in it, especially if the Japanese company decides to announce a full-blown takeover." Jay knew Oliver would be livid, but this was a chance to shine in front of the chairman. He wasn't going to let the opportunity get away, even at the risk of pissing off Oliver.

"Then why the hell haven't you bought any shares yet?" McCarthy demanded.

"I wanted to do a bit more work on it before I mentioned it to anyone." That ought to placate Oliver. Now McCarthy wouldn't know that he had already passed on the opportunity.

"What's the share price right now?" McCarthy asked.

"It closed at twenty-two and a quarter yesterday."

"How many shares does TurboTec have outstanding?"

"About ten million."

"Buy two hundred thousand shares first thing in the morning," McCarthy ordered. "Tonight, if you can get them in the off-hours markets. Use three or four brokers. Two hundred thousand is enough to make us a substantial profit if you're right, but not enough to draw any real attention."

"I agree."

"If this TurboTec thing pans out, Jay, I'll take back everything I've been saying to Oliver about how you've been doing nothing but taking up space on the arbitrage desk." McCarthy was beaming. "I've got a feeling this kid might make us some money after all," he said, turning to Oliver. "I guess your instincts were right."

Oliver nodded coolly.

"Where the hell was Abby today?" McCarthy asked suddenly, taking a sip of coffee.

Jay's eyes shot to Oliver, then to Barbara. For a brief moment he thought he detected the same sadness in her face he had seen at the estate. Then she lowered her head and fidgeted with her napkin.

"I left Abby a message on her voice mail early this morning. I wanted her to get me some information, but she never called back," McCarthy went on. "That's very unlike her."

"I believe she was ill today," Oliver said. "Something about a stomach virus," he said, motioning to Bullock. "Isn't that right, Badger?"

"Yes," Bullock answered firmly. "Apparently it was pretty bad, but she thinks she'll be in tomorrow morning."

"I see." McCarthy took another sip of coffee, then grinned lewdly. "I've always thought I'd like to get a piece of her tail," he said.

Just as he made the remark, an uncomfortable hush fell over the table. McCarthy had uttered the comment loudly enough for everyone to hear.

Jay picked up his water glass, took a large gulp, and began to cough loudly, as though he had swallowed the wrong way. That broke the painful silence and deflected people's attention away from McCarthy.

McCarthy leaned toward Jay, handed him a napkin, and slapped him gently on the back.

"Bill, whatever happened to your partner, Graham Lloyd?" Jay asked, still coughing. He'd wanted to ask that question since coming to the firm. Now seemed like a good time.

McCarthy put his coffee cup down slowly and shook his head, glad to have been rescued from his embarrassing situation. "He was lost in a boating accident in the Caribbean." McCarthy's voice was sad. "He was sailing from New Orleans to the Bahamas, and his boat was capsized by a rogue wave. One of those huge waves that comes from nowhere, you know?"

Jay nodded. "I've read about them."

"Awful thing," McCarthy said ruefully. "The Coast Guard confirmed that he never had a chance. They found the boat floating upside down. Never did find his body."

"That's terrible."

"It is." McCarthy's voice cracked slightly. "And what makes it worse is that it didn't have to happen. I pleaded with him not to go. I told him it was too dangerous. But he was a stubborn son of a bitch. He rarely took advice from anyone. Said he had faith in himself and his own instincts. Ultimately that attitude cost him his life."

Jay stared at McCarthy. The memories seemed difficult. "It must have been tough on you when all of that happened."

"It was." McCarthy's expression remained grim for a few moments, then he forced a smile. "But there's no need to dwell on all this talk about Graham's death. That might put a damper on what has been a most enjoyable evening."

"I agree," Oliver spoke up quickly, lifting his wineglass. "Here's to Graham, the old son of a bitch." He took a long drink. "Now, how about those Yankees?"

McCarthy chuckled as Oliver and Bullock began arguing about the team's prospects for winning another World Series at the end of the summer. "Not much seems to dampen Oliver's spirits," he said to Jay.

"That's very true." Jay hesitated. "Would you excuse me?"

"Got to use the facilities?"

"Yes."

"They're that way"—McCarthy pointed toward the door—"then down the hall and to your right."

"Thanks." Jay rose and walked through the dining room to the men's room. It was almost ten o'clock, and they'd been drinking steadily for almost three hours. He stared straight ahead, trying to determine how much the alcohol was affecting him. He felt only slightly dizzy—the room didn't seem to be spinning too fast—but suddenly he could think of nothing but Sally. The more wine he consumed, the more often he found himself stealing glances at her. He'd been disappointed that she hadn't been able to sit beside him at dinner, but Oliver had organized the seating, making certain that Sally sat next to him, and as far away from Jay as possible. It seemed that Oliver had noticed on the porch that there was something going on between them.

Jay zipped up, walked to a sink, and began washing his hands. He hadn't had a steady girlfriend since college, and that relationship had died when he had come to New York City. In New York he'd immersed himself in his work, soaking up everything he could about Wall Street and finance, and he hadn't found time to date seriously. Now, after all this time, he was interested in someone at the same firm—in the same department, for Christ's sake. At a time when he should be working harder than ever. He shut off the water, grabbed a towel, and dried his hands. He was interested in Sally Lane. There was no point in denying it. But pursuing her was out of the question. No good could come of dating someone you worked closely with, particularly the competition. And if they did try to see each other and Oliver ever found out, both he and Sally would probably be fired. Much as he wanted to see where it would lead, he'd have to ignore his attraction to her. He pulled open the bathroom door.

"Hi." Oliver stood a few feet away.

"Hi yourself." Jay held open the door, assuming Oliver was headed inside. "Here."

Oliver glanced over his shoulder. "Take a walk with me."

"Okay." Oliver seemed affable enough, but he had to be steamed about the impromptu TurboTec presentation. "Thanks for tonight. Dinner was delicious."

"My pleasure." Oliver guided Jay into a small room off the main hallway and closed the door.

"Listen," Jay began, "about TurboTec, I'm—"

"Don't worry," Oliver interrupted. "I didn't realize you had such good information. You should have told me about your contact in Tokyo. Do as Bill directed, buy the shares."

"All right."

Oliver cleared his throat. "Listen, there's something I want to talk to you about."

"Oh?"

"Yeah." Oliver tapped his thigh.

"What is it?" Jay prodded gently. He could see that Oliver was having a difficult time.

"It's about Barbara . . . and me."

"What?"

"We're having problems." Oliver met Jay's stare halfway. "Marital problems."

"I see." Jay glanced away, instantly uncomfortable. "That's too bad."

"You're right. It is." Oliver rubbed his chin for a moment. "I really do love her. I want you to understand that." He laughed nervously. "I love her enough that I'm going to attend counseling sessions with her starting next week. I never thought I'd do that."

"It's good that you're willing to make the commitment."

"It is, isn't it?"

Jay detected an unsteadiness in Oliver's voice. "Yes."

"I just wanted you to know. You probably figured it out while we were on the boat."

"I didn't." It had been obvious, but it seemed better not to let Oliver know that.

"It's better that you know," Oliver said firmly. "Because there can't be any secrets on a trading floor. We work together so closely."

"We do."

"Besides, I consider you a friend. Someone I can talk to." Oliver's gaze dropped to the floor. "I know I'm hard on you sometimes, Jay, but it's my nature. I'm not singling you out. It's just that our business is tough. Kill or be killed and all that crap. It's trite, but there is truth to it. Despite the money we make on the arbitrage desk, McCarthy's on me all the time. As he said, he's been riding me constantly about hiring you. And that's just one example of the pressure. Sometimes it gets to me and I take out my anger on exactly the people I shouldn't," he said quietly.

"I can see where McCarthy could be difficult to work for."

Oliver exhaled loudly. "When you're going through something like this with your wife, the stress can cause you to do things you shouldn't. Like seek companionship from other women."

"Uh-huh." Jay stared at Oliver. Bullock had to have said something about the storage room incident.

"At least, that's what I've heard." Oliver raised his eyes to Jay's. "I hope it doesn't happen to me."

"I'm sure it won't." The message had been relayed and received. He was to tell no one about the marital problems.

Oliver smiled. "Enough of this." He reached into his blazer and produced an envelope. "Here."

"What's this?" Jay asked.

"The money I said I was going to loan you. A hundred thousand dollars. I want you to buy that BMW. I don't want you driving around in that beat-up piece of junk anymore."

Jay thought of asking Oliver how he knew about the Taurus, but that seemed obvious. He shook his head. "I can't accept this."

"You can and you will," Oliver said firmly.

Jay glanced at the check, made out to him for one hundred thousand dollars.

"It's a loan," Oliver said. "Like I said, you can repay me in January."

Jay swallowed. He didn't want to accept the money, but his checking account balance had dipped dangerously close to zero in the past few days. The cut in salary he had accepted to join McCarthy & Lloyd was having its effect. It didn't feel completely right to accept the charity, but there didn't seem to be any real harm in it. "Thanks."

"You're a friend. I like to help my friends." Oliver produced the keys to the Austin Healey. "Speaking of which, why don't you drive the Healey back into the city tonight?"

Jay glanced up from the check. "I can take the train."

Oliver shook his head. "Nah, trains suck. Take the Healey. Park it in a garage, give me the keys tomorrow, and I'll have Barbara pick it up the next time she's in New York. She's in the city every few days." He smiled. "Besides, this way you can give Sally a ride back to the city and have some time alone with her."

Jay grinned, embarrassed at how transparent his attraction to her must be.

"I saw the chemistry today," Oliver said. "And look, as long as you two keep it out of the office, it's all right with me."

"Don't worry, I won't—"

Oliver held up his hands. "I've said what I'm going to say."

"Oliver, you've been very decent to me." Jay's voice was raspy. He'd never been good at this kind of thing. "I really appreciate what you've done." Oliver was a good man. A man who had caved in to temptation, but realized now that he needed help. And that was the first step. "I hope I can repay all of your kindness someday."

"Just repay the loan on bonus day. And find me some

takeover stocks soon." Oliver turned to go, then hesitated. "One more thing."

"What's that?"

"I'm going to be late to the office tomorrow morning. Will you do me a couple of favors first thing?"

"Sure. Name them."

"First, execute the Simons trade we talked about yesterday morning. I know Bill said it was a boring company in a boring industry, but I like it." He raised an eyebrow.

Jay's gut was telling him no, but Oliver was the boss and he'd just accepted a hundred thousand dollars of the boss's money. "Okay."

"Good."

"What else?"

"I want to buy a big block of shares of another company."

"Which one?"

Oliver hesitated. "Bell Chemical. Use Jamie and buy three hundred thousand shares at the market as soon as you get in."

Instantly Jay recognized Bell Chemical as the name on the piece of paper in the Austin Healey's glove compartment. "Okay," he agreed hesitantly.

"Good." Oliver moved toward him, patted him on the shoulder, then headed toward the door. "Come on," he urged, holding it open.

Standing in the hallway outside the door were two silver-haired men dressed in conservative gray suits and holding snifters of brandy. Physically, they resembled each other closely. "Hello," one of the men said stiffly to Oliver. The other simply nodded, a pained expression on his face.

"Hi, Harold." Oliver shook hands with the man who had spoken to him. "Harold, this is Jay West. He's recently joined the arbitrage desk at McCarthy and Lloyd."

Oliver turned to Jay. "This is Harold Kellogg, my father-in-law, and his brother, William."

Both of the older men nodded, but neither offered his hand.

Jay nodded back. He had heard that together the Kellogg brothers were worth well over a billion dollars.

"Still going to pay me back for the property someday, Oliver?" Harold piped up, an impudent grin on his face.

"Yes," Oliver said quietly. "And it will be the happiest day of my life."

"My real-estate people tell me that property is worth close to fifty million dollars these days. And you've lived there for seven years, so we'll call that another thirty million in interest." Harold laughed, but his jaw was tight. "I can't wait."

"I'm sure you can't."

"Oliver, when did you become a member here?" William asked.

"He isn't," Harold answered. "Barbara's the member."

"Oh, that's right. I remember now. We had to campaign heavily, didn't we? The members would allow them in only if she was the member of record."

Jay saw that the brothers had consumed a great deal of alcohol. "Come on, Oliver." Jay touched him on the arm. "Let's go."

"Oh, Oliver," Harold called.

Oliver turned around slowly. "Yes?"

"I'm sure some people appreciate your attempt to be stylish," Harold said sarcastically, pointing at Oliver's bright red shirt. "But tone down your act when you come around here, will you?" Harold nudged his brother. "You know what they say, Billy?"

"What?" William asked, finishing his brandy.

"They say—"

"They say you can take the boy out of the Bronx, but you can't take the Bronx out of the boy," Oliver interrupted, his voice wavering. "I should know. I hear it every damn time I see you."

CHAPTER 8

"Why didn't Abby go into the office today?" Barbara asked, slamming her pocketbook down on the pristine, white kitchen counter, her voice shaking. It was the first time she had spoken since they had left the yacht club. "What was the real reason?"

"She was sick," Oliver answered calmly. "You heard Bullock."

"She wasn't sick," Barbara snapped, turning to face him. "She was probably just exhausted."

"What are you talking about?"

"I know you were with her last night. I'm not stupid. She probably couldn't walk this morning, she was so sore." Barbara's fingers curled into tight fists as the image of Oliver with Abby flashed through her mind.

"Sweetheart, I—"

"Do you take me for an idiot?" Barbara shrieked, losing control. "Do you really think you fool me when you don't get home until eleven at night and I haven't been able to reach you at McCarthy and Lloyd all day?"

Oliver fidgeted with the Suburban's keys.

"I called you yesterday at three o'clock, but you were off the desk." Barbara's body was shaking. "That adolescent bastard of a fraternity brother of yours, Carter Bullock, said you were in a meeting, but he couldn't seem to tell me where or with whom."

"I was with several outside consultants. Bill has put me in charge of an important project, a big-picture thing."

"I tried calling Abby, but Bullock picked up again," Barbara continued, ignoring Oliver's explanation. "He said she was in a meeting, too, though not the same one as you, of course. He was very careful to mention that fact. But what do you know—once again he couldn't tell me where she was or with whom."

Just keep denying, Oliver told himself. *She can't prove anything, and she doesn't really want you to admit it. She's just venting.* "You're blowing this way out of proportion."

"Am I?" Barbara banged the counter with her fist. "I found a little note from Abby a couple of weeks ago in your suit."

The color drained from Oliver's face. Despite his objections, Abby was constantly writing those damned things. He was usually so careful to rip them up and throw away the tiny pieces in several different trash cans around the trading floor. But this one had slipped through the cracks because one of the equity traders had rushed up to him with an emergency only moments after Abby had placed the folded piece of paper in front of him. He'd stuffed it in his pocket, then forgotten about it.

" 'I love you so much.' " Barbara's voice became dramatically sarcastic, repeating the words of Abby's hand-scribbled note. " 'I can't wait to have you again. All of you.' " She grabbed two fistfuls of her hair.

"Barbara, I don't know what to . . ." Oliver swallowed his words, his chin-out defiance evaporating.

"How could you do this to me?" she screamed, tears streaming down her cheeks. "I've tried to be so good to you. I've tried to love you, tried to understand you."

"I know. I'm terrible," he said hoarsely, holding his hands out, a signal that he was guilty as charged. There was no use trying to defend himself any longer. It was time to raise the white flag and plead for mercy, a strategy that he knew tugged powerfully on her heartstrings and had never let him down before. "I need help. I think we should go to a marriage counselor together. Please," he begged.

"You need more than a marriage counselor."

"What are you talking about?" he asked tentatively. Usually the mention of a counselor calmed her down.

Barbara rushed to a kitchen drawer and yanked it open, causing several implements inside to clatter to the floor. From far back in the drawer she pulled out a tiny piece of paper folded into a small triangle. She held it out in front of her. "I may be naive," she sobbed, teeth clenched, "but I know what's inside this. Cocaine."

Oliver reached out again, this time moving forward a few steps. "What the . . ." His voice faltered.

"I found this in the same suit as the note, you bastard! You and your girlfriend must have had quite a party."

"I don't have any idea how that got there," he said, his voice shaking.

"Liar!"

"I swear."

"Admit nothing."

"What?"

"The guiding principle of your life," she sobbed. "Never admit anything incriminating, because then there's always that seed of doubt in other people's minds as to your guilt even if the evidence is overwhelmingly against you. Jesus, you probably wouldn't even admit that you're really nothing but a poor boy from the Bronx who's scratched, clawed, and married his way into wealth and society." The wine from dinner was affecting her, and she was slurring her words. "You've probably deluded yourself into believing that you didn't actually begin life in a nasty little sixth-floor apartment overlooking a trash-strewn parking lot, watching your daddy get drunk every afternoon on cheap malt liquor." She ripped open the paper triangle and sprinkled the white powder on the floor. "I hate you, Oliver." She dropped the shredded paper, turned, yanked a butcher knife from the drawer, and hurled it at him.

He dodged the knife, then dashed forward and grabbed her.

"Let go of me!" she screamed.

"No."

"I'm going to my father," she warned, sobbing uncontrollably. "I'm going to tell him everything."

"No, you aren't," Oliver snapped. "You hate him as much as I do. You know if you go to him, he'll just laugh and tell you how right he's been all along. How you've screwed up your entire life. How he can't believe you're really his daughter. How he thinks you must have been adopted." Barbara's father had never said that, but Oliver had told her of overhearing Kellogg make the comment to a friend at a cocktail party, and she'd believed him.

"No!" Barbara pressed her hands over her ears tightly. "I hate you both."

"You're not going anywhere." Oliver released his grip on her, and she sank to the floor, her head coming to rest against the counter. He had always been able to manipulate her any way he wanted to, the way he could manipulate almost anyone now. He had tried to convince Barbara that she hated her father all these years, to drive a wedge between them, and now, just at the moment he needed it most, it had worked and she believed him. She was defeated, just a quaking mass of empty threats.

There had been no reason to worry. He could conquer anything. "You're going upstairs and you're going to bed. And we're never going to speak about this incident again."

"You've lost your mind, Oliver," she murmured forlornly, her lips pressed against the wood.

"Shut up." Suddenly he felt the urge to wrap a tie around her neck and watch her eyes bulge and the veins in her neck rise.

"I didn't know for certain until this afternoon when I watched you crank Jay West up the mast," she whispered. "You love forcing people to do things they don't want to do." Barbara wiped tears from her face and sniffed. Her sobs had abated. "My God, you've probably never enjoyed Abby as much as you enjoyed hoisting that young man seventy feet into the air. You adore power, Oliver. No, you crave it. It's driving you insane."

"We were just having fun. I wouldn't put a friend in danger."

"You don't have friends," Barbara whispered sadly. "You have disciples. That poor young man is trying his best not to become one. I can see it in his eyes. But you have this way, this horrible, sick way about you that sucks people in. Jay's a fine young man, but I pray for him. He doesn't know who you really are. He doesn't know how far you'd go. I should do him a favor and tell him," she said, laughing sarcastically, "but he wouldn't believe me."

"You've had way too much to drink, Barbara. I can always tell when you've reached your limit because you become melodramatic." He jabbed at her leg with his shoe. "Let's get you up to bed so you can sleep it off."

"I'm surprised you hired Jay," Barbara said groggily. "He doesn't fit the profile, and that disgusting friend of yours Bullock obviously doesn't like him at all." Her eyelids fell slowly shut. The long day of drinking and hot sun had exhausted her, and it was all she could do to remain conscious. "I thought you two didn't let anyone you didn't like play in your sandbox."

CHAPTER 9

"Do you like the beach?" Jay asked, taking a deep breath of salt air.

"I love it," Sally answered, clutching her sandals in one hand as she walked beside Jay, cool, dry sand pushing between her toes. "I didn't have much of a chance to enjoy it as a little girl."

"But I thought you grew up in Gloucester."

"I did," she agreed quickly. "But the ocean water up there is cold even in the summer, and a lot of the beaches are rocky. And you know when you live near something, you don't take full advantage of it. Like most New Yorkers have never been to the Statue of Liberty or the observation deck of the Empire State Building."

"I have."

"God, look at the moonlight on the water." Sally touched his arm gently. "It's beautiful."

Jay watched Sally enjoy the brilliant reflection, gazing at her profile in the faint light. She was something else. He felt himself becoming more attracted to her by the minute. She had suggested that they take a walk after bidding good night to Oliver and Barbara outside the yacht club, and he'd accepted immediately even though it was getting late and they both needed to be at McCarthy & Lloyd early in the morning.

He groaned to himself. Dating a woman with whom he worked was a recipe for disaster, and ultimately he wouldn't allow himself to become involved—at least not as long as Sally was at McCarthy & Lloyd. He knew himself too well. He was too career-oriented to allow a personal relationship to endanger the opportunity that lay before him.

But he was lonely. He'd realized that when he'd held her in the ocean and felt her skin against his as they awaited the *Authority*'s return. As they'd joked and laughed in the bow of the sailboat on the trip back to shore, drinks in hand and their ankles intertwined, Oliver and Barbara far away in the cockpit.

Sally spoke up. "I've never really done much in New York City."

"Well, it isn't as if you've had much time," Jay pointed out. They caught each other's eye and looked away. "You've just started at McCarthy and Lloyd, and you were in San Diego before that."

"That's true." She kicked at the sand. "You know, one thing I'd really like to do is get a good view of the city from way up high. From the top of a tall building or something. And not from the Empire State Building or the World Trade Center towers, where everybody else goes. From a place off the beaten track."

"My building has a great view of midtown."

"Oh?"

"Yes."

Sally smiled flirtatiously. "Does it really, or is this part of an intricate plan to get me back to your—"

"You could come by after work sometime," he cut in, aware of what she was thinking. "Before the sun goes down on a day when we can sneak out early. Before Oliver and Bullock turn into vampires."

"I didn't know time of day made a difference to the two of them as far as bloodsucking went." She laughed. "From what I hear, they work people to the bone twenty-four hours a day."

"It's a grind at McCarthy and Lloyd," Jay admitted. "No doubt about it. You better be ready."

"I am." She hesitated. "But I'd love to come by one day and check out the view."

Jay sensed a trace of disappointment in her tone. "Would you prefer a night view?"

She gave him a sidelong look. "Definitely a night view."

"How about a tonight view?" He cleared his throat, aware that his voice sounded strained.

"Perfect."

They turned and started back toward the club, and as they did, she stumbled, falling against him. He caught and steadied her, wondering if the fall had been accidental.

An hour later they were on the roof of his sixty-story Upper West Side apartment building, side by side, elbows on the brick parapet, gazing at the skyline. It had taken Jay a few minutes to coax Sally to the low wall—the street was more than six hundred feet below them, and the parapet hadn't seemed sturdy—but now she was comfortable enough to make it to the edge.

"There are so many lights," she remarked. She slid her hand to the back of his arm. "It's beautiful."

This was insane, Jay thought. The next morning they'd have to go to work and act as if nothing were going on. However, it had been Sally's idea to come to the roof. And after all, the touch of her fingers was exactly what he wanted. He was still waiting for the rational side of his brain to take over and convince him of how stupid this was.

"Oliver's quite a character," she remarked.

"He really is." Oliver's hundred-thousand-dollar check lay neatly folded in Jay's shirt pocket, and for a moment he wondered if Oliver had given Sally the same deal that night. "A tough man to figure out."

"Exactly. I've already seen that he can be a real—" She stopped short.

"A real what?"

"You'll think I'm terrible."

"No, go ahead," Jay urged.

"He can be a real pain," she said. "I can see that even after being around him for such a short time. I mean, that business of forcing us overboard in the middle of Long Island Sound. And sending you up the mast with the waves as nasty as they were. Ridiculous."

Her fingernails dug gently into his skin, sending chills up his spine.

"But," Sally continued, "he's got this way about him. Just when you think you're starting to really dislike him, he does something that turns your emotions completely around."

"I know," Jay agreed. "He's quite a charmer." *So charming he would accost a subordinate in a storage room,* Jay reminded himself. "Did you see those elderly women at the table on the porch tonight?"

"Yes." Sally laughed. "They wanted to strangle him at first.

You could see it. But by the time he took the chair, they loved him." She hesitated. "Did you notice anything strange about Oliver and Barbara?"

"What do you mean?"

"She was trying to get his attention all day, but he completely ignored her."

Jay nodded. "I heard her say she loved him a couple of times, but he didn't respond. He must have heard her, though. They were standing right next to each other."

"Exactly. He doesn't seem very happy with her."

"I don't know." Oliver had made it clear that Jay wasn't to discuss this issue. If Oliver wanted to tell Sally about his marital problems, he would.

"It's as if they don't look right together."

"What?" Jay turned quickly to look at her.

"You know how most couples sort of look right together?"

"I guess." So she'd noticed, too.

"I pictured Oliver with someone different."

"How so?"

Sally thought for a moment. "Someone sexier. I mean, Barbara's very attractive," she said quickly. "Don't get me wrong. But in a matronly, still-trying-to-hold-on-to-her-prime way." She gave Jay a strange look. "Why are you laughing?"

"Because I noticed the same thing."

"Really?" She smiled at him, happy that they were on the same wavelength.

"Yeah, I thought Barbara would be a little more exotic."

"Exactly." Sally squeezed his arm. "Do you think Oliver and Abby have something going on?"

"Huh?"

"Oliver must have called her five times yesterday while he was taking me around the firm. He'd cup his hand over the phone while they were talking so I couldn't hear, and he was giggling like a teenager."

"I don't know." Jay wanted no part of this discussion. "Why do you ask?"

"Barbara's nice. I feel bad for her. It's pretty clear to me Oliver would like to be with anyone but her."

"Maybe your interest is sparked by something else," Jay teased, smiling at her suggestively. "Maybe you're looking for an opportunity."

"You're terrible." Sally punched him on the arm.

"You never know."

Sally rolled her eyes. "Oh, yes, Oliver and I have actually been secretly seeing each other for months, and that's why he's picked now to hire me. We have this place over in Brooklyn Heights. We meet at Henry's End for dinner several times a week, then go to Basement of Blues for some mood music before hustling back to our little love nest and wrestling the sheets off the mattress."

Jay tilted his head and gave her a long, inquisitive look.

"What?" she asked self-consciously. "I was only kidding."

"I know," he said quietly.

"What is it, then?"

"Henry's End and Basement of Blues are kind of out-of-the-way places. How do you know about them?"

"What are you talking about?"

"For a woman who hasn't spent much time in New York City, you sure know about some obscure spots. Spots I doubt many natives even know about."

"I've visited the city a few times."

"And you went to Brooklyn?" he asked curiously. "Nothing against the borough, but most tourists stay in Manhattan."

"I read travel magazines. I don't think it's a big deal."

"You're right, it's not."

She glanced away and pointed toward Central Park South. "Which building is the Plaza Hotel?"

"You can't see it from here. It's on the far corner of the park, and it's blocked by that building there," he explained, motioning toward a high-rise to their left.

"How about New Jersey?" she asked. "Can you see New Jersey from here?"

"Why?"

"My apartment is in Hoboken."

"Really?" he asked, taking her by the hand and moving toward the west side of the building.

"Yes, and don't give me that look of pity." She slipped her fingers into his as they made their way around a huge, rusting compressor. "It's not as bad as you think—"

"I know," Jay interrupted. "Some areas of Hoboken are pretty nice."

"Then what's the problem?"

"I didn't realize I was going to have to drive you over there," Jay answered. "It's already after midnight. By the time I get you home it'll be past one."

"You don't have to drive me home."

Jay shook his head. "I'm not letting you ride a train by yourself at this time of night, and a cab would cost seventy bucks."

"Who says I have to go home?"

He stopped a few feet short of the parapet. "Well, I—"

"I brought a change of clothes. Business things I can wear tomorrow. They're down in the bag we left in the Austin Healey. Oliver said it might be a long day, so I came prepared."

Suddenly he was fighting the feeling of physical arousal.

"I know your place is a one-bedroom," she continued, "but I assume you have a couch in the living room."

"Of course I do. I'll take the couch and you can have the bedroom." Now he fought disappointment, cursing himself for even considering the possibility of sleeping with her.

"I accept." She smiled at him sweetly. "That's very nice of you."

"Sure." For a few moments they stared at each other, then Jay dropped her hand and jogged toward the parapet.

"What are you doing?" she screamed, hands over her mouth. "Stop!"

But he didn't. When he reached the parapet, he jumped up, putting one foot on the bricks, then pulling himself to a standing position atop the low wall, wavering for a second before regaining his balance. Then he turned, crossed his arms over his chest, and gave her a triumphant nod.

"Get down right now!" she ordered. It was all she could do to look up at him standing on the parapet, his body silhouetted against the inky sky. "You're scaring the hell out of me, Jay."

He smiled, dropped nimbly back down to the roof, and ambled calmly back to her.

"You're insane," she said gravely. "You could have killed yourself."

"Nah."

"I'll never understand men," shc said, rolling her eyes.

"It has nothing to do with being a man." He brushed hair back off his forehead and quickly passed a fingertip over the scar beneath his eye.

"Then what does it have to do with?"

"It doesn't matter."

She peered up at him. "Why do you do that so much?"

"Do what?"

"Touch that scar beneath your eye."

"I don't do it *so* much."

"Yes, you do. How did you get it?"

"High-school football. Now come on." Jay guided her toward the doorway leading back inside. "It's getting late."

Minutes later they were in Jay's bedroom.

"Well, this is it," he said, gesturing around the small room. "It's not much, but it's home." He moved toward the closet. "Let me get a few things and I'll be out of your way."

"Take your time." She walked over to his personal computer, set up on a table in one corner of the room. "Are you on-line?" Her eyes flashed around the tabletop. Two boxes of disks sat beside the CPU.

"Isn't everybody?" he called, gathering his things. "All right, I've got what I need. I'm taking the alarm clock out into the living room with me. I'll wake you up in the morning."

"Okay." She turned away from the computer and met him at the door. "I had a wonderful time today."

"So did I."

For several moments they said nothing, then she placed her hands on his shoulders, lifted up on her toes, and kissed him on the cheek, allowing her lips to linger.

Jay could resist no longer. He slipped his arms around her, pressed his lips to hers, and kissed her deeply. He felt her response instantly—her hands at the back of his neck, her mouth pressing back, the skin of her legs against his. After several moments he pulled back, but she brought his mouth back to hers immediately. Finally their lips parted.

"I liked that," she whispered.

"Me too."

She rubbed the backs of her fingers over his cheek until they came to the scar. "Now tell me how you really got that."

"I already told you."

"You told me a story, but you didn't tell me the truth."

"How did you get so good at determining whether or not someone is telling the truth?"

"Tell me," she said, ignoring the question.

He drew in a long breath. "It's nothing you'd be interested in."

"Let me be the judge of that."

"Okay," he said, setting his jaw. "My younger sister drowned in an abandoned quarry near my home in Pennsylvania. We used to swim there in the summer. I was sixteen and she was nine at the time. Her foot got trapped in some old mining equipment way below the surface. I tried as hard as I could to free her." He hesitated and swallowed, touching the scar without realizing it. "The second time I went down she grabbed on to me. I was running out of air and I pulled her hand away. I had to. She was wearing a ring and it cut me as she was trying to keep me with her. When I got back down she was gone."

"I'm sorry, Jay." She wrapped her arms around him and kissed his cheek. "I shouldn't have pushed."

"I've got to get some sleep," he said brusquely. "The phone is by the bed if you need it."

"Okay."

He pulled away from her embrace and exited the room, closing the door behind him. For several moments he stood there, amazed that Sally had been able to pull the drowning story out of him. It was the first time he had spoken of it since the day it had happened, ten years before.

■ ■ ■

She worked by the light of the computer monitor, tapping on the keyboard as quietly as possible while she retrieved the file. After what seemed like an eternity, words and numbers finally flashed onto the screen. She scanned what was there, then began printing, working quickly for fear that he would wake up.

CHAPTER 10

The living room came slowly into focus as gray light filtered through the window blind, unadorned by curtains because his was a typical bachelor's apartment. Curtains weren't a priority.

Jay's mind drifted toward full consciousness and he realized that his body felt oddly constrained. There seemed to be a wall on one side of him and an edge of nothing on the other. Then he remembered. He was sleeping on the couch. Sally Lane was in the bedroom.

He stretched his long legs, extending his feet further over the worn and faded fabric of the couch's arm. After trying to find a comfortable position all night and catching only a couple of hours of sleep, he was exhausted, and now it was time to head into a killer day that wouldn't end until eleven o'clock that night—if he was lucky.

He began to rise from the couch, then groaned and fell back, not yet ready to face the day. In the back of his mind he had hoped that at some point during the night Sally would steal out into the living room, awaken him with another passionate kiss, then lead him back to the bedroom and make love to him over and over. He pulled a pillow from behind his head, ground it into his face, and groaned again. Christ, they'd only met two days earlier. Yes, they had kissed the previous night, but so what? Sally didn't strike him as the kind of woman who fell into bed with a man after one kiss. And he didn't want her to be that kind of woman.

Her perfume had haunted him all night—a subtle scent he had first noticed on the club's porch, then later filled his senses as they kissed and embraced in his bedroom. He pulled the pillow aside and sniffed his arms—the scent was still there—and smiled as he remembered the touch of her soft lips against his. A wonderful kiss, full of passion, that told him she had much more than a passing interest in pursuing a relationship.

Jay swung his feet to the floor and stood, clad only in light blue boxers. There was no need to dwell on how much he had enjoyed the previous day with Sally. That would only make the day in front of him even longer.

He stretched once more, raising his hands far above his head, then padded toward the bedroom door. It was slightly ajar. Maybe Sally was already using the bathroom. He hadn't heard her get up, but perhaps he had been sleeping so soundly during the last hour that he hadn't been able to hear anything. He glanced down the hallway. The bathroom door was open and the lights were off, and there was no scent of shampoo or perfume or any warmth from residual steam drifting from that direction.

"Sally," he called in a low voice. No answer. He knocked gently on the bedroom door, then rapped louder. "Sally." Still no answer. He pushed the bedroom door open and peered through the doorway. The bed was made and Sally's bag was gone.

He moved down the short hallway past the kitchen to the bathroom and checked the shower. It was dry, obviously unused, which seemed strange. He doubted that she would have gone into work without a shower, so she must have headed all the way back to her Hoboken apartment.

Jay walked back to the bedroom and stood in front of the linen chest at the foot of the bed. The cordless phone wasn't nestled in its stand where he had left it to recharge. Now the phone was on the night table.

Jay clasped his hands at the back of his head, his focus now on the computer in the corner of the room. Something seemed different about it or the table on which it was positioned. He scanned the table and the computer several times. Next to the CPU were the two boxes of wafer disks, one red and the other silver. They had been rearranged. The silver box was now in front of the red one. He always left the red one in front.

He moved across the floor to the table and stood before the computer for a moment, then leaned forward and placed his palm on top of the monitor. It was warm.

■ ■ ■

Victor Savoy stood at the edge of a forest near a grove of oak trees looking up at the steep hills rising around him on three sides like an amphitheater. He wore sunglasses, a thick black mustache, a dark blue baseball cap with U.S.S. *New Jersey* embroidered in gold lettering on the front, and padding beneath his shirt and pants to make himself appear overweight. He was with people who were supposedly allies, yet he still wore a disguise. He had learned that if you wanted to survive in this business, you trusted no one. A friend could become a foe in a heartbeat if he suddenly discovered your true identity.

After completing his bargain with Karim in Konduz, Savoy

had negotiated the winding dirt roads of the Hindu Kush to Kabul in a beat-up Yugo, flown from Kabul to Amsterdam on a private jet, barely made a United flight bound for JFK airport in New York City, then immediately hopped aboard another private jet for the hour-and-a-half flight to Richmond, Virginia. At the Richmond airport he'd rented a car under the name Harry Lee and driven an hour southwest of the city to the remote farm in the Virginia countryside. He had taken a roundabout route to make certain that he wasn't being followed.

It had been a grueling eighteen-hour trip. But now he was refreshed and alert after only a few hours of sleep on the United flight. He was pleased to be back in the States, particularly Virginia, because it was a homecoming of sorts. He had been born and raised in Roanoke, a small town a few hours to the west, though he'd left at sixteen to begin his life of "alternative procurement," as he liked to call it, and never looked back. He was also pleased because watching the exercise made the end of the mission and an extraordinary paycheck finally seem close at hand. He only prayed to whatever gods existed that his second in command on the other side of the Atlantic could procure the weapons in Konduz and transport them to Karachi without incident, then load them on the tramp freighter waiting to set sail for Antwerp. There were so many things that could still go wrong.

Savoy grabbed a handful of sunflower seeds and stuffed them in his mouth. He glanced around as he spat out shells, checking the positions of his marksmen on the hills with a powerful pair of binoculars that hung from his neck by a leather strap. Then he looked up at the sky. Ominous thunderheads were building in the west, fed by the sweltering heat and humidity suffocating the eastern seaboard of the United States. No matter. They'd be back in the house within fifteen minutes, well before the storm unleashed its fury.

Savoy turned and nodded over his shoulder toward the grove of oak trees. Moments later an accomplice appeared pulling a young woman along by one wrist. She was clad in a short, tattered dress and stumbled forward zombielike behind the man. The prostitute, whom Savoy's accomplice had lured into his car the previous day, had been force-fed a sedative a few hours earlier. Now she was glassy-eyed and almost incoherent, barely able to stand.

The accomplice led the woman to a chair next to Savoy and placed her hands on the back of it. She grabbed it, swaying slightly from side to side, a gentle breeze blowing filthy brown hair across her pale face.

Savoy spit out a few remaining shells and lifted the binoculars to his eyes once more, checking each position. He had been told that the men were good, but he wanted to see for himself. He had learned not to give anyone the benefit of any doubt.

He nodded at his accomplice and they jogged back to the grove of oaks together. From behind a large tree he checked each position a third time. The rifles were up and ready. He let the binoculars fall to his chest and glanced at the young woman. She was struggling to maintain her balance, leaning forward against the chair exactly as one might do behind a podium.

"Fire," he said quietly into the microphone.

Before he had finished the command the shots rang out as one, like a cannon blast, shredding the serenity of the Virginia afternoon with appalling force. Four .30-caliber slugs tore into the young woman's frail body, and she tumbled backward, coming to rest facedown in some long grass.

Savoy sprinted out from behind the tree to where the dead woman lay, noting with satisfaction that the back of her head was completely gone. He rolled her over and inspected two neat holes in her face, one in the middle of her forehead, the other just beneath her still-open left eye. Finally, he pulled her dress up and gazed at two more holes between her breasts.

Savoy smiled as he inspected her ravaged body. They really were that good.

■ ■ ■

Jay gazed at the hand-scribbled note. It had been waiting for him when he arrived at McCarthy & Lloyd a little past seven, taped to the seat of his chair.

> Buy shares of those two companies we talked about as well as shares of whatever that Boston company was you pitched to McCarthy last night over dinner. Do it in the share amounts we discussed and do it first thing this morning. Don't screw this up, Jay. I don't want to have to give the job to Sally. That would really piss me off.
>
> Cordially,
> Oliver

Jay had placed the buy orders at eight-fifteen, excited about TurboTec, less so about Simons, and not at all about Bell Chemical. McCarthy had agreed that Simons wasn't an exciting play, so he wasn't going to be happy about the purchase. And Jay knew nothing about Bell Chemical. He hadn't had time to research Bell and substantiate Oliver's claim that the company was an attractive takeover candidate. The only thing Jay knew about Bell Chemical was that it had been the name on the paper inside the envelope he had discovered in the Healey's glove compartment.

He had executed the trades anyway, and now his fingerprints were all over the transactions. And only *his* fingerprints, he realized ruefully, rereading the note. Oliver hadn't even specified Simons and Bell by name. But what the hell was he supposed to do? He couldn't ignore Oliver's direct order. He'd agreed to execute the share purchases for Oliver the previous night after dinner. And he wanted his million bucks. He didn't want to give Oliver any excuse to fire him if indeed Bullock was correct and the contract had outs.

He dropped the note on the desk, leaned back in his chair, closed his eyes, and groaned. He was dead tired from his night on the couch, and he was hungry as hell, too. It was two o'clock in the afternoon and he hadn't eaten anything since dinner the night before. Plus, the day had been crazy since the opening bell, and he'd been the only professional on the desk most of the time, the only one available to manage the chaos. The secretary had informed Jay that Oliver was working on a project for McCarthy and had taken Sally with him to midtown for a meeting. Bullock had been on and off the desk all day—mostly off—and Abby hadn't come in once again. He couldn't stifle a wide yawn, and covered his mouth with his hand.

"Hey there."

Jay opened his eyes. Sally stood on the other side of the bulkhead. Oliver was nowhere in sight. "Hi," he said coolly, trying not to think about how much fun he'd been having at this time the day before. He was irritated at her for having left the apartment with no warning that morning.

"Why are you so tired?" she asked quietly, looking around to see if anyone had heard her. "God, someone might think you spent the night on a lumpy couch last night," she teased, her smile widening.

"Someone might at that." He could hear the irritation in his own voice.

Sally walked around the end of the bulkhead to where he was sitting and leaned against the edge of the desk. "I had a wonderful time yesterday," she whispered.

"So did I." He allowed himself a quick look up into her eyes. They were beautiful.

"And I appreciated the fact that you opened up to me about your sister."

"Yeah, well . . ." He gazed off into the distance.

"I'm sorry I used the express checkout option this morning at Hotel Jay West, but you were fast asleep," she explained. "I didn't want to wake you." She checked the immediate area, then reached forward and quickly stroked his hand. "I wanted to say goodbye. I really did."

"It's okay." He flashed her a quick grin, aware that sulking wouldn't win him any points. "What time did you leave?" he asked, forcing himself to be jovial.

"Around five. I woke up and couldn't get back to sleep, so I decided to get going."

"You should have called me into the bedroom. Maybe a little exercise would have helped you get back to sleep."

"Exactly what kind of exercise did you have in mind?" Her eyes narrowed slightly, but the corners of her mouth turned up.

"Nothing unusual. Just a little something to get the blood pumping."

"Uh-huh."

"Did you go all the way back to Hoboken?" Jay asked.

She nodded, hesitating a moment before answering. "Yeah, I . . . I noticed that I'd forgotten to pack some things, so I went home."

"How did you get there?"

"I took the subway down to the World Trade Center and caught the PATH train from there." She scanned the trading floor again and spotted Oliver and Bullock deep in discussion on the corridor paralleling the floor. "The trains weren't crowded that early in the morning, and the trip didn't take long."

"I thought maybe you had called McCarthy and Lloyd's car service," Jay said.

"Why?" Sally asked, her eyes flashing from Oliver to Jay.

"I noticed that you used the phone. It was off its stand. I had left it in its stand to recharge."

She hesitated once more. "You're right, I did call the service. But the dispatcher said it was going to be forty minutes until he could get a car to your apartment. So I decided to be daring and take the train."

Jay felt a strange sensation crawling up his spine—the same thing that had happened when Oliver had asked him to purchase Bell Chemical after dinner the night before. "What did you use the computer for?"

"What?"

Maybe it was his imagination, but she seemed to be stalling. "My personal computer was warm when I woke up. I was wondering why you used it."

She laughed without a hint of amusement. "This is quite the third degree."

"No, it—"

"I went on-line and checked out the morning headlines and what happened in the financial markets in Asia overnight," she interrupted. "Oliver and I had this meeting in midtown first thing, and I wanted to be prepared. The papers don't always report the overnight Pacific Rim closing numbers."

"I know." Now it was Jay's turn to hesitate. "It's just that—"

"Come on, people!" Oliver shouted coming up behind Jay, Bullock in tow. "Let's go. Meeting right now in the conference room. And I mean *right* now."

Sally puffed out her cheeks and rolled her eyes once Oliver and Bullock had blown past. "Here we go. He's on the warpath."

"What's the problem?" Jay asked, rising from his seat.

Sally shrugged. "I don't know. He seemed fine at our meeting this morning."

Moments later the four of them were seated around the conference table. Oliver was at the head of the table, Bullock to his right, with Sally and Jay facing each other on either side.

"Close the door," Oliver ordered, pointing at Jay. His hair was slightly tousled and there were bags under his eyes. He rubbed his bloodshot eyes and took a deep, exasperated breath.

Jay rose and moved slowly to the door. The large, comfortable bed in his apartment seemed to be calling all the way from the Upper West Side.

"Before fucking Christmas, pal," Oliver yelled.

The night before, Oliver had acted like a close friend. Now he was back to being Captain Bligh.

After stopping and starting several times, Oliver finally spoke up. "Abby has resigned," he said flatly.

Jay looked up, suddenly wide awake. He had noticed the same strained quality in Oliver's voice the previous day when Oliver had rushed up to him at the liquor store.

"There was . . . there was a letter delivered this morning to me," Oliver explained, reaching into his leather portfolio and removing an envelope, holding it in the air for the others to see as if he were a defense attorney holding up a piece of evidence for the jury. "By . . . by courier."

Jay had always been impressed with Oliver's glib demeanor and smooth delivery, even in pressure situations. But that demeanor was gone. Jay scrutinized him carefully. Oliver seemed preoccupied, and his normally sleek appearance had faded.

"I wanted to tell everyone as soon as I could." Oliver's voice softened. "I wanted to tell you all at the same time."

"Did she take another job?" Jay asked.

Oliver didn't respond. He was staring at the wall, his eyes fixed on something.

"Oliver." Bullock nudged Oliver with his elbow.

"I'm sorry." Oliver shook his head. "What was the question?"

"Did Abby take another job?" Jay asked again.

"I don't know. The letter simply said that she was resigning for personal reasons." Oliver glanced at Bullock—almost for moral support, Jay thought.

Oliver drew himself up in the chair. "We're all going to have to work very hard until Bullock and I can find a replacement for her," he said. "Abby was an extremely valuable member of our team. She took a lot of pressure off us by attending to details and doing the grunt work. I don't know how we'll replace her." Oliver placed the envelope back in his portfolio, his hands shaking. "That's all I have to say," he mumbled. "I'm sorry to take up your time." He glanced at Sally, his eyes misty. "Would you excuse us? Bullock and I need to talk to Jay alone."

"Sure." Sally picked up her notebook and exited the room quickly.

Jay studied Oliver's face, noticing age lines he'd never seen before. His permanent tan seemed to have paled as well, and the bags under his eyes were obvious. Something had happened since Jay and Sally had left Oliver at the club. Maybe it had to do with Abby, or perhaps Oliver and Barbara had gotten into it at home. Whatever it was, it was deeply affecting him.

"We need to go over your one-month review, Jay," Bullock announced when Sally was gone.

"One-month review?" Jay looked at Oliver, who was slouched down in his seat. "No one ever told me anything about a one-month review."

"It's standard stuff," Bullock said. "Every new employee gets one of these things." He reached into his notebook and produced a single piece of paper, inspected it briefly, then passed it across the tabletop to Jay. "Read what's there, then sign it at the bottom of the page. And don't worry too much about the specifics of the review."

Jay scanned the paper quickly. He had received an overall rating of two out of a possible five. Bullock had filled out the report. His name was at the bottom. "I don't understand. This indicates that I'm not working to my full potential. It seems to infer that I'm not pulling the hours I ought be. I've been here until at least eleven o'clock almost every night since the day I started. Sometimes later."

"Then you need to work more efficiently," Bullock retorted. "And you need to pull the trigger on a few trades."

"I placed three orders this morning," Jay replied evenly.

Oliver opened his eyes and straightened slightly in his seat.

"Which companies?" Bullock asked.

"TurboTec, Simons, and Bell Chemical."

Suddenly Oliver sat straight up and snapped his fingers. "Let me see that review," he ordered.

Jay slid the paper across the table. Oliver scanned it briefly, then glanced at Bullock. "A two?" he asked incredulously. "I think this is way too low. Raise it to a four."

"A *four*?"

"That's what I said. A four." Oliver pointed at Jay. "Are you comfortable with a four?"

"I suppose so."

"Good." Oliver shoved the paper back at Bullock. "Do it right away, Carter," he directed, then walked out of the room.

Moments later Bullock rose from his seat and stalked wordlessly from the room as well, furious.

Jay rubbed his eyes when Bullock was gone, then headed

back to his position on the desk. When he got there, Bullock wasn't on the desk, but Oliver and Sally sat next to each other on the far side of the bulkhead, speaking into their phones. Jay eased into his chair, pulled open a drawer, and retrieved the employee home-phone list for the arbitrage desk, something Bullock had given him his first day. As Bullock had explained, everyone needed to be available at all times, because deals didn't have nine-to-five schedules and even a brief lack of communication could cost the desk millions.

Jay located Abby's home number and dialed, listening to the ring at the other end of the line while he watched Sally move off holding a piece of paper. After five rings Abby's answering machine picked up. Jay listened to the greeting, then cut the connection without leaving a message. For a few minutes he gazed at the computer monitor in front of him, numbers on the screen blinking continuously as the on-line program updated the stock prices he was following closely. Then he rose from the chair, moved around the bulkhead, and stood beside Oliver.

"What is it?" Oliver snapped, finally looking up from the memo he had been reading.

Jay pulled out the keys to the Austin Healey, a clear image of Oliver forcing himself on Abby racing through his mind. "Here." He tossed the keys down on the desk, then reached into his shirt pocket, pulled out the check Oliver had given him the previous night, and dropped it beside the keys. "I appreciate your generosity, but I think you better keep this."

Then he turned and headed for the soda machine, feeling Oliver's eyes burning holes in his back, wondering why Sally had lied to him about using his computer that morning to go on-line to check out the Asia close. He wasn't hooked up to the Internet at home.

CHAPTER 11

McCarthy eased into the back of the long black limousine and sat down on the bench seat beside Andrew Gibson, deputy chief of staff for the president of the United States. McCarthy had taken a Delta shuttle down to Washington that afternoon from New York because his private Learjet was undergoing routine maintenance.

Gibson directed the driver to proceed northwest out of National Airport on the George Washington Parkway toward the Capital Beltway. "I'm glad you could come down to Washington today on such short notice," Gibson began. "The president sends his regards. He says he's looking forward to seeing you in New York."

"Yes, it should be a great event," McCarthy agreed proudly. He liked Gibson. They were about the same age and held similar political views. Gibson was short, slight, and perfectly manicured, from his neatly clipped straight gray hair to his crisp dark suits and conservative ties.

"It will be a tremendous couple of days," Gibson said emphatically. "And your ability to coordinate the governor's and mayor's offices has proven very helpful. There is quite a rivalry between those two, and they both want to take credit—for political reasons, of course. It was good of you to step in and remind them that the president is the host. It's their state and city, but they needed to have the whip cracked a little. Thank you. And those thanks come from the president as well."

"Certainly."

"There is one bit of bad news," Gibson offered hesitantly.

"What's that?" McCarthy asked.

"I'm afraid I couldn't get you at the president's table at the dinner."

"Ah." McCarthy waved his hand as if that piece of information was of no concern. "I don't give a damn. I'm glad to be of help to the president any way I can. Besides, I'll see him the next day downtown."

"Yes, you will," Gibson assured McCarthy. "You'll be right there on the dais."

"That would be nice, but I won't count on it."

Gibson patted McCarthy's knee with his small fingers and smiled. "That's why the president likes you so much, Bill. That's why he'll always take care of you. He knows that you have your eye squarely on the big picture. So many of his supporters don't," Gibson groused. "So many of them come to Washington with their hands out, looking for charity. You aren't like that. You're a team player, and we appreciate that."

"Thank you." McCarthy glanced out the limousine's tinted window at the Key Bridge spanning the Potomac River, and at Georgetown on the bluffs beyond.

"The president wants you to come to Camp David in the fall," Gibson announced. "He's going to be hosting a very private forum on the U.S. economy and needs you to attend. He wants an insider's perspective in a relaxed setting. There will be only about ten of you there. The CEO of General Motors, the CEO of ATT, IBM's chairman . . . you get the picture."

"Yes, I do." It was the kind of access to political power few people in the world possessed, and McCarthy fought to keep his satisfaction hidden.

"He won't take no for an answer, Bill," Gibson warned good-naturedly.

"I'll be there," McCarthy assured Gibson. "I wouldn't miss it for the world."

"Good."

The limousine headed up a long incline into the dense forest on the south side of the Potomac River. McCarthy and Gibson fell into a discussion of the current state of the economy, the rapid consolidation of the financial services industry, and where McCarthy saw interest rates heading over the next few months. All so Gibson could brief the president later.

When the vehicle moved past the headquarters of the Central Intelligence Agency on the left, the driver lowered the partition. "We're coming up on the Capital Beltway, Mr. Gibson. What would you like me to do?"

"Get on the Beltway going north and cross the river," Gibson instructed. "Then turn around at the first exit and get us heading back toward National Airport on the GW. Right back the way we came."

"Yes, sir." The driver raised the partition again.

Gibson pushed a button on the wood-grain console built into the door and turned on classical music. "Now we get to the heart of the matter. Why I needed you to come down to Washington today, Bill."

McCarthy felt his heart begin to pound. Not one who had

ever been able to hide his emotions well, he swallowed hard and felt the perspiration covering his palms. He wiped his hands on his suit pants.

"Steady, Bill," Gibson urged gently. He had known McCarthy long enough now that he could easily sense the other man's discomfort.

"What is it?" McCarthy asked. "Why did I have to come down here today?"

"It has to do with Oliver Mason."

"Oh?"

"Yes." Gibson turned the music up slightly louder. "When the fireworks are over, you're going to have to let Oliver go. He can't remain at McCarthy and Lloyd."

"But I thought—"

"I've had two extensive conversations with my friend at the Justice Department. You know she is very powerful."

"Yes." McCarthy bowed his head deferentially.

"She has the president's best interests at heart, and therefore yours."

"I understand."

Gibson blinked several times quickly and ground his teeth. This reaction was his personal Achilles' heel, a certain indication that he was feeling uncomfortable himself, and the reason he would never be more than deputy chief of staff. Washington's top appointee positions were available only to those who never revealed any of their emotions unless they wanted to. "She has discussed everything again with her point person in New York, and while he has promised not to prosecute Oliver," Gibson explained, "he isn't willing to allow him to continue as head of your arbitrage desk. It would simply be too transparent. Too blatant an abuse of power. He can't even stay at McCarthy and Lloyd to work on special projects, as we had discussed. In fact, he's going to have to take a long hiatus from the securities industry and simply be happy he won't be spending that time in a federal penitentiary."

"I see," McCarthy said. "I'll only say that he's a good friend. He's done a lot for me, and by extension, he's done a lot for the president. Some of the contributions I've made have come from money Oliver has made me."

"Don't ever connect the president to this situation again," Gibson warned.

McCarthy glanced up. He had never heard that tone from Gibson. "Oliver has promised not to engage in any insider trading once this is over, Andrew," McCarthy pleaded. "I believe him. And if he ever violated his promise, I'd personally help you put him away."

"It doesn't matter," Gibson answered. "You will quietly let Oliver go once the lamb has been sacrificed. You will let Carter Bullock go as well. In fact, you will shut down your arbitrage desk permanently. We had talked about a six-month cooling-off period and then a restart, but that isn't in the cards."

McCarthy felt himself fighting for breath. That directive from Gibson presented unimaginable complications. "But—"

"Don't fight it, Bill," Gibson warned. "You should feel very fortunate the way this has all worked out. We are confident that you didn't know what was going on at the arbitrage desk, but you know how these insider-trading investigations can start snowballing if somebody gets a bug up their ass."

McCarthy hung his head. "I certainly do." Everyone on Wall Street knew that insider-trading scandals mushroomed faster than the cloud from an atomic bomb.

"They can turn into goddamn witch-hunts, with people making all kinds of deals to protect themselves and accusing anyone the prosecutors tell them to accuse in order to save their own asses, whether or not they really have information on the others." Gibson shook his head. "It can get really nasty. Innocent people can have their good names dragged through the mud," he said ominously. "We don't want that to happen to you. The president cares about you. As I said, he'll always take care of you, but that promise can be kept only as long as you maintain your end of the bargain. We've made a deal. You must accept the terms, even these new ones."

"All right." McCarthy looked out the window. The limousine was back on the George Washington Parkway and heading toward National Airport. He was searching frantically for answers, but he wasn't finding any. "I'll give Oliver a hefty severance package." He had to agree to the directive. Any hesitation and Gibson might pull out of the whole thing. "Bullock too."

"I think that's wise." Gibson said. "I'm glad that's settled." He held up his hand. "I would wait to tell Oliver about his disassociation with McCarthy and Lloyd. I wouldn't want him causing problems at this point."

"Okay," McCarthy agreed submissively.

The Key Bridge appeared again, and a few minutes later the limousine coasted to a stop in front of the Delta Airlines drop-off area.

Gibson shook McCarthy's hand. "Keep your head up, Bill. It'll all work out. In a couple of months everything will be back to normal."

"I know," McCarthy mumbled.

"Remember," Gibson called as the driver opened McCarthy's door, "not a word to anyone about what's happening in New York in a couple of weeks. We must keep it under wraps for as long as possible. Particularly the downtown affair. Security and all that."

"Right."

"One more thing, Bill," Gibson called out.

"What?"

"Get a haircut."

McCarthy smiled wryly, remembering his order to Jay. Then he stepped out of the air-conditioned limousine into the sweltering heat. To the west he noticed dark clouds looming on the horizon. He hoped the storm wouldn't delay his trip back to New York.

CHAPTER 12

Oliver lay on the couch—the same couch on which he and Abby had shared a gram of cocaine only a few days earlier. A cool wet washcloth was draped across his forehead, the top button of his pinstriped shirt was undone, he had pulled the knot of his tie almost halfway down his chest, and his tasseled loafers lay on the floor. Oliver rolled onto his side, causing the washcloth to fall to the floor. He stretched to pick it up and groaned.

"What's wrong, Oliver?" Kevin O'Shea sat in a wingback chair a few feet from the couch, sipping iced tea. Despite the air-conditioning, the room still seemed muggy in the midst of the heat wave throttling New York.

"Nothing," Oliver answered glumly.

"Come on," O'Shea urged. "Tell me what's bugging you." The situation notwithstanding, he had come to like Oliver Mason.

O'Shea had dark red hair, green eyes, and fair skin. He was

over six feet tall with a broad chest, not quite so toned now that he was two years past his fortieth birthday and had no time to work out. His stomach was starting to bulge as well, thanks to his affection for McDonald's cheeseburgers—his way of combating the stress of his new job responsibilities. He pinched his midsection between his thumb and forefinger to see if the crash diet his wife had forced on him the past few days had done any good. His expression turned grim. The belt seemed tighter around his waist than ever, and the fleshy roll above it seemed larger.

"Stop kidding yourself, Kevin," Oliver said from the couch, rolling onto his back and replacing the washcloth on his forehead. "It's a losing battle for a guy like you. That belly is there to stay. It's only going to become a bigger friend the older you get. But at least it's a friend you'll never lose, which is more than you or I can say about most of our acquaintances," he said bitterly.

"Thanks, Oliver," O'Shea said, sipping his iced tea. He made a mental note not to touch his stomach in public again. People noticed what you were doing, even when you thought they didn't. "I appreciate those uplifting words."

"My pleasure." Oliver heaved a long sigh.

"So what's the matter?" O'Shea asked. "You seem down in the dumps tonight, not your usual chipper self."

Oliver grimaced. "Just thc normal domestic crap."

"Wife problems again?"

"Maybe. Hey, I want to know something." Oliver's voice changed pitch as he switched gears.

"What's that?"

"Is that a little bit of an Irish accent I hear?"

"Aye, laddie," he answered, exaggerating the Belfast accent. "My father was second generation in this country. When I was growing up you could barely understand him if you weren't accustomed to the way he spoke," O'Shea explained, his voice returning to normal, just a faint trace of his father's influence still audible. "You don't really hear it, do you?"

"Sometimes," Oliver said absentmindedly.

O'Shea finished his iced tea and placed the glass on a table beside the chair. "Enough small talk, Oliver. Bring me up to date on the latest developments."

Oliver tossed the washcloth toward the bathroom door and wiped moisture from his forehead. "Jay West made the share purchases this morning. He bought large amounts of Simons and Bell Chemical, as well as something called TurboTec."

"What's TurboTec?" O'Shea asked suspiciously. "That doesn't sound familiar. That isn't one of the stocks your pals gave you a tip on, is it?"

"No." Oliver shook his head. "Jay came up with TurboTec all on his own. He has some college buddy who works at the company."

"I suppose that's okay," O'Shea said, repeating the name to himself several times. He was afraid to write anything down at this point. "I'll check it out. If it turns out Jay did anything illegal there, it'll make the whole thing even easier." He paused. "Did we get what we needed?"

"Yup." Oliver pulled himself to a sitting position on the couch, then reached beneath it and produced an envelope. "Here." He tossed it to O'Shea. "The disk is inside."

O'Shea caught the envelope, checked inside, and placed it in his suit-coat pocket. "How about the other thing? How is that going?"

"Fine."

"Good." O'Shea relaxed. Things were falling into place.

"So the trap is set," Oliver said dramatically. "The lamb has been led to the altar, and all we have to do is wait for the takeovers to be announced. Right?"

"That's right," O'Shea agreed. "Speaking of which, when do you think that will happen?"

"That's the million-dollar question, isn't it?"

"Have your contacts ever been wrong?" O'Shea asked. "Have they ever given you tips, but then the deals never happened?"

"Sure," Oliver admitted. For a moment he thought about Tony Vogel and the three other insiders, all employees of prominent Wall Street brokerage firms. They had been passing him illegal information on pending takeovers for the last five years in return for a very special arrangement. "Deals crater all the time. You should know that, Mr. Assistant U.S. Attorney."

O'Shea rolled his eyes. "Great. That would really screw this thing up if one of those deals isn't announced. Bell Chemical or Simons, I mean. Then we'd be right back to square one. And Jay West might be suspicious at that point. He might not execute trades again just because you tell him to."

"Don't sweat it," Oliver said reassuringly. Tony and the other men were rarely wrong. In the past five years only a handful of tips hadn't panned out. "Everything will be fine." Oliver put his feet up on the coffee table. "Why did you become a lawyer for the government, Kevin? What the hell possessed you to do that?"

O'Shea suppressed a smile. As a law enforcement officer, he should have despised Oliver. The guy was no better than a common street thief. Worse, in fact, because he had cheated so many people out of so much money. But Oliver had a fascinating way of looking at life, and an uncanny ability to make you like him even though you knew he was always looking out for himself and no one else. "My father was a cop, and his six brothers were all either cops or construction workers," O'Shea explained. "The ones who were construction workers were always complaining of back pain. That didn't seem like much of a way to earn a living to me. The justice system always appealed to me, but I had no desire to be shot at like my father. Plus cops and construction workers didn't make much money. So I went to law school."

"But that's what I don't get," Oliver said. "I understand wanting to be a lawyer, even though lawyers are still basically hourly laborers," he pointed out. "What I don't understand is why you'd want to be a government lawyer. You work your ass off to get the same degree as the big corporate boys at Davis Polk or Skadden Arps, but you get paid dog shit in comparison."

"My family taught me when I was very young how important it is to do the right thing and not make everything about money. They stressed balance. They said there was nothing wrong with making money as long as you made a contribution to society at the same time." Over the last few years O'Shea had been pondering more and more often the question Oliver had just posed. After a long and grueling career, O'Shea had finally struggled his way up the ladder to the position of a senior-level assistant U.S. attorney in the Manhattan office. He was a respected member of the office and earned ninety-two thousand dollars a year working for the Justice Department. But with four children, he still couldn't seem to get ahead. "I guess I get enough of a charge out of stopping guys like you from ripping off the American people not to care about the financial sacrifice," he said defiantly.

"Enough of a charge not to be jealous of some of your Fordham classmates who are probably earning millions of dollars a year?"

And living in huge houses in Rye and Greenwich, O'Shea thought. "My only regret is that I won't be able to put you away on this one," O'Shea said with a smile. "You'll still be free to trade. But I'll be watching."

"I'm sure you will," Oliver said dryly. "But I can assure you that once this is over, I'll never be guilty of insider trading again. I've learned my lesson."

O'Shea laughed sarcastically. "No, you haven't. You're just like a common street junkie. Addicted. You don't get insider trading out of your system overnight. I've seen it before. You'll be setting up another ring within a year." O'Shea pointed a finger at Oliver. "And when you do, I'll be there." His eyes narrowed. "At that point you'll be facing jail time yourself, not setting up someone else to take your fall. Maybe then you'll give us McCarthy."

"There's nothing to give," Oliver answered quickly. "Bill didn't know anything about what I had arranged before your people approached him. He's clean."

"Uh-huh." O'Shea didn't believe that for a second. Bill McCarthy was a Wall Street veteran. He must have known that Oliver couldn't turn the kind of huge profits he'd been consistently earning for the firm without insider information. You just didn't pick the right pony as many times as Oliver had over the last five years without somebody in the stable telling you whom to bet on. But it wasn't his place to rock the boat. The decision concerning the situation at McCarthy & Lloyd had been made many levels above him, probably in a limousine on the Beltway or in an out-of-the-way alcove buried deep in the Capitol. He was simply a foot soldier carrying out the general's orders. "Are you certain Carter Bullock knows nothing about what's going on?"

"Positive," Oliver said firmly. "Bullock is completely in the dark about what's going on. Believe me."

"And West?"

Oliver clenched his jaw. Jay had answered that idiot Tony Vogel's call on the cell phone the day before, and Oliver was sure he had discovered the envelope in the Healey's glove compartment with Bell Chemical's name inside. But Jay had still made the trades that morning. "Nothing," Oliver said softly. "Jay knows nothing. He's too busy doing whatever I tell him. He's focused on the million-dollar bonus and nothing else. He's a disciple."

Oliver's mind flashed back to the previous night's terrible fight with Barbara.

"Do I detect a trace of regret?" O'Shea asked. "Do you feel a little guilty about what you're doing?" It was important that there be no last-minute second thoughts.

"Hell, no!" Oliver snapped.

"Are you sure?"

"Yes." Oliver rose from the couch and shuffled to the suite window overlooking Central Park.

O'Shea stood up. "All right, Oliver. It sounds to me as if everything is under control. I've got to get going." He turned and moved to the door. "If there are any developments, you call me at that number I gave you last week. Never downtown. Do you understand?"

"Yeah, yeah." Oliver didn't look away from the window.

"Okay, sweet dreams, baby doll," O'Shea called, opening the hallway door. A moment later he was gone.

"Fuck you, asshole," Oliver mumbled. "God, I'd love to take him down."

For a long time Oliver stood before the window, watching tourists climb into horse-drawn carriages parked along the far side of Fifty-ninth Street five stories below him, considering Kevin O'Shea's observation that he wouldn't be able to keep himself from trading on the inside once things had calmed down. That once Jay West had taken the fall and been whisked away to Leavenworth for the next twenty years, Oliver wouldn't be able to resist the lure of easy money. That McCarthy's power and influence would all go to waste because the government couldn't be expected to agree to such an amiable arrangement the second time around. Contacts only went so far. Even ones as influential as McCarthy's.

Oliver gazed at the carriages a moment longer, then turned

and walked slowly back to the couch. He reached into his shirt pocket and removed a piece of paper folded into a neat triangle. His fingers shook as he carefully opened the paper and placed it on the coffee table. His mouth turned dry as he stared at the pure white powder. This was stupid, but it made him feel so damn good. It provided that sense of power and invulnerability that he craved so badly—things he had been missing since he had met with McCarthy and O'Shea that March afternoon in the privacy of McCarthy's Park Avenue apartment and had his world blown to bits in a matter of seconds.

Oliver reached beneath the couch and picked up a small framed painting he had taken from the suite's bedroom wall. He dumped the powder onto the glass, then began chopping it with a straight razor he withdrew from his shirt pocket, slicing the cocaine crystals into finer and finer grains and beginning to arrange the powder into two lines. Last March in McCarthy's apartment, when O'Shea had explained what was going on, Oliver had been certain he was going to be carted away to jail immediately, hands cuffed behind his back. The U.S. attorney's office had identified at least three cases in which the authorities felt certain that Oliver, or someone on the arbitrage desk, had traded on inside information. Out of respect for McCarthy and his White House connections, the office had approached McCarthy first, and he had appealed to his high-powered friends in Washington, who had quietly brokered a very attractive deal. For political reasons the arbitrage desk at McCarthy & Lloyd would have to offer up a sacrificial lamb to publicly take a fall, then sign a consent decree stipulating that they wouldn't engage in the equity arbitrage business for six months. That would placate the Justice Department and leave the major players unscathed. During that six-month period Oliver would perform special projects for McCarthy, and when the cooling-off period was over, the arbitrage desk could start up again, but it would have to act legitimately. There would be no more insider trading.

Oliver stopped cutting the cocaine for a moment. He was certain he could refrain from any inside plays. Of course, he'd promised himself that he'd never take that walk through Central Park's northern section to meet his drug connection again, either. But he had. Maybe O'Shea was right. Maybe he wouldn't be able to go straight. Oliver took a labored breath. Fuck O'Shea. O'Shea didn't know what making real money was all about. He had no conception of the pressures associated with bringing in that kind of bucks. O'Shea had lived a dull, protected life for the last fifteen years, never taking any real chances, sheltered by the federal government's cocoon, being satisfied with a shithole town house in shithole Queens. O'Shea had no idea what it was like to have to eat only what you killed, no idea what it was like to try to measure up to a man like Harold Kellogg.

Oliver picked up a straw from atop the glass, leaned down, and prepared to snort the drug.

A sudden banging on the hallway door caused him to drop the straw, then stand and hold his hands up as if he were about to be arrested.

The door burst open and Bullock stood in the foyer.

Oliver had been certain that he'd been set up by Kevin O'Shea, certain that O'Shea didn't really care about insider trading but wanted to arrest Oliver on drug charges. That somehow O'Shea had found out about his cocaine habit and alerted the FBI or the New York City police or whoever the hell made drug busts. Oliver's paranoia and insecurity had reached such levels that he'd even believed Abby was involved and that her disappearance was linked to the banging on the door, that she'd become a witness. He stared at Bullock, relieved to realize that another bullet had been dodged.

"What are you doing?" Bullock nodded at the cocaine.

"Nothing," Oliver snapped, back in control. "Close the door. Make sure you lock it."

Bullock obeyed, then walked slowly across the room until he was standing behind the wingback chair O'Shea had vacated only a few minutes before. "So this is what you're doing when you disappear for the afternoon."

"Shut up." Oliver sat back down on the couch and snorted an entire line of cocaine. "Here, take some," he offered, head tilted back to keep powder from falling from his nose. He held the straw out for Bullock.

"No."

"How the hell did you know I was here?" Oliver asked suspiciously, dropping the straw beside the second line. He hadn't told anyone where he was going.

"I followed you."

"Why?"

"I wanted to know where you were going."

"Why?" Oliver asked again.

"Just curious."

"Has your curiosity been satisfied?" Oliver allowed his head to fall back against the couch.

"No. Who was the guy that just left here?" Bullock asked.

"Kevin O'Shea." There was no reason to be coy with Bullock about O'Shea's identity. Bullock was in this thing as deeply as Oliver was, all the way up to his eyeballs. He knew everything about the investigation and the deal. There were no secrets between them. O'Shea was a moron for believing otherwise. "Assistant United States attorney for the southern district of New York." The cocaine was beginning to have its desired effect. He was beginning to feel that power surging through his body. "The man who's going to put Jay West behind bars and leave us free to trade." Oliver smiled. He could feel the rush thrusting him forward like an avalanche. Life was good again. If only Abby were waiting in the bedroom for him, naked beneath the covers. Then life would be perfect. He missed her so much. It was frightening for him to realize that. He'd never missed anyone in his life.

"So that's O'Shea." Bullock moved in front of the chair and sat down. "Did you tell him that Jay pulled the trigger on the trades?"

"Yes." There was that familiar postnasal drip. He swallowed several times in rapid succession, pulling the drug-laced saliva down. "He seemed very happy."

"I bet."

"Did you put that one-month review into Jay's human resources file?" Oliver asked, speaking more quickly now that the cocaine was taking over. "The one with the rating of two?"

Bullock smiled. "Absolutely. And I included a note explaining that Jay had refused to sign it, citing our out in his contract. That should make O'Shea happy, too." Bullock laughed snidely. "I've been telling Jay how you're going to fire him or Sally. How the contract has outs. It's perfect."

Oliver shook his head. "Poor kid. He has no idea what's about to happen to him. No idea that a freight train is bearing down on him. Kevin O'Shea will take him down so easily."

"I hope so."

For several moments they were silent. Finally Oliver glanced at Bullock. "What do you think happened to Abby?"

"I don't know, Oliver, but it scares the crap out of me. If what you told me is correct, she knows about our partners. About Tony and the others. If she went to somebody who isn't privy to what's been arranged downtown, we could have real problems."

Oliver exhaled loudly, frustrated with his inability to contact her. "Carter, I've got to find Abby."

CHAPTER 13

"Hi," Sally called, following the maître d'. She clasped Jay's arm as they came together, kissed him on the cheek, then sat in the chair he was holding out for her. "I'm sorry I'm late," she apologized, slightly out of breath.

"Don't worry about it." Jay sat in the chair beside hers at a small table next to the window, unable to take his eyes off her. The short, low-cut black dress clung to her slim body, revealing most of her long, toned legs and delicate shoulders. Adorning her soft lobes were simple diamond earrings, shimmering in the chandelier light. When he looked away, he noticed that several men in the restaurant were paying close attention to her. "You look great."

"Thanks. I'm ashamed to say it, but I've been getting ready since five." She moaned. "And I'm still late." She reached across the plates, silverware, and glasses and squeezed his fingers. "I've missed you all week."

Jay gazed into her eyes. The pace on the desk had been frantic, and they'd hardly had a chance to speak. But Friday at five o'clock he'd answered one of his phone lines and been surprised to hear Sally's voice. She was calling from a conference room, requesting a Saturday-night date. Dinner at the River Cafe. Eight o'clock. Just the two of them. He'd glanced at Bullock, sitting a few feet away reviewing a memo, and accepted the invitation with a simple "sure" so Bullock wouldn't suspect. Sally hadn't returned to the desk after the call, and when she hadn't arrived at the restaurant on time, he was certain that he'd been stood up. But there she was, looking even better than she had at the yacht club, if that was possible. He realized how much he'd been looking forward to this.

"I'm glad you called yesterday," he admitted.

"That was pretty courageous, wasn't it? I surprised myself."

A waiter arrived with a bottle of chardonnay, served it, and retreated without a word, sensing that the couple would be taking their time that night.

"Here's to us," Sally said, picking up her glass.

"To us," Jay repeated, touching his glass to hers. It was so easy with her. He tried to stay focused on the fact that he had several important things he needed to ask her. But that was going to be difficult. He didn't want to spoil the mood.

"It's beautiful." She nodded out the window at the skyline of lower Manhattan towering above them across the East River. Lights inside the office buildings were illuminated brightly even though it was Saturday evening. "Don't you think?"

"Yes."

They sat in silence for a moment, then Sally spoke up. "Did anyone ever hear from . . ." She paused. "What was the young woman's name who mailed her resignation to Oliver this week?"

"Abby," Jay answered. "Abby Cooper."

"That's it. I met her in passing on Tuesday. She seemed very nice."

"She is," he agreed. "And no, I don't believe anyone has heard from her."

"Do you find that strange?" Sally asked, taking a long drink of wine.

Jay watched the wine disappear. She seemed nervous. "I do." For a moment he considered telling Sally about what he had witnessed in the storage room, but decided against it. "Abby wasn't the type of woman to mail in her resignation. She is a very responsible person, not the kind to let people down."

"Did you know her well?" Sally asked, finishing what was left in her glass.

Jay picked up the wine bottle from the ice bucket and refilled her glass. "I've only been at McCarthy and Lloyd for about a month, but we got pretty close in that time. In a friendly way," he added.

"Have you tried to contact her?"

"I've left several messages on her answering machine at home, but I haven't heard back from her."

"I don't mean to be an alarmist, but maybe it makes sense to contact a relative. Human resources must have the name of someone to call in an emergency."

"That's a good idea." Jay didn't tell Sally that he had already found the number for Abby's parents in Brooklyn before people from human resources had come down Thursday afternoon to clear out her position on the desk. He didn't want Sally to know how concerned he was. "You were kind of sneaky about arranging this date," Jay said, changing the subject, "calling from the conference room."

She toyed with her earrings for a moment. "I didn't want Bullock to get the wrong idea. He's so damn nosy, especially with you," she said. "He listens to every word you say when you're on the phone. He tries to act as if he isn't listening, but I can tell he is. It must be very annoying."

"It is."

"I'm not worried about Oliver," Sally said. "He wouldn't care if he knew we were out tonight. In fact, he'd probably be very happy for us. But Bullock's another matter."

"Why did you say that about Oliver?" Jay asked. "About Oliver's being happy for us."

She took another sip of wine and shrugged. "When he and I were coming back from our meeting in midtown last week, he told me that he and Barbara had noticed . . ." Sally hesitated.

"What?" Jay prodded.

"It's a little embarrassing."

"Come on."

"He said it was obvious that you and I had enjoyed each other's company on the sailboat. And at dinner." She looked straight into his eyes. "He said he wouldn't have a problem if we saw each other socially, as long as we kept it out of the office."

"He said that to you?" Jay broke into a grin.

She pointed at Jay. "You too?"

Jay nodded. "After dinner at the yacht club."

Sally laughed. "That's just like Oliver. He can be such a jerk sometimes, but then he can be really great, too."

"Exactly." Jay watched the diamonds sparkle. "What did you mean when you said you didn't want Bullock to get the wrong idea? What's the *right* idea?"

She put her elbows on the table and rested her chin on the back of her hands. "Would you mind if I said something very forward?"

"No."

"I'm not sure exactly what the right idea is, but I do know I want to find out." She paused, still locked onto his eyes. "It's been a long time since I've been really attracted to anyone," she said. "And don't worry, I'm not rushing into anything or asking you to, and I'm very conscious that we have to be careful because we work together. But I would like to see you outside the office."

"Sounds good. I couldn't have put it better myself."

For a moment they stayed on each other's eyes, then they looked away at the same time, both aware that things had suddenly become much more complicated.

"Tell me more about yourself." Jay finally broke the silence.

"What do you want to know?" Sally was staring at the skyline across the river, now fully shrouded in darkness.

"You said you were from Gloucester."

"Yes, I grew up on the south shore of Cape Ann. It was a very nice place to live. I was fortunate. My family had money, I won't deny it. After prep school I went to Yale. The fact that my father was an alumnus and a regular donor to certain scholarship funds certainly didn't hurt my application. He helped me get into Harvard Business School as well."

"Did he help you get your job at that financial firm in San Francisco after Harvard?" Jay asked.

She shook her head. "No, I got that on my own."

"How did you hear about the job at McCarthy and Lloyd?"

"A headhunter." She took a long swallow of wine, and a melancholy expression came to her face. "I wish my parents could have known about my getting this job. They would have been proud of me."

"I'm sure," Jay agreed. He shook his head sadly. "It's terrible about your mom and dad. You said it was a plane crash, right?"

"Yes."

"Two years ago?"

"Mmm." She finished her wine and put the empty glass down on the linen tablecloth. "Again, bartender."

Jay poured each of them another glass, then gestured to the waiter, indicating that they needed another bottle.

"Do you have any more questions for me, Perry Mason?"

Jay thought he detected a faint trace of aggravation in her voice. "Prying too much?" he asked. "Am I being too Bullockesque?"

"No, just persistent." She picked up her glass and moved it slightly from side to side, watching the wine sway.

"Are you involved with anyone?"

"What?" she asked, surprised by his blunt question.

"Is there someone in San Francisco?" Jay pushed.

"Now that's a Bullock question."

"Just the same."

Sally hesitated. "There was," she said slowly. "But there isn't anymore."

The waiter returned to serve the second bottle of wine, and they fell silent.

"Now it's my turn," Sally said when the man was gone.

"Okay."

"What about you? Is there someone in New York I should know about? Someone who wouldn't be happy if she knew we were out tonight?"

Jay shook his head. "I've dated a few women, but no one of any consequence. No one I've become serious with. I've been too busy working." He waited for another question, but nothing came. "That was easy."

"Oh, I'm not finished."

"Fine. Ask me anything you want."

"Okay, why do you insist on being a daredevil?"

He gave her a strange expression, uncertain what she was getting at. "I don't understand."

"On Wednesday you jumped out of the bosun's chair from seventy feet. That night you went up on top of that wall when we were on the roof of your building." She searched his eyes. "There must be a reason that you did those things."

"You're crazy. I think you must have stayed out in the sun too long when you visited your parents down in South Carolina one time. Wasn't that where you said they went when they moved from Gloucester?"

Sally put her glass down slowly and focused on the candle flame. "Why do you keep doing that?" Her voice was trembling slightly.

"Doing what?" he asked innocently.

"Why do you keep testing me on my background?"

"Huh?"

"It's as if you're checking me out, or trying to trap me."

"What are you talking about?"

"You alluded to my living in San *Francisco* before coming to M and L. I told you on Wednesday that the firm I was working for was headquartered in Los Angeles, but I worked in the San *Diego* office."

"Sally, I—"

"Then you referred to my parents' airplane crash occurring two years ago. I told you before, it happened *one* year ago. Now you're trying to trick me into saying that my parents lived in South Carolina after leaving Gloucester. I distinctly remember telling you they moved to Florida." She shook her head. "I know your memory is quite good. I've seen that over the past few days on the desk. Bullock even said something about it. I was willing to believe that you slipped the first two times, but the South

Carolina thing is too much. It's stupid. Why are you putting me through this?"

"I'm sorry, Sally." There was no reason to deny what he had been doing. She was absolutely right, and he would look foolish by continuing to protest. "I have no excuse."

"But why did you do it?"

"I don't know," he said lamely. He couldn't explain to her how disturbing he found the events of the past week. The Bell Chemical coincidence, the way Oliver had pressed him into making the Simons and Bell trades, her familiarity with New York despite claiming never to have spent much time in the city, the phone off its base, the warm computer, and her claim that she'd used the Internet on his computer when he wasn't on-line. "Maybe I'm feeling strange because all of a sudden I'm interested in someone for the first time in a long time. You know?"

"No, I don't," she said flatly, staring at him, searching for the truth.

■ ■ ■

The freighter churned steadily through the warm Indian Ocean waters, sliding southwest through the night over calm seas toward the southern tip of Africa and the Cape of Good Hope. From there the captain would turn the ship north and begin the long voyage up Africa's western shore toward Antwerp, his destination.

He peered out from the bridge at the horizon, searching for any lights that might warn of an unfriendly situation—an authority interested in searching his ship for the cache of automatic weapons, grenade launchers, surface-to-air missiles, and mortars hidden below. He was a veteran of gun-running trips, and he knew that situation was unlikely in these waters. Here it would more likely be pirates who would board his freighter searching for treasure. But he was ready for that possibility as well. Unless the pirates possessed an overwhelming force, they would be dead ten minutes after boarding, their bodies tossed to the sharks and their boat sunk without any risk of legal retribution. The same authorities who would imprison him and confiscate the weapons in his hold would turn a blind eye if he did away with ten or fifteen modern-day Blackbeards.

When the ship neared Europe the next week, he would begin to worry more about navies and coast guards. Years ago, only a deckhand at the time, he had been aboard the *Claudia* off the coast of Ireland when it had been captured on the last stage of its voyage from Libya full of arms for the provisional wing of the Irish Republican Army.

■ ■ ■

The lights of lower Manhattan loomed over Jay and Sally as they walked slowly down the Brooklyn Heights promenade, a half-mile brick walkway overlooking the East River in the fashionable neighborhood of million-dollar brownstones and tree-lined streets.

Sally's arms were crossed tightly over her chest, the way they had been all through the end of dinner. "Look, I'm really sorry," Jay began, glancing around through the streetlights' soft glow. There were only a few other people on the promenade. "I really am."

"It's all right," she said coldly.

He reached out, took her by the arm, and guided her to the wrought-iron railing at the edge of the walkway. Far below them the black waters of the East River flowed silently into New York Harbor. "I want to tell you something."

On the walk from the restaurant she had let her hair down, and a wisp of a breeze pushed several blond strands across her face. She brushed them out of her eyes. "What?"

He could see that she wasn't really interested. He hoped what he was about to say would change that. "The crack you made about me always being a daredevil. Jumping from the bosun's chair and up onto the wall."

Sally glanced up from the railing. "Yes?"

"You're very perceptive."

"Oh?"

Jay nodded. "I do stupid things sometimes."

"To impress people?"

"I don't think so," he said slowly.

She moved slightly closer. "Then why?"

He hesitated. "My little sister was a wonderful athlete."

"The one who drowned."

"Yes," he said quietly. "She and I were alone at the quarry that day. My parents had forbidden her to go there, even with me, but she was an incredible swimmer, almost as good as me even though she was so much younger. I mean, she could hold her breath forever, she could dive from the high board, she could—"

"I believe you," Sally said gently, sliding her hand into his.

Jay cleared his throat. "It was terribly hot. One of those July days that makes you sweat while you're just sitting in your chair. Our house didn't have air-conditioning. It was like a furnace, and Phoebe kept—"

"Phoebe?"

"Yes."

"That's a pretty name."

"She was a pretty girl." Jay gazed across the river. "Anyway, she kept begging me to take her to the quarry, and I kept telling her we couldn't go. But finally I gave in. She had that effect on me. She could get me to do anything. I had so much confidence in her."

"But she got trapped underwater."

"Yes." Jay's voice became hoarse. "The water was gin-clear, and I saw she was in trouble about fifteen feet down. I tried to help her, but by the time I got her to the surface . . . she was gone."

"I'm so sorry, Jay." Sally squeezed his hand tightly. "You still feel guilty, don't you?"

"Yes."

"But you shouldn't. It wasn't your fault."

"I was responsible for her."

"Not so responsible that you should try to kill yourself by jumping up onto a parapet six hundred feet above the street."

He shook his head. "It isn't that. That's not why I do those things."

"Why then?"

"If I'd been braver, I might have saved her."

"What do you mean?"

He took a deep breath. "I was timid as a kid. To get to her I had to swim through some of the old equipment. I was afraid that I'd get stuck myself." He drew himself up. "I was afraid."

"I can see why."

"No, I mean I was afraid of a lot of things. I was not a courageous person. I backed down from a fight in front of the entire high school one time. It was humiliating." He took a deep breath. "I hesitated going after Phoebe." He clenched his teeth. "Those few seconds may have cost her life."

Sally reached up and touched his scar. "So now you feel you have to prove to people that you aren't afraid of anything."

"I don't care about other people. Just myself. I need to keep proving it to myself."

For a long time they were quiet, listening to the sounds of the city.

"I'm glad you felt you could share that with me," Sally finally said.

"I've never told anyone that."

"But you still haven't told me why you were trying to catch me in a lie during dinner," Sally said softly.

Jay tapped the railing, then stopped when he remembered that Oliver did the same thing when he was nervous. "Do you recall when we were leaving Oliver's place in the Austin Healey? I asked you to check the glove compartment for the registration."

"Yes. I thought that was kind of silly because I knew you had already driven the car. I saw you come up the driveway."

Jay nodded. "Yes, I was at the liquor store picking up a bottle of gin for Barbara. When I pulled into the store's parking lot, I heard a cell phone ringing in the glove compartment. I answered the call thinking it was Oliver or Barbara, but it wasn't."

"Who was it?"

"A guy named Tony who thought I was Oliver and blurted out something about not being able to use some information. When Tony realized I wasn't Oliver, he hung up very fast." Jay watched the green and yellow lights of a tugboat churning upriver. "When I put the phone back, I saw an envelope and I opened it."

"What was in it?"

"A single piece of paper with the name Bell Chemical on it. Bell is one of the companies Oliver had me purchase shares of last week."

"Did you ever ask Oliver about the phone call or the envelope?"

"We talked about the phone call, but not the envelope. You should have seen Oliver when I told him the guy had said not to use the information. He looked like a deer in the headlights. He claimed the call had something to do with a condo he's trying to buy in Manhattan, but I'm convinced that was crap." Jay exhaled heavily.

"I don't understand why you didn't simply ask him about the envelope if you were so concerned."

Jay's eyes narrowed, then he smiled, a quick half grin that was barely discernible in the dim light. "Let's be honest with each other, Sally. Oliver has guaranteed me a million dollars next January. The same amount he's guaranteed you." Jay paused, waiting for her acknowledgment. "Bullock tells me that McCarthy and Lloyd can extricate itself from the contract they made each of us sign. He claims there are safe harbors in it. Maybe you had an attorney review yours, but I was warned not to, and foolishly, I obeyed."

Sally shook her head. "No, I didn't have a lawyer look at mine, either. I got the same warning."

"Well, according to Bullock, Oliver wants to pay only one of us in January."

Her eyes widened. "What?"

"Yes. At least that's what Bullock said. I don't like the guy much, but he seems to have Oliver's ear." Jay looked away. "You may not want to hear this, but if what Bullock says is true, I want that bonus to come to me."

"Don't think I'm just going to step out of the way and let you take it," Sally warned. "I'm going to try to get it as hard as you are."

"I don't want to jeopardize my relationship with Oliver," he said, choosing to ignore her challenge, "and given the type of person he is, questioning or not carrying out one of his direct orders would be tantamount to mutiny."

"Probably," Sally agreed.

"I stalled as long as I could, but when it came down to it, I had to pull the trigger on the Bell shares."

"And now you're regretting it."

"Very much." He pursed his lips. "I just want a few weeks to go by without a takeover announcement concerning Bell or Simons, then convince Oliver to dump the shares."

She turned back toward the promenade railing. "I don't think you have anything to worry about, but I can understand why all those things taken together could disturb you. And I truly appreciate your confiding in me." Her voice turned tough again. "But I still don't understand why you would be trying to catch me in some kind of lie. The only explanation I can come up with is that you think there's some sort of conspiracy and I'm part of it," she said bitterly. "That I'm working with Oliver to railroad you or something. Why else would you grill me about the phone being off the base and the computer being warm?"

He put his finger beneath her chin and turned her face back toward his. "If I believed there was a conspiracy—which I have to admit sounds a little silly when you say it like that—and if I believed you were part of it, would I have said all this to you?"

"I don't know," she snapped, angry again, pulling away from him. "I thought I did, but now I'm not sure."

"That's not fair. I'm just being careful."

"You shouldn't have to be careful with someone you care about."

"I know."

"Then why—"

Before she could finish, Jay grabbed her and pulled her to him, locking his strong arms around her, pressing his lips to hers.

For a moment she struggled, fighting him, but then slowly she slipped her hands around his neck, pressed herself against him, and kissed him deeply.

CHAPTER 14

At five minutes past eight on Monday evening Jay rang the doorbell of a modest two-story brick house in a blue-collar Brooklyn neighborhood. The sun was setting, casting long shadows over a neatly manicured lawn stretching a short distance from the house to the narrow, car-lined street behind him. The doorbell made a buzzing sound inside, and after a few moments Jay heard footsteps moving toward the door. He stepped back on thc concrete stoop as the front door opened. Before Jay stood a short man with gray hair and bloodshot eyes.

"Mr. Cooper?"

"Yes," the man answered in a low voice.

It was dark inside the house except for a faint candle that was burning atop a foyer table. "My name is Jay West."

The man's face remained impassive. "Oh, yes, Abby mentioned you to us several times. You worked with her at McCarthy and Lloyd."

"That's right."

The man glanced over his shoulder into the darkness, then stepped out onto the stoop and closed the front door. "Bob Cooper," he said, offering his hand in a subdued manner.

Jay shook Abby's father's hand. "I'm glad to meet you."

"Likewise."

"Look, I realize this may seem a little strange," Jay said. "My coming to your house unannounced, I mean."

The man shrugged but said nothing.

"I didn't want to call," Jay continued, "because I felt that if I did that, I might alarm you, and I don't think there's any cause for that."

"What do you mean?"

"Abby hasn't come to work for a few days," he explained. "I've tried to reach her at her apartment several times, but she's never there, or doesn't answer. I've left several messages for her, but she hasn't returned any of them. I wanted to see if you had heard from her."

Cooper's eyes dropped. "She won't be returning your calls." His voice was barely audible.

"What do you mean?"

He swallowed hard. "She's dead," he said, choking back tears.

The vision of Oliver forcing himself on Abby flashed back to him again. "What happened?" he gasped.

Cooper wiped tears from his eyes. "I don't know. My wife and I were only notified this afternoon. The police found Abby's body in a Dumpster in the Bronx. She'd been strangled."

"God, no." Jay placed a hand on Cooper's narrow shoulder. He could feel the man shaking.

"Yes." Cooper looked up at Jay, then away. "I'm sorry I can't ask you in, but my wife's in there with her sister. They're pretty torn up. I don't think they could handle visitors right now."

"I understand."

Abby hadn't come into work on Wednesday, the day Jay and Sally had joined Oliver and Barbara on the sailboat. The afternoon before, he had watched Oliver and Abby in the storage room. As he stood on the stoop staring at Cooper, Jay replayed what he had heard and seen standing outside the storage room, as he had so many times in the past few days. There was something he should be remembering, something that might have significance. It was the same feeling he had experienced staring at his computer the morning Sally had left his apartment without awakening him. The sense that something was amiss.

Then Jay remembered. As he had first glanced through the tiny aperture between the door and the wall, he had heard Oliver say something to Abby about meeting him after work at the Plaza. Oliver might have seen Abby right before she was killed. In fact, he might have been the last person to see her.

■ ■ ■

Bullock sat in the conference room, feet up on the long wooden table, leaning back in his chair. Oliver sat slumped in a seat on the opposite side of the table, fiddling aimlessly with his tie.

"What did you want to tell me, Oliver?" Bullock asked impatiently. He was suffering from a sore throat and a slight fever, and he still had a pile of paperwork to get to before he could head home.

Oliver flung the end of his tie over one shoulder. "Kevin O'Shea called me an hour ago."

Bullock looked up from the cuticle he'd been picking. He had heard panic in Oliver's voice. "And?"

Oliver took several labored breaths in rapid succession, as if he was trying to remain calm.

Bullock removed his feet from the table, and they landed on the carpet with a dull thud. "Come on, Oliver. Talk to me."

"O'Shea was calling to tell me that this afternoon two New York City police officers found . . ." Oliver swallowed his words and had to regroup. "They found Abby's body in a Bronx Dumpster. Personal effects, including her purse, were also in the Dumpster, so it wasn't a problem identifying her." Oliver felt his lower lip beginning to tremble. "She'd been strangled."

Bullock placed both hands on the table, the pain in his throat and the fever forgotten. "You're kidding," he mumbled.

Oliver shut his eyes tightly. "Do you think I'd kid about something like this?"

"No," Bullock said quietly. "I'm sorry, Oliver. I know you cared about her."

Oliver nodded. "I did, I really did." For the first time in many years he felt himself surrendering to tears. "I don't think I knew how much I cared about her until right now."

"How did O'Shea find out about Abby's body being discovered?" Bullock asked shakily. It unnerved him to see Oliver so upset.

"How the hell should I know?" Oliver yelled. "All those law enforcement people talk to each other." He could barely think straight. "Maybe it came across his computer or something."

"What did O'Shea say when he talked to you?" Bullock pressed. "What were his exact words?"

"He was very quick. He just said that they'd found her body." Oliver glanced at Bullock. He had recognized a strange tone in Bullock's voice. "What's your problem?"

"I think it's odd that he called you so fast. How would he

know the Abby Cooper they found in the Dumpster was the same Abby who worked here?"

"He knows about everybody in the group, Carter. He's done thorough background checks on all of us. He would have recognized her home address and put two and two together." Oliver tapped the table. "I think he was simply giving me an FYI. He's carrying on an investigation of our group, if you really want to call it that, and he probably wanted me to know what was going on so that I wasn't taken off guard when I heard about it. There's a lot happening around here." Oliver tapped the table harder. "He was probably worried that if I was taken off guard, I might slip up or something. Remember, his ass is on the line, too. He's the point person on the investigation. If the lid is blown off this thing and the media finds out what's really going on here, he'll take the fall. I know he's only a cog in this whole thing, but you better believe the higher-ups won't take the blame for the arrangement." Talking seemed to help. Suddenly Oliver felt a little better.

"Maybe," Bullock said, not totally convinced. "I still think it's odd that he called you right away."

Oliver put his elbows down on the table and rubbed his forehead. His entire body had gone numb. "Oh, God."

"What is it?" Bullock saw Oliver's hands trembling.

"Carter, I've got a problem."

"What is it?"

Oliver felt his emotional foundations giving way. "I was with Abby on Tuesday evening," he whispered.

"With . . . Abby?"

"Yes, at the Plaza."

"With her, as in sleeping with her?" He had known for some time that Oliver was having an affair with Abby.

"Yes."

"Jesus, Oliver." Bullock rolled his eyes and slammed the table.

"I know." Oliver grabbed his hair. "I'm an idiot, but what the hell am I going to do?"

"Did you use protection?"

Oliver shook his head. "No."

The room fell silent except for the hum of the fluorescent lights overhead.

Finally Bullock spoke. "They'll do an autopsy," he warned. "They'll find your semen inside her."

"Yes." Oliver nodded, staring wide-eyed at Bullock.

"But they'll have to know to look for you. Does anyone other than me know you were having an affair with Abby?"

"Barbara suspected."

"Well, that's—" Bullock stopped speaking.

Oliver glanced up. "What?"

Bullock didn't answer.

"Carter, what is it?" But he already knew what Bullock was thinking. He could see the look of horror in the other man's expression. "No, Carter."

"When did you last see Abby?" Bullock asked quietly.

"Eight, nine o'clock Tuesday night. Sometime around then. We finished in bed and I left almost right away. She said she was going to stay for a while."

"Did anyone see you leave?"

"No, I don't think so."

"Do you think that resignation letter was authentic?" Bullock asked. "The one you showed us last week."

"Hell, yes, I think it was authentic." Oliver's stomach was churning. He could feel the nausea building. "Why wouldn't I?"

"Did Abby sign it?"

"Yes—no . . . I'm not certain." He couldn't remember. His mind was tumbling into vapor lock. Bullock was a friend. Why the hell was he asking these questions and looking at him that way?

"Get the letter," Bullock ordered. "Let's see it."

Oliver shook his head. "I can't."

"What do you mean?"

"It's gone." His voice was trembling. "I had it locked in a drawer. Now it's gone."

Bullock's eyes narrowed. "Do you really expect me to believe that, Oliver?"

"Why wouldn't you believe it?" he yelled. "It's the truth." His body went limp and he slumped back into a chair. Bullock wasn't buying anything. "Carter, I didn't kill her," he whispered. "You have to believe that."

Bullock stood up slowly. "I think you have a problem, Oliver." He stared at Oliver for a few seconds, then walked from the room.

Oliver let his head sink to the table and for several moments kept his eyes shut tightly. Then he raced for the men's room, clutching his stomach.

CHAPTER 15

It was just before midnight and the cavernous McCarthy & Lloyd trading room was deserted except for a man cleaning the carpet at the far end of the floor where the bond traders yelled and screamed over telephones all day, buying and selling multimillion-dollar pieces of paper they never saw. Jay walked down the corridor paralleling the floor, then threaded his way through the clutter to the arbitrage desk. Despite the lack of people, the room was brightly lit. Half-full coffee cups stood in front of chairs pulled out from the long workstations, and most of the computer monitors remained on, graphs, memos, and reports glowing on the screens. It was as if everyone had filed out for a fire drill, Jay thought as he reached his position on the desk. Or the place had been hit by a neutron bomb.

He tossed his suit coat over the bulkhead and sank down into his seat, exhausted and emotionally drained. He had spent the last few hours with Abby's father, accompanying him as they walked slowly through his darkened Brooklyn neighborhood, talking about everything but Abby. Bob Cooper's best friend had died recently, Jay found out, and only then did it become clear why the older man had asked him to stay a while as they stood on the concrete stoop together. He needed someone, anyone, to talk to after losing his only child. At that moment on the stoop Jay had been the only person in the world for him to turn to.

Jay leaned back in the seat and closed his eyes. He'd agreed to stay. The poor man was clearly beside himself, and even though they hadn't known each other ten minutes, Jay wasn't going to leave any human being alone in such a vulnerable state. At the end of the walk he'd accompanied Cooper inside and met Abby's mother. She was short and attractive, an older version of Abby. The sister had left a few minutes earlier, and it was time for Cooper and his wife to grieve together. And time for Jay to go.

Now, as he sat alone on the trading floor, Jay realized that he hadn't come to grips with Abby's death himself. He'd been too busy comforting her father to grasp the fact that she was gone. He'd met Abby only a month earlier, but he'd felt an instant bond of friendship with her. She was one of those people you didn't have to expend a great deal of energy to get to know. She was open, energetic, and compassionate, a woman who wanted to make people feel comfortable in new surroundings and help others in any way she could.

Jay glanced past Bullock's seat at Abby's position. Now she was gone. That quickly. Just like Phoebe. He shook his head, his expression grim. He hoped that at some point the authorities would discover that they had made a terrible mistake and Abby would turn up, absolutely fine. He glanced at her chair once more, then rubbed his eyes. Perhaps this was what the psychoanalytical types termed denial. Perhaps it would take time before her death would sink in. But then, Phoebe's still hadn't.

He leaned forward and began typing commands on his keyboard. The computer clicked several times before images flashed on the screen. He had come back to perform research on Bell Chemical and Simons. He was the uncomfortable owner of a large stock position in each company, and though the decision to buy shares had already been made, at some point he might have to defend his purchases with hard data. He knew he couldn't count on Oliver to back him up if no takeover bids were announced and the share prices of each stock dropped. He'd have to face McCarthy's wrath alone.

The research was work he could have started the next morning, but he didn't want to go home yet. His apartment would feel even lonelier than this deserted floor, and he had the feeling that once he got into bed, he'd simply stare at the ceiling and think about Abby—and Phoebe.

He had tried to call Sally from Brooklyn, but there was no answer at the number she had given him Saturday evening. Perhaps she had stayed late at work and was still on her way home.

Jay punched in a few more commands on the keyboard, then headed toward the soda machine while the computer contacted an on-line service that would provide him with research material regarding Bell and Simons. When he returned, he noticed someone standing at the arbitrage desk. Jay stopped and took a sip of soda, watching while the short, dark-haired man reviewed a document. After a few moments the man slid the document into a manila envelope and put it down in front of Bullock's position. He knelt, removed a key from beneath the desktop, then slid the key into the lock in Bullock's stack of drawers and opened the middle one.

"Hi, Paulie."

Paul Lopez stood up quickly and glanced around. "Oh, hi, Jay." He spoke in a high-pitched whine.

Paul was one of the firm's late-shift back-office employees—quartered two floors up—who made certain that the hundreds of millions of dollars flowing through McCarthy & Lloyd on a daily basis reached their intended destinations. These operations people didn't begin their shifts until ten o'clock at night and often were just going home as the first traders were arriving on the floor in the morning. They couldn't leave until all the money wires satisfying the previous day's trades had been sent out or received and any problems with other financial institutions concerning transfers not received had been resolved.

"What are you doing here so late?" Paul asked, checking his watch. "Man, Oliver must be busting you. It's midnight."

Jay saw Paul almost every evening around ten o'clock. It was then that Paul made his rounds to collect the last batch of order tickets—tickets traders filled out detailing every purchase or sale of securities they had made during the day. He and Paul had gotten to know each other fairly well and often spent a few minutes talking about the Yankees or Mets before Paul continued on.

"Yeah, Oliver's a slave driver," Jay answered innocuously.

"That's what I've heard."

"What are *you* doing here, Paulie?" Jay asked. "Does anybody ever do a trade at this time of night?" By eleven, when he usually left, he was one of only a few people—if not the only person—remaining on the floor.

"Nah. I'm delivering something to Carter Bullock. I need his signature on it."

"Oh?"

"Yeah, he's an officer of a company that McCarthy and Lloyd owns."

"Really?" No one had ever mentioned anything about Bullock's having a second job.

"It's a travel agency."

"Here in New York?"

"No, it's in Boston."

"Why does M and L own a travel agency in Boston?"

Paul shrugged. "Got me. I don't know much about the company except that we send money up there every once in a while. It's funny, though."

"What is?"

"We don't ever get money back, at least not that I know of."

"How is Bullock involved?" Jay asked, trying not to sound too eager.

Paul nodded at the envelope lying on the desk in front of Bullock's position. "Carter authorizes the money transfers from M and L to the travel agency. That's why I need his signature. I think he's actually listed as the chief financial officer on the official advice—the hard copy detailing the transfer that we send to the payee. He goes up there every so often, probably to check the books."

"Up to Boston, huh?" So that was where Bullock went. Jay had never received a satisfactory explanation for Bullock's six separate absences in the last few weeks. The secretaries had no idea where he was, and Oliver would say only that Bullock was visiting "some company." Typically, if you were traveling, you had to be reachable at all times so that the desk could contact you if there was an emergency with a deal you were working on. That hadn't been the case with Bullock during his absences. "To check the books," Jay repeated.

"I guess so. Isn't that what a chief financial officer does?"

Jay grinned. "Yeah, Paulie, that's what a CFO does."

"Well, I gotta go," Paul said. He picked up the manila envelope, placed it in Bullock's middle drawer, and pushed in the lock. "At this rate I won't be out of here until nine in the morning," he groaned, bending down to replace the key on the small sill beneath the desk.

"Pretty careful about all this, aren't you?" Jay asked.

Paul rolled his eyes. "Carter's orders. If you ask me, he's being paranoid. There's nothing anyone could do with that advice even if they got hold of it." He stood up, groaning again. "See you later." Paul chuckled. "Probably tomorrow night, knowing how hard you work."

"Probably. Hey, Paulie?"

Paul stopped and turned around. "Yeah?"

"How long have you been with McCarthy and Lloyd?"

Paul thought for a second. "About three years. I came over from Chemical after the Chase merger."

"Were you given a performance appraisal after your first month here?"

"You mean a review? Like how I'm doing on the job?"

"Yes."

"Hell, no. I haven't had a formal review since I got here. This place is pretty lax about all that stuff. Ask any of the traders." He waved at the empty chairs. "Why do you want to know?"

"Just wondering."

"Don't worry—if you're screwing up, they'll let you know." He waved. "See you later."

"Yeah, bye."

Jay watched Paul disappear into an elevator, then checked the trading floor. He was alone in the huge room. He glanced at the elevator doors once more, then quickly moved to Bullock's position, pulled the chair out, knelt, and slid his hand beneath the desktop. At first he felt nothing but lint and dust, but a moment later he located the key. He grabbed it, pulled it out, and slid it into the lock. A quick turn to the left and the lock popped out. He took one more look around the trading floor, then pulled the drawer out, removed the manila envelope, withdrew the advice, and scanned it.

The name of the firm receiving the money was EZ Travel and the amount of the money transfer was five million dollars. The numbers blurred in front of his eyes. Why the hell did a travel agency need five million dollars? A travel agency was nothing but a couple of people sitting in front of computers booking flights and hotels. And Paulie had said that funds were transferred from McCarthy & Lloyd to EZ Travel on a regular basis. If this was a typical transaction, how much money had already gone to this Boston address?

Jay made a mental note of the post office box number, then slid the advice back into the manila envelope and replaced it in the drawer. He was about to close the drawer when something caught his eye. In the back of the drawer was another envelope that seemed vaguely familiar. Affixed to the top left corner of it was a label decorated with a floral pattern, and inside the floral pattern was Abby's home address. Jay had watched Abby attach that same label to a stack of bills one afternoon a few weeks earlier.

His heart beat furiously. If Paulie came back or someone else saw him rifling through the drawer, Bullock would probably find out. Then there'd be hell to pay.

He pulled the envelope from the drawer and studied it intently. The letter had been sent to Oliver Mason at McCarthy & Lloyd, but there was no stamp. The top of the envelope had been ripped open, and Jay pulled the paper from within, his fingers shaking. It was Abby's resignation letter. The same letter Oliver had held up in front of them the previous week in the conference room. Abby's name was typed at the bottom with her title beneath, but she hadn't signed the letter.

Jay slid the letter back into the envelope and replaced it in the drawer. He rose, turned around, and froze. Bullock stood only a few feet away.

"What the hell are you doing?"

"Replacing your calculator," Jay replied, his voice raspy. "I . . . I borrowed it because I left mine at home and I know you keep yours in this middle drawer. I've seen you get it out of there a hundred times." He gestured at the drawer. "I was doing research and I needed to run some figures," he explained haltingly.

"You were doing research at midnight? Do you really expect me to believe that?"

"One of your comments on my review was that I wasn't getting enough accomplished. Remember?"

"How the hell did you get into the drawer? I left it locked."

"No, you didn't. There's the key." Jay pointed at the key protruding from the lock. "You must have thought you locked it. Anyway, I didn't think you'd mind if I used your calculator."

"You were looking at a letter," Bullock hissed, moving toward Jay, flexing his right fist. "I saw you."

Jay held up his hands, backing up until he touched the desk. "I swear I was using your calculator." He glanced down. "I did check out one of your payroll stubs." He had noticed the blue stub next to a box of staples. It was the same stub everyone at M&L received from the company that processed the firm's payroll. "I shouldn't have done that. I'm sorry."

Bullock stood only inches away, hands on his hips, his face twisted in rage. Suddenly he grabbed Jay and pushed him aside roughly. "Get the hell out of here!"

"Easy, Carter."

"I said get out!"

"All right." Jay hustled to his position, placed several things in his briefcase, then headed for the elevators.

When Jay was gone, Bullock pulled the manila envelope from his drawer and gazed at it. If Jay had inspected the contents, he now knew about EZ Travel. When the takeovers were announced and Jay realized how desperate his situation had become, he would remember this evening.

Bullock glanced at the elevator doors once more, his eyes narrowing. The Bell Chemical or Simons takeover needed to happen quickly. Just one of them. Then O'Shea could make the arrest, and once Jay West was in jail, his life would come to a quick end. Jay would be found dangling from the ceiling of his cell, a sheet around his neck, and all would be well. The authorities would term the death a suicide and the link would be cut.

Bullock dropped the manila envelope into his briefcase, then retrieved the resignation letter from the drawer and placed it into the briefcase as well. He closed the drawer and the briefcase, then hurried toward the elevators. He wouldn't feel completely secure again until Jay was dead.

From beneath her desk on the other side of the bulkhead, Sally rubbed one calf. Her legs were tucked underneath her in the alcove and they were beginning to cramp. The pain was intense, but she couldn't move until Bullock was gone. She was certain Bullock wouldn't leave anything of consequence in his desk, especially now that he had caught Jay rifling through the drawers, but she had to check. She hadn't made any progress, and her superiors were becoming anxious.

CHAPTER 16

The heavens opened up, hurling an early-morning deluge of rain and mothball-size hail down onto Wall Street amid the boom of thunder and crackle of lightning. Jay sprinted the last hundred yards to the McCarthy & Lloyd entrance, holding a copy of the *Wall Street Journal* over his head against the torrent, dodging umbrellas as he ran. He burst through the firm's front door, nearly knocking over Paul Lopez on his way home after the graveyard shift.

"Sorry, Paulie." Jay dropped the soggy paper in a trash can. "Looks like you had a tough night," he said, noting Paul's sour expression.

"It wasn't too bad," Paul replied tersely, "until about fifteen minutes ago."

"What do you mean?"

"I got a call from Carter Bullock as I was about to leave. Literally as I was getting up from my chair to go home."

"Oh?"

"Yeah. Seems he was in a conference room doing some work when you and I saw each other last night on the trading floor. When he came back to his desk, he found somebody going through the drawer I put the money transfer advice in." Lopez pointed a finger at Jay. "That somebody was you."

"I needed his calculator, Paulie," Jay explained calmly. "I told him that."

"I don't care what the hell you needed or what you told him. Your going through his desk got me in a lot of trouble. I know I locked the drawer before I left the desk, and you told him it was open."

"I'm sorry." Jay's face lighted up. "How about if I get you some box seats for a Yankee game? Would that make you feel better?"

Paul shrugged. "Maybe."

"Good. I'll arrange it." Jay darted past Paul and into an elevator just as the doors were closing. When it stopped at the trading floor, he walked briskly to the arbitrage desk. It was only seven-thirty, but everyone else had arrived.

"Good afternoon," Bullock said sarcastically as Jay put his briefcase down.

"Hello."

Sally smiled at Jay from the other side of the bulkhead, but Oliver didn't acknowledge him. The head of the arbitrage desk sat in his chair, slumped down, staring at his computer screen from beneath his dark eyebrows, hands clasped tightly in front of his mouth.

"Morning, Oliver," Jay called.

Still Oliver said nothing.

"You and the boss are getting along really well these days," Bullock observed dryly. "That should help you at bonus time."

Jay started to say something, then spotted Ted Mitchell ambling across the trading room floor toward the arbitrage desk. Mitchell brokered stocks for high-net-worth individuals.

"Hello, everyone," Mitchell said pleasantly, stopping between Oliver and Sally. "Oliver, I thought you might want to hear about a couple of rumors our desk has picked up so far this morning."

"What rumors?" Bullock asked when it became apparent that Oliver wasn't going to respond.

"The Street is talking about a leveraged-buyout group on the West Coast that's about to announce a huge takeover bid for Bell Chemical," Mitchell answered. "A bid that will be well above yesterday's closing stock price. At least that's the early word."

Mitchell blurred in front of Jay as the words "Bell Chemical" buzzed in Jay's ears like a swarm of angry hornets.

"And the other rumor concerns some company in the Midwest," Mitchell continued. "I think the name is Simons. I've never heard of it before."

Jay felt his mouth go dry. He stood up slowly and gazed over the bulkhead at Oliver, who was still staring blankly at his computer screen.

"Let's check this out," Bullock suggested, tapping commands onto his keyboard and pulling up company news on Bell Chemical. "Yup, it says right here that trading of Bell shares will be delayed at the nine-thirty opening of the New York Stock Exchange pending an announcement by the company," Bullock read. "There's a huge imbalance in orders for its shares." Bullock slammed the desktop happily. "The reason for the imbalance has got to be a takeover announcement."

"Are you guys long on Bell shares?" Mitchell asked.

"Sure as hell are!" Bullock shouted. "Shares of Simons, too. We own a large block of each company, thanks to this guy," he said, pointing at Jay. He was giddy, like a young boy on Christmas morning who'd just been given the pony he'd been begging for all year. "Our new guy, Jay West, seems to have the Midas touch."

Mitchell smiled at Jay. "That's incredible, picking two takeovers like that. Congratulations. Bill McCarthy will be a happy man."

"Thanks," Jay muttered, not taking his eyes from Oliver, who still hadn't moved.

Mitchell nudged Oliver's chair. "This ought to be a nice ride, Ollie. You haven't had a couple of big hits like this in a while. Not since the spring, right?"

Jay's eyes flashed to Mitchell's. It was the first he'd heard of any slump on the arbitrage desk.

"That's right," Bullock agreed. "I guess Jay was exactly what we needed." He slapped Jay on the back. "Way to go, pal. I know Oliver and I weren't very supportive when you went out and bought those shares on your own, but you certainly proved us wrong."

Mitchell smiled at Jay. "Let me be the first one to shake your hand," he said, leaning over the bulkhead.

But Jay wasn't listening. He was watching Oliver, who had risen from his seat and was walking slowly toward the elevator.

Bullock nodded at Sally, who scrambled from her seat and raced after Oliver.

"What the hell is wrong with everybody around here?" Mitchell asked, pulling his hand back and giving Jay an irritated look. He glanced at Bullock, then grunted an obscenity and walked away.

"You bastard, Bullock," Jay whispered. "Why the hell did you tell Mitchell that I went out and purchased the shares on my own? You know that's not true."

"I wanted you to get some much-needed credit," Bullock answered. "If McCarthy hears that the stock purchases were your idea, it'll be good for you."

"You don't care whether I get any credit," Jay snapped. "You and Oliver—"

"Hey!" Sally was back. Her face was ashen. "Oliver got on the elevator and pushed the button for the top floor." She was speaking in a harsh whisper. "He wouldn't respond to me. Something's wrong."

Bullock rose from his seat and ran for the elevators, Jay and Sally right behind him.

"What could be the matter with him?" Sally asked as the elevator doors closed and the car began to climb. She, Bullock, and Jay were the only occupants. "He was like a zombie."

"He's got pressures at home," Bullock answered, watching the numbers light up over the doors, banging his fist against the wood paneling of the car. "I think he's on some kind of medication, too. He'll be all right. He probably won't even be up here."

Jay studied Bullock's face. For the first time since Jay had known him, Bullock seemed unnerved.

The elevator doors opened onto the fifty-seventh floor of the building, the reception area of a law firm. The name of the firm hung in bold black letters on the mahogany wall behind the receptionist, who gave them a quizzical look as they spilled out of the car and headed toward a sign pointing to the stairs.

At the top of the steps they burst through a metal door onto the roof. The wind howled as Jay put a hand above his eyes to shield them from the lashing rain and scanned the roof for any sign of Oliver.

"There!" Sally yelled.

Jay followed Sally's gesture and saw Oliver sitting on the wall running around the perimeter of the building. Instinctively Jay sprinted toward him.

Oliver sat facing them, his back to the sickening drop on the other side. He was rocking back and forth, his feet not touching the roof, ankles crossed. "Hello, everyone," he said loudly, a strange smile on his rain-streaked face. The smile faded as they came nearer, and his eyes flicked rapidly several times from side to side. "Don't come any closer!" he warned.

"Stay away from him, Bullock," Jay yelled. Bullock was ignoring Oliver's pleas, heading right for him. "Christ, you'll make him jump."

"I know what I'm doing," Bullock snarled, hesitating for a moment, then moving forward again more slowly this time.

As Bullock inched forward Oliver stood up, legs spread wide and hands out, his body soaked and shaking, the wind tearing at his clothes.

"Carter, stop," Sally begged, hands over her mouth.

"If he looks down, he might lose it!" Jay yelled. "He may not even know where he is right now."

"He knows," Bullock hissed, edging closer, now only a few feet from Oliver.

Jay followed, just behind Bullock.

"Don't take another step," Oliver yelled. "Please, Carter. Leave me alone. Don't do this to me."

"I'm saving you, Oliver," Bullock answered through gritted teeth. "You know this is for the best."

"Don't do this to me! Please!" Oliver raised his arms and spread them wide, then leaned back and gazed straight up at the black sky.

"Bullock, he's going to go over!" Jay shouted. "Stay back!"

But Bullock lunged forward, wrapping his arms around Oliver's legs. Oliver's arms flailed as he lost his balance and began to fall backward.

As Bullock let go of Oliver's legs, Jay clamped down on

Oliver's forearm, breaking his backward momentum. For a second they were perfectly balanced, Oliver's body out over the edge with nothing between himself and Wall Street, Jay braced against the wall, and Bullock kneeling below them.

Then Jay felt a tremendous weight against his shins and searing pain, and for a moment he lost his grip as Oliver's wet shirt shredded in his fingers. But he lunged and grabbed Oliver once more, hauling him back toward the roof, not letting go until he lay on top of Jay on the roof in a drenched heap. For a moment they stared into each other's eyes.

"I can't hold on much longer," Oliver whispered.

Before Jay could say anything, Bullock was pulling Oliver up and escorting him toward the door, his arm around Oliver's shoulder.

"Are you all right?" Sally knelt beside Jay as he rose on one elbow.

"Yeah," he groaned, his right knee throbbing.

"You saved Oliver's life." Her eyes were wide open and she was breathing hard. Rain and wind were whipping through her hair. "God, I thought you were both going over. You could have been killed." She threw her arms around him and held him tightly.

"It was a reflex, and probably a stupid one," Jay said. "I didn't even think about it. If I had, I might not have done it." He glanced up into her face and saw her terror. "It's over, Sally. I'm fine."

She nodded. "I know."

"What is it, then?" She was staring off into the distance, her mouth wide open. There was something else. "Talk to me."

She looked down at him and ran her fingers through his dripping hair. "Did you feel anything against your legs when you were holding on to Oliver?"

Jay thought back to those seconds, suddenly aware of a throbbing in his knee. "Yes, I think so, but I'm not certain what it was. It must have been the wall as I braced myself against it."

"It was Bullock," she whispered.

"What?"

"He was trying to make it to his feet—to help, I thought—but then he fell, or maybe he slipped. The roof was wet, but . . ." Sally looked away.

"But what?"

She hesitated, not certain she wanted to continue. "It looked as though he fell against your legs on purpose. Almost as if . . ."

But her voice faltered, or her words were swallowed up by a roll of thunder. When the rumble faded, they rose slowly and headed toward the door leading back into the building. Jay was never exactly certain which had occurred—whether Sally had held back or the thunder had drowned out her words—but it didn't matter. He knew what she was trying to say.

■ ■ ■

The young woman tucked the bedspread tightly beneath the pillows, chopping at the crease with the back of her hand. When she finished, she checked the room once more, nodded to herself, and headed toward the door. It was ready for another customer. She sighed as she pulled the door shut. The next day she would clean the same room the same way.

"Hello."

The maid shrieked softly, startled by the tall stranger standing before her in the hallway. He looked disheveled, as if he'd been caught outside in the morning storm that had buffeted the city. She clutched her chest, her heart pounding.

"I'm sorry if I surprised you," Jay apologized.

"It's okay," she answered nervously, placing two used towels down on the cart beside her. "You caught me a little off guard. That's all."

Jay checked the hallway. They were alone. "I need to ask you a couple of questions. It won't take long, I promise."

"Look, I've got a lot of rooms to—"

Jay pulled a twenty-dollar bill from his shirt pocket and held it out.

The young woman shook her head. "I'm not that kind of girl, mister. And if the Plaza management ever heard that I did something like that, I'd be fired. I need this job."

"What?" For a moment Jay didn't comprehend, and then suddenly he understood. "Oh, Jesus, no. I don't want you to come to a room with me. I really do want to ask you a few questions."

"Now it's a *few* questions." She grabbed for the twenty, but Jay pulled it away before she could snatch it. "Before it was a couple."

"You don't get the money until I get answers."

"Okay, but hurry," she said, irritated at the imposition. "My boss could show up any second."

"One of the other maids said you were working this floor of the hotel Tuesday a week ago," Jay said quickly, pointing over his shoulder at the suite behind him. One of the secretaries on the arbitrage desk was aware that McCarthy & Lloyd had been renting it for years and had told Jay when he asked. "Is that right?"

"I came in at four and left at midnight. So what?"

Jay removed two photographs from his suit pocket. The first was of Abby, a picture Abby's father had given him at the end of their walk the night before. "Do you recognize this woman?"

The maid took a quick glance at the picture. "Yes, I saw her going into that suite a couple of times over the past few months."

Jay showed her the second photograph. "Take a look at this one," he ordered. It was the picture of Oliver sitting between

Sally and Jay on the sailboat. "Do you recognize anyone in this photograph?"

The young maid snatched the picture from Jay and scanned it briefly. "Yeah, you." She shoved it back at him.

"A longer look," he directed.

She looked at it again. "Him." She pointed at Oliver. "He was with the woman in the last picture." She gestured at the suite door again. "I nearly ran into him getting on the elevator as I was getting off it last Tuesday evening around nine o'clock, but that was down in the lobby." She started to hand the picture back to Jay, then stopped. "He was with her."

Jay gazed at the photograph. The young maid was pointing at Sally.

CHAPTER 17

"Hey, pal!" Oliver shouted across the trading room.

Jay checked his wristwatch. It was only six-thirty in the morning. What the hell was Oliver doing there? Usually he didn't arrive until seven at the earliest.

"What an incredible morning," Oliver exclaimed, laying his briefcase on the desk. "It's still hot as Hades out there. I thought the cold front that went through here yesterday morning and brought us all those storms might have cooled things down. But it didn't." He was talking quickly and confidently, as if the events of the previous morning had never happened. "In fact, I think it's hotter this morning than it's been all summer." He sniffed several times in rapid succession. "And we aren't even into August yet." He tossed his jacket over the bulkhead. "But it's still damn good to be alive, Jay."

Jay gazed at Oliver from his seat on the other side of the bulkhead. The man had to be in complete and utter denial of the incident on the roof. The self-preservation sector of his steel-trap mind must have kicked in and convinced the rest of him that his close call had been nothing but a terrible nightmare, Jay thought. That was the only explanation. Less than twenty-four hours earlier the man had been standing at the edge of an abyss, literally—staring down from a precipice into a valley of certain death. And here he was acting as if he hadn't a care in the world. Acting as if nothing had happened.

"I'm going to get a cup of coffee," Oliver announced. "Want some?"

"No."

"Okay, pal." Oliver turned to go, then paused. "For a guy who's the talk of the trading floor after picking two takeover stocks in one day, you certainly aren't very cheerful." He leaned over the bulkhead and lowered his voice even though there was no one else within earshot. "By the way, if you want to thank me for the information on Bell Chemical and Simons at some point, don't bother, just throw cash. As I've always said, Jay, cash is king." He put his head back and laughed obnoxiously. "By the way, I didn't see TurboTec on the takeover wire yesterday."

"What's your point, Oliver?"

"Nothing," he said smugly, cocaine drenching his nasal cavities. He had snorted several huge lines in the back of his limousine on the way into Manhattan. "See you in a minute." He turned and headed off toward the coffee machine.

Jay watched Oliver make his way through the floor, stopping to slap early arrivals on the back and make small talk. *A complicated son of a bitch,* Jay thought, *in a complicated situation.* He only wished he knew more about that situation. Perhaps Oliver's breakdown the day before had to do with his marital problems, or what was happening on the desk—whatever that was. Or maybe all those forces and others Jay wasn't even aware of had come together that morning and caused the emotional implosion he had witnessed Oliver endure. Whatever it was, Oliver had to be hanging on by one very thin thread.

Jay began printing out the research material he needed for his trip—the only reason he had even bothered to come in at all that morning before heading to La Guardia Airport. When the printer finished, he placed the information in his briefcase, tucked the briefcase in his travel bag, and zipped the bag shut. He stood up and picked up the bag.

"Where are you going?" Bullock was moving across the floor to the desk.

"Nashua, New Hampshire," Jay answered, cursing silently. Bullock was the last person he wanted to see.

"What the hell is in New Hampshire?" Bullock glanced down at Jay's bag.

"TurboTec."

"Why do you need to go all the way up to New Hampshire? Why don't you just speak to someone at the company by phone?"

"I'm meeting tomorrow with a friend of mine from college who works for the firm. I think the meeting could provide some very helpful insights. And he wants to see me in person."

"Does Oliver know you're going?"

"No." Jay took a step toward the elevators. "I thought I was free to do whatever field research I needed to do."

"I think we better talk to Oliver first." Bullock moved in front of Jay, blocking his path.

"Why?"

Bullock smiled. "He's the boss. I care about what he thinks."

Jay shook his head. "You don't give a damn about what Oliver thinks. In fact, you don't give a damn about Oliver, period."

"What do you mean by that?" Bullock dropped his briefcase and stepped toward Jay.

"Exactly what you think I mean," Jay replied calmly, standing his ground as Bullock moved closer.

"Spell it out for me," Bullock challenged.

"Let me put it this way. If Oliver had slipped through my fingers yesterday and splattered all over Wall Street, something tells me you wouldn't have gone into mourning."

"You better reconsider that statement." Bullock's face suddenly flushed a brilliant red. "Oliver's one of my best friends. I would never want anything to happen to him."

Jay dropped his traveling bag. "Then why did you fall against my legs while I was holding on to him?"

"You stupid—" Bullock didn't finish. His temper overpowered him and he took a swing at Jay.

Jay blocked Bullock's punch and countered with a quick left to the stomach. As Bullock recoiled from the impact, doubling over and gasping for breath, Jay struck again with a compact right to Bullock's chin, splitting his lower lip wide open. Bullock fell to the floor, clutching his stomach with one hand and his bleeding lip with the other. "Have a nice day," Jay hissed, glancing around. Several of the traders were standing and staring at Bullock, who was moaning on the floor. Out of the corner of his eye Jay noticed Oliver emerging from the coffee room. He grabbed his bag and headed for the elevators.

When the doors had shut, Jay checked his knuckles. Blood was seeping from one, but he could move it. It wasn't broken. He licked the blood away and laughed, a nervous release after the confrontation. He had felt an incredible tension between himself and Bullock since the interview at McCarthy & Lloyd over a month before, as if Bullock had been wanting this physical exchange ever since they had met. But Bullock had gotten more than he bargained for, Jay thought. He was probably still doubled over on the trading room floor or leaning over a bathroom sink trying to stop the bleeding.

There would be a price to the exchange for himself as well, Jay realized. When he returned from New England, the seat on the arbitrage desk would no longer be his. He was certain of that. Bullock had taken the first swing, but Oliver would stick up for his friend. If Oliver only knew what Bullock had tried to do the previous day on the roof . . . Jay shook his head, suddenly uncertain. Or maybe Bullock hadn't. Perhaps Bullock had just slipped. But Sally had seen Bullock's action and confirmed his intent.

Of course, where were her loyalties in all of this? She had been with Oliver immediately after he had left Abby in the Plaza Hotel room. Now Abby was dead.

The hell with it, Jay thought. *The hell with Oliver, Bullock, McCarthy and Lloyd, Sally, and the million-dollar bonus. The hell with everything.* He was going on this trip, and when he got back, he'd deal with the situation the best he could. If there was no longer a job for him at McCarthy & Lloyd, so be it. He'd had enough of the damn place.

The elevator doors slid open, and Sally stood in front of him.

"Where are you going?" she asked, looking at the bag.

"On a business trip," he snapped, brushing past her into the lobby, moving against the tide as people streamed into the building.

"I called you several times last night." She trotted beside him, dodging people. "Why didn't you call me back? I was worried about you."

"Sorry. I was out." That wasn't true. He'd been at home all evening, paying bills and working at his computer. It was then he had realized that one of his disks was missing—a disk that stored a record of all personal checks and cash withdrawals he had written or made in the previous year. It was not something he would have noticed was missing, except that he still couldn't shake the nagging feeling that Sally had rifled through his boxes of disks. So he'd gone through them carefully. He couldn't prove she had taken the missing disk, but no one else had been in the apartment in three months.

Sally had called three times after he discovered that the disk was gone, and he'd listened to her voice carefully. Her tone seemed to grow more urgent with each message.

"Tell me where you're going," she insisted, grabbing his arm.

"Nashua, New Hampshire. TurboTec. The company I pitched to Bill McCarthy at the yacht club." Jay paused at the front door. "Goodbye." Then he was gone.

Sally started to move through the door to go after Jay, but she stopped. It wasn't worth it. He wasn't going to tell her anything else of importance, and she had what she needed. She watched him hail a cab, throw the bag inside, and pile in. When the taxi was out of view, she grabbed a cell phone from her bag and began dialing frantically.

■ ■ ■

Victor Savoy sat on a park bench beneath a grove of elm trees munching contentedly on a pastrami and rye sandwich, watching the lower Manhattan lunch crowd flash past. He loved pastrami but ate it only when he was in New York City because there was a particular deli on Williams Street called Ray's that served a sandwich that literally melted in his mouth. Ordering pastrami from any other place in the world had always turned out to be a bitter disappointment. Savoy savored the last bite of the sandwich, then crumpled its wrapper and glanced to his left.

City Hall was fifty yards away. It was a three-story structure built of smooth white stone with eleven steps leading down from a portico to a small open area where the mayor occasionally welcomed visiting dignitaries or gave away keys to the city. In front of the open area was the candy end of a lollipop-shaped driveway crowded with blue Town Cars constantly dropping off or picking up city officials.

Savoy rose from the bench and began to walk. City Hall was located a half mile north of Wall Street, facing the small park Savoy was now ambling through. Broadway ran past City Hall's west side, and another street ran diagonally left to right until it reached Broadway, creating a triangle in front of the building inside of which was the park. On the outside of the triangle skyscrapers towered over the cozy swath of grass and trees, creating an amphitheater effect with City Hall on the stage.

Savoy stood at the edge of the driveway, noting that there were several uniformed New York City policemen milling around, casually checking him out every few moments. When none of them was looking at him, he walked quickly out from the shade of the elm trees past two concrete barriers and moved across the driveway. As he reached the open area in front of the steps leading up to the portico, he stopped and turned. The Woolworth Building soared sixty floors skyward on his right, while shorter buildings encircled the rest of the park several hundred yards away.

He leaned back and examined the Woolworth Building. Someone in an office near the top of the neo-Gothic structure would have a perfect view of the open area where he now stood, one unobstructed by trees. Views from most of the other buildings around the perimeter would be at least partially blocked. The problem with the Woolworth Building, and most of the other buildings encircling the park for that matter, was that the Secret Service, the FBI, and British intelligence would have snipers and lookouts posted everywhere. A rifleman at the top of the Woolworth Building would be discovered quickly, as officials would be constantly scanning the area with high-powered binoculars. He'd have to come up with something else.

Savoy turned left, due south, and suddenly saw the opportunity. Almost a half mile from where he stood, a tiny piece of One Chase Manhattan Plaza was visible. Its dark outer structure protruded from behind a closer building rising up around the park's perimeter. Only a tiny strip of the huge building that served as headquarters for one of the world's largest banks was visible, but that would be enough. A person in one of those offices would have an unobstructed view of the dais, which on the critical day would be positioned exactly where he was now standing. And oddly, the treetops in the park parted in Red Sea fashion between the Chase Building and this spot. The sniper would stare right down a natural funnel into the open area. It would be a long shot, perhaps eight hundred yards, but Savoy had witnessed firsthand the proficiency of his hired guns. They would have no problem hitting the target.

One of the policemen moved quickly toward Savoy. "Hey, what are you doing?"

"Admiring the view." Savoy was wearing another disguise and wasn't worried about the officer thinking back to this day at some later date and remembering him. He might remember the conversation, but not the face. Not a face that mattered.

"Well, this area is off-limits to the public. Move along," he ordered.

"Yes, sir," Savoy said politely. There was no need for confrontation. If the officer got a bug up his ass, he'd find several different passports in Savoy's pockets as well as plane tickets under the aliases. EZ Travel could get him anywhere in the world he wanted to go under any name he gave them.

A half hour later Savoy had talked himself onto the fifty-fourth floor of the Chase Building. He wanted to make certain that the view from the building down to City Hall was as good as the view from City Hall up to the building. It seemed logical that if the view was good from one direction, it ought to be good from the other as well. However, that wasn't always the case.

The fifty-fourth floor was empty because the law firm that had rented the space from the bank had recently moved. From high above lower Manhattan, Savoy gazed down from the vacant northwest corner office at the open area in front of City Hall. He could clearly see officials hopping in and out of cars and the black Explorer parked in the driveway. Bingo. As soon as he could get to a secure phone, he'd call the people in Virginia and tell them to abandon the farm and make the move to New York City.

Savoy thanked the janitor who had graciously allowed him entry to the deserted floor in return for fifty dollars, and headed toward the elevators. He had to fly to Antwerp to meet the freighter that was now steaming its way up the west coast of Africa.

CHAPTER 18

Jay stood on the porch of a large Victorian home overlooking the Atlantic Ocean. A few hours earlier he had landed at Boston's Logan Airport after leaving Sally at McCarthy & Lloyd's front entrance and grabbing the cab to La Guardia. Upon landing at Logan, he'd rented a car and driven an hour and a half northeast of Boston to the end of Cape Ann and the tiny fishing village of Gloucester. He'd eaten a crab-cake lunch at a small seafood place on the docks, and learned from his waiter where the Lanes had lived. They had been well known in town, and the waiter confirmed that they had died in a plane crash a year ago and that their only child, Sally, was living on the West Coast. The last he had heard, there were no longer any Lanes living in Gloucester.

Jay glanced over his shoulder at the rental car. He had told everyone on the arbitrage desk that he was visiting his friend at TurboTec, but he had no intention of going to New Hampshire.

He was going to spend the next two days searching for answers about whatever the hell was going on. His eyes narrowed as he gazed at the lush gardens lining each side of the driveway. Since landing at Logan he'd been fighting the prickly sensation that he was being watched.

Before leaving McCarthy & Lloyd that morning, Jay had gone on-line and reviewed several articles from back copies of the *Boston Globe.* He had printed out Joe and Patsy Lane's obituaries as well as an account of the airplane crash and their double funeral. The funeral article reported that a man named Franklin Kerr had delivered a stirring eulogy for Sally's father at the service. And Kerr's wife, Edith, had done the same for Sally's mother. The article had described the Lanes and Kerrs as lifelong friends and neighbors. Jay stared at the door. This seemed the best place to start looking for answers.

He rapped on the Kerrs' door with his left hand—the knuckles of his right still throbbed from the impact with Bullock's chin. Moments later he heard footsteps and the door swung open.

"Can I help you?" The elderly woman wore a sleeveless white blouse, green slacks, and a wide-brimmed sunbonnet. A yellow ribbon hung down from the side of the brim onto her gray hair.

Jay noticed that her head and age-spotted hands shook constantly, a sure sign of Parkinson's disease. "Mrs. Kerr?"

"Yes, I'm Edith Kerr."

"My name is Jay West. I was a classmate of Sally Lane's at Harvard Business School." He hoped Edith wasn't too familiar with Harvard, because he'd never been there and wouldn't be able to answer even the most basic questions about the grounds.

Edith smiled and stepped forward, opening the door wider and extending her hand. "How do you do?"

"Fine, thanks." Jay took her hand, fighting the pain as she squeezed his fingers.

"Do you live in Gloucester now?" Edith asked. "You don't look familiar. Not that I get into town much these days."

"No. I was passing through Boston on business," Jay explained. "I've never been to Cape Ann, and I've heard Sally say many times how pretty it is. I thought I'd see for myself."

"What do you think?"

"Sally was right. It's beautiful." It was, too. The coastline was a picturesque mix of rocky cliffs and sandy beaches. Gorgeous old homes dotted the cliffs as well as the rugged, heavily wooded hills inland. The village was a collection of small, weather-beaten clapboard homes and churches centered around a south-facing harbor filled with fishing vessels hanging long black nets off tall booms.

"What can I do for you?" Edith asked.

Jay gestured to his left. Several hundred yards away was the Lanes' house. "Sally had given me her address here in Gloucester. I stopped by the house but no one was home. In fact, the house looks as if it isn't occupied." Jay smiled self-consciously. "I know it's a shot in the dark, because she probably doesn't live around here anymore, but I was hoping to see Sally. I've lost touch with her since Harvard, but we were kind of . . . well, I liked her very much. I thought I could at least say hello to her parents while I was out here, even if she isn't around. I had dinner with them on several occasions when Sally and I were in school. They were very nice."

Edith placed her hand on Jay's arm. "Why don't you come in?"

"Thanks." Jay followed Edith into a den off the main hallway and sat opposite the older woman in a large chair. "Have you lived in Gloucester long?" he asked.

"All my life. I grew up here. My husband, Frank, and I were Joe and Patsy's neighbors and close friends for almost forty years." She placed her hands on her lap and looked down. "Frank passed on a few months ago. Now I'm all alone."

"I'm sorry to hear that."

"My gardens keep me busy."

Jay paused. "You must have known Sally pretty well."

"Very well. I watched her grow up. Frank and I were her godparents." Edith stood up, walked to the fireplace, and picked up a silver frame from the mantel. She gazed at the picture for a moment, then moved to where Jay sat and handed the frame to him. "There's Sally."

Jay glanced at the photograph. Sally stood between an older couple. "With Joe and Patsy." It was only a guess that the other two people in the picture were her parents.

"Yes," Edith agreed quietly.

Jay studied the picture a little longer. Suddenly the images blurred before him. "I'd really like to see them again." His pulse was racing and he was doing his best to keep his voice steady. "Just to say hello, you know?"

"Sure," she said quietly.

"Is something wrong?" he asked. Edith's expression had turned somber.

She motioned toward the hallway. "Why don't we take a walk?"

"All right," he said slowly, handing her back the frame, which she replaced on the mantel.

Edith moved from the hearth into the hallway, and Jay got up to follow. But he hesitated at the den's doorway and glanced at the picture once more. He was almost certain that the young blond woman in the picture wasn't Sally Lane. A very close likeness, but not Sally. Not the one he knew from McCarthy & Lloyd.

Twenty minutes later Jay and Edith stood on a sandy beach, admiring a large stone home rising before them. Constructed on a rocky bluff at the end of a point overlooking the Atlantic, the Lane house wasn't as grandiose as Oliver and Barbara's mansion, but it was impressive, particularly because of the magnificent view it commanded.

Large swells rolled in continuously, pounding the rocks at the base of the bluff below the mansion. Jay felt cool drops from the spray, even from this spot a hundred feet away. With the hot sun beating down on him, the spray was refreshing.

He glanced to his right toward a line of old oak trees at the edge of the beach. He was almost certain the dark blue sedan had been tailing him all the way from Logan Airport. The sedan had exited the highway just before Gloucester, but Jay was sure he'd seen the same car pass several times in front of the restaurant where he'd eaten lunch. He squinted and held his hand up against the sun's bright rays. There was no one in the woods, not that he could see, anyway. He glanced back up at the house on the hill.

"It's beautiful, isn't it?" Edith commented.

"Yes," Jay agreed. "The Lane family is in the fishing business, correct?"

"They were," Edith confirmed. "Joe's great-grandfather started the business. Joe sold the company for a good deal of money two years ago."

They lapsed into silence, both staring up at the house.

"Was there something you wanted to tell me, Edith?"

"What do you mean?"

"I couldn't help but notice the strange tone in your voice every time you mention the Lanes." He nodded up at the house. "And I thought maybe you were going to take me to their house when we left your place, but I doubt we'd get over that fence from here." A ten-foot-high chain-link fence ran around the base of the bluff.

Edith clasped her hands together. "I should have told you before, but it's still so difficult."

"What is?"

"After Joe sold the business, he and Patsy moved to Florida."

"I see. I guess I won't get to—"

"They were killed in a plane crash a few months later."

"Oh, no," Jay whispered.

"Yes."

"My Lord, was Sally—"

"No, no," Edith interrupted. "She's fine. I believe she's working for a firm on the West Coast."

"Thank God."

A long pause ensued before Jay finally broke the silence. "Did Joe Lane own a red sports car?"

"A sports car?" she asked hesitantly.

"Yes, a British sports car called an Austin Healey." He knew the question sounded strange, but he wanted to confirm his suspicions.

Edith put her hand to her mouth, trying to remember. "I don't think so. Why do you ask?"

"I've always been interested in British sports cars, and Sally once told me that her father owned a Healey when she was young," Jay continued, trying to sound convincing. "But she said the salt air out here chewed it up pretty badly, and he had to sell it. I was wondering if the car was still in town, because I might want to buy it."

"The salt and the weather out here are rough on everything," Edith agreed. "But I don't remember Joe owning any British sports cars. He certainly could have bought one. He had enough money. But he wasn't really interested in cars. Any he bought were made in this country. He was a big believer in buying American."

Jay shrugged. "I must have been wrong. I must have been thinking of someone else." He reached into his shirt pocket and touched the Polaroid Barbara had taken on the sailboat. "Sally sure is a pretty girl, isn't she?"

"Beautiful. She always was, from the time she was little. You know how sometimes girls go through that awkward stage during adolescence? That never happened to Sally. She was beautiful all the way through."

Jay pulled out the Polaroid. "I still have this picture of her."

"Let me see." Edith moved closer so that her arm was touching his. She studied the photograph intently, then stepped back, a strange expression on her face.

"What's wrong?" he asked, watching her eyes narrow, as if she were taking a mental picture of him. He sensed that suddenly she wasn't certain she wanted to continue their conversation.

Edith pointed a shaking finger at the photograph. "That's not Sally," she said crustily.

"Are you certain?" he asked, his voice barely audible over the pounding surf.

The elderly woman checked the photograph once more, then nodded. "Yes. Oh, the woman in your picture looks a lot like Sally, almost the spitting image of her, but it isn't she."

"How can you be so certain?"

"For one thing, Sally had a scar on her chin. It was noticeable. Enough that you'd see it in this picture. It was her only imperfection. She tripped on the front walkway when she was thirteen and hit her chin. Split it wide open. Frank and I took her to the hospital because Joe and Patsy had gone out to run an errand. It was July, right about this time of year." She pointed to the picture once more. "The woman in your photograph doesn't have a scar."

Jay thought back to Saturday evening on the Brooklyn

Heights promenade. He'd touched Sally's chin as he stared at her, but he couldn't remember seeing a scar. "Maybe she had plastic surgery to fix it."

Edith shook her head. "No. Sally was deathly afraid of doctors. I had suggested plastic surgery once at the Christmas Eve party Joe and Patsy used to host every year. Sally wouldn't hear of it." Edith laughed. "I think she was a little irritated that I mentioned it. She was so afraid of doctors. And water," Edith added.

Jay's eyes flashed to Edith's. "Sally was afraid of water?" The Sally he knew had jumped off Oliver's boat in the middle of Long Island Sound.

"Deathly afraid," the elderly woman said. "She wouldn't go near it. She wouldn't even get on a boat. It's ironic when you think about where she grew up and what her family did."

Jay put the photograph back in his pocket and glanced out over the ocean. For the last week he had been trying to determine the name of the financial firm Sally had taken a job with on the West Coast after Harvard. He had tried to pry the name out of McCarthy & Lloyd's human resources department but had run into a stone wall there. Strangely, neither Oliver nor Bullock would tell him the name of the firm, and Harvard had been no help, either. When he first contacted the school, a clerk in the placement arca had promised to find the name of the firm, agreeing that it ought to be on record. However, the man had called back the next day to say that they had no record of the name of the firm, nor a forwarding address for Sally. Jay had ordered a yearbook and was going to try to contact classmates to see if any of them knew the name of the firm, but perhaps there was no need to follow that angle any longer. He already had his answer. The woman he had come to know was a fraud.

"What business did you say you were in again?" Edith asked.

"I didn't." Jay glanced away from the water and looked Edith straight in the eye. "The truth is that I work with the woman in the photograph I showed you. She claims to be Sally Lane, but I guess she isn't."

"Why would she claim to be Sally Lane if she isn't?"

Jay saw a flicker in the elderly woman's eyes, as if she had a great deal to say but wasn't certain she should. "I don't know, but I intend to find out."

They were silent for a few moments, then Edith bid Jay goodbye. "It was nice to meet you."

"Thanks."

"I hope you find answers to your questions," she said over her shoulder.

"Me too," Jay muttered. He'd had a nagging feeling that something was amiss ever since coming to McCarthy & Lloyd. An alarm had gone off the day before when Ted Mitchell had ambled across the trading room to announce that Bell Chemical was being taken over. Now it was screaming at him.

"It's funny," Edith said loudly over the sound of the waves. She had stopped twenty feet away.

"What is?" Jay asked, walking quickly toward her. "Please," he urged, still sensing her hesitance. "If you have something to say that you think might be important, I really wish you would."

"The people in town will say that I'm just an old gossip, but there was always something strange about Joe Lane. I hate to sound so catty about a man who was my best friend's husband, but it's true."

"What do you mean, strange?"

"Every once in a while people would come to the Lanes' house in the middle of the night." She pointed toward the bluff. "Not often, maybe a couple of times a year. They'd come after midnight and leave before dawn. And sometimes Joe took telephone calls in the middle of dinner parties he and Patsy were hosting. He'd leave the room and be gone for an hour while we finished."

"You could say it was rude of him to leave the party, but not strange," Jay observed. "As far as middle-of-the-night visits go, he was a businessman. It's difficult to say those kinds of visits are strange." He was challenging Edith because he wanted her to dig deeper.

She drew herself up. "My husband knew a man on the docks who claimed that the fishing vessels Joe Lane owned weren't always used for fishing. Most of the time they were, but not always." She nodded triumphantly, as if she'd proven her case.

"What else were they used for?"

"He didn't know, or wouldn't say, but—"

"Well, I don't think—"

"But"—her voice rose as she interrupted Jay—"he did say that occasionally the men on other boats saw Lane's vessels heading *away* from the fishing and lobstering grounds. He said that there were crew members on board Joe's boats that weren't from Gloucester. Men with soft hands and no dirt under their fingernails who dressed the part of a fishing boat crew but obviously hadn't done a lick of physical labor in their lives. He also said things were loaded on those boats in the middle of the night that didn't look much like fishing equipment. And sometimes the boats wouldn't return for weeks. Typically the boats are out for a day, or maybe a few days, but never weeks at a time."

"What do *you* think was going on?" Jay asked quietly.

"I don't know," she replied. "But I do know that every time I brought up the midnight visits or the rumors on the docks with Patsy, she got very quiet. One time she almost opened up to me. I felt as if she was going to tell me something important, then she backed off." Edith paused. "After that I never asked her about Joe's business again."

Jay glanced out to sea. When he looked back, Edith was walking toward the woods. He started to go after her, to press her for more, but then stopped. She had given him all he could ask for.

A few minutes later Jay slid behind the rental car's steering wheel. He was now certain that the Sally Lane he knew had never lived in the house on the bluff. But now there were more questions. Such as what Abby had meant when she told Oliver she knew about his friends. Who were the people she had claimed would take care of her in return for the information she could provide? Who had strangled her, and why?

Jay checked the rearview mirror and froze. A blue sedan was moving slowly past Edith's house—a sedan matching the one that had followed him from Boston to Gloucester and passed the restaurant where he'd eaten lunch at a booth by the window. For several moments he gazed into the mirror, intensely aware of the blood pounding in his ears. Edith's description of the activity on Joe Lane's fishing boats and the midnight visits had raised his suspicions to a new level. There wasn't any proof of anything, but the anecdotal evidence was piling up, causing him to question everything and everyone. He started the engine, put the car in gear, and headed down the driveway. He was about to put that anecdotal evidence to a test.

He guided the rental car onto the wide two-lane road that followed the coastline, turning left, away from Gloucester. There was no sign of the blue sedan. He picked up speed, then saw it parked in a driveway. As he sped by, he checked the rearview mirror. The blue sedan was coming after him.

At the bottom of a steep hill the road veered sharply right. Jay saw another, narrower road leading off into the dense forest, and he leaned on the brakes and wrenched the steering wheel to the right. The rental car fishtailed crazily, then the car skidded sideways. He lifted his foot off the brake for a moment; instantly the car straightened out, and he gunned the engine, flying over the narrow, twisting lane, constantly checking his rearview mirror, twigs and pebbles being kicked up behind him.

The road crossed a tiny raised bridge over a meandering creek, then dove back down again. The rental car went airborne, all four tires losing contact with the road, hurtling toward a ninety-degree left turn at the bottom of the short hill. Jay jammed the brake pedal to the floor out of reflex, but the car flew uncontrollably toward a massive oak tree. With just a hundred feet between Jay and the tree, the car regained contact with the pavement, bouncing crazily as it bottomed out. He twisted the wheel left and pumped the brakes, hypnotized by the huge tree trunk. He was so close he could see the scars on the bark where other drivers had hit it.

At the last moment the front end pulled left. The back right fender smacked the huge tree, partially ripping the bumper from the car and smashing the taillight. Jay careened left, bouncing away from the tree. He came to rest facing the way he had come. He punched the gas, steered the car to the right behind another large tree, came to a stop, and waited.

Seconds later another car roared over the bridge. At first Jay couldn't see it because of the tree he was hiding behind. But he didn't have to wait long. The blue sedan flashed in front of him, sideways, as he had been. But the driver of the sedan wasn't able to regain control of the vehicle. It skidded past Jay and slammed into the massive tree trunk with a sickening crash.

Jay gunned the rental car's engine and headed back up the hill the way he had come, the rear bumper of his car dragging along the road, barely connected to the car. At the top of the bridge he hesitated, but when he saw the driver of the sedan emerge slowly from the door, he took off. He'd call the police to report the accident when he made it to a pay phone that was well away from Gloucester.

CHAPTER 19

Bill McCarthy ran a hand through his hair as he sat at the kitchen table looking out a window of the small three-bedroom house. Dusk was falling on the middle-class neighborhood. "I need a damn haircut," he announced.

"You sure do." Kevin O'Shea sat on the opposite side of the table, sipping unsweetened iced tea. "You're starting to look like a hippie, like a sixties throwback or something."

"That'll be the day," McCarthy groused.

O'Shea chuckled. "All you'll need pretty soon is a pair of bell-bottom jeans and a tie-dyed T-shirt." The top button of O'Shea's shirt was unbuttoned, the knot of his tie was pulled down, and his dark red hair was tousled and frizzy. The humidity had reached 90 percent that afternoon and the temperature had soared to almost a hundred degrees. The small house they were using for the meeting didn't have air-conditioning. "What do you think about Bill's hippie look, Oliver?"

Oliver sat beside O'Shea, slumped in his chair.

"Did you hear me?" O'Shea nudged Oliver with an elbow.

Oliver grunted something unintelligible but refused to look up. His mood had darkened since that morning. The mental walls were closing in around him again, as they had the day before. Abby was dead, and he had an ominous feeling that the plan he was counting on to get him out of the insider-trading mess was developing cracks. Someone was out there putting chinks in his armor.

And his crutch was gone. His supply of cocaine had run dry.

"Why did we have to come all the way up here?" McCarthy asked gruffly, annoyed at the prospect of a long trip back to the city. "Christ, this shit-heel town must be fifty miles from Wall Street."

"Sixty," O'Shea answered sharply. "And it isn't a shit-heel town. It's a very nice town. My in-laws live here." McCarthy was turning out to be a real horse's ass, O'Shea thought. "We're here for security reasons." The three of them had been driven to the small town of Milton, New York, on the banks of the Hudson, in separate cars by professionally trained drivers who had made certain that no one was following. Federal law enforcement authorities maintained a network of homes in residential neighborhoods across the country for meetings like this one. "We've come too far to blow this thing at the eleventh hour because somebody happens to overhear something they shouldn't."

"Who the hell would overhear us?" McCarthy asked. "And what was up with all of that cloak-and-dagger driving around and doubling back we did on the way? Christ, I think I threw my back out because of one of those CIA-wheel-man turns my driver made."

"So sue me," O'Shea snapped. "I felt it was necessary, and what I say goes. I'm driving this bus." He picked up an apple from the table and took a huge bite. He was starving. He'd eaten nothing but rabbit food for the last few days. But it didn't seem as if the diet was having any effect on his waistline.

"Fine, but can we get on with this thing?" McCarthy complained. "I'd like to get back to the city. I'm flying down to New Orleans on Friday and I haven't even packed yet."

"Oh?" O'Shea's radar flipped on. "New Orleans?"

"Yeah, I need some R and R, so I'm going out to my place on the bayou."

O'Shea nodded. His initial thought had been that McCarthy ought to remain in New York, given what was about to happen. But now that he considered it, perhaps it would be better for McCarthy to be away from the action so that the public-relations people could handle damage control on their own, with no need for him to wade into unfamiliar waters. McCarthy had very little experience dealing with reporters, so maybe it was best for him to be away, at least initially. At some point he would have to face the music. O'Shea snickered. That was all McCarthy was going to have to do: face a few zingers from a couple of reporters. He knew McCarthy despised the press, but answering their questions for a few hours was a small price to pay for the sweet deal the government was offering. By all rights he ought to be taking a fall. Maybe in the end he would. "You'll leave a number, Bill," O'Shea ordered.

"No, I won't," McCarthy said petulantly. "If you need me, you can call my executive assistant at the firm. I don't want to be bothered when I'm down in Louisiana. It's my time to get away from everything. My time to completely relax. I'll take a cell phone with me, but Karen Walker will be the only one with the number for the place."

"Okay," O'Shea said slowly, rolling his eyes. If McCarthy wanted to be obstinate, the hell with him.

"Now tell me what this is all about," McCarthy demanded, his southern accent growing sharper.

O'Shea took a deep breath. "Next week I'm going to arrest Jay West on insider-trading charges," he explained. The room became pin-drop still except for the whirring of a small fan on top of the refrigerator. "In front of everyone."

"If you're lucky." It was the first thing Oliver hadn't mumbled since arriving.

"What's that supposed to mean?" O'Shea asked, picking at a seed lodged tightly between his top front teeth.

"Jay took a trip this morning."

"I know," O'Shea said. "He went to New Hampshire to see some company."

"TurboTec," Oliver specified. "But how did you know?"

"I've got my sources," O'Shea replied nonchalantly. "He'll spend the night and come back tomorrow or Friday. We aren't moving on him until next week. It's all right."

Oliver shook his head. "Jay never made it to New Hampshire. He told Sally he was going to see a guy named Jack Trainer who's in the marketing department at TurboTec, but according to Trainer, Jay never went there. I had my secretary call the guy. He had no idea what she was talking about. Jay had never even madc an appointment with him."

O'Shea pushed out his lower lip, acting as if he were deep in thought. He couldn't tell Oliver that he knew Jay had gone to Gloucester, because that revelation might push Oliver over the edge—Oliver knew about Sally's cover. He'd seen the coming-apart-at-the-seams signs in people before, and Oliver was definitely exhibiting them. "If Jay isn't back on Friday morning, we'll go looking for him. You know I can find him. I have the resources."

"But we wanted to arrest Jay at McCarthy and Lloyd to get

the biggest bang for our buck," McCarthy broke in anxiously, as if rain clouds were looming over his parade. "I thought you said someone from your office was going to give the media advance warning concerning the arrest so that the cameras could be outside the front doors waiting when you lead him away in chains. Then our public-relations people will talk about how we've been cooperating with your office, and your people will say that Jay's actions are an isolated incident. And McCarthy and Lloyd will be in the clear. That was the plan."

"It still is." O'Shea glanced at Oliver, who had lapsed into silence again and was hunched even further down in his chair. It was almost as if Oliver was regretting the fact that he had set up Jay, even though by doing so Oliver was saving himself. Perhaps Oliver didn't want to be saved, O'Shea pondered. He turned back to McCarthy. "But if we have to arrest Jay elsewhere, we will. We can't have him on the run."

McCarthy leaned back in his seat, pushing it up on two legs, balancing himself by placing one foot against the table leg. "I also thought that we were going to wait awhile after the Bell Chemical and Simons deals had been announced to arrest Jay. A couple of weeks, anyway." McCarthy rolled up his shirt sleeves. "Christ, the deals were only announced yesterday. Isn't it kind of quick to go after Jay next week? Won't people be suspicious?"

"No," O'Shea answered quickly. "We'll reveal that we received a tip from an unnamed source deep inside McCarthy and Lloyd. That's perfectly acceptable. These things happen that way all the time. When we arrest Jay next week at M and L, we'll already have been through his apartment, where we will have discovered the computer disk containing all kinds of incriminating evidence pertaining to Bell Chemical and Simons. Evidence proving that he planned the insider trades all along." O'Shea patted his shirt pocket, indicating that the disk was inside. "The disk we discover will be the same one we obtained from Jay's apartment, the one containing his entire personal financial file for last year. The disk will link him directly to insider trades. Of course, we will have put all the stuff about Bell Chemical and Simons on the disk, but Jay's lawyer won't know that for certain, and neither will the jury." O'Shea laughed. "By the way, Jay had kind of a rough year last year, and he doesn't have a net worth to speak of." O'Shea nudged Oliver. "But I guess you already knew that. You knew the smell of a million bucks would make him do anything."

Oliver said nothing, barely reacting to O'Shea's elbow.

"Is the disk in your pocket?" McCarthy asked incredulously.

"There are more copies of it," O'Shea assured McCarthy, anticipating his concern.

"But the original one has Jay's fingerprints on it."

"That's why I have it in an envelope and a plastic bag," O'Shea said. "In case you're worried."

McCarthy relaxed. That was exactly what he'd been worried about. They had gone to great lengths to acquire a damning piece of evidence that would link Jay directly to Bell and Simons when O'Shea had entered the planted evidence on it. "I still think it seems kind of soon to move on Jay."

"No," O'Shea said firmly. They had to move right away. He didn't want Jay doing any more digging. The kid had turned out to be one sharp customer, and sooner or later he'd figure out what was really going on. Unlike Oliver and McCarthy, who were too wrapped up in their own egomaniacal worlds to see the bigger picture. "We have plenty of evidence to make the case appear airtight. Individuals from my office who have no idea what's really going on will execute the search warrant. They'll be accompanied by officers from the New York Police Department. The disk will be planted in Jay's apartment minutes after he leaves for McCarthy and Lloyd one morning next week, and minutes before the authorities arrive. By the time Jay is arrested we will have in our possession records of the calls to Bell and Simons made from his home telephone." O'Shea smiled. "We've got him."

"Good." McCarthy was smiling, too.

"Yeah, great!" Oliver shouted. "The kid will spend twenty years in jail. He'll probably be raped in his cell a few times if we can get him sent someplace really nice. Aren't we just the smartest, greatest, most upstanding assholes in the world?" Oliver slammed his hand down on the table, almost spilling O'Shea's iced tea.

"Damn it!" O'Shea reached for his glass, snatching it just before it toppled over.

"What the hell's wrong with you, Oliver?" McCarthy roared.

"Nothing. Not a damn thing," Oliver replied curtly.

McCarthy took a deep breath and glanced furtively at O'Shea, then at Oliver. Now didn't seem like a great time to drop the bomb, but he had no choice. Andrew Gibson had called from Washington that morning to make certain McCarthy had followed through on the order. McCarthy glanced at O'Shea once more. The powers above O'Shea must have told him about the edict. "Oliver, there's something we need to discuss."

O'Shea took a sip of iced tea. "Do you want me to leave, Bill?"

"Yeah, give us a second."

Oliver looked up curiously, watching O'Shea walk into the living room.

McCarthy removed a handkerchief and wiped his forehead. He was perspiring profusely. He'd put this task off as long as he could, but the time was at hand.

"What is it?" Oliver asked, his voice weak. He saw McCarthy's discomfort. "Tell me."

McCarthy cleared his throat and drew circles on the Formica

tabletop with his fingertip. "Oliver, when all this is over—when Jay has been arrested, I mean—you are going to have to resign from McCarthy and Lloyd. Or I'll fire you."

"What?"

"It has to be that way."

"I don't understand." Oliver felt the room beginning to spin. His entire self-worth—what few shreds remained—was entirely wrapped up in his association with McCarthy & Lloyd. He was a god at the firm, and without the adulation of his coworkers he was nothing. He would be just another hack on Wall Street trying to make a living trading pieces of paper—assuming he could catch on with another firm, which, he realized, wasn't a sure thing. The other firms would know why he had been let go from McCarthy & Lloyd and wouldn't touch him. "Please don't do this to me, Bill," he begged.

"*I'm* not doing it to you, Oliver. You know that." McCarthy wiped his forehead again. "The order came down from the mountain, from way above O'Shea." McCarthy nodded toward the living room. "The people who have arranged this exit for you simply couldn't allow you to remain at McCarthy and Lloyd. It would have been too much of a kick in the teeth. They've been investigating you for a while, and only with my help have they agreed to what we have arranged. Otherwise you'd be in deep trouble."

"But I thought I was going to work on special projects for you, then restart the arbitrage desk in six months," Oliver protested, his eyes flicking around wildly.

"You were, but that isn't how it's going to play out. The people in charge felt your crimes were too great. There were just too many cases of insider trading." McCarthy took a labored breath and allowed shock to register on his face. "I couldn't believe it when O'Shea showed me the extent of what you've been doing. I mean, there are at least fifty incidents of blatant insider trading over the past five years. Incidents in which your desk bought shares or call options only days before the announcement of a takeover. It's obvious what was going on, and it stinks, Oliver." McCarthy shook his head sadly. "It's appalling."

Oliver gazed at McCarthy, hatred festering inside him like an infected sore. What was appalling was that McCarthy would attempt to paint himself as some innocent bystander in all of this. McCarthy had known all along what was happening on the arbitrage desk, and Oliver had the proof. But if he presented that proof to authorities, the head of McCarthy & Lloyd would execute a scorched-earth strategy and he'd lose his godfather. McCarthy would cut him loose like excess ballast in a storm and convince the authorities not to protect him anymore. It would be him alone against McCarthy and his influential friends in Washington, who didn't want to see McCarthy's political-contribution jet crash and burn because of something trivial like insider trading, which Oliver knew many people in Washington considered a victimless crime. Hell, they'd probably all engaged in it at one time or another. He'd lose the fight with McCarthy and end up in jail, while McCarthy would remain free. And he couldn't handle jail. He really would jump off a building before he would ever spend a night behind bars.

But Oliver couldn't resist one final jab. He was a fighter by nature, and a man who could not easily control his urges. "Bill, you've known all along what was happening on the arbitrage desk," he said tersely. "When I came to McCarthy and Lloyd five years ago from Morgan, that was the arrangement. You told me you wanted me to set the ring up. You instructed me to do it. You said that you had to raise money quickly, that your partners were pressuring you."

Color surged into McCarthy's fair cheeks. "God help me, I'll destroy you, Oliver. If you think things look bad now, just wait."

"Bill, we had an understanding!" Oliver yelled, ignoring McCarthy's warning. "You said you would protect me."

"Which is exactly what I'm doing," McCarthy hissed under his breath, glancing toward the living room fearfully. O'Shea was nowhere in sight, but the place was probably bugged. If Andrew Gibson heard about this, there could be hell to pay. There was always the chance that Gibson might recommend to the president that he wash his hands of the entire affair and find another large donor. "I'm going to give you a very nice severance package, Oliver. You'll be taken care of."

"I w-want to stay at McCarthy and Lloyd, Bill. I-I'm begging you," Oliver stammered.

"It can't happen."

"Bill . . ."

"You'll go to jail," McCarthy said through clenched teeth. "You'll rot in there, do you understand me? I'll see to it myself. And nothing will happen to me."

Oliver knew everything that McCarthy had said was true, and it made him furious. But there was nothing he could do about it. He just had to lie down and take it like some calf being hog-tied at a rodeo. He stared at McCarthy, his mind out of control. Perhaps there was another option. The conversation he and Tony Vogel had engaged in at the Plaza Hotel suite door flashed back to him. "What kind of financial settlement did you have in mind?" he asked quietly, doing his best to control his emotions. "Tell me the amount."

"Five million dollars."

"That's ridiculous!" Oliver pounded the table, furious again. "I got a five-million-dollar bonus for last year alone. Now you want to buy me out for good for that amount. I want more than five million."

"I don't care what you want!" McCarthy roared. "It isn't about what *you* want. Five million is what you're going to get, and there won't be any negotiating. Remember, you have our other arrangement."

"Which I may not be able to collect on for quite some time," Oliver pointed out.

"I certainly hope not," McCarthy muttered, making the sign of the cross over his chest.

"My partners aren't going to be happy about this," Oliver warned, noticing McCarthy's gesture. Once more he thought about Tony Vogel.

"Fuck them. They're in it up to their nose hairs. They'll have to wait for their shares just like you," McCarthy said defiantly. "And if they screw with me, they'll go to jail. You tell them that in no uncertain terms, Oliver. But be sure to tell them I'll come visit them every Sunday behind bars. Because I'm such a hell of a nice guy." A smug smile tugged at the corners of his mouth. "And I don't want to hear you crying poverty. Don't try to tell me that five million dollars isn't enough to support the lifestyle you've become accustomed to. You've got plenty of money." He paused. "Or should I say, Barbara and her father have plenty of money. They'll take good care of you."

Oliver seethed. He wanted to grab a bat and smash McCarthy's broad face in, smash it to a bloody pulp. For the first time in his life he wanted to kill. He put his hands beneath the table and made tight fists, squeezing his fingers until he thought they would break. Finally he unclenched them and sat back, barely able to hold himself together. "Fine," he said calmly, despite the storm raging within.

"Good." McCarthy stood up. That hadn't been so bad. "Next

week will be your last, Oliver. McCarthy and Lloyd will announce that you and Bullock are out, a few hours after they drag Jay out of the building in chains."

"Whatever."

McCarthy hesitated a moment, staring down at Oliver. The man had made him millions, hundreds of millions, but he felt no compassion. Oliver had simply been a pawn, and it was time to sacrifice the pawn to protect the king. He turned and walked into the living room. O'Shea sat on a couch reading the *Daily News.* "I'm ready to go," McCarthy announced.

O'Shea tossed the newspaper aside and stood up. "How did Oliver react?" He had learned that morning from his Washington contact that Oliver wasn't going to be allowed to remain at McCarthy & Lloyd after Jay was arrested. O'Shea had initiated the Washington call to request that they accelerate plans to detain Jay. The young man was getting too close.

McCarthy grinned. "I'm still alive."

Because unfortunately good things happen to bad people, O'Shea thought. "Your car is waiting outside."

McCarthy turned to go.

"Bill," O'Shea called.

"Yes?"

"Make certain you're back in New York City by the end of next week. Thursday at the latest. You'll have to talk to the press at that point."

"Yeah, fine." McCarthy headed out the door toward the waiting car.

O'Shea watched him through the window, then walked into the kitchen. Oliver was leaning forward, his chin resting on the tabletop. "Head up, Oliver. Everything will be all right."

Oliver rose up slowly and rubbed his eyes. "No, it won't," he replied softly. "I've been fired."

O'Shea moved to the chair next to Oliver's and sat down. "I know."

"Of course you do," he said forlornly. "I'm the only one in the dark. Just a puppet on a string."

"It could be worse."

"Please tell me how."

"You could be going to jail."

Oliver felt his breath becoming short. He was fighting the urge to let go. Abby's face kept flashing through his mind. It was crazy, but all he could keep thinking was that they should have been together. He put his face in his hands. He needed that white powder so badly.

O'Shea saw Oliver's eyes glaze over, and looked away. Even though he had come to detest McCarthy because of his callous disregard for anyone's feelings but his own, he had also come to like Oliver. Not that Oliver was a saint; far from it. Oliver was an egomaniac like McCarthy and had committed despicable acts over the past few years, just as McCarthy had. But somewhere deep beneath Oliver's flashy exterior and cavalier attitude was a vulnerable man who had been caught up in a bad set of circumstances. A man who desperately wanted to be good, but didn't have the strength to fight off the evil influences and temptations constantly swirling around him.

And there was regret in Oliver. Regret for setting up Jay West, and regret for what had happened to Abby. O'Shea had learned to spot that emotion during his years with the U.S. attorney's office, and he could see it now in Oliver's expression. McCarthy, on the other hand, harbored no regret at all.

O'Shea stared out the kitchen window. The detectives investigating Abby Cooper's death wanted to talk to Oliver, but because of what was going on at McCarthy & Lloyd, that conversation had been delayed. The coroner had found semen inside

Abby's corpse and the detectives were certain it was Oliver's, as was O'Shea. He had known about the affair long ago, well before the detectives had dug up a maid at the Plaza Hotel who had seen Oliver and Abby enter the suite together several times, including one night the past week—the last night anyone had seen Abby Cooper alive. Abby had probably pressed Oliver to leave his wife that evening—they had located and read several of her discarded love letters to Oliver. He had refused Abby's demand, and in a fit of rage she had threatened to call his wife and reveal everything. Then she had suddenly disappeared until the police had found her strangled body in the Bronx Dumpster.

Oliver had motive and opportunity, and he was already the prime suspect. The detectives were certain they had their man even though the labs hadn't performed any scientific tests to prove the semen was Oliver's because they couldn't interrogate him and obtain a sample. They were champing at the bit to get at him.

"What will happen to my partners?" Oliver asked, desperation in his eyes. "The four men who have provided me tips on takeovers for the past five years."

"I'll call each of them down to Federal Plaza in lower Manhattan, one at a time of course, and give them the come-home-to-Jesus speech."

"What the hell is that?"

"I'll sit them down in my office, making certain the handcuffs are obvious on my desk, and lay out everything I know about the dark side of their lives. I'll spend a full thirty minutes describing in detail the insider-trading case I have against them. Then I'll pick up the handcuffs, play with them for a few seconds, and continue. I'll detail things I know about their personal lives. I'll tell them about women I know they've cheated on their wives with, taxes they haven't paid, and so on. All the usual stuff. When

I'm sure I see the fear of God *and* the devil in their eyes, I'll tell them that today is the luckiest day of their lives. For reasons they don't need to understand, the government won't prosecute as long as they keep their mouths shut." O'Shea smiled. "It's at that point that people generally fall down on my office floor and praise Jesus, no matter their religious denomination." He studied Oliver's puzzled expression. "What's wrong?"

Oliver shook his head. "I don't understand why the government would make that deal. It's a ring that involves some very prominent brokerage houses. It would be a coup for your office. Has McCarthy really given so much money that he's untouchable?"

"Yes. And he's pledged to give a lot more."

"So it comes down to cash."

"It always does. You know that." O'Shea checked his watch. "Listen, I've got to get back to the city."

"Kevin."

O'Shea looked up. He had heard the hopelessness in Oliver's voice.

"Have you learned any more about the investigation into Abby Cooper's murder?" Oliver's voice cracked.

O'Shea hesitated. There was nothing he could say. "No."

Oliver nodded and stood up. "Okay, I'll get going."

O'Shea escorted Oliver to the front door, whispered a word of encouragement in his ear, then watched him disappear into the gathering gloom.

CHAPTER 20

"This is the TurboTec Corporation. May I help you?"

"Jack Trainer, please." Jay checked the gas station parking lot for anything suspicious as he spoke into the pay phone to the TurboTec receptionist. He had his cell phone, but he didn't want to turn it on. He knew that if he did, the phone company could track him down.

"One moment."

"Thanks." Since the wild ride through the Gloucester forest the previous day, Jay had become infinitely more careful, almost to the point of paranoia. He had stayed at the Boston Hyatt the night before under an assumed name. And he was making this contact with a calling card he had purchased with cash.

"Hello."

Jay recognized Trainer's voice. "Jack, it's Jay West."

"Where the hell are you?" Trainer wanted to know.

"Los Angeles," Jay lied, in case the line at TurboTec was

tapped. "Hey, did you get any calls for me yesterday or today?" He had heard irritation in Trainer's tone and was almost certain of the answer.

"You bet I did. Two yesterday and ten more today," Trainer replied angrily. "People are jumping down my throat demanding to know where you are. They said you were supposed to be meeting with me yesterday or today. What the hell is going on, Jay?"

Before Jay had left New York he had considered warning Trainer about the possibility of receiving calls, but it had seemed better to leave him in the dark. "Jack, I had planned to come up and see you next week, but I mistakenly wrote down on my calendar that I was going to New Hampshire this week. I got LA and New Hampshire switched on the schedule, and the secretaries saw that and were understandably confused," he explained. "I'm very sorry. It's my fault."

"The people calling here are crazy," Trainer said, aggravated. "I mean, screaming at me. Like finding you is a life-or-death situation."

"I'm caught up in a couple of deals with short fuses. There's lots of money involved. Wall Street, you know."

"Yeah, yeah," Trainer said, unimpressed. "So are you really coming up to see me next week? We talked about that possibility a while back, when you were first looking at investing in TurboTec."

"That's why I'm calling."

"Good. I'm looking forward to seeing you. It's been a long time."

Jay made the appointment with Trainer but doubted he'd be going to New Hampshire the next week. His real reason for the call had been to see if people were checking up on him. There had been only two calls to Trainer the previous day, but there had been *ten* that day. Since shaking the blue sedan in Gloucester, interest in his whereabouts had increased dramatically. Perhaps he wasn't being so paranoid after all.

He turned and began walking through the streets of South Boston, known by the locals simply as "Southie." It was a working-class part of the city inhabited by a cross-section of ethnic populations living within well-defined neighborhoods, like squares on a quilt. Only the squares weren't all the same size here in South Boston. At this location, Jay was deep inside Little Ireland, one of the largest squares.

That morning Jay had tracked down EZ Travel. It was located in a strip mall in Braintree, south of the city limits, and he'd spent several hours watching it. The office was staffed by four people at metal desks who helped a trickle of customers but mostly talked to each other or played computer games. Nothing unusual had happened, and he didn't have time to waste on a dead end.

Frustrated by his lack of progress, Jay had returned to his now bumperless rental car—he'd pulled the twisted piece of metal off after getting a few miles away from the crash—and headed for South Boston. He had one more lead to check out. It probably wouldn't amount to much, but he had to give it a shot.

The post office was located only two blocks from the gas station where Jay had placed the call to Trainer, and he found the building quickly. It was an old brick structure flying a tattered United States flag on a rusted pole. The flagpole rose from a small, dusty courtyard crisscrossed by crumbling sidewalks. Behind a tall chain-link fence topped by barbed wire he could see a dozen or so white postal delivery trucks parked in a lot to the left. He checked his watch. It was twenty to five. There was still time for someone getting off work to check mail.

Jay walked through the front door and moved over scuffed

gray tiles to a tall, wide bank of boxes, quickly locating the box number that matched the address on the wire transfer Paul Lopez had brought to the trading floor Monday evening. Jay leaned down and glanced through the glass of the old-style box. There was mail inside. He moved off to a counter and pretended to be writing an address on a large label.

A few minutes before five Jay glanced at the front door. A postal employee was loitering around it, talking loudly to a woman wearing a floral print dress, alternately holding then dropping a key that dangled from a chain attached to a belt loop of his gray standard-issue pants. It was probably the key to the front door, Jay realized. A door that was about to be locked for the evening. He shook his head. Christ, he'd just wasted an entire day in Boston. Of course, he was probably unemployed by now after decking Bullock on the trading floor, so wasting a day in Boston didn't matter. And maybe he didn't want to go back to McCarthy & Lloyd now that he knew beyond any doubt that someone was tracking his moves and that Sally Lane wasn't who she said she was.

The front door burst open. For a split second Jay locked onto a short blond man with piercing blue eyes and a light complexion wearing a diamond stud in his left ear, then quickly looked back down at the label on which he had been drawing aimlessly to pass the time. In his peripheral vision he followed the man to the mailboxes, then glanced around when he was certain the man had come to a stop. The man had halted directly in front of the bank of boxes that included the one corresponding to the number on the advice address. From where he stood Jay couldn't tell exactly which box the man was opening, but it didn't matter. None of the other boxes around the critical one contained mail. He'd checked each of them before moving to the counter.

Jay walked through the lobby to the front door and moved through it casually, trying not to draw attention to himself. When he was out of sight of those inside, he sprinted down the crumbling sidewalk and around the corner of the building. There he stopped, peered back at the entrance, and caught his breath. He had found nothing at EZ Travel, but perhaps he would now learn the answer to one very simple question: Why the hell would the advice of a money transfer from McCarthy & Lloyd to EZ Travel be sent to a post office box in South Boston, a working-class neighborhood located on the other side of the city from the travel agency?

The short blond man with the diamond earring emerged from the post office clutching several envelopes and strode directly toward the corner of the building behind which Jay was hiding. Jay turned and sprinted further down the sidewalk, then darted out into the street between a Chevy van and a green Ford. He knelt down beside the van's front left tire. Moments later he recognized the man's red-and-black Nikes moving past the van. He waited ten seconds, then rose slowly. Already forty yards away, the man was moving at a brisk pace despite a limp Jay hadn't noticed in the post office.

"You got a problem or something, mac?"

Jay jumped back, startled by an older man sitting behind the van's steering wheel smoking a cigarette. He hadn't bothered to see if anyone was in the van. "No, sorry." He turned, trotted to the far side of the street, and followed the blond man, staying fifty yards back, hoping he wouldn't suddenly jump into a car and tear off.

But there was no need to worry. Five blocks later the blond man ducked into a pub located on one corner of a quiet intersection. Jay hesitated halfway down the block, eyeing the dark green door beneath a sign that read Maggie's Place. The man might easily recognize him from the post office, but Jay knew he had to follow him inside.

It was dark inside the pub, and for the first few seconds Jay could see little after being in the bright sunshine. As he moved to the bar and sat on a wooden stool, he became aware of the reek of stale beer, the feel of sawdust beneath his shoes, and the sound of Irish music in the background.

"What'll you have?" the stout bartender asked in a thick Irish accent.

"Whatever lager you recommend."

"Aye." The bartender moved away, picked up a chilled glass, and began to fill it from a tap.

Jay stared down at the sawdust on the floor beneath his stool. His eyes were slowly adjusting to the dim light. A few stools away two men were carrying on a loud conversation about a soccer game and seemed headed toward an argument.

The bartender returned and placed the glass of lager in front of Jay. "I think you'll like that one."

"Thanks."

"That'll be three dollars."

"Sure." Jay pulled a five from his shirt pocket and handed it to the bearded man. "There you go. No need for change."

"Aye." The bartender nodded, placed the five in an old cash register, withdrew two ones, dropped them in a plastic pitcher, and rang a gold bell loudly.

Jay winced. He could do without the fanfare. Then he noticed the red-and-black Nikes on the floor beside his stool. Jay picked up the glass and took a sip.

"Hello, Patrick," the bartender said loudly, hands spread wide on the sticky, scratched wooden bar.

"Hi, Frankie." The short blond man had a gravelly voice, as if there were something stuck in his throat. "Give me one of what he's having," Frankie ordered, pointing at Jay's glass. He spoke with an Irish accent as well.

"Okay."

Jay heard the conversation a few stools away becoming more heated.

"Haven't seen you in here before," Patrick said, turning toward Jay.

This was the moment of truth, Jay realized. He glanced into Patrick's eyes, watching carefully for any signs of recognition. "I'm visiting a friend. I'm from out of town."

Patrick picked up his beer and took a long drink. "Where you in from?"

"Philadelphia."

"The city of brotherly love."

"That's what they call it." Jay had noticed a distinctive rise in the man's voice at the end of his sentence, as if Patrick had been asking a question when in fact he had been making a statement. Patrick was from Northern Ireland. An uncle who had fought in World War II with several Irish immigrants had once explained to Jay that people from the north typically ended their sentences with that distinctive rising tone, question or not.

"You look familiar," Patrick observed.

"I doubt it," Jay said calmly.

"Who you visiting?" Patrick asked, staring steadily at Jay. His gravelly voice had gone ice cold.

Jay felt his pulse quicken. "An old college friend."

"Who might that be?"

"Jimmy Lynch. We went to Boston College together."

"Don't know him." Patrick took another gulp of beer. "I know plenty of Lynches, some named Jimmy, but none of them went to Boston College."

"You can't know everybody."

"I do," Patrick said confidently.

Jay shrugged. "I don't know what to tell you."

"Tell me what you might be doing here, mister," Patrick demanded.

"I told you, I'm waiting for a friend."

For several seconds the two stared at each other. Then the front door opened, bathing the pub in bright light. The door closed quickly, and another man moved past Patrick, touched him on the shoulder, and gestured toward a stairway at the back of the bar. Patrick gave Jay a long look, then turned and headed toward the stairway. When he reached the bottom step, he hesitated and looked back at Jay once more, then finally climbed the stairs.

Jay sat on the stool for another ten minutes, sipping his beer, then walked to the small bathroom. When he reemerged he moved to a pay phone on the wall and faked a call. After hanging up the receiver, he moved back to the bar and gestured at Frankie, who sauntered over.

"Will you do me a favor?" Jay asked.

"Maybe."

The two men a few stools away were now standing and shouting at each other. Jay glanced at them and rolled his eyes, making it clear to Frankie that he was leaving because of the commotion and not because of Patrick's grilling, which Jay knew Frankie had overheard. "When my friend Jimmy Lynch gets here, he'll ask for me. Will you tell him I've gone back to my motel?"

Frankie gazed at Jay. "I will," he answered after a few moments.

"He can call me there. He has the number."

"Okay."

"Thanks." Jay turned and headed toward the door. When he was outside, he leaned against the brick wall beside the green door and exhaled loudly. Patrick had obviously sensed that something was amiss with Jay. And Jay had sensed the same about Patrick.

CHAPTER 21

Oliver walked slowly through Central Park, dodging roller bladers and joggers making the most of the late-afternoon sunshine. As he strolled, he reflected on how it had all happened. How he had become involved in this ugly business.

Five years ago he and Bill McCarthy had met on a cool, rainy April evening in a smoky, out-of-the-way-of-anyone-from-Wall-Street bar in Greenwich Village and hatched a plan to make themselves fabulously wealthy. The scheme would be laced with risk, but the rewards could be tremendous.

Oliver, then a member of J. P. Morgan's fledgling equity-trading group, had problems. Morgan executives were uncomfortable about several large stock trades he had recently executed. He was being hit with sticky questions from the executives concerning whether or not he had obtained the proper internal approvals and therefore even had the authority to make the trades. More important, there were whispers among coworkers that

Oliver had obtained material, nonpublic information concerning the pharmaceutical company in question before purchasing its shares, then quickly sold the stock a month later at a huge profit when the company announced Food and Drug Administration approval of a new blockbuster drug.

Morgan's senior officers were understandably concerned because they realized that the firm's stellar reputation would come under attack from the press and competitors if a major insider-trading scandal broke. The old-line commercial bank was gearing up at that point to make a full-scale push into the investment banking business, and the last thing the executives wanted was a scandal splashed all over the front page of every newspaper in the world. On the evening Oliver first discussed the plan with McCarthy, he had just come out of a meeting with his superiors at Morgan about the trades in question, and he was feeling the heat. He was ready to leave Morgan, and they were ready to see him go. And at that point Oliver resented his father-in-law so intensely he would have done anything to make enormous amounts of money on his own.

Bill McCarthy had recently lost his longtime business partner and best friend, Graham Lloyd, in a boating accident. Now he had new partners. McCarthy was the owner of record of Lloyd's 50 percent stake in McCarthy & Lloyd, purchased from Lloyd's widow per an automatic buy-sell agreement executed by the two men when they had founded the firm in 1989. But a shadowy European group was the real financial muscle behind the transaction, because McCarthy didn't have the money to pay for Lloyd's shares. The stock hadn't cost much—M&L was on the verge of bankruptcy—but McCarthy had next to nothing in his personal bank accounts, so he had taken on partners.

The new partners wanted McCarthy to generate cash quickly, and they weren't particularly concerned about how he did it. A year before the meeting, McCarthy & Lloyd—upon McCarthy's personal order—had made a disastrous investment in a Florida high-tech company. The declining financial performance of the Florida company and the inability of its executives to raise fresh capital had almost wiped out the value of McCarthy & Lloyd's investment, which in turn would have wiped out McCarthy & Lloyd's own thin capital layer. But ultimately the firm had survived—with help from the new partners. McCarthy had been guardedly optimistic about the sudden, seemingly positive turn of events, but his new partners, who had originally claimed they would be passive investors, instantly became aggressive, demanding more from him than he could have ever imagined.

Within days of their meeting in Greenwich Village, Oliver and McCarthy had agreed to the terms of Oliver's employment at M&L. Oliver would become the head of a new equity arbitrage desk and receive a one-million-dollar annual salary, substantial annual bonuses, and a piece of Bill McCarthy's share of McCarthy & Lloyd—the Europeans weren't willing to bargain with their 50 percent stake in the firm. In return for his huge compensation package, Oliver would put together a small, discreet ring of Wall Streeters with access to nonpublic information concerning companies about to be taken over, and the McCarthy & Lloyd arbitrage desk would execute the trades and earn the substantial profits the information would generate.

The obvious risk embedded in the scheme was that law enforcement authorities would uncover the ring. Oliver knew that the easiest way for the authorities to prove that an insider-trading ring existed was to identify personal connections within the ring and find a money trail leading from individual to individual. So he carefully instructed the insiders to make calls only from pay phones when arranging face-to-face meetings, which were kept at a minimum. The insiders would receive their compensation for the information they provided Oliver in the form of McCarthy & Lloyd stock, which, upon Bill McCarthy's death, would be distributed to an offshore partnership entity the insiders had formed. After the insiders or their heirs had received their shares from the partnership, the stock would be repurchased by McCarthy & Lloyd over a four-year period at a price to be determined using a preset multiple of McCarthy & Lloyd's book value. Oliver and the other insiders would essentially become shadow equity owners of McCarthy & Lloyd.

Within six months Oliver had recruited four men to become insiders. Instead of approaching investment bankers who were working on deals in secret and knew about them before the rest of the market, Oliver had recruited four back-office people who worked in compliance areas of brokerage houses and investment banking firms on Wall Street. Investment bankers earned huge bonuses and typically came from monied families to begin with. Oliver reasoned that they had far less incentive to trade on the inside and put themselves in legal jeopardy. Back-office people, on the other hand, earned much less. They had a great deal more incentive.

Oliver knew that compliance areas maintain highly confidential lists of companies in which individuals at the investment bank cannot trade for the firm or themselves. As a matter of policy, investment bankers who arrange takeovers notify their firms' compliance areas about companies involved in takeovers on which they're working as soon as a deal is in the works—well before it becomes public knowledge—so people at the firm, specifically equity traders, won't deal in the shares of either the target or the attacker. The Securities and Exchange Commission and other federal and state authorities take a dim view of brokerage firms that trade in the shares of companies for whom they are arranging financial transactions in the weeks before those transactions are announced. The brokerage firms can easily anticipate sharp rises or drops in stock prices that the rest of the market can't—clearly insider trading. Even the appearance of impropriety can cause trouble for the firms.

The compliance groups attempt to make certain no one at the firm trades in the shares of such companies by putting out a "gray list"—a list of stocks that can't be bought or sold by the firm as long as they remain on the list. Professionals at the firm have access to the gray list and could use the list to secretly trade in the stocks and make themselves exceptional profits, except for one small detail: Some stocks on the gray list are decoys—stocks that aren't involved in takeovers and which won't necessarily generate huge overnight profits. This snag helps keep people honest and assists the firm in identifying individuals who violate the gray list. Only a few people in the compliance group know exactly which stocks are hot and which are decoys. That kind of knowledge makes those individuals invaluable—and vulnerable—to a person such as Oliver Mason.

The four men Oliver recruited into the ring—Tony Vogel, David Torcelli, Kenny Serrano, and Peter Boggs—were midlevel executives in compliance groups at major Wall Street investment houses. The men had large immediate families—at least four children each—and therefore large bills to pay. Oliver picked them carefully, as he had Jay West, making certain that each man had a significant financial need without family money to fall back on. Nothing about the ring was ever recorded, and the only tangible evidence of its existence was the alteration of Bill McCarthy's will by his personal attorney to include the insiders' offshore partnership entity as an heir. However, the insiders had no say at all in the management of McCarthy & Lloyd. Each man was provided with a copy of McCarthy's new will as well as a separate document, signed by all six parties, whereby McCarthy agreed not to change the terms of the will without written approval of each insider. This caveat would allow McCarthy to buy them out early if that made sense for all parties involved.

In its first full year of operation Oliver's insider-trading ring earned McCarthy & Lloyd fifty million dollars. After that, profits only improved. The already booming takeover market on Wall Street accelerated with the strong economy. By the late nineties the annual value of takeovers in the United States had grown to almost one trillion dollars—plenty of volume for a small arbitrage shop at a boutique investment bank to make unsightly profits on sure-thing bets.

For Oliver, it became like shooting fish in a barrel, only easier. In fact, the shooting became so good, he began intentionally picking a few losers—stocks he had no inside information on and actually hoped *wouldn't* increase quickly in value—to throw anyone who might be watching too closely off the track. He was careful, buying as far in advance of the takeover as possible, and spreading his purchases over a wide number of brokers. There was never even a hint of trouble.

The only negative for the insiders—other than for Oliver, who received his annual million-dollar salary and huge bonuses—was that they received no cash for the valuable information they provided to the arbitrage desk. On paper, however, they were millionaires. Since its low point five years before, the value of McCarthy & Lloyd had skyrocketed. Once back on his feet with the fifty million Oliver had earned in the arbitrage desk's first year of existence, Bill McCarthy had beefed up the staff in every area of the firm, and now it was competing against the bulge-bracket firms in corporate finance and sales and trading and making serious money. But Oliver remained the cash cow, and his reputation within the firm became legendary to the point where some simply referred to him as "God."

Though the value of the insiders' shadow ownership in McCarthy & Lloyd had risen dramatically, it wasn't an asset that provided any immediate value. It hadn't put anything in their pockets, and they couldn't use it as collateral because the partnership didn't actually take possession of the shares until McCarthy was dead. They had all rationalized that they were doing this for their children, building a huge nest egg for them. But cash needs grew for the four men. There were bigger houses and newer cars that had to be purchased; their children were approaching college age, and there would be staggering tuition bills very soon. The insiders had taken huge risks and decided it was time to see the fruits of their labor. The hell with the future and a nest egg later on. They wanted their piece of the pie now.

Oliver had deftly defused dissension in the ranks with annual five-figure cash loans, which he delivered to each man in briefcases filled with small bills. Oliver funded these loans out of his own pocket, carefully withdrawing the money from many different accounts over time so nothing could be traced. The men never deposited the money from Oliver. They kept it at home, literally under their mattresses. Fire and theft were constant risks, but they had no choice. Putting the cash in a bank might have alerted the IRS to the scheme during an audit. The men were temporarily placated, and the profits kept piling up at McCarthy & Lloyd.

Oliver had believed that the success of the arbitrage desk would continue forever, even as he had sat in the living room of Bill McCarthy's Park Avenue apartment the past March wondering why McCarthy had needed to see him so urgently. Even as the tall man with dark red hair and green eyes, wearing an inexpensive-looking wool suit, followed McCarthy into the room, Oliver had remained his typically brash and confident self. He had believed paradise would last forever—until the moment

McCarthy had uttered the words "Kevin O'Shea, an assistant U.S. attorney for the southern district of New York." With those words Oliver's world had shattered, because he knew exactly why O'Shea was there. The insider trading at McCarthy & Lloyd had been uncovered.

For several heated seconds Oliver had actually considered bolting past the other men and heading for the apartment door and a life on the run. He saw no handcuffs on O'Shea's belt, but Oliver was certain he was about to be led downstairs in shackles and loaded into a police cruiser, where he would sit on his hands and stare at the backs of two policemen through a metal screen as they drove him downtown for booking.

But he had come to his senses and realized that running was out of the question. He probably wouldn't make it out of the building before being apprehended, and if he did, they'd find him sooner or later. He had no idea how to remain one step ahead of the law and no stomach for being hunted. Besides, he had figured out as he stood staring open-mouthed at the Justice Department official that there must be something to listen to, as O'Shea hadn't snapped the cuffs on him right away. He'd been right.

O'Shea explained that he had uncovered several situations where certain trades appeared suspicious—where the McCarthy & Lloyd arbitrage desk had purchased stock immediately prior to a takeover, and where he was certain he could prove insider trading. However, the word had come down from on high that no one wanted Bill McCarthy to get caught up in a nasty situation. McCarthy had major-league political connections, and those connections wanted him and his contribution money to remain clean, so O'Shea was ready to offer Oliver a deal. The arbitrage desk would have to offer up a sacrificial lamb to take the heat for the insider trading, and it would have to abstain from any arbitrage activities for six months. If subsequent instances of insider trading were uncovered, everyone, including McCarthy, would be locked up. The sacrificial lamb would be a junior person, marketed as a rogue trader acting outside the bounds of his authority, and his or her arrest and prosecution would pacify those at the U.S. attorney's office who had already spent time on the investigation.

The only catch was that Oliver would have to identify and entrap the lamb. It was a small price to pay for freedom—and for what he thought at the time would be the ability to remain at McCarthy & Lloyd—so he had readily agreed. Over the next several months Oliver had lured Jay West into the ambush.

Since the meeting in the Park Avenue apartment in March, two things had nagged at Oliver. It was apparent to him that O'Shea had no idea how intricately involved McCarthy was in the situation—no idea that McCarthy had originally hired Oliver with a mandate to engage in insider trading. O'Shea had never even asked about McCarthy's possible role in the situation. Oliver had been forced to give O'Shea the names of his information sources—the four insiders—but he had never volunteered that McCarthy was in on the ground floor.

McCarthy had explained after the meeting in the apartment that Oliver was never to reveal his involvement, and that if Oliver did, he would go to jail. Keeping McCarthy's name out of the subsequent discussions with O'Shea had been a no-brainer capitulation for Oliver: stay free versus go to jail. An easy choice, except that it irritated Oliver when, a few weeks after the initial meeting with O'Shea, McCarthy suddenly began acting as if he really hadn't known what was going on. As if he had convinced himself that he was innocent. Just Oliver Mason's victim.

McCarthy's transformation from coconspirator to innocent bystander annoyed Oliver but wasn't particularly important beyond its effect on his psyche. Something else troubled Oliver a great deal more. At the March meeting, and in all subsequent discussions, O'Shea would never reveal how he had uncovered the insider trading on the arbitrage desk. Oliver had asked about the origin of the discovery several times, but O'Shea would never come clean. In addition, O'Shea never brought anyone else from the office with him when he and Oliver met, nor would he be specific about the "others" he kept referring to who had worked on the initial investigation. This lack of disclosure bothered Oliver so much that he checked to make certain Kevin O'Shea actually was an assistant U.S. attorney in Manhattan. He was, but the haziness surrounding what was going on first irritated Oliver, then frightened him more and more.

Now, as Oliver walked past the Children's Zoo on the east side of Central Park, he couldn't shake his depression, which was deeper than ever. A sensation of dread had enveloped him since the morning, as if he'd just awakened from a nightmare. He spotted Tony Vogel and David Torcelli standing at the appointed place and moved toward them, wondering if it was too late to lead that life on the run.

"Hello, David." Oliver shook David Torcelli's hand firmly, forcing himself to seem untroubled. In addition to the general malaise he found himself mired in, he'd been specifically worried all day about how tight-lipped O'Shea had been the previous night concerning the investigation of Abby's murder. But he didn't want to show any sign of weakness to Torcelli or Vogel. They had no idea what was going on, and it had to remain that way. "How are you this afternoon?" he asked.

"Not so good, Oliver." Torcelli sat down on a wooden bench overlooking Wollman Rink. The rink was tucked into the south-east corner of Central Park, in the shadow of the Plaza Hotel. During the winter it would have been crowded with ice skaters, but now it was open to in-line skaters. The men had originally agreed to meet at the Plaza suite McCarthy & Lloyd rented, but at the last second Torcelli had decided it would be better to meet on neutral territory. Over the last twenty-four hours he had become extremely careful.

Tony Vogel stood beside Oliver. Torcelli motioned for him to sit down beside him on the bench, and Vogel obeyed with the speed and loyalty of a military aide.

During the five years of the insider-trading ring, Oliver had always been the unofficial leader of the group. Suddenly allegiances seemed to have changed, he noticed. "What's wrong, David?" Oliver knew exactly what was wrong, but he played the game anyway, wanting to delay the confrontation as long as possible.

"I told David how you reacted when we met last week up there." Vogel gestured over his shoulder at the Plaza looming behind them, providing the explanation for his new leader.

"Tony told me you wouldn't even listen to what we had to say. That you wouldn't consider what we wanted." Torcelli was a huge man, six and a half feet tall, with a barrel chest and a tough Brooklyn accent. "I was very disappointed, to put it mildly."

"I understand," Oliver agreed quietly, glancing at a young woman who seemed too interested in their conversation as she walked past. He waited until she was out of earshot. "I should have listened more carefully to what Tony had to say."

Torcelli and Vogel looked up from the bench in unison, surprised by what they had just heard.

"We've always operated as a loose democracy," Oliver said. "Perhaps we should revisit the issues now."

"R-Right," Torcelli stammered, wondering why Oliver had

suddenly changed his mind and what his angle was. "As a compliance officer, I've made friends over the years with some of the government people downtown. I keep hearing from them that something is going down at McCarthy and Lloyd. Something very big and very bad."

"Like what?" Oliver asked unsteadily. He couldn't keep receiving bad news and hope to keep himself together.

"That's the odd thing," Torcelli answered, looking around furtively. "They don't know. People at the highest levels are involved in some sort of investigation, but no one is talking. No one knows. My contacts suspect some kind of insider-trading investigation, but they don't know for certain."

Oliver glanced at the petrified expression on Vogel's sad face. "What do you think we should do, David?" Suddenly Oliver didn't want to be the one in charge. Suddenly he wanted to hand the reins over to Torcelli.

Torcelli put his hands behind his head and tried his best to give the impression that he was taking control. He sensed that Oliver was ceding power. "First, we need to stop all trading. Don't use the Bell Chemical or Simons tips."

Oliver and Vogel exchanged a quick glance. They hadn't talked about Jay West's inadvertent interception of Vogel's call to the phone in the Austin Healey. And obviously Vogel hadn't told Torcelli about it.

"Okay. I won't." Oliver noticed Vogel's shoulders slump with relief.

Torcelli would have gone ballistic if he had known that Jay West had rooted through the glove compartment of the Austin Healey and probably found the envelope with Bell Chemical's name written on the page inside, Oliver thought. But Jay had purchased the Bell and Simons shares, even though he must have been suspicious. O'Shea had been correct in his analysis the previous night in Milton, Oliver realized. Jay West had been willing to do anything to get his million dollars. Oliver swallowed hard and glanced down at the pavement. All Jay was really going to get for his trouble was a twenty-year stay in a hotel room with steel-bar walls.

"Good," Torcelli said enthusiastically, happy with Oliver's unexpected acquiescence. "I think we should shut down the operation altogether."

"I see no alternative, either," Oliver agreed submissively.

Torcelli leaned forward and motioned for Oliver to come closer. "And I think we should put an end to the life of William McCarthy. It's time to collect what's ours. I don't trust him further than I can throw him, which isn't very far."

Oliver gazed at Torcelli, blood pounding in his ears, wondering how the hell life had so quickly spun out of control.

Torcelli's eyes narrowed, and a tight grin turned up the corners of his mouth. "I've already spoken to someone who is willing to help us."

Oliver nodded almost imperceptibly. He'd always figured that none of the other insiders would have the stomach for murder. Torcelli had proven him wrong.

■ ■ ■

Oliver sat at one end of the screened-in porch of his Connecticut mansion. He sat in the dark, in a comfortable upholstered chair, looking out over meticulously manicured rose gardens illuminated by a half moon, sipping his fifth gin and tonic of the evening. Before meeting Torcelli and Vogel in Central Park, he had spent the day on the arbitrage desk receiving congratulations from half the trading floor as the share prices of Bell Chemical and Simons skyrocketed. Another bidder, a European conglomerate, had emerged as a second suitor for Bell, and Bell's stock price had doubled in the last twenty-four hours. Simons stock was 50 percent higher than the price at which Jay had purchased its shares a week earlier, and rumors were swirling through the markets that a second bidder was about to make a higher tender offer, which would send its stock price sailing into nosebleed territory.

Like congregations paying homage to the pope, traders from other areas had filed past Oliver's seat to kiss the ring. He gulped down what remained of the gin and tonic—mostly gin—and poured himself another from a pitcher sitting on a small table next to his chair. He had accepted their adulation with the knowledge that very soon he would be viewed no longer as a god but as a fallen angel—or the devil. Sometime the next week, after Jay had been arrested and carted away, Oliver would be fired. Not accused of anything illegal, but simply accused of a lack of control. No one would ever know that he had made most of his money on the arbitrage desk over the past five years illicitly, but that didn't matter. All that mattered to him was that he would be gone, shunned into a life of lounging around the house in his bathrobe, watching talk shows and soap operas, while the rest of the world passed him by and Harold Kellogg laughed. Shunned into what he knew would be a haze of alcohol and drugs in which he was solely dependent on Barbara, because no Wall Street firm would touch him after this. He was to be shunned into a life of quiet desperation by someone in Washington whom he had never met, a nameless, faceless son of a bitch who was going to allow Bill McCarthy to go completely free because the president wanted to keep receiving those wonderful contributions. Contributions made from the money Oliver had earned McCarthy on the arbitrage desk. He took another swallow of gin.

"Oliver." Barbara stood in the porch doorway, silhouetted by a light from inside. "Why are you drinking so much?" she asked tentatively, inching a few steps out onto the porch.

"None of your damn business," he answered sullenly.

A tear trickled down one cheek, and she muffled a sob. "Why do you hate me?"

Oliver flinched and took a huge gulp of alcohol. She was right. He did hate her, though he wasn't really certain why. He'd asked himself that question many times, but he'd never come up with a satisfactory answer. Perhaps it was because she seemed to whine about everything these days, or because she was always trying to get him to pay more attention to her. Or because her face so resembled her father's. Or because she reminded him of a time in his life when things seemed simpler, all his goals still within reach. Whatever it was, the hatred had become intense. "Go to bed," he mumbled.

"Are you sleeping in the guest room on the second floor again tonight?" Barbara no longer attempted to hide her sobs.

"Go to bed," Oliver snarled.

"Are you sad because Abby is dead?" She hadn't wanted to ask the question, but she couldn't help herself. The possibility that Abby's death was somehow connected to Oliver had occurred to her as soon as she heard the news.

Oliver looked up at her dark form. "How did you find out about that?" he asked, his voice wavering. He knew reports of Abby's murder hadn't yet hit the newspapers.

"My father told me. He has contacts."

Once more Harold Kellogg was playing God. "Get out of here."

"It wasn't because he knows about you and that girl. I've never told—"

"I said get out!" Oliver roared.

"I want to help," Barbara cried. "I don't care what you've done with her."

"Leave me!" he yelled, hurling his glass at her.

The glass shattered on the floor behind Barbara, but still she held her ground. "Please." She was sobbing uncontrollably now, choking on her tears.

"I'm not going to say it again!" Oliver rose from his chair and stepped toward her.

That was enough. Barbara turned and raced away into the house.

Shaking, Oliver sat back down in the chair. After staring into the darkness for several moments, he reached beneath the chair, picked up a .38-caliber revolver, and put the barrel to his head. Just one of the gun's six chambers was loaded. He put his finger on the trigger, shut his eyes tightly, and squeezed.

■ ■ ■

Barbara raced up the stairs to her bedroom, dropped to her knees in front of her wardrobe, and yanked open the bottom drawer, pushing aside several sweaters until she found the envelope. She picked it up and gazed at it as it shook wildly in front of her. The very next day she would deliver it. She had nothing to lose now.

CHAPTER 22

Jay struggled to bring his hands to his eyes, but the motion was difficult because he was jammed so tightly into the freezing, cramped space. *Maybe this is what hell is like,* he thought as he finally managed to depress a tiny button on his watch and check the time in the eerie blue light of the liquid crystal display. It was almost four o'clock in the morning. The loud music and voices had faded away an hour earlier, and as far as he could tell, the pub was empty. However, he was still reluctant to crawl out of the duct and down into the men's bathroom of Maggie's Place. While using the pub's bathroom that afternoon he had noticed the vent. It was then that the idea had occurred to him.

At eleven o'clock, when the pub was jammed with locals enjoying a Thursday night out, he had stolen inside as inconspicuously as possible, the brim of a Red Sox baseball cap pulled low over his eyes. He had walked directly to the door of the small bathroom, entered when he was certain it was empty, closed the wooden door without sliding the small bolt lock into place, stepped up onto the top of the urinal closest to the vent, and pulled himself headfirst into the narrow opening.

He'd barely fit and was worried that someone would see his shoes. Seven feet inside the duct, the sheet metal had turned ninety degrees to the right, and he'd been unable to move any farther forward. He'd pulled his legs up as far up as possible, but there was no way to tell if he was visible. Fortunately, no one had detected him, though the bathroom had been used many times since he had crawled into the space. He'd counted the creak of the door hinge each time it opened because he needed something to keep his mind occupied.

Jay exhaled to make his chest smaller, then pushed backward until first his feet and then all of his legs were clear of the vent. Feeling around with one shoe, he found the top of the urinal, then eased his torso and head out of the space and jumped to the floor. He shivered, stretched, and inhaled deeply. It was damn nice not to have that air-conditioning blowing in his face and to be able to take a normal breath. He hadn't known going in whether he was claustrophobic. Though he'd come close to panic a few times, the ordeal hadn't been as difficult as he had anticipated.

He moved to the door, pressed a hand against it, then hesitated. It was going to creak loudly. He'd heard that creak so many times this evening. But he couldn't stay inside the bathroom all night. If anyone was left in the bar, he'd act drunk and claim he'd passed out, then leave quickly.

There was no need to worry. The pub was deserted. Stools and chairs lay upside down on the bar and tables, and the only bulbs still illuminated were a spotlight over the bar and a long thin fluorescent bulb hanging over a pool table in one corner of the place. The floor was strewn with beer-soaked sawdust, but everyone was gone. He moved quickly across the floor to the steps he had watched Patrick climb that afternoon.

At the top of the steps Jay found exactly what he had expected—a locked door. He jiggled the knob several times, then inserted one end of a straightened paper clip into the keyhole and moved it around. But the door was shut securely. From his jacket he removed a small crowbar and hammer he had purchased at a local hardware store a block from the post office, inserted the sharp end of the crowbar between the door and the jamb, smacked the end of the crowbar with the hammer twice, and with a violent wrench broke the door open. For several seconds he stood statue-still, listening for any sounds other than his own rapid breathing and heart pounding. This was insanity. He was guilty of breaking and entering. But he had to understand the connection between this obscure pub in South Boston and McCarthy & Lloyd.

Jay switched on the small flashlight hanging from a chain around his neck, leaned inside what appeared to be a ramshackle office, and scanned it. Positioned between two windows on the far wall was a large wooden desk. He took one step into the room and heard a snort, then a heavy sigh. He extinguished the flashlight instantly, backed out of the office onto the top step, and listened to heavy breathing turn to a loud snore.

When he was confident that the person inside was asleep—or passed out—Jay moved into the office again, flicked on the flashlight, and directed the beam around the room. From the desk, which was straight ahead, he moved the beam to the left and illuminated a long brown leather couch that had clearly seen better days, and a man stretched out on it who had once been in better shape before, too. It was Frankie, the bartender. He was on his back, one shoe off, still wearing his stained green apron, arms folded across his chest and head to one side in what looked like an extremely uncomfortable position. On the floor beside the sofa was a half-full liquor bottle, cap off.

Jay doused the flashlight and listened to Frankie snore, intent upon making absolutely certain that the man wasn't pretending to be asleep. The snores seemed too loud and too perfect.

In midsnore Frankie stopped, sighed, made a clicking sound with his lips and tongue, groaned, and began snoring again in the same deep, measured, back-of-the-throat way. Jay turned on the flashlight again, pointed it at Frankie, and saw a tiny trail of glistening saliva coursing from the corner of his mouth to several old shirts he had bunched together to use as a pillow. Frankie was definitely down for the count. Somehow he'd managed to climb the stairs, lock the office door, and crawl onto the couch, but it didn't look like he was going to be much use to anyone for at least another few hours.

Jay checked the bottle on the floor beside Frankie. A fifth of premium Irish whiskey. "Shouldn't drink out of the bar's good stock like that, Frankie," Jay muttered. "Somebody might be able to break into your office without your knowing." He stood up and walked across a tattered Oriental rug to the desk. He kept one ear tuned to Frankie. If the snoring stopped or even altered slightly, he'd bolt.

The desk reminded Jay of McCarthy's. It was littered with dated newspapers, old coffee cups, notebooks, and miscellaneous pieces of paper. Jay picked up a thin yellow sheet. On it were scrawled numbers. He flashed the beam on Frankie—still sleeping like a baby—then back on the paper. It was a receipt for liquor deliveries. Jay dropped the receipt back on the desk and inspected other papers. More receipts. He leaned down and opened the top right drawer of the desk, where he found nothing but pencils, pens, paper clips, and a box of St. Patrick's Day memorabilia.

He knelt down and attempted to pull out the bottom drawer, but it was locked tightly. He inserted the crowbar and pried it open. The lock gave way with a splintering crack. At the sound of the crack Frankie snorted several times in rapid succession and groaned loudly. Instantly Jay turned off the light and took several quick steps toward the door. But even the crack of the drawer giving way couldn't rouse Frankie from his single-malt slumber. Jay turned the flashlight on once more and padded back to the desk.

Unlike the rest of the office, this drawer was meticulously organized, containing a cigar box, a marble notebook, and a three-ring binder. Jay pulled out the binder and flipped it open. It was separated into two sections. The first contained nine transfer advices concerning funds wired from McCarthy & Lloyd to EZ Travel, including the one Paulie had delivered to Bullock's drawer Monday night on the trading floor. All were stapled to plain white pieces of paper bound to the notebook rings. Jay quickly totaled the amounts on the advices—approximately one hundred million dollars.

He flipped to the second section of the binder. On these pages he found the names of several foreign banks, headquartered in Antigua, Switzerland, Liechtenstein, Saudi Arabia, England, and Ireland. The names were followed by long sequences of numbers—sometimes several for each institution.

Jay carefully removed several of the pages and put them in his pocket, then placed the binder on the desk, reached for the marble notebook, and opened it. At the top of the first page the words "Project Hall" were written. He skimmed the notebook but couldn't decipher any of the text. It was written in a language, or a code, he couldn't understand. Then he found what appeared to be a hand-sketched road map at the back of the book. A small square at the upper right-hand corner of the page was labeled

"Richmond Airport," and another spot was labeled "Farm." He ripped this page out of the notebook and put it in his pocket as well. Adrenaline poured through his system. He was tunnel-visioned on the task and was aware of nothing else now, including the drunken man's snores.

Jay picked up the cedar cigar box and opened it. Inside were several photographs of men—including Patrick—dressed in camouflage, arms around each others' shoulders and smoldering cigars hanging from their mouths. Jay skimmed through the pictures and was about to put them back when he came to the last one. In it four men were kneeling in the foreground and four more were standing behind them. Trees towered above the men, and to one side were pitched canvas tents. Each man wore camouflage, and each held a rifle. Jay peered at the picture in the beam of the flashlight, then let out an audible gasp. Standing in the back row beside Patrick, brandishing his weapon, was Carter Bullock. Jay's eyes narrowed. Beneath the men were scrawled the words "Donegall Volunteers."

"What in the hell is going on?"

Jay whipped around and aimed the flashlight directly at Frankie, who held his hand up against the glare.

"Patrick?" Frankie muttered. He tried to rise, but groaned and fell back on the sofa. "What are you doing here? Why are you bothering me in the dead of night?" he grumbled in his thick Irish accent. "God, I think I'm going to be sick. Why the hell did you make me drink so much of that fuckin' firewater?"

Frankie wouldn't be difficult to evade, Jay knew, but there was no reason to stick around any longer than was absolutely necessary and give the other man the opportunity to recognize him. That possibility seemed unlikely, given Frankie's still-inebriated condition, but the men in the pictures were brandishing very nasty weapons and he wanted no part of them.

"Patrick! Oh, God!" Frankie suddenly leaned his head over the side of the couch and regurgitated the poison sloshing in his stomach.

Almost instantly a foul stench reached Jay. He held his breath and stuffed the photograph of Bullock, Patrick, and the other men into his pocket, then put the rest of the pictures back into the cigar box. As he replaced everything in the drawer, he heard a loud banging from downstairs. The front door of the pub had been hurled open. He heard Frankie groan and fall back on the couch, then loud voices downstairs and people rushing through the bar. They must have spotted the flashlight beam from the street.

Jay bolted to one of the windows, threw up the blind and the lower half of the window, and stopped short. His escape was blocked by a row of metal bars on hinges kept tightly shut by a padlock attached to the window jamb. "Damn it!" he muttered. For the first time Jay felt his life might actually be in danger. He doubted whoever was downstairs would hold him until the police arrived. Judging from the pictures in the cigar box, they'd probably take justice into their own hands.

He aimed the flashlight on the floor beside the desk, raced back to the spot where he had been kneeling, grabbed the hammer, tore back to the window, and smashed the lock like a deranged serial killer attacking a victim. The lock was giving way, but he could hear people bounding up the stairs. They would be on him in a matter of seconds. With one final maniacal blow he crushed the lock and it tumbled to the floor. He pushed back the bars, then felt arms wrapping around his chest and instantly smelled the stench of vomit. Even in Frankie's drunken haze he had realized that something was wrong, and he was doing his best to keep Jay from getting out the window until the others arrived.

Jay smashed Frankie's soft belly with a hard elbow, and the

bartender tumbled backward into the boots of the other men, who had just made it to the top of the stairs. Jay scrambled up onto the window ledge—just as someone snapped on the overhead light—and threw himself forward, lunging for a telephone pole rising from the sidewalk two stories below. The pole was five feet from the window and he hit it hard, wrapping his arms around it tightly like a shipwreck victim grabbing for anything that floats. The sharp smell of creosote suddenly replaced the stench of vomit.

The open window was instantly filled with the heads of two men, shouting over their shoulders to comrades within to get back down to the street. Jay was vaguely aware of the hulking forms in the window as he let go of the telephone pole and plummeted down, catching himself just before he hit the sidewalk. Sharp splinters pierced his palms and arms, but he ignored the searing pain. He let go again, tumbling onto the concrete. He was on his feet instantly, aware that his left elbow was suddenly paralyzed and that people were spilling out of the front door of Maggie's Place only twenty feet away. He turned and raced off into the darkness, sensing the pack panting behind him like a prey animal that knows one misstep or stumble means the end.

There was no hope of reaching the rental car. It was parked in the opposite direction, only two blocks away. Even if he could evade his pursuers, the car was too close for him to circle back. He needed to put as much distance as possible between himself and Maggie's Place as fast as he could.

He darted between two cars, raced across the street, and sprinted into a dark alley with the pack in pursuit.

■ ■ ■

In the early-morning darkness of his small living room, O'Shea sat in his favorite easy chair nursing a beer in the television's flickering light. His eyes kept darting to the VCR's digital clock. It was almost five o'clock. He glanced at the telephone on the table beside the chair. They had promised to notify him as soon as they had reestablished contact with Jay West after losing him Wednesday afternoon in the woods outside Gloucester. At that point they'd been confident it wouldn't take long to find him. But it was now two days later, and they hadn't been able to track him down.

Jay had turned out to be quite an adversary, not the naive sacrificial lamb he had hoped for. The men who had been following Jay had sworn that they had stayed well back of his car on the trip from Boston to Gloucester, yet Jay had identified and evaded them, evaded men who were skilled trackers—and killers. He'd left them smashed against a tree, then had the galling courtesy to call local authorities to report the accident.

O'Shea's expression turned steely. There was only one reason for Jay to have traveled to Gloucester, only one reason for him to go poking around Sally Lane's old neighborhood. O'Shea hoped he hadn't learned too much.

The assistant U.S. attorney shook his head, finished what was left of his beer, stood, and headed upstairs. If they didn't find Jay soon, everything could fall apart.

■ ■ ■

Crouched beneath the deck, Jay held his breath as he peered out from his hiding place. The deck had been built off the back of a modest house and rose only a few feet from the ground. Exhausted, he had crawled beneath it after leading the pack on a fifteen-minute chase through South Boston. He had sensed that his pursuers were closing in, so he had ducked down an alley, hurdled a wooden fence into a small yard, and scrambled beneath the deck. Moments later the pack—at least ten men—had raced past into the next yard.

He began to crawl over the dirt. It had been five minutes since his pursuers had bolted past. They'd soon realize that they had lost their quarry and would begin backtracking. He wanted to be long gone before that happened.

Jay had almost reached the edge of the deck when he stopped short. Through the darkness he noticed a pair of legs only a few feet away, standing near the deck, feet shod in red-and-black Nikes. They were illuminated by the gleam of a floodlight affixed to an eave of the two-story home. He froze as the man knelt down and inspected the space beneath the deck. It was Patrick. The diamond stud in his ear sparkled, and Jay recognized the dim features of his face. Jay held his breath, waiting for the blinding flashlight beam that would give away his hiding place. It had to come, he thought. Patrick would remove a light from his pocket, aim it at him, and then everything would be over.

But the light never came. Patrick finally rose and walked slowly in the direction the pack had gone.

Jay watched the Nikes disappear around the end of the deck, counted to fifty, then dragged himself from beneath the deck and onto the lawn. He should have waited longer, but there wasn't time. Something told him the pack would be coming back soon.

He scrambled to his feet and started to sprint in the opposite direction of his pursuers. But Patrick was on him instantly, screaming as he leaped over the deck's railing. They fell to the ground as one and rolled across the grass, coming to a stop with Jay on the bottom. They wrestled wildly until Patrick lifted up and slammed Jay with a hard right to the face. White and green lights exploded in Jay's vision, but he managed to heave the smaller man away and scramble groggily to his knees.

Patrick whipped a long Gerber hunting knife from its sheath on his belt and sprang at Jay. But before Patrick could reach him,

Jay pulled the hammer he had used to break into the office from his coat pocket and hurled it, hitting Patrick flush in the mouth and nose with the forged steel end. Patrick went down screaming, clutching his mouth, spitting blood and teeth onto the grass.

Seconds later Jay was over the fence and gone.

CHAPTER 23

Jay glanced up at the hot Virginia sun, then knelt down, picked a bone fragment off the grass, and examined it. It was slightly larger than a quarter and stained with blood. What appeared to be filthy strands of human hair clung to it. He glanced around. Scattered around were more bone fragments and a great deal of dried blood on the ground. Suddenly he dropped the fragment as pain seared through one finger. He'd managed to extract most of the splinters from his hands and arms with a pair of tweezers a steward on the early-morning flight from Boston to Richmond had provided, but the cuts still hurt. Fortunately, his left elbow, which had cracked the pavement hard during his fall, was working again.

Jay's expression turned grim. The pack had almost caught him in the alley, and Patrick had almost killed him in the yard. But he'd survived. After eluding Patrick, he'd caught a ride with a taxi heading into the city for a morning shift and directed the cabby to Logan Airport. The guy had given him a couple of strange looks, but he'd taken Jay to the airport with no complaints or questions.

Jay squinted up again at the hot sun, beating down on him through high clouds, then at the hills overlooking what he assumed was a target area, judging by the trees at the edge of the field, which were pocked by hundreds of bullet marks. He gazed at the bone fragments once more. Not a target area. A killing field.

With the map he'd taken from Maggie's Place, it hadn't been difficult to find his way from the Richmond airport through the rolling Virginia countryside and thick forest west of the small city to the "Farm." After locating his objective, he hadn't steered immediately up the driveway in the rental car—leased from Avis, since he had left the bumperless Alamo car abandoned in South Boston. He was aware that the men who had chased him through the Irish neighborhood must have discovered by now that he had taken the map, and they might be waiting for him here. So he had driven past the entrance to a dirt road a few hundred yards down the small country lane and parked the car in a clearing. He had walked through thick brush and trees until he'd found the driveway, then paralleled it on foot, staying back in the woods, hidden from anyone who might be heading up or down the rutted path through the forest. He hadn't heard any cars during the twenty-minute trek, and there were no cars parked in the area around the run-down clapboard home at the end of the mile-long driveway. He'd waited and watched the house for an hour from behind a grove of trees, but it had seemed deserted. Finally he'd stolen across the shaggy grass, entered the home—nothing more than a shack with a filthy kitchen, a bathroom, and a few bunk beds—and inspected it. He hadn't found anything of interest except hundreds of empty boxes of large-caliber ammunition.

Now, as Jay stared up at the hills towering above the target area, he couldn't help wondering if Carter Bullock had knelt up there and aimed a high-powered weapon down at this spot. The picture in the cigar box proved that Bullock was involved with the people at Maggie's Place. He had probably been informed by now that someone had broken into the office, since he was the one responsible for diverting the money out of McCarthy & Lloyd to EZ Travel—a firm that was clearly just a front for something very dark. Something related to the Donegall Volunteers.

Jay glanced at his scarred palms. No one had gotten a good look at him during the chase through the neighborhood. He was confident of that. His back had been turned to them as he'd jumped from the office onto the telephone pole, and it had been much too dark on the streets and alleys for anyone to identify him there. He had no fear that Frankie had recognized him during their brief struggle, because Frankie was too drunk. And it was too much of a stretch to think that Bullock would automatically make the connection and realize that Jay was the one who had broken into the office. Bullock probably knew by now that the trip to TurboTec was a farce, but he wouldn't have any idea of what the real destination was—unless he was in touch with the men in the blue sedan who had crashed into the tree outside Gloucester. Or Patrick, Jay thought, remembering the young man from Maggie's.

"Get your hands up!"

Jay thrust his fingers up in the air immediately, strangely aware that he'd never been ordered to do so before.

"Turn around," the young male voice ordered in a high-pitched southern accent. "No sudden movements, either."

Jay turned around slowly. Twenty feet away stood a blond boy, no more than eleven, Jay guessed. The boy wore a ratty T-shirt, grungy jeans, and a pair of green rubber hunting boots.

He was holding the stock of a double-barreled shotgun tightly to his right cheek and aiming the other end directly at Jay's chest. "What seems to be the problem?" Jay asked calmly. The shotgun was almost as big as the boy.

The boy decided that the intruder was of no immediate danger and brought the stock down to his hip, keeping the barrel aimed at Jay. "I thought y'all were gone."

"Who are you talking about?"

"The people who rented my grandfather's property for the last month," the boy answered.

"I'm not one of those people." Jay brought his hands slowly down. The boy didn't object.

"How do I know that?"

"If I was one of them, would I walk around here without my gun drawn?" Jay took a chance on the logic. He assumed the boy had seen the men and also assumed that they were constantly carrying weapons. "And have you ever seen me here before?"

The boy seemed satisfied and allowed the barrel of the gun to drop further. "No." He shook his head. "I haven't."

"What's your name?" Jay asked.

"Ben."

"Ben, I'm Jay."

"If you aren't onc of them, then what are you doing here?" Ben asked suspiciously.

"I'm trying to track them down," Jay answered. "They're bad people."

"How do you know?"

"I'm pretty sure they killed a friend of mine."

"Really?" Ben's eyes widened.

"Yes."

Ben glanced down at the barrel of his shotgun. "They're planning to kill somebody else, too."

Jay looked up into Ben's eyes. "How do you know that?"

"I overheard them. I was out checking my deer stands one night last week, and I snuck over to the tenant house they had rented. I got real close to them, but they never saw me. I heard every word they were saying." Ben stuck his chin out, as if he had disobeyed orders by going to the house but was proud of it. "They were cooking hamburgers and steaks on the grill, and it smelled good. I heard them talking about kill shots and trajectories and how the body of the man they were going to shoot would explode. I heard them laugh and say how they were going to enjoy watching the blood spill and how it would turn the tide."

"What man's body would explode?"

Ben shrugged. "I don't know. They didn't say."

"Did you tell your grandfather what you heard?"

Ben shook his head. "My grandfather told me not to come over here. Besides, he wouldn't have believed me anyway." The boy turned and waved toward a ridge barely visible in the hazy afternoon through a break in the trees. "I live with him over there about five miles. He owns all the land around here. Our family has for a long time. Since before the War."

"But you didn't tell him," Jay repeated.

"He would have whipped me," Ben responded matter-of-factly, allowing the barrel of the shotgun to point straight down. "He said the people paid him cash to use the place and that it was their right to do whatever they wanted here for as long as they had paid for it."

"Cash?" Jay could see that the boy wanted to talk.

"Yeah, lots of it. I saw the envelope on my grandfather's desk. It was stuffed with twenties."

For a moment Jay considered asking Ben to take him to see his grandfather. But he realized that the men had paid cash so they couldn't be traced. Talking to the boy's grandfather would be a waste of time. These people wouldn't have left a trail. He glanced at Ben. Kids were prone to exaggeration—he'd told a few stories in his youth—but Ben's account seemed plausible because of the details, and because of what Jay had found in Boston. "Did you overhear anything else?" Jay asked.

Ben thought for a moment, started to shake his head, then nodded. "I heard one more thing," he said, smiling, proud of himself for remembering.

"What?"

"They said they were looking forward to seeing the war start up again."

■ ■ ■

O'Shea ended the secure call. That morning Jay West had boarded a 6:50 Continental flight en route from Logan Airport to Richmond, Virginia, where he'd rented a Grand Am at the Avis counter. And he had booked himself on a 5:45 flight that evening back out of Richmond bound for La Guardia Airport and New York City. The good news in all of this was that Jay was using his credit cards again, making him easier to track. The bad news was that by the time they had been notified of the credit card use, Jay had landed in Richmond and disappeared into Virginia without a trace.

O'Shea reached for the phone and began to punch a number into it, then stopped and slammed the receiver back down. It was still too early to call and see if any progress had been made.

■ ■ ■

Jay directed the cab driver who had brought him into the city from Newark Airport to the left side of Amsterdam Avenue, a block north of the service entrance to his Manhattan apartment building. The plane had lifted off from National Airport in Washington, D.C., an hour late, and now it was almost ten o'clock. He'd slept for a few minutes during the short flight, but he was still exhausted and all he could think about was climbing into bed and getting some sleep.

When the taxi had come to a stop, Jay dragged himself out of the back, handed the driver two twenties through the open window, and headed toward the back door of the building, keeping his eyes peeled for anyone suspicious, even though he could barely keep them open. He only wished he could have seen the faces of those who were trying to follow him when the Richmond flight for La Guardia took off without him on board. He had booked that reservation to throw his pursuers off the track one more time and—he hoped—enjoy an uninterrupted night of sleep.

Jay slipped in through the service entrance with a key one of the janitors had given him in return for a nice Christmas bonus the year before, and headed to the elevators. When the doors opened on his floor, he walked slowly down the hall, stopped in front of his door, pulled out his key, and began to insert it in the lock.

"Jay."

"Jesus Christ!" He stepped back from the door as if the lock had hit him with an electrical charge, then whipped to his right and saw Barbara Mason emerge from behind the stairwell door. "What are you doing here?" he asked, his heart still pounding.

"I have something I have to give you," she answered calmly.

"What?" He took a deep breath. After the last few days he had tried to condition himself not to be surprised by anything, but Barbara's voice, coming from the shadows, had shocked the hell out of him.

Barbara dug into her alligator-skin purse and pulled out an

envelope. "Take this." She hesitated for a moment, then handed it to him. "I think it's important." She tried to move past him, but he caught her by the wrist.

"What's inside?" he asked.

"Let go of me."

She attempted to break free, but Jay held on tight. "No, you aren't going to hand me something like that and just leave. You're going to give me an explanation."

Barbara gazed into Jay's eyes for a moment, then looked down.

"What's the matter?" he asked.

A tear spilled down her face as the pain of the last few years overcame her. "Oliver has lost his way," she whispered, trying her best to maintain control of her emotions. "I think he's done some very bad things." She tapped the envelope with a fingernail. "I think he's been trading stocks using inside information. In that envelope are the names of people I believe are Oliver's accomplices, and stocks I think he's purchased at McCarthy and Lloyd using information from those accomplices." She sobbed.

Jay touched Barbara's arm gently. "Barbara, I—"

"It's all right," she said, pressing a tissue to her eyes and coughing. "I'm all right." She shut her eyes tightly for a moment, then opened them and stared back at him. "Oliver thinks I don't know anything. He thinks I'm just a naive woman who doesn't understand business and couldn't turn on a computer to save her life." Her posture stiffened. "But I'm not naive, and I know how to use computers." She paused. "A couple of months ago I found a computer disk in his shirt pocket along with . . ." She swallowed several times, then steadied herself against the wall.

Once more Jay touched her arm. "Would you like to come inside and get a drink of water?"

"No." She shook her head. "I found the disk in his shirt

pocket along with a love note," she continued in a raspy voice, "from Abby Cooper."

Jay froze. So Barbara had known about Oliver and Abby all along. He could see the bitterness oozing from her. Perhaps Abby's murderer was standing before him. Perhaps the Donegall Volunteers weren't responsible after all, as he had assumed.

"Abby thought she could take Oliver away from me," Barbara continued, a forlorn smile coming to her face. "But she didn't understand that there was something in the mix she couldn't compete with, something no one can compete with when it comes to Oliver Mason: money. Oliver would never trade money for love. It isn't in him." Her smile disintegrated and her chin dropped. "I had no idea what was on the disk. I thought maybe there were more love letters or something, I don't know. And I don't know why I would have wanted to look at more of her adolescent drivel. It would have made me sick to my stomach. But I brought up the files on our home computer and printed out what was on them. In there is everything." She pointed at the envelope in Jay's hand.

"Why would Oliver have put anything on a disk if he was trading stocks using insider information?" Jay was leery of what Barbara claimed to be giving him. Abby was dead, but perhaps Barbara still wanted revenge and Oliver was the only one left to exact it from. That would make perfect sense, and the charges would have more credibility coming from someone Oliver worked with as opposed to a jilted wife. "It seems to me he would have done his best *not* to make records."

"Why did Richard Nixon make tapes?" Barbara was suddenly infuriated. "Every man has a fatal flaw. You should know that, or maybe you're still too young to understand. Maybe you need a few more years of seasoning."

"Why are you giving this to me?" Jay held up the envelope, ignoring her reproach. Barbara was looking up at the ceiling, and he could see the tears welling in her eyes, about to let loose in a torrent.

"You seem like an honest man," she said. "I know something about business, but not enough. You'll figure out how to best use this information." Barbara shook her head, and the tears streaked down her face. "I can't be the one to turn him in to the authorities," she admitted sadly. "I can't go that far. For whatever demented reason, I still love him, and I simply can't be the one to actually turn him in." Her expression suddenly turned to one of determination. "But I have to save myself and my child. Oliver is out of control. He's close to the edge, Jay, and he's dangerous. I don't want to do this to him, but I don't know any other way." With that she bolted to the elevator.

Jay turned and raced after her, begging her to come into the apartment and talk further, but she wouldn't. When the car doors finally opened, she stepped inside and stood with her back against the wall, refusing to look at Jay as the doors slid shut.

Jay stared at the closed elevator doors, then trudged back down the hallway to his apartment and went directly to his bedroom. He groaned as he glanced at his answering machine. Fourteen calls were registered on the display. He moved to the nightstand, punched the play button on the machine, and sprawled onto his bed.

The list of callers was predictable. There were several messages from Sally wanting to know where he was. During the fourth and final message she asked him to get together with her for dinner Saturday night if he was in the city. Oliver had called five times, also wanting to know where Jay was, at one point admitting that he knew Jay and Bullock had scuffled on the trading room floor Wednesday morning before Jay had left. In the message Oliver went to great lengths to point out that trading floors were high-stress environments where tempers sometimes flared out of control, and that Jay needn't have any concern about his job at McCarthy & Lloyd. Oliver made certain Jay understood that he knew Bullock had started the fight, then begged Jay to call him. There were three blank messages from a caller or callers who had hung up without leaving messages, and one from Jay's mother wondering if he would be coming home anytime soon.

As the messages continued to play, he rolled onto his side and pulled out the three pieces of paper from the envelope Barbara had just given him. On the first page were the names of four individuals he didn't recognize and the brokerage firms for which he assumed they worked. He recognized the names of the firms. They were several of the largest brokerage houses on Wall Street.

On the next two pages was a list of companies, with the name of one of the four individuals from the first page behind the company name. As Jay's eyes scanned the first page of company names, he recognized them as stocks Oliver and Bullock had purchased—at one point Abby had shown Jay a list of all the stocks Oliver and Bullock had purchased since Oliver had started the arbitrage desk. As Jay's eyes hit the bottom of the second page he caught his breath. The two names there were Simons and Bell Chemical, behind both of which was the name Tony Vogel.

Barbara Mason couldn't have manufactured this list on her own, Jay realized. She was telling the truth about stumbling onto the disk and making copies. But there was still something that bothered Jay. Why would Oliver create a computer disk file concerning something illegal, a disk that might fall into the wrong hands—as indeed it had?

Jay replaced the three pieces of paper in the envelope, then stopped and looked at the answering machine as the last message began to play. The man's voice was unfamiliar to Jay, but the barely controlled anger of his tone, his unfriendly words, and the sounds of traffic in the background caught Jay's attention. When the man identified himself as the treasurer of Bell Chemical, the room blurred before Jay's eyes. When the message finished, Jay scrambled to the answering machine, rewound the tape, and played the message again.

There was static for a moment, then the man's voice came on, trembling with anger. "Look, Mr. West, I don't know who the hell you think you are, but you better call me back. I've called you three times and you haven't been home, so I'm going to leave a message this time. This is Frank Watkins, the treasurer of Bell Chemical, and I want you to call me as soon as possible *at home*." Watkins recited the phone number quickly. "Never call me at Bell again!" he shouted as a truck rushed past the phone he was using. "And I'll tell you something, Mr. West: I don't respond well to threats. Just because you think you have something on me concerning my past doesn't mean I'm going to give you any information." There was a long pause, and Watkins's voice became more conciliatory. "Please call me."

Jay stared at the machine as it clicked off. He'd never met a man named Frank Watkins in his life, much less called the man and threatened him. But Watkins clearly thought he had heard from Jay. Slowly Jay rose from the bed and moved to the corner of the room and his computer. Carefully he went through the two boxes of disks standing beside the CPU—as he had done several times since the night Sally had slept there. He was hoping that somehow he'd simply missed the disk detailing his personal financial transactions for last year, that it would be there this time. But it wasn't.

He put the box down and glanced back at the answering machine. He was in deep trouble.

■ ■ ■

O'Shea grabbed the phone before the first ring had ended. "Hello!"

"Got him."

"Where?"

"His apartment. He went in a back way, through a service entrance. But we got him."

"Good." O'Shea let out an audible sigh of relief. "Whatever you do, don't lose him."

"Never happen."

Sure, O'Shea thought. *It wasn't supposed to happen in Boston, either.* "Keep me apprised of where he goes for the rest of the weekend. I don't want any hitches on Monday."

"I understand."

"I'll talk to you later."

"One more thing."

"Yeah?"

"Barbara Mason went into West's building a little while before he got there. Then she came out about ten minutes after he went in."

O'Shea felt his pulse quicken. Monday morning couldn't come fast enough.

■ ■ ■

Victor Savoy watched as the men hurriedly unloaded the long wooden boxes from the backs of the trucks and stowed them in the warehouse located on a lonely side street of Antwerp. An hour earlier, in the dead of night, they had surreptitiously unloaded the freighter at the Belgian port.

When the last box had been stored, Savoy paid the men their cash. Seconds later they were gone. Different men would arrive in a few nights to load the arms onto smaller boats, which would take the cargo on its last leg—a short voyage across the North Sea, around the northern point of Scotland, and down to Ireland. He smiled as he padlocked the door, listening to the trucks roar off. The smuggling route had worked perfectly, and the infrastructure was in place. As soon as he had finished the job in the United States, he could begin wholesale shipping of the small arms—and make himself a large fortune.

Savoy glanced at his watch and hurried away. He had a little over an hour to make the flight to New York.

CHAPTER 24

"What's the problem, Jay?" Vivian Min pushed the chair she was sitting in away from her desk with the toe of her running shoe. She was dressed in shorts and a T-shirt. She was planning to jog from her Rockefeller Center office back to her Upper East Side apartment after finishing some paperwork that was easier to accomplish on weekends, when the phones weren't ringing off the hook. "Why the need to see me so urgently on a Saturday?" Vivian was a partner at Baker & Watts, a small but prestigious midtown Manhattan legal firm specializing in transaction law and securities work.

Jay hesitated. Vivian was young, attractive, hardworking, and a firecracker—never without a punch line. He had become friends with her during his time at National City, when she had provided legal counsel on many of his transactions. "I have a friend," he began lamely.

Vivian rolled her mahogany eyes, flipped her long jet-black

hair over one shoulder, and smiled knowingly. "Okay, tell me about this friend," she said.

"He's in kind of a tough spot," Jay continued, still trying to figure out the best way to put this.

"Oh, really?" She twirled a pencil around her thumb like a baton, a sure signal that she was quickly losing interest. For all of her virtues, she had little patience.

"This friend of mine thinks he's being set up to take a fall for an insider-trading charge at his investment bank," Jay explained.

The pencil stopped twirling. "Why does he think that?" Vivian's voice had lost its disingenuous tone.

Jay glanced down. "His boss pushed him into buying a couple of stocks that ended up being takeover targets only days after this guy purchased them."

"I'm not an expert with respect to insider trading," Vivian reminded him. "You know that."

"But you do a great deal of securities work," he pointed out. "You may not be an expert, but you know a lot about it."

"More than I'd like to right now," she mumbled, pulling a pack of Marlboro Lights out of her desk drawer and lighting one. "Just because your friend—"

"All right," Jay interrupted, shaking his head. "There's no need to continue the charade. The friend is me."

"Sorry to hear that." Vivian took a puff. "Did your boss write down his order to buy the shares of the two stocks?"

"Yup," Jay said, aggravated with himself for making such a stupid mistake. He liked to think of himself as at least halfway intelligent, but this little maneuver had shaken his self-confidence. "He wrote me a nice long note in his own handwriting."

"What's his title at McCarthy and Lloyd?" she asked.

"Senior managing director."

"And what's yours?"

"Vice president."

"So he's clearly your superior."

"Yes."

"Did you keep the note?"

"Yes."

Vivian's expression brightened. "Then what's the problem? You were simply acting on his orders and you have the note to prove it." She smiled. "Let's go have a beer and celebrate."

Jay shook his head. "Nowhere in the note does my boss actually specify the names of the stocks he wanted me to purchase. He refers to them in passing as 'stocks we talked about last night.' "

"Oh." Vivian rubbed her nose. It was what she always did when she was deep in thought. "Did anyone ever overhear you two discussing these stocks?"

Jay thought for a moment. "Nope. We were always alone when we talked about them." Oliver had been very careful that way. Jay cursed under his breath. He should have seen it coming. It had been like a freight train bearing down on a crossing, but he'd paid no attention to the flashing red lights.

Vivian leaned back in her chair and inhaled. "Didn't you get a little suspicious when he didn't name the stocks in the note?"

"A little."

"Then why in the world did you buy them?"

"I didn't want to irritate him. I'd already stalled on the purchases for a few days."

"So you put yourself in this position because you didn't want to irritate him?" she asked incredulously.

"It isn't as simple as it sounds."

"What do you mean?"

Jay let out an exasperated breath. "I signed a contract when I went to work at McCarthy and Lloyd stipulating that I had a guaranteed bonus next January."

"Is the amount significant?"

Jay hesitated.

"Don't waste my time," Vivian warned good-naturedly. "After all, I'm giving you free advice here. Now how much is your guarantee?"

"A million dollars," Jay answered.

Vivian whistled. "I should be an investment banker, not a lawyer. Suddenly I'm very attracted to you," she teased.

"Come on," Jay growled.

"Okay, okay." She glanced at the ceiling, considering Jay's situation. "The million is guaranteed, right?"

"Yes."

"Unconditionally guaranteed?"

"Yes—at least I think so," he replied tentatively. He had never gotten around to reviewing the McCarthy & Lloyd contract as thoroughly as he should have. "Why do you ask?"

"If the bonus is unconditionally guaranteed, it would help your situation because it would demonstrate that you had no incentive to do anything shady. Not that I think you did." She glanced out her fourth-story window overlooking the Rockefeller Center ice rink, home to a restaurant in the summer. "Why don't you bring the contract to me on Monday and I'll review it? That'll cost you a nice dinner, but considering my normal hourly rates, you'll be getting a very good deal."

Jay reached down for the manila envelope leaning against the leg of the chair he was sitting in. "Here." He stood up and placed the envelope on her desk.

"Oh, no," she groaned. "I want to get out of here."

"Please, Viv."

"All right." She picked up the envelope. "But you will buy me dinner."

"I will," he agreed. "It might have to be in a prison cafeteria, though," he muttered.

For ten minutes Vivian carefully reviewed the document, then slid it back into the envelope, shaking her head. "That isn't good."

"What do you mean?" he asked.

"Two things," she said. "First, it says in the contract that you could earn *more* than a million dollars if you perform well, so you certainly have incentive to perform, that is, to pick stocks that are winners." Vivian finished her cigarette and snuffed it out in a glass ashtray on her desk. "Second, and more important, there is a provision in the contract stating that McCarthy and Lloyd may give you a performance review after the one-month anniversary of your starting date, and again after three months. If you receive unsatisfactory ratings on those reviews, your manager can terminate you. The provision is buried as an addendum to the boilerplate, and the language is actually typed on the back of one of the contract pages, which I find very strange. But it is there." She pointed at the envelope. "Without the addendum the bonus is clearly guaranteed, which is good," Vivian said. "But with the clause, buried though it is, your bonus is not guaranteed, which is bad. Therefore, in the eyes of a court, you would have incentive to perform. Again, incentive to pick winners." She pursed her lips. "And a court might view a million dollars as a pretty big incentive. Enough to . . ." Her voice trailed off.

"What are you saying?" Jay asked quickly, sensing that she wasn't telling him everything.

"I'm saying that you might have a little problem."

"I appreciate your bedside manner, Viv. You sound like a doctor telling a patient he might have cancer when the doctor's already seen the test results and knows the patient has only a few months to live. But I don't need my bad information sugarcoated."

"How long have you been at McCarthy and Lloyd?" she asked.

"Almost six weeks."

"Did you receive that one-month review?"

"Yes."

"And?"

"Initially I received a very poor rating, but then it was changed to a favorable one. For good reason," he added. "I've worked hard since I've been there."

"Did you ever receive a copy of the new review with the changed rating?"

Jay thought for a moment. Bullock had never actually gotten around to giving him a copy of the new review. "No," he admitted quietly.

Vivian let out a frustrated sigh. "As I said, you might have a problem." She tapped the desk with her long fingernails. "Has anything else occurred that makes you feel uncomfortable with respect to what we're discussing?" Her tone became more formal.

"Yes."

"What?"

He looked up. "Are we protected by attorney-client privilege at this point?"

Vivian nodded.

"Okay. Apparently someone claiming to be me called the treasurer of one of the companies I had purchased the shares of and threatened to expose something in his past unless he revealed insider information about the company."

"How do you know that's true if it was someone else who called him?" Vivian asked.

"Because the treasurer left a message on my answering machine at home telling me that he wasn't going to be bullied into giving away any sensitive information, and that I better stop harassing him or he'd take the appropriate action, whatever that was. Although at the end of the message his conviction didn't sound nearly as solid as it had at the beginning."

"It seems strange that he'd leave a voice message for you," Vivian observed. "He had no idea who might hear what he said on an answering-machine tape."

"He sounded pretty panicked, as if there really was something in his past he didn't want outed. And he said he'd already tried to get me three times."

"How do you know this man?"

"I don't," Jay said loudly. "That's the point. I've never spoken to him in my life. I wouldn't know him from a hole in the wall."

Vivian pulled out another cigarette and put it in her mouth without lighting up. "So you think someone called this man from your home number, claiming to be you?"

"Yes."

"How could someone use your home phone without your knowing?"

"They must have broken into my apartment when I wasn't there." Jay didn't want to tell Vivian that he had a damn good idea who had made the calls. Vivian would want to investigate Sally immediately, and he wasn't ready for that. "It would be easy. Hell, I'm never there. I'm always at work."

Vivian glanced at the envelope. "Then your concern is that now there's a record of phone calls going back and forth between you and the treasurer of the company."

"Exactly. Don't authorities look for things like that to prove insider-trading allegations?"

"Absolutely," Vivian confirmed.

"Great," Jay groaned.

She lit the second cigarette. "Is there anything else that's made you suspicious?"

"Yeah," Jay answered quickly. "There's a computer disk missing from my apartment."

"What's on it?"

"My personal financial files for last year. A record of every check I wrote and every cash withdrawal I made."

"Only things you would know," Vivian said to herself. "Someone could plant a file on that disk having to do with your plans to trade on certain stocks, linking you to what was going on."

"That's true," Jay agreed. The exact same thought had occurred to him on the flight from Washington as he was dozing in his aisle seat.

"And your fingerprints are on that disk."

"Yes."

She took an extra-long drag from the cigarette. "Huh."

"What does 'huh' mean?" Jay asked nervously.

"It means that when you started telling me all this, I thought maybe you were just being paranoid. Now I'm not so sure."

"I can't tell you how happy that makes me."

Vivian glanced out her window again. "Why would someone want to set you up?"

"I doubt I could reasonably estimate how many times I've asked myself that same question in the past twenty-four hours." He shook his head. "I don't know. Unless . . ." His voice trailed off.

"Unless what?"

"It's only a guess."

"Go on," she urged.

"I think that there's been a pattern of insider trading at McCarthy and Lloyd's equity arbitrage desk over the last five years. Maybe I'm being set up as a scapegoat to take the fall so others won't have to."

"What makes you think that the pattern of insider trading exists?"

"Someone gave me information to that effect."

"Someone reliable?"

"Yes."

For a few moments they were silent.

"How does an insider-trading investigation work?" Jay finally asked. "Who has authority over it?"

"The Securities and Exchange Commission and the United States attorney's office for the southern district of New York," Vivian answered. "There are other people involved. Each of the stock exchanges has a watchdog group that looks for unusual patterns of activity in the trading of company shares or options, but the SEC's division of enforcement and the U.S. attorney's office are the primary players. The SEC is responsible for civil cases in which the guilty parties pay hefty fines, and the U.S. attorney's office pursues criminal cases where they want to put people away. Typically, it's an either-or situation, civil or criminal."

"What determines whether the case is civil or criminal?"

Vivian heard the concern in Jay's voice. "The SEC and the U.S. attorney's office work very closely on these things and share all information. Higher-profile cases usually become criminal prosecutions. Cases where people have engaged in a pattern of insider trading and bilked investors out of lots of money." She hesitated. "But you never know."

"Well, I'm innocent," Jay said defiantly, "so it doesn't matter."

"I'm sure you are," Vivian agreed delicately. She'd always known him to be honest to a fault. He was a full-disclosure person, as she liked to say about certain individuals. "But sometimes that doesn't matter."

"What do you mean?"

"Insider-trading cases are like traffic court. You're guilty until proven innocent. If the authorities show up with handcuffs, you're in a world of hurt. It means they've identified a pattern of trading and other things like phone calls and that disk you were talking about. It becomes very difficult to defend yourself against that kind of investigation, as well as extremely expensive. The really insidious part about the whole ordeal is that people tend to settle with the government in terms of jail time or money because they simply can't afford the cost of a protracted defense, even if they are innocent. Because once the government comes after you in these cases, typically they come after you with everything they have, and they will keep you in court as long as they have to."

"But I bought the stocks for my firm, not my personal account," Jay pointed out. "It seems to me that this fact, in and of itself, would keep any prosecution in the civil realm."

"That doesn't matter," Vivian replied. "You have a substantial bonus as an incentive to perform well."

Jay felt a burst of panic.

"Look, you're probably just imagining things," Vivian offered, sensing his fear. "There's probably no need to worry."

Jay knew better. "What can I do to help myself?"

Vivian finished the second cigarette and snuffed it out in the ashtray. "It sounds bad, but most of the time the feds want to go after the most senior people they can find. Career reasons, you know. They want to pursue the alpha dogs. No offense, Jay, but in most cases they'd rather take down a senior managing director who has engaged in a pattern of insider trading over five years than a vice president who traded in two stocks. If you have information that implicates someone higher up, or you can get hold of it, I'd advise you to do so, because these cases become like the Salem witch trials. People start pointing fingers at anyone the feds want them to in the name of cutting a deal. And if you have hard evidence, it will enable you to negotiate from a much stronger position."

Jay gazed down at the manila envelope. "Do you have someone here at Baker and Watts who specializes in insider-trading cases?"

"Yes. Bill Travers. He's very good."

For a moment Jay thought about the pub in South Boston and the photograph of the Donegall Volunteers. "I'd appreciate it if you would talk to Mr. Travers first thing Monday morning."

CHAPTER 25

Despite a breeze kicking up off the harbor, the city air was muggy and unpleasant. Beyond the Statue of Liberty and the petroleum tank farms of northern New Jersey, lightning crackled in the night sky as a line of thunderstorms bore down from the west. Jay leaned over the railing of the Staten Island ferry, raincoat slung over his shoulder, and stared into the black water sliding by.

"What's wrong, Jay?" Sally stroked the back of his neck and leaned against him lightly. "You've been so distant tonight."

Sally had requested that they repeat the events of last Saturday night—dinner at the River Cafe and a walk along the promenade. But Jay wanted no part of that. He needed to remain in the shadows so the boys in the blue sedan couldn't find him. Toward that end he had checked into a no-amenities hotel in Brooklyn on Friday night after Barbara's visit, using a sizeable cash payment to avoid the use of his credit card. He was going to hole up there until Monday morning, when he could sit down with Vivian's partner, Bill Travers, at Baker & Watts. There they would figure out the best legal strategy for dealing with his crisis.

He had met Sally at Castle Clinton, a colonial fort constructed at the southern tip of Manhattan, where they had talked for a few minutes. But he was nervous about remaining too long in one place, so they had walked to the ferry terminal and headed for Staten Island. He realized it was probably just an active imagination playing with his mind, but he could have sworn he had seen someone following him as he left the subway station in Brooklyn on his way to meet Sally.

The time with her had seemed surreal. They both knew there were many things to say, yet neither of them had said anything of substance so far. Jay glanced past her down the deck but saw nothing suspicious. He had watched each of the few passengers board the craft, and none of them had seemed particularly interested in him. But if necessary, he was prepared to go into the water.

"Talk to me," Sally insisted.

"There's nothing wrong," he answered curtly, slowly moving his hand along the railing so she could no longer reach it. He wanted to relax and be himself, but he kept reminding himself that the woman standing next to him had a secret, that she wasn't really Sally Lane. "I'm fine."

"I know that isn't true. You haven't been yourself at all tonight." She pulled away and turned her back. "I can't believe you won't tell me where you were for the last few days. I know you weren't in New Hampshire. I called TurboTec and you never showed up. I was worried sick. What's the big secret, anyway?"

"Why are you so eager to find out where I was?"

Sally sighed. "Here we go again with the third degree. Why

are you suspicious of me?" she asked. "What have I ever done to make you question my motives?"

Let's start with a phone call made from my apartment to the treasurer of Bell Chemical, Jay thought. *Then we could move to a missing computer disk. To top things off, you could tell me your real name.*

Sally turned around and took his hands in hers. She caressed his fingers for a few moments, then gazed up at him. "I really care about you, Jay," she said softly. "You have to believe that."

He stared into her eyes without responding. She looked so beautiful in the dim light. Slowly his gaze moved down to her chin. Even in the low light he could see that there was no scar. "Who are you?" he asked.

■ ■ ■

The phone screeched like an ambulance siren. Oliver opened one eye, groaned, and reached through the darkness. "Hello."

"Oliver?"

"Yes." He turned on a lamp and rubbed his eyes.

"It's O'Shea."

His head was killing him. "What time is it?"

"Three o'clock. Sorry if I woke up your wife."

Oliver grimaced. He and Barbara hadn't slept in the same room in months. "Barbara's a sound sleeper." He had often wondered over the past few months if O'Shea had bugged the mansion, but during his paranoid and typically drunken searches he'd never found wires or microphones. "She always has been."

"Good." O'Shea smiled grimly. Oliver had no idea that the walls of the house were indeed filled with needlelike microphones and that O'Shea knew all about their sleeping arrangements.

Oliver rose on one elbow, the taste of lime and tonic still in his mouth. "Why are you calling me so late?"

Despite Oliver's groggy state, O'Shea could hear the despondency in his voice. "I had to make certain I got hold of you. For all I know you'll be out on your sailboat tomorrow and I won't be able to reach you."

"I'm not going anywhere—"

"We move on Monday morning," O'Shea interrupted. "I wanted you to know that as soon as possible."

"Okay," Oliver said slowly.

"But we won't do it at McCarthy and Lloyd."

"Oh?"

"No. There's been a change of plans."

"Why?"

"That's all I can tell you." O'Shea hesitated. "If Jay contacts you, let me know immediately."

"I will," he said obediently.

"Goodbye, Oliver."

The phone clicked in Oliver's ear. As he put the receiver down, he thought about Abby and the fact that this would be his last week at McCarthy & Lloyd. He glanced at the revolver lying on the nightstand. He'd had the courage to pull the trigger just once that evening.

■ ■ ■

McCarthy stretched in the front doorway of his small clapboard lodge, raising his hands far above his head. He moved slowly down the short wooden walkway to the dock, holding a cup of steaming coffee. To the east the sun was just beginning to lighten the sky. It hadn't yet reached the horizon, but it was already turning the low-hanging clouds beautiful shades of red, orange, and yellow.

McCarthy took a deep breath of the Louisiana morning

air. He loved Bayou Lafourche. The property had been in his family for years, and he went there whenever he could get away from New York. It was Sunday morning, but it might as well have been the middle of the week. Out there, days of the week were irrelevant.

He loved everything about the bayou, from its rugged beauty, briny smell, and prehistoric-seeming predators to the sound the water made lapping against the hull of his Boston Whaler, moored to the dock. But more than anything he enjoyed the sense of absolute isolation—there were no other houses within ten miles. At least none that were occupied. What was left of Neville LeGaul's home lay in shambles two miles away on the next canal over, rotting from disrepair and the war the elements constantly waged against homes on the Gulf Coast. Neville had killed himself one night five years previously with a bullet to the brain.

McCarthy shook his head. Experienced in moderation, total isolation was a positive thing. It allowed a man to come to terms with a major decision in his life or clear his mind before a battle. But in large doses, isolation could wreak horrible consequences—as it had in Neville's case.

Poor Neville, McCarthy thought. A simple man eking out a break-even existence living off the bayou. They had been acquaintances for thirty years, checking in on each other's places every once in a while. McCarthy's eyes narrowed. It was strange how Neville's suicide had so closely coincided with Bullock's trip to the bayou to feed Graham Lloyd's body to the alligators. McCarthy had always wondered if the two events had been more than coincidence, but Bullock had sworn that he'd had nothing to do with the Cajun's death.

McCarthy searched the calm water in front of the dock for a few moments and finally found what he was looking for—a pair of sinister eyes rising a few inches above the surface, staring back at him from across the canal. Dawn was breaking, but the thermometer hanging in a corner of the lodge indicated that the temperature had already climbed past eighty degrees. He would have enjoyed a swim—the lodge had no running water, and a bayou bath would have been just the ticket. He knew, however, that the canal was infested with alligators, and he wanted no part of a large male eager for a human breakfast.

"Good morning, Mr. McCarthy."

McCarthy recognized the voice and turned around slowly, not at all surprised. Victor Savoy stood before him, smiling. "When did you get here, Victor?"

"About an hour ago." Savoy motioned toward the canal. "My boat is tied up around the bend. I didn't want to awaken you."

"Ah, so kind of you," McCarthy said sarcastically. "Did you have any trouble finding the place?"

Savoy shook his head. "No, your directions were quite good."

"Wonderful."

"When will the prime minister arrive in New York City?"

McCarthy spat. "Nine o'clock tomorrow morning." That was what his Washington contacts had told him.

"And you have been given the seating arrangements for the Wednesday ceremony at City Hall?"

"Yes," he said, gazing at a white heron flying majestically overhead.

The day after next would be McCarthy's last on Bayou Lafourche for quite some time, and he was already sad at the prospect of leaving. Tuesday afternoon he would head back to New Orleans, then fly to New York to face the press and answer questions about Jay West's insider-trading charge, as well as co-host a dinner for the British prime minister and attend a ceremony for the man the next morning at City Hall. A ceremony that would end in a chaotic hail of bullets, leaving the prime minister dead, and within hours reigniting the horrible bloodshed in Northern Ireland when the Donegall Volunteers—a splinter group of the Irish Republican Army's provisional wing—claimed responsibility for the assassination.

CHAPTER 26

Something didn't feel right, but he couldn't put his finger on exactly what it was. He'd seen nothing suspicious while he was with Sally Saturday evening or all day Sunday, but now as he moved through the lobby of the shabby Brooklyn hotel he was overcome by a strange sense of foreboding. Maybe he was feeling this way because Vivian had sounded glum over the phone when she instructed him to be at the Baker & Watts offices at eleven sharp. Normally she was so upbeat.

Jay looked up as he moved outside into daylight. The front that had passed through the day before hadn't brought cooler air with it. In fact, it seemed hotter and more humid than ever. And the clouds on the horizon were ominous, even at this early hour.

"Jay West."

Jay turned quickly in the direction of the voice. Standing twenty feet away was a man with dark red hair wearing a charcoal-gray suit. The man was holding up a large gold badge affixed to a black wallet. Behind the redhead were several other men wearing suits, as well as three New York City policemen, one of whom was holding handcuffs.

"Mr. West, my name is Kevin O'Shea," the man said loudly, snapping the wallet shut as he moved forward. "I am with the U.S. attorney's office, and I'm here to arrest you on two counts of insider trading. The names Bell Chemical and Simons should ring a bell."

Jay's mouth fell open as he heard the charges.

"Mr. West, you have the right to . . ."

O'Shea's voice turned to a hum of indecipherable babble as adrenaline began tearing through Jay. The officer holding the handcuffs was moving past O'Shea, and suddenly Jay's reflexes took over. He clasped his briefcase tightly—inside were the papers and the photograph he had taken from Maggie's Place in South Boston—and raced in the opposite direction.

"Stop! You're under arrest."

Jay paid no attention to the order. He tore down the sidewalk, barely avoiding an elderly lady and her grocery-laden shopping cart.

The policemen bolted after him.

Jay sprinted out into traffic, dodging two cars that skidded sideways to miss him, and headed into the subway station, descending the steps three at a time. He could hear the policemen ordering him to stop as they gave chase. He leaped onto the landing in front of the token booth just as the double doors of the train in the station were closing. He hurdled the turnstile and jammed his fingers between the doors, frantically trying to pull them apart, vaguely aware of the horrified expressions of the passengers on the other side of the glass. But it was no use. The train began to move. He heard the officers clambering down the stairs.

He darted back to where that car joined the next one,

pulled the protective railing between them aside, and stepped onto the narrow platform above the coupler. He'd learned this trick to boarding a subway on days when he was late for work and the cars were too full to enter through the doors. The Transit Authority discouraged riders from using this method because it was dangerous as hell—one wrong move and you were down beneath the cars, and dead. But it was effective.

The train picked up speed quickly, and Jay watched with satisfaction as one of the officers slammed the side of the moving train in anger, unable to follow him as it glided out of the station.

Jay didn't see one of the officers remove his walkie-talkie and request assistance at the next stop. Nor did he realize that the officers could contact the next station and have the train held.

Even so, the officers at the next station would come up empty-handed. Several hundred yards into the tunnel Jay pulled the emergency brake—a small cord dangling at one end of each car—then jumped from the train after it had come screeching to a halt, and headed back the way the train had come. The officers who had chased him down into the first station had already gone.

■ ■ ■

At three minutes after nine o'clock the British prime minister's jet touched down on the JFK runway. When it came to a stop on the tarmac and the staircase was in position, he was greeted by the U.S. secretary of state in front of a large contingent of the international press corps. He read a prepared statement describing his appreciation for America's contribution to the continuing peace in Northern Ireland, then answered a few questions and posed for photographs with the secretary of state. Then the two world leaders were whisked into a waiting limousine and escorted onto the Belt Parkway and into Manhattan by twelve black sedans crammed with members of British intelligence and the Secret Service, as well as fifty New York City police officers riding motorcycles. The convoy wreaked havoc with the city's late-morning traffic, but the prime minister reached the British consulate without incident.

■ ■ ■

Jay sprinted through the woods, dodging and ducking pine branches. He'd parked his beat-up Ford Taurus down the road because he didn't want to alert anyone that he was coming. Up ahead he saw a break in the trees and hesitated as he reached the edge of the woods. The estate lay before him across fifty yards of perfectly manicured lawns and gardens.

He put his briefcase down and for several minutes hunched over with his hands resting on his knees, his lungs sucking in much-needed fresh air. He'd been on the run for three hours, fueled by adrenaline and reacting by reflex. Now the significance of what he'd done began to sink in. Guilty of insider trading or not, he'd resisted arrest by losing himself in the subway system and melting into the crowded streets of New York City. He exhaled heavily, picked up the briefcase, eyed the mansion once more, and broke out of the trees.

He sprinted across the lawn and in seconds reached the side of the huge house, near the kitchen door he'd entered the day he had gone sailing. He hugged the stone wall of the mansion and made his way around to the back of the house. A man dressed in blue overalls was working in a rose garden toward the edge of the trees, but Jay managed to slip into a basement stairwell without attracting attention. The door at the bottom of the stairwell was unlocked, and he quickly moved into a large workroom filled with tools and stacks of lumber. He moved through it, taking several wrong turns before finally locating the stairs. He climbed them rapidly, hesitating at the door to listen. He heard nothing, so he opened it and slipped into the mansion's main hallway. Instantly he ducked into the formal dining room. Twenty-five feet away a maid was about to vacuum the rug that ran the length of the long hallway.

For several minutes he stood in the dining room, listening to the hum of the vacuum cleaner. Then the sound faded and he heard footsteps moving down the hall toward the dining room. He pressed himself flat against the wall and watched wide-eyed as the maid passed by, heading toward the kitchen. When she had disappeared, he moved out of the dining room and stole down the hall. It turned left and right several times, and he checked each room as he passed. Finally it ended at the open doorway to Oliver's massive study, off which was a small porch overlooking the lawn.

Vivian had compared insider-trading cases to the Salem witch trials of the seventeenth century and advised him to gather as much evidence as he could against senior people involved in the ring. This would be his bargaining chip, with which he could cut a deal with the feds by implicating others whose necks would be more prized by prosecutors. He was certain that, given the opportunity, he could find something in Oliver's personal papers that would exonerate him completely. Here was the opportunity. The variable was time.

He moved to a tall black file cabinet beside Oliver's rolltop desk and pulled out the top drawer. Oliver had maintained a computer file concerning his informants and the deals they had provided him, so there was every reason to believe that he'd have more backup data stored somewhere. Jay rifled through files in the top drawer but found nothing except old tax returns. He had to find something to corroborate what Barbara had given him Friday night outside his apartment. Her testimony would certainly help him, but he needed more than that possibility because there was no reason to be sure she would testify. She had admitted that the reason she was giving Jay the envelope was that she couldn't be the one to put Oliver away, and no one could force a wife to provide testimony against her husband. The list of insiders and deals was of no use to Jay without Barbara. In fact, it might serve to strengthen the prosecutor's case against him. The prosecutor would argue that Jay couldn't know about the insiders and their deals without being intimately involved in the ring. If Barbara denied giving him the lists, he'd be as good as locked up.

Jay heard voices coming from the hallway. His eyes darted around the study frantically. The voices—one of which he recognized instantly as Oliver's—were quickly growing louder, and now he could hear their footsteps. He closed the file cabinet drawer, knelt down and slid his briefcase underneath Oliver's desk, then stood back up and desperately searched for a place to hide.

■ ■ ■

"Right in here." Oliver moved to the side of the study door so the other men could go ahead of him. David Torcelli and Tony Vogel entered the large room. "Have a seat," Oliver said, following. Torcelli and Vogel sat next to each other on a large couch. Oliver sat across from them in a Chippendale chair. "Would either of you care for something to drink?"

Vogel began to make a request, but Torcelli interrupted. "No," he said curtly.

"All right." Oliver nodded deferentially. "Why are you here?" His voice was weak, and he could not meet Torcelli's fierce gaze.

"I couldn't get you on the phone," Torcelli snapped. "I tried all day yesterday. I kept going out to pay phones every half an hour, but the line just rang and rang. My wife thought I was out of my mind."

"I'm sorry, I'm sorry." Oliver held his hands up. He hadn't the strength left to deal with anyone after the call from O'Shea, so he had ignored the phone. "What do you want?"

"You know what I want, Oliver," Torcelli said sternly. "I need to know how to get to Bill McCarthy's place in the Louisiana bayou."

Oliver's mouth ran dry. The walls were closing in on him from all sides, and there was little room left to maneuver. He'd thought he had the stomach for murder. But without the confidence the cocaine provided, he didn't.

"We all agreed what we were going to do," Torcelli reminded Oliver. "McCarthy needs to suffer his accident now, and the bayou is the perfect place for that accident to occur."

"Yes, of course it is," Oliver mumbled, trying to think of a way out. He could lie to Torcelli about the location of McCarthy's lodge, but that would come back to haunt him quickly. There was nowhere to turn. He was out of choices.

"Oliver, you told me that McCarthy took you down to his place on the bayou two years ago to hunt alligators," Torcelli said.

"Yes," Oliver admitted softly. McCarthy had invited him down to the bayou as a reward for the many millions the arbitrage desk had earned, thinking Oliver would love the experience as much as he did. Oliver had reluctantly agreed to go because McCarthy was the boss and controlled the bonus-purse strings. He hadn't enjoyed the crude lodge at all, and had breathed a happy sigh of relief when the limousine had brought him back to his estate in Greenwich after the flight from New Orleans.

"Tell me how to get to the place," Torcelli urged. "I need to provide directions as soon as possible."

Oliver hesitated a moment longer, then related as best he could remember how to get to the lodge, starting with the tiny shrimping town of Lafitte, fifty miles from New Orleans. "I can't remember exactly, of course," Oliver remarked, his voice just a low whisper.

"That's all right," Torcelli said, studying what he had written down on a page of his date book. "All I needed was the general location of the place. The bayous are flat as hell. Our contact can rent a plane or a helicopter to pinpoint the site of the lodge, then go in by boat and do what needs to be done." Torcelli looked up from the page. "Oliver, I will take a drink now. Orange juice, please."

"All right," he said, despair overtaking him.

"I'll have a Coke," Tony said nervously. He wasn't at all convinced that the killings were the only way out, but Torcelli was his leader now, and he wasn't going to protest at this stage.

After Oliver had shuffled out, Torcelli rose from the couch and made a call using the phone on Oliver's desk. When he had finished relating directions to McCarthy's bayou lodge to the party at the other end of the line, he returned to the couch, sat down, and smiled triumphantly at Vogel.

■ ■ ■

"Come on, Junior," Barbara called, reaching into the backseat of the Suburban for a grocery bag, wondering why the boy hadn't responded. She pushed the Suburban door closed with her back and began to turn around slowly, careful not to touch the Austin Healey. She knew that if she ever scratched that damn car, Oliver would throw a fit. She shook her head. They needed to widen the parking area closest to the kitchen door. It was the area they used most for the cars, and it was too narrow to accommodate the Suburban, the Healey, and the Mercedes. One of these times she was going to ding that damn sports car. She just knew it.

As she turned, she almost ran into a hulk of a man she had never seen before. He wore blue overalls embroidered with the insignia of a landscaping company, but it wasn't the company she paid to maintain her gardens. Instantly she knew she was in terrible trouble. She dropped the bag and tried to run, but he caught her before she could take a step and forced her to the gravel, shoving a handkerchief in her mouth, then securing her wrists behind her back and lashing them to her ankles tightly with a single length of rope. In seconds she was immobilized.

Junior lay on the other side of the car, bound and gagged as well, crying silently into the cloth stuffed into his small mouth.

■ ■ ■

Torcelli and Vogel stood up when Oliver returned with their drinks. "Thank you, Oliver," Torcelli said politely.

Vogel only nodded as he took his glass, constantly checking the study door through which Oliver had just come.

"What's wrong, Tony?" Oliver asked. The ice in Tony's glass was shaking wildly.

"Nothing." He glanced down at his feet, unable to meet Oliver's gaze.

Oliver took a deep breath, then, out of the corner of his eye, saw the hulk in blue overalls standing in the study doorway holding a revolver. "What the—"

"I'm sorry, Oliver." Torcelli took a sip of orange juice, then calmly placed the glass on an antique coffee table. "Over the last few weeks I've taken matters into my own hands. I had to. It was the only way."

"I—I don't understand," Oliver stammered.

Torcelli glanced at the man in the overalls. "Is everything under control?" he asked.

The man nodded. "The woman and the boy are in an upstairs bedroom," he said gruffly. "So is a maid. There's no one else here."

"Good."

Despair suddenly turned to rage. "You fucking bastard!" Oliver lunged at Torcelli, but the man in the overalls stepped into the room and aimed the revolver at Oliver's chest. The action stopped Oliver dead in his tracks, and he stared at the end of the gun, as though hypnotized.

"It's over, Oliver," Torcelli said. "You've become a liability. You are mentally unstable. The other insiders and I can't take the chance that you'll crack under the pressure and give us all away. I'm not going to jail because of you," he said firmly. "It will look like a robbery. There will be things missing from the mansion that will show up later in Brooklyn and the Bronx. The police will assume that the burglars had planned to commit the crime while everyone was out of the house, but the maid surprised them, then the family came home unexpectedly. Unfortunately, you and your family don't make it." Torcelli's lip curled. "There just isn't any other way, Oliver. Although from what I know of you, the only murder you care about is your own." Torcelli motioned to the man in the blue overalls. "Tie him up."

"David, please," Oliver begged. "I'll never say a word. You know that."

"No," Torcelli hissed.

The man whipped a length of rope from his pocket and forced Oliver down on the floor, pulling his hands behind his back roughly. For a second the man placed his revolver down on the rug as he bound Oliver's wrists.

In that second Jay thrust the screen door aside and burst into the study. He had been out on the porch for almost half an hour, his back tightly pressed against the rock wall beside the sliding door, barely obscured from those within. Jay fell against the man in the overalls, taking him by surprise, knocking him away from Oliver and the revolver. Jay scrambled to the gun.

For a split second the man gazed at Jay. Then he smiled, rose to his feet, and lunged, certain Jay wouldn't fire the weapon.

He was wrong. Jay aimed carefully at the man's left thigh and calmly squeezed the trigger, hitting his leg and smashing the bone. The man toppled to the floor, grabbing his wounded leg and screaming wildly. The explosion sent Vogel cowering onto the couch.

For several seconds no one moved and the only sound was a long, steady moan from the man on the floor. Blood was pouring from his bullet wound.

Jay reached down and freed Oliver without taking his eyes off Torcelli. "Tie that guy up," Jay directed, nodding at the man on the floor and tossing the rope to Oliver.

Oliver obeyed quickly.

"Now go get more rope," Jay directed. "It's down in the basement where you keep lumber." He had noticed several coils hanging from nails on the wall on his way into the mansion. "And check upstairs for your family and the maid."

Oliver raced from the room, panic-stricken.

"Hey, kid, think about what you're doing!" Torcelli shouted. His calm demeanor was gone.

Vogel sat on the couch sobbing, his face in his hands.

"What will it take?" Torcelli pleaded. "Money? How much? We'll cut you in. I swear it."

Jay laughed out loud. Torcelli's plea was so utterly pathetic he couldn't help himself. "No way, pal."

Oliver returned moments later with two long pieces of rope. First he bound Torcelli, then Vogel. When the two of them were tightly restrained, Oliver turned to Jay. "Thank you," he said. "My family is fine. A little shaken, but fine." He looked away. "I don't know how I can ever repay you."

"I do," Jay said coldly. "A man named Kevin O'Shea from the

U.S. attorney's office showed up this morning to arrest me for insider trading." Jay raised one eyebrow. "I believe he mentioned Bell Chemical and Simons."

Oliver grimaced. "Oh?"

"How could you set me up that way, Oliver?"

Oliver shook his head. "I've asked myself the same question so many times. Each time all I get is a blank." He put his face in his hands. "I'm sorry, Jay. I wish I could help you."

"You can. You can give me everything you have on your insider-trading ring." Jay pointed toward the couch. "On Torcelli and Vogel here, and the other two as well."

Oliver glanced up. "How do you know about it?" he asked dejectedly.

Jay shook his head. "It doesn't matter."

"Okay," he agreed meekly. He hesitated a second, then moved to his file cabinet and removed a slim envelope. He gazed at it for a moment, then walked to Jay and handed it to him. "Here, take it. I don't want it anymore. Everything you could want is in there, including a copy of Bill McCarthy's will."

"Jesus Christ!" Torcelli shouted. "You're going to screw us giving him all of that, Oliver. We aren't going to have a chance in court."

"McCarthy's will?" Jay asked incredulously, ignoring Torcelli.

"That's how we were to take our share of the profits," Oliver explained. "When McCarthy died, the five of us were to receive stock in McCarthy and Lloyd, which the firm would then buy back from us. That way we had an incentive to produce. In fact, the ultimate number of shares each man was to receive depended on the number of tips he gave me and how profitable those tips were. We formed a partnership so we could allocate the shares proportionally."

"You had to keep a record of each tip provided and who

gave you the tip so you could know how many shares to allot to each man at the end," Jay mused. So that was why Oliver had created the file on the computer disk with the names of the insiders and the companies.

"Yes," Oliver confirmed. "It was capitalism at its best. Once we were into it, once everyone had provided a tip, no one was going to rat the others out, because that would have meant jail for the rat, too. And there weren't any money trails. It was beautiful," he said wistfully.

"Shut the hell up!" Torcelli yelled.

"Incredible," Jay said quietly.

"Yes, it was."

"That was a big risk for McCarthy to take," Jay observed. "To make the insiders part of his will, I mean."

"Why?"

"You all had quite an incentive to see him die right from the start."

"Not necessarily. Bill brought in a great deal of business to McCarthy and Lloyd. He was a hell of a rainmaker. Remember, we had shadow shares in the entire firm. We weren't just taking our cut from the arbitrage desk. At the time we made the deal, M and L wasn't worth much. We wanted to see the firm grow. Without him, it might have failed." Oliver hesitated. "And have you ever seriously thought about killing someone, Jay?"

"No."

"Well, I have. Killing isn't as easy as television and movies make it out to be. It isn't natural to take another life. Plus there's always a trail, no matter how careful you are. Especially if you hire someone else to do it. And the death of someone as well connected as Bill McCarthy would have mobilized a lot of law enforcement officials who might have found that trail."

"Not if his death was assumed to be an accident."

"Mmm."

"What?" Jay could see that Oliver was holding something back.

Oliver glanced at Torcelli, then back at Jay. "Bill wasn't stupid. He had told an attorney he knew very well to independently investigate his death no matter what the police report said. Bill made certain I knew that so nobody would try anything stupid. Of course, he never told me who the attorney was."

It occurred to Jay that Barbara had probably called the police by now. She was a practical woman and she would have heard the gunshot, even upstairs in the huge house. But he had several more questions he had to ask Oliver. "What about the money McCarthy and Lloyd sent to EZ Travel in Boston?"

Oliver looked up, a blank expression on his face. "What are you talking about?"

"The travel agency in Boston that M and L owns. The one Bullock is CFO of. Why does M and L send so much money to it?"

"I don't know what the hell you're talking about."

Jay glanced at Torcelli and Vogel. They wore puzzled expressions as well. Then it hit him. "Are you certain McCarthy is in Louisiana?"

"Yes, but don't go down there," he said, anticipating Jay's next move.

"One more question, Oliver," Jay said quickly, ignoring the warning. "Why did you set me up to take the fall?"

Oliver glanced down at the Persian rug. "It was you or me, pal," he whispered, "and that's all I know."

Jay shook his head and turned to go, then hesitated. "Oh, by the way, Oliver, I heard on the news this morning that a Japanese company made an all-cash takeover bid for TurboTec. The offer price was triple Friday's close."

Five minutes later Jay was tearing down the long driveway in the Suburban past a blur of white fences. On the passenger seat beside Jay was his briefcase, now stuffed with material that would prove his innocence as well as indict the insiders. He'd left Oliver in charge of Torcelli, Vogel, and the wounded man in the blue overalls—which probably wasn't very smart—but he had no choice. The police would reach the estate soon, and he had one more place he had to get to without any delays.

As the Suburban crested a rise in the driveway, Jay saw a silver sedan heading straight at him. He slammed on the brakes, skidding to a stop on the driveway less than a hundred feet from the silver car, which had screeched to a stop as well.

Sally jumped from the passenger side of the sedan before it had stopped moving and sprinted toward the Suburban. "Jay!" she screamed. "It's me!" Ten feet from the Suburban she came to a halt, frozen by what she saw—Jay pointing a revolver at her. "What are you doing?"

"Don't come any closer," he warned.

"Jay, let me explain," she begged. "I'm not who you think I am."

"I know that," he said icily.

"You have to listen to me," Sally yelled frantically. "We need your help. You're inside and you don't even know it."

"I know all I need to know."

"I'm here to help you."

"You set me up. That's a hell of a way to help."

"Jay, I—"

He didn't wait any longer. He punched the accelerator and swerved onto the freshly mowed grass between the driveway and the fence, barely avoiding Sally as the vehicle lurched forward.

As the Suburban roared toward the silver sedan, the sedan's driver's-side front door opened and Kevin O'Shea jumped out, pistol drawn. For Jay, it seemed the last few feet to the sedan took an eternity. He watched O'Shea pull the gun up and take aim.

The Suburban suddenly seemed to be standing still even though he had the accelerator pressed to the floor. Everything seemed to be happening in slow motion.

Suddenly O'Shea scrambled on top of the sedan without firing and the Suburban raced past, tearing the sedan's door away as if it were attached by paper hinges. And Jay was gone in a whirl of sticks, stones, and dust.

"Damn it!" O'Shea shouted, jumping down. He tried to get into the car but couldn't. The seats were covered with shattered glass. And the car wouldn't have been able to keep up with the Suburban because the back left tire had been blown out by the impact of the crushed door against it. He glanced at Sally, who was kneeling on the ground. "Let's get up to the house and call for backup."

■ ■ ■

Oliver gazed out over the Connecticut countryside from the roof of the mansion. He didn't know why, but he liked high places these days. The only problem with the view from up there was that if he looked hard, he could just make out his father-in-law's chimney across the treetops.

"Oliver, what are you doing?" Sally climbed onto the roof twenty feet away, steadying herself uncertainly on the five-foot-wide flat area that ran the length of the top of the mansion. She was followed onto the roof by O'Shea. A hysterical Barbara had directed them up there. "Come down," Sally pleaded.

For a long while Oliver stared at them as if he wasn't quite certain who they were. Then he raised the revolver and pressed the barrel to his head. Abby was gone, his career was finished, his reputation was destroyed, and Junior would leave with Barbara. There was nothing left.

Once a day for the last five days he had pressed the barrel of this gun to his head and squeezed the trigger, and five times the gun had only clicked. Only one of the gun's six chambers was loaded, and the first five had proven empty. It was fitting, he thought as he squeezed, that the gun hadn't fired before now. Then everything went black.

Sally screamed and turned away, putting a hand to her mouth as Oliver's limp body tumbled from the roof. As the corpse hit the ground the sound of the shot echoed away through the trees.

CHAPTER 27

The tiny shrimping town of Lafitte wasn't difficult to locate. It was right there above the Sportsman's Paradise logo on the map Jay had purchased at the New Orleans airport. A fifty-mile shot straight south from the city led through a dense swamp on a lonely twisting road that brought Jay right to the town's waterfront and Henry's Landing—Lafitte's combination general store, watering hole, and boat launch. After a few ice-cold beers—on Jay's tab—the grizzled commercial fishermen sitting at the bar were only too eager to provide him directions to a small lodge they claimed to know about deep in Bayou Lafourche on the other side of the bay. The men agreed on directions to the lodge up to a point, then opinions diverged when disagreements arose concerning canal names, courses, and bearings. When the disagreements escalated to the point of no return, Jay quietly paid his tab and slipped out of the establishment. As near as he could tell, the men's directions were very close to those he had overheard Oliver give that morning to the two men sitting on the couch in his study.

By the time he slipped out of the bar at Henry's Landing, it was after ten-thirty at night, too late to fire up the ski boat he'd rented and head west across the bay to search for Bill McCarthy—there were unlighted wellheads out there that could send a boat to the bottom in seconds. So he rented a room for twenty-nine dollars at a motel two doors down from the landing, careful to set his wristwatch alarm for four o'clock the next morning. He was physically and mentally exhausted after driving from Oliver's estate in Connecticut to Philadelphia—to evade authorities who might be waiting for him at the three New York metropolitan airports—and then flying to New Orleans and driving to Lafitte. The last image in his mind as he drifted off to sleep only moments after collapsing onto the motel bed was the wild look on Sally's face as he'd ignored her plea to stop the Suburban and listen to her explanation.

■ ■ ■

After buzzing across the bay in the gray light of dawn at forty miles an hour and navigating a maze of waterways, Jay felt he was close. He'd headed up several isolated canals off a larger channel, but they had ended abruptly after a mile or so. However, this one seemed to hold better prospects. It was a little wider and deeper, and floating on the water's surface he noticed several shredded lily pads, signs that a boat had been through there recently. He glanced up into the moss-covered branches, then at the black mud bank as a small alligator slipped into the water, startled by the boat.

Jay slowly rounded a bend and saw the lodge. On the dock, sitting in a green lawn chair smoking a cigar, was Bill McCarthy.

As Jay drew near, McCarthy remained seated, puffing on the cigar. Jay steered the ski boat to the dock, jumped up onto the pier, and lashed cleats at the boat's bow and stern to cleats affixed to the dock.

"Hello, Bill," he said calmly.

"Hello, Mr. West."

McCarthy's southern accent seemed suddenly more acute, as if his speech had been affected by being out in the bayou. "Nice morning."

"It certainly is." McCarthy surveyed the landscape, then pointed the smoldering cigar at Jay. "You're quite a resourceful young man."

"Thanks," Jay responded evenly, inspecting the area around the lodge for anyone who might be lurking in the dense woods surrounding it on three sides.

McCarthy leaned over and spat into the murky water swirling slowly toward the bay with the outgoing tide. "I assume you've traveled out to my little corner of the world to ask me a few questions. But, more important, to warn me about an assassin who's coming to kill me," he said, wiping his lips with the back of his hand.

Jay blinked in amazement. "How did you know?"

"I always figured the insiders would cave when the pressure got bad. That was always the risk. But the reward was worth the risk. They made me quite a bit of money."

"Well, I guess I don't have to warn you, then."

"No, you don't. I heard the assassin's boat last night about ten minutes before he got here, just like I heard yours." McCarthy laughed and pointed at the water in front of the lodge. "He's out there somewhere, probably in a couple of pieces by now. Gators like human meat, though they tend to let the water soften it up for a few days before they consume it. They tear a body into a few pieces, wedge them under rocks or logs, then come back later to gorge."

Jay checked up and down the canal. It occurred to him that the assassin's boat should have been in view. He assumed that the Boston Whaler moored to the dock was McCarthy's.

"Even though I told him about the attorney, Oliver sent the man to kill me," McCarthy said to himself, puffing on his cigar. "But I knew he would someday." His voice rose. "That was always the key. I knew he would."

"It wasn't Oliver."

"No?" McCarthy seemed surprised.

"No. It was another member of the ring."

McCarthy's eyes narrowed. "Must have been Torcelli. He's the only other one of them with the balls to pull off a stunt like that."

Jay shrugged. "I only know the names."

"Torcelli's a big guy. About six and a half feet tall." McCarthy gestured with his hand.

"That sounds right."

McCarthy smirked. "I never did like Torcelli."

"You knew about the ring the whole time, didn't you?" Jay asked.

"Of course. My name's on the door. I know about everything that goes on there." McCarthy checked his wristwatch. "Speaking of which, you must have done quite a job evading Kevin O'Shea and his friends from the New York City police department. If I'm not mistaken, he was going to arrest you yesterday."

"He tried."

McCarthy laughed again, this time loudly. "Like I said, you are a very resourceful young man." McCarthy flicked an inch-long ash into the water. It hissed when it hit the surface. "How in hell did you find out about them sending the assassin down here?"

Jay quickly related pieces of the previous day's events.

"I knew they'd come after me sooner or later," McCarthy repeated. "I mean, it only made sense. Ultimately, that should have been their plan. It would silence me permanently and get them their money." He glanced up at Jay. "I assume you know about the will and all of that."

Jay nodded. There was silence for a few moments, then he spoke. "Why was I set up?"

"That's the sixty-four-thousand-dollar question, isn't it?" McCarthy was enjoying the conversation, with each man trying to determine exactly what the other knew. "There's a simple explanation, but that simple explanation leads to a whole different world, which is so much more complex." His voice changed slightly. "Do you know about that world?"

"I have an idea."

"Damn." McCarthy shook his head, impressed and for the first time slightly uneasy. "I had a bad feeling about you that day Oliver brought you into my office. He said you were sharp. I should have gone with my gut and never hired you." He gazed at the sun, now above the horizon. "Was that you who broke into Maggie's Place in South Boston a couple of days ago?" he asked.

"Yes."

McCarthy grunted. "Well, the simple answer to your question is that you were set up to take the insider-trading fall for political reasons. As you know, I'm pretty well connected in Washington, and I've made significant contributions to my political party, on the order of ten million dollars a year for the last few years. The Justice Department uncovered Oliver's insider-trading ring back in March, but I was able to arrange a deal using my contacts in the capital to soften the blow."

"And I was the fall guy."

"That's right," McCarthy affirmed. "By the time I found out about the investigation into insider trading at M and L, it had already reached a point where someone had to be indicted, and of course my friends couldn't allow McCarthy and Lloyd to continue to operate its sinfully profitable equity arbitrage desk. The agreement was that we would halt the operation and offer up a sacrificial lamb, as the feds termed it. As I said, it was all politically motivated." He hesitated. "The investigation was turned over to Kevin O'Shea after I arranged my deal. He knew exactly what was going on and kept things contained. You were hired for the express purpose of taking the fall."

"Sally Lane was involved as well, I assume."

McCarthy nodded. "Oh, yes. She worked for O'Shea. She obtained a computer disk of yours and made several incriminating telephone calls from your apartment."

"I know."

"That way, when you purchased Bell Chemical and Simons, O'Shea would have an airtight case against you."

"I would have rotted in jail," Jay said, tight-lipped.

"I believe they were talking about a twenty-year sentence," McCarthy said indifferently.

"I can't believe my government would do that to me."

"Believe it, Jay," McCarthy said smugly. "Scientists might tell you that the world revolves around the sun, but they're lying. It revolves around money." McCarthy exhaled slowly. "It wasn't anything personal, Jay. It never is."

"But that isn't the real story, is it?"

McCarthy shook his head. "No, it isn't."

"The real story involves South Boston, EZ Travel, the Donegall Volunteers, and destroying a peace process. Isn't that right, Bill?"

McCarthy grimaced. He'd thought it only fair to answer Jay's questions about the insider-trading ring, but now he was feeling uncomfortable. "Yes," he replied tersely.

"How did it start?"

McCarthy leaned forward and began to stand up, then relaxed into the chair again. What the hell—Jay West wasn't leaving Bayou Lafourche alive. "Five years ago McCarthy and Lloyd was in terrible financial trouble, and so was I. The firm was struggling, and I had directed our equity group to make an all-or-nothing bet on a company down in Florida that I thought would save us. I thought that company's stock was about to take off, but I was wrong. In fact, the company tanked very soon after we invested in it. The company's executives attempted to attract other investors to keep it afloat, but they were unsuccessful and the company spiraled down toward bankruptcy." McCarthy pursed his lips. "If that Florida company had gone down, McCarthy and Lloyd would have gone down as well."

"What happened? How did you keep the company out of bankruptcy?"

"The company's executive team traveled to the island of St. Croix to meet with a wealthy individual investor, but he decided against the opportunity after a day-long presentation." McCarthy swallowed hard. "After the presentation the executives boarded a Gulfstream and headed back to the United States. Thirty-two minutes after takeoff, the plane blew up, killing all of them," McCarthy said calmly.

Jay anticipated the motivation for the bombing. "There must have been key-man insurance policies on the executives."

McCarthy nodded. "Yes, there were huge life insurance policies on each executive. The total proceeds from the policies were enough to pay off all the creditors and make a large dividend payment to McCarthy and Lloyd. It didn't make M and L wealthy, but it tided us over." His upper lip curled. "There were investigations into the crash, but nothing ever came of them. What was left of the plane and the bodies fell into an area of the Atlantic Ocean that was very deep and was known for its strong tides. There was nothing left to find by the time investigators arrived."

"I wouldn't have guessed that you knew people capable of doing something like that."

"I didn't," McCarthy said firmly, as if that was worth something. "They approached me. They blew up the plane. They killed Graham Lloyd, because he never would have agreed to anything like that. They purchased his fifty percent interest from his widow. They did it all." He hesitated. "None of it was my idea."

"Who are 'they'?" Jay asked quietly, amazed that McCarthy could rationalize away his culpability so easily.

McCarthy gazed out at the water. He loved this place so much, yet he wouldn't see it again for a long time, possibly never. "The Donegall Volunteers," he finally said. "It's a splinter group of the provisional wing of the Irish Republican Army. Let's just say they didn't agree to the peace accord ratified last year."

"Named for Donegall Square, the central square of Belfast, the capital city of Northern Ireland." Jay had done his research Saturday at the library before meeting Sally.

"That's right," McCarthy said. "My family is originally from Northern Ireland, and I still have many relatives there. Six years ago one of those relatives introduced me to a man who said he could help me out with my problems. I didn't pay much attention to him the first time we met, but as the situation at McCarthy and Lloyd became worse, I had no choice but to listen." He shook his head. "Sometimes I wish I'd never laid eyes on him."

"The Donegall Volunteers must have been very well funded," Jay went on, digging for as many answers as McCarthy would yield.

"Not at all. They actually had very little in the way of financial resources at that time. The entire faction consisted of less than a hundred people," McCarthy explained. "In fact, the entire reason for their interest in becoming my partner was to amass wealth. They saw Wall Street as a way to accumulate a war chest very quickly."

"How could they have afforded Graham Lloyd's fifty percent if they weren't well funded?"

"McCarthy and Lloyd was worth almost nothing at that point. The Donegall Volunteers quietly scraped together three million dollars. Graham Lloyd's wife was ecstatic when we offered her that much. You can't continue to fight a war on three million dollars, but you can buy into a failing investment bank. Now M and L is worth close to a billion dollars. And they can have their war."

"So you hired Oliver specifically to arrange an insider-trading ring."

"That's right. On orders from the Donegall Volunteers. They saw insider trading as a way to jump-start the firm, and they didn't care that it was illegal. If the firm was caught trading on the inside, the Donegall Volunteers would simply fade into the shadows. It wasn't as if they were scared of committing a white-collar crime. Hell, they were out killing people like my partner and the men in the Gulfstream."

"But what about EZ Travel and the pub in South Boston? What were they all about?"

McCarthy drew himself up in the chair. "Once McCarthy and Lloyd began making serious money, my partners wanted to start taking cash out of it to fund their war, particularly as the peace accord became more real."

"You mean they wanted to start purchasing weapons?" Jay asked.

"Of course that's what I mean," McCarthy snapped. "We actually own five other businesses, including a string of service stations and some grocery stores, all cash-intensive businesses that we can flush money through before it goes to Antigua, then to Europe."

"How does a travel agency fit?"

"The Donegall Volunteers send individuals all over the world to procure arms. Individuals the international law enforcement community would love to get their hands on. Travel agencies can make it very easy for an individual to get around without having to give away his identity."

"But why send the money through a bar in South Boston?"

McCarthy looked at his watch. It was time for him to head out. "A great deal of the money that has flowed from this country to Northern Ireland to support the war effort has been funneled through Boston. And I'm not talking about just the Donegall Volunteers now. The total amount is in the hundreds of millions over the past two decades, maybe more. There is quite a contingent of sympathizers up there. Lots of splinter groups. The Donegall Volunteers are no different. From a group of one hundred people five years ago, it has grown to almost five thousand members today. Half of those members are in Northern Ireland, and the other half are in this country, many in Boston. It's a force to be reckoned with. I'll admit that having the main office of your U.S. operation on the second floor of a pub may seem a little crude, but it worked for them, and for many other crews. Maggie's Place is far from a unique setup."

"Do you think Oliver ever knew what was really going on at McCarthy and Lloyd?" Jay asked.

"No. He was too focused on himself to take even a cursory look around." McCarthy took one last puff, then tossed the cigar stub into the water. "Jay, it's been great, but I have to—" He broke off as he gazed down at the revolver.

Jay had purchased the gun for two hundred dollars from a dealer in Jefferson Parish the previous afternoon before driving to Lafitte. He had traveled to New Orleans on business several times, and was aware that anything you wanted was available on a couple of streets in the parish west of the city, as long as you had cash.

He clasped the weapon tightly. "Bill, put your hands behind your head and turn around slowly."

McCarthy chuckled. "You think I'm going to go quietly with you to the authorities, boy? Just like that?"

"You don't have much choice."

"He's got a few options left." Carter Bullock rose up slowly from the bow of the Boston Whaler, a twelve-gauge shotgun aimed at Jay. "Throw your gun in the water," he ordered.

Jay hesitated.

"Now!" Bullock shouted.

The gun splashed on the water's surface, then sank quickly to the bottom of the bayou.

McCarthy smiled as he watched the revolver disappear. Even with Bullock aiming the shotgun at Jay from only a few feet away, he hadn't felt completely comfortable. The kid might have had something up his sleeve. "Jay, meet Seamus Dunn, also known as Carter Bullock," he said. "Seamus is the commander of the Donegall Volunteers' U.S. operation. And my on-site partner at McCarthy and Lloyd."

Bullock stepped onto the dock and stood beside McCarthy. "Hello, Jay. Best of the morning to you," he said sarcastically. "Okay, men," he yelled. Four men in camouflage uniforms stepped out of the lodge, automatic weapons slung over their shoulders.

Jay felt the breath sucked from his lungs at the sight of the soldiers. This wasn't some kind of half-assed paramilitary effort. He had unwittingly stepped into a professional operation, and suddenly his expectation of making it out of the situation nose-dived. He glanced into Bullock's eyes. "What was the farm in Virginia all about? Who are you planning to kill, Badger?"

Bullock grinned. "The British prime minister as he sits in front of Manhattan's City Hall tomorrow," he answered proudly. "Northern Ireland will never be the same. The British and the fuckin' Protestants will declare war on us." His grin broadened. "But we'll be ready."

"You've already gotten quite a bit of money out of the United States, haven't you?"

"Absolutely," Bullock confirmed. "Enough to finance a hell of a war."

"And provide me a very comfortable life for as long as I need it," McCarthy reminded Bullock.

"Yeah, sure," Bullock said. McCarthy was going to be alligator bait very soon.

"Sooner or later someone will figure out McCarthy and Lloyd's involvement and the U.S. government will shut the firm down," Jay pointed out.

"They would have done that soon anyway," McCarthy said ruefully. "It was only a matter of time."

"We've gotten as much money as we could out of it," Bullock added. "We've fooled the regulators for the last month by playing shell games with its capital. The firm is on the verge of collapse. We wanted to keep the operation going a little longer, but the investigation accelerated a shutdown plan we already had in place." He nodded over his shoulder to the men standing in front of the lodge door.

Incredible, Jay thought, watching the men move toward the

dock. In five years the Donegall Volunteers had grown a three-million-dollar investment into hundreds of millions. Enough money to sustain a significant guerrilla warfare effort for the foreseeable future. They could easily tear apart the uneasy Irish peace that had taken years to bring about. "Did you kill Abby Cooper?" he asked bluntly.

Bullock walked to where Jay stood. "Yes, I did. Oliver had told Abby all about the insider-trading ring during one of their cocaine sessions at the Plaza. He never could keep his damn mouth shut, and he always thought she was absolutely loyal to him. I was never as naive as Oliver. I couldn't take a chance on her loyalty. Abby could have fucked up everything if she'd gotten pissed off at him and gone to law enforcement officials. We could control O'Shea, but not necessarily someone outside the circle. I killed her, then sent the resignation letter to Oliver." He hesitated. "By the way, I really was trying to push Oliver over the wall that day on the roof." Bullock smiled. "And this is for that day last week on the trading floor." He slammed Jay in the stomach with the butt of the gun.

Jay dropped to the wooden slats of the dock instantly, clutching his stomach, unable to breathe. Despite the intense pain, he still heard the helicopters tearing over the bayou, skimming across the treetops, and—as he had been instructed—he managed to roll into the water.

He had been rudely awakened the night before in his motel room at two o'clock, aware of nothing at first but chaos. People dressed in navy blue windbreakers and matching baseball caps were pouring into the small room, guns drawn. Then Jay had noticed Kevin O'Shea and Sally Lane—or, as O'Shea had explained, Victoria Marshall, a senior operative of a joint FBI-CIA cell working closely with British intelligence. The woman he had known as Sally Lane wasn't just some junior assistant in the Justice

Department assisting O'Shea. Vicky was a high-ranking intelligence agent working on an even more important mission.

As it turned out, Jay hadn't been as shrewd about evading the authorities as he had thought. Oliver's estate was bugged, and they'd listened to the tapes of the conversations in the study and realized where Jay was headed. As Vicky had explained, it hadn't been difficult to find him in Lafitte. In fact, several FBI agents had already made it to town before he arrived. They'd watched him rent the boat and temporarily disabled it while he was sitting at the Henry's Landing bar in case he'd decided to do something stupid like head out across the bay at night.

Now Jay struggled to swim beneath the ski boat. Bullock's punch had knocked the wind out of him, and he swam with one arm while he held his gut with the other. Lungs screaming for air, he pulled himself along the smooth hull and burst through the surface on the far side, gasping for breath. Automatic gunfire, shouts, and the deafening roar of helicopter rotors directly overhead filled the air. With spray pelting his face, he took a huge gulp of air, ducked beneath the surface again, and pulled himself forward.

His fingers touched muddy bottom and he propelled himself to the surface once more. He was only a few feet from the bank and he struggled forward, running in slow motion in the mire and waist-deep water, grasping wildly at branches hanging over the water. Finally he scrambled up the bank and pulled himself onto land, then took a step toward the thick woods. But Bullock was there, directly in front of him, clutching the shotgun, blood pouring from a bullet wound in his shoulder.

"I can't let you live!" Bullock shouted through the deafening din and blinding spray. "You know too much," he yelled, lifting the shotgun's barrel and squeezing the trigger.

Jay felt the heat of the blast blow by his arm, but sensed no pain. Then he saw Bullock down on the ground, writhing in his death agony.

Vicky Marshall sprinted to where Bullock lay, Beretta 9-mm drawn, and touched his neck. There was no pulse. She picked up the shotgun and hurled it into the water, then ran to Jay. “Are you all right?” she yelled. She was dripping wet, having jumped into the water near the bank from one of the army helicopters.

Jay nodded, still dazed.

“Did they talk?” she shouted.

“They didn’t shut up.”

“Good.” Vicky handed him her weapon, then reached down, pulled up his shirt, and tore off the tiny waterproof tape recorder taped to his chest. “Good job.” She grabbed the Beretta and slogged back down the muddy bank toward the lodge.

Jay sank to a sitting position against a huge tree, watching her go. “Thanks,” he whispered.

CHAPTER 28

As the dignitaries took their seats, he carefully checked the photographs he'd been provided, then gazed through the binoculars from the fifty-fourth floor of One Chase Manhattan Plaza. That was the mayor on the left side of the area in front of City Hall, and beside him sat the governor. According to what he'd been told, the secretary of state would be next to appear, followed by the British prime minister, who would be accompanied by the president of the United States. He took several quick breaths to calm his nerves. He had killed people before, but never a world leader.

The assassin pressed the electronic listening device further into his ear, then turned, picked up his rifle, wrapped the leather strap around his left arm, and aimed through a tiny opening in the window that he had cut a few minutes before. Affixed to the top of the rifle was a powerful telescopic sight through which he would aim at the second button of the prime minister's dark blue chalk-stripe suit coat. The prime minister would be over eight hundred yards away, yet the assassin was confident of putting the first shot directly through his target's heart. He'd done it several times in Virginia from even greater distances.

He was so focused on his task he never heard them. The rifle was torn from his hands and he was hurled to the floor, his face pressed into the coarse carpet of the empty office.

Vicky Marshall smiled as the men of her joint FBI-CIA command hustled the would-be assassin out of the room. It had taken her team less than four minutes of interrogation to break Bill McCarthy and ascertain exactly what was happening. The tape from the recorder Jay had worn alerted them to Bullock's admission that the British prime minister was the target. But they wanted details, and McCarthy had been quick to provide them. The poor son of a bitch had no tolerance for pain.

■ ■ ■

Savoy stood on the running board and waved to the convoy of four trucks behind him, motors running as they waited on the wet sand in the mist. The weapons were loaded and the boats were already heading back out into the North Sea. He glanced up at the cliffs overlooking this remote section of the Irish coast, then sat down and slammed the door shut. "Let's go," he said gruffly to the driver.

The truck's engine roared and the convoy began climbing the narrow gravel road leading from the beach up into the hills. They were almost home, Savoy thought.

The driver saw the roadblock first—manned not by police but by regular British Army troops—and slammed on the brakes. Savoy followed the driver's gaze. There were hundreds of troops, armed with automatic weapons. He clenched his jaw and made a conscious decision. He would not be taken alive.

He shoved the door open with his shoulder and ran. He was cut down less than ten feet from the truck.

EPILOGUE

Jay sat on the Central Park bench, enjoying the warmth of the late afternoon. "I'd like to ask a few questions, Sally—I mean Vicky." He grinned, letting her know that the slip had been intentional.

Vicky took a sip of Coke. "I'll answer what I can. If it's classified, I'll simply say 'next.' " She was trying to be tough, trying not to think ahead.

"Okay." Jay nodded. "Is Kevin O'Shea part of your FBI-CIA cell?" He was aware that this was one of those questions she probably shouldn't answer.

"No. He really is with the U.S. attorney's office."

"But you and he were working together."

"Yes."

"I don't understand."

Vicky finished what was left of her Coke. "Six months ago British intelligence alerted the Central Intelligence Agency that the New York investment banking firm of McCarthy and Lloyd had turned up in several communiqués that their national security people had intercepted. The usual informants were queried, and several interesting facts emerged about M and L—but not enough to allow us to move against them," she explained. "At that point the higher-ups decided to go covert and put someone inside the firm under deep cover."

"You."

"Me," she confirmed. "But of course we needed to make certain I would definitely get into the firm, and that I'd have access to senior people. We ascertained that a preliminary insider-trading investigation was going on, and we contacted the Justice Department to arrange the deception. The president was informed, and we went to work."

"But you didn't know exactly what you were looking for."

"We had an idea, but that was all. We tried for a short time to figure out what was going on from the outside, but that didn't work." Vicky gazed out across the Sheep Meadow, a large grassy area of the park stretching out before them. "A senior White House official approached Bill McCarthy to let him know that Justice was initiating an insider-trading investigation, but that an agreement could be reached that would make the investigation go away without too much pain. McCarthy readily agreed."

"Of course he did," Jay said, laughing.

Vicky paused, gazing at Jay's handsome face. "I like it when you laugh."

Jay took her hand. They had spent the last three days together sharing everything New York City had to offer—and sharing each other as well. And though it made him uncomfortable to admit it, he had fallen for her very hard.

She glanced away. "You know most of the rest. We made McCarthy and Oliver think that Kevin O'Shea was in charge of an insider-trading investigation that would end up taking you down. Both of them believed I was with the DOJ. They bought the whole thing hook, line, and sinker. But you broke things wide open before I had a chance to," she admitted.

"You took the computer disk from my apartment. And made the phone calls to the treasurer of Bell Chemical."

"Yes."

"But the treasurer would have heard your voice, and I doubt you would have sounded masculine to him," Jay pointed out. "Definitely nothing like the voice he would have heard on my answering machine at the apartment when he called back."

"I never actually left a message for the treasurer when I called from your apartment. I had his direct line and I simply stayed on the line long enough for a record to register at the telephone company. The actual threats were made by an associate of mine at the agency who sounds very much like you. And he made those calls from a phone that blocked Caller ID."

Jay grinned. They had worked it all out. "I assume you really did have something on that poor treasurer from Bell Chemical."

It was Vicky's turn to laugh. "Oh, yeah."

"What was it?"

"Next."

"Come on," Jay protested, "that can't be classified."

"I really can't tell you," she said firmly. "We did those things to make the whole deception seem more real, to get McCarthy and Oliver to believe the insider-trading investigation story was absolutely true. It worked perfectly. But as I already said, you tore the whole thing wide open."

Jay smiled, proud of himself. "I did, didn't I?"

"Yes."

"Then I was never really going to jail."

"No. We would have hidden you away for a while and explained most of what was going on. But you wouldn't have gone to jail." She tried to stop herself, but it was impossible. She leaned over and kissed him.

"Is that legal?" Jay asked when she pulled away. "What with your being intelligence and all."

"It's fine." She tried to smile, but it was difficult. They had become so close in the last few days. "What other questions do you have?"

"I want to know about Bullock. I did some digging while I was interviewing for the job at McCarthy and Lloyd, and I found out that he was raised in Pennsylvania, in a town near where I grew up."

"It was just his cover. Some of the terrorist groups we deal with are very good at that sort of thing." She reached over and caressed the back of his neck.

"Bullock killed Graham Lloyd." Jay caught her hand and kissed her fingers.

"Yes. He killed Lloyd outside New Orleans in 1994 and threw him to the alligators near McCarthy's lodge." The feeling of his lips on her fingers was arousing. "Then he sailed Lloyd's boat out to sea and set it adrift. He was picked up by an associate. The Coast Guard found the boat capsized after a storm." She pulled her hand away. She couldn't take it anymore. "You were very brave at McCarthy's lodge," she said quietly. "You didn't have to go in there wearing the wire."

"It seemed like the only thing to do. You told me there were lives at stake."

"Many," she said.

"I hope it helped."

"Your actions helped a great deal. I talked to my superiors this morning and—"

"I assume that was when you went down to the street to get

coffee." They had stayed at the Four Seasons the past three nights. "Even though room service could have brought it up to us."

"Yes," she said, smiling self-consciously. "Anyway, British intelligence has already taken the Donegall Volunteer leaders into custody and shut down their weapons supply line. Yesterday they intercepted an arms shipment on a remote part of the Northern Island coast and took a man named Victor Savoy into custody. We've been trying to catch up to him for years."

"Great." He'd been holding this question for the end. "Were you and Oliver ever . . ." His voice drifted off.

"Ever what?"

"You know."

"How could you possibly think that?" she asked.

"A maid at the Plaza identified you as having been there with him. I showed the woman that picture of the three of us on the sailboat."

"I met him there one night," Vicky explained. "But that was just to go over the details of my new 'job' at M and L." She moved close to Jay, slipped her arms around him, and kissed him again. "I promise."

"You saved my life," Jay said, holding her tightly. "Bullock could have killed me."

"I would never have let anything happen to you," she whispered.

"Somehow I don't doubt that for an instant."

"You shouldn't."

He kissed her soft cheek. "What happens now?"

She had known he was going to ask that question sooner or later, but she still wasn't prepared for it. "We give the real Sally Lane her life back," she said hoarsely.

"What?" He looked at her curiously.

"She's been down in Argentina for six months while we used her as cover."

"Really?"

Vicky nodded.

"Why did you use her?" Jay asked.

Vicky knew she should reply by saying "next," but Jay deserved answers. "Sally's father operated a fleet of fishing vessels."

"Right. It was the family business."

"It was also a cutout. The business was legitimate, but his boats were occasionally used by the United States intelligence community."

Jay nodded. What the elderly woman on the Gloucester beach had said now made perfect sense.

"Joe Lane was extremely patriotic, as is Sally," Vicky explained. "We asked if we could use her as a cover six months ago because she and I had such a strong resemblance. She agreed immediately."

"You dodged my question," Jay pointed out. "What I meant by what happens next was, what happens to us?"

Vicky pressed a finger to his lips. "I'm going to get another Coke. I'll be right back."

"Another one? You're going to float away if you keep drinking."

She kissed him once more, then took his hands and kissed them, too. "I really do love you, Jay West." For a long time she stared into his eyes. "See you in a minute."

"Hurry back." He lay down on the bench. The sun felt good, and he was exhausted. That night they were going to dinner and a Broadway show. And the next day it would be out to the Hamptons for a day at the beach. If only life could go on like that forever.

The sun had dipped below the buildings on the west side of

Central Park when Jay finally awoke. He rubbed his eyes and checked his watch. Almost eight o'clock. They were going to be late for the show. Still groggy, he rose unsteadily from the bench and looked around. She was nowhere in sight. For a few moments he stared straight ahead, then slowly sank onto the bench as it hit him. She wasn't coming back.

Jay glanced down at his hands. She'd kissed them as she bid him goodbye.

He took a long breath and looked up at the sun setting behind the buildings on Central Park West. Somehow he'd always expected her to go. He just hadn't known when.